Note: This novel contains a scene where Alfred
must consummate the marriage during dire circumstances,
which may be a trigger for some readers.

Also by This Author

Henry's Spare Queen Trilogy:

Lady Margaret's Escape Book One

Lady Margaret's Challenge Book Two

Lady Margaret's Disgrace: Prequel to
Henry's Spare Queen Trilogy
Release Date: 1 September 2021

Find Victoria online and on social media:
Author Website: *victoriasportelli.com*
Facebook: facebook.com/victoriasportelli
Instagram: vcsportelli
Pinterest: VictoriaSportelli

Dear Reader:

The author will be most grateful
if you leave an honest review online.
Thank you so much!

LADY MARGARET'S
FUTURE

Henry's Spare Queen Trilogy Book Three

VICTORIA SPORTELLI

Creazzo Publishing
Sioux Falls, South Dakota

Creazzo Publishing
Sioux Falls, South Dakota
401 E. 8th Street Suite 214-1194
Sioux Falls, South Dakota 57104
USA

ISBN: 978-1-952849-10-7 (paperback)
ISBN: 978-1-952849-08-4 (ebook)

Credits:
Cover Design: Jennifer D. Quinlan
Interior Design: *www.wordzworth.com*
Map and Illustration: Lindsey A. Grassmid
Editor: Margaret K. Diehl

Publisher's Cataloging-In-Publication Data
(Prepared by The Donohue Group, Inc.)
Names: Sportelli, Victoria, author. | Grassmid, Lindsey A., illustrator.
Title: Lady Margaret's future / Victoria Sportelli ; [map and illustration: Lindsey A. Grassmid

Description: Sioux Falls, South Dakota : Creazzo Publishing, 2021. | Series: Henry's spare queen trilogy ; book 3 | Interest age level: 017-018. | Summary: "So that King Henry's spare queen will no longer be a threat to her throne, Queen Matilda sends for Lady Margaret to marry her off once and for all. With no option to deny the Queen's demand, Margaret must marry a man without rank or title and surrender control of her lands and wealth to her new husband, the Saxon upstart, Alfred ... As the intrigues of Henry's court follow the newlyweds, Alfred and Margaret find themselves in the middle of a dangerous game that could find them both dead"–Provided by publisher.

Identifiers: ISBN 9781952849060 (paperback) | ISBN 9781952849077 (mobi) | ISBN 9781952849084 (ePub)

Subjects: LCSH: Henry I, King of England, 1068-1135–Juvenile fiction. | Ladies-in-waiting–England–History–To 1500–Juvenile fiction. | Arranged marriage–England–History–To 1500–Juvenile fiction. | Great Britain–History–1066-1687–Juvenile fiction. | CYAC: Henry I, King of England, 1068-1135–Fiction. | Ladies-in-waiting–England–History–To 1500–Fiction. | Arranged marriage–England–History–To 1500–Fiction. | Great Britain–History–1066-1687–Fiction. | LCGFT: Historical fiction. | Romance fiction.

Classification: LCC PZ7.1.S7174 Laf 2021 (print) | LCC PZ7.1.S7174 (ebook) | DDC [Fic]–dc23

For Jim,

My Beloved Husband

Contents

England, 1103 A.D.

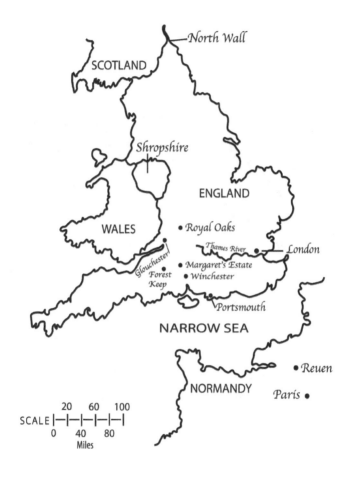

North Wall

SCOTLAND

Shropshire

ENGLAND

WALES

• Royal Oaks

Thames River — London

Glouchester

• Margaret's Estate
Forest
Keep   • Winchester

Portsmouth

NARROW SEA

• Reuen

NORMANDY   Paris •

SCALE
20 60 100
0 40 80
Miles

Lady Margaret's Estate

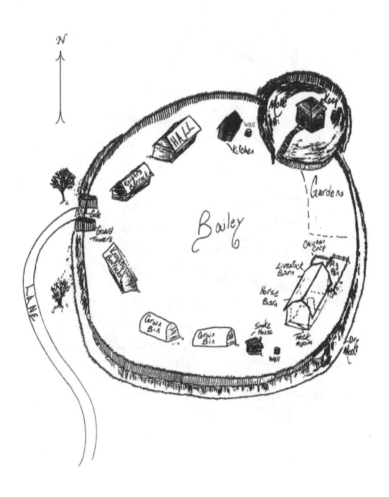

A Royal Family

William I (the Conqueror) m. **Matilda of Flanders**
b. 1028 - d. 1087 A.D.   b. 1031 - d. 1083 A.D.
King of England 1066 - 1087 A.D.

Children:

Richard (Deceased)

Robert
Duke of Normandy

William II
b. 1056 - d. 1100 A.D.
King of England 1088 - 1100 A.D.

Henry m. **Matilda of Scotland**
b. 1068 A.D.   b. 1080 A.D.
King of England 1100 A.D.

Children:

Princess Matilda
b. 1102 A.D.

Prince William Adelin
b. 1103 A.D.

A Noble Family

Charles   m.   **Rosamonde**

b. 1064 - d. 1102 A.D.   b. 1069 - d. 1099 A.D.

Lord, Royal Oaks Estate 1086 - 1102 A.D.

Children:

Margaret

Charles   m.   **Cleanthe**

b. 1087 A.D.   b. 1091 A.D.

Lord, Royal Oaks Estate 1102 A.D.

Child:

Charles

(called Young Charles)

b. 1103 A.D.

Father Raymond

Cecily

Characters

Normans

Arnaud. Knight errant.

Bertrand. Knight errant.

King Henry. Became King of England 3 August 1100 after his brother King William II died in a hunting accident. He renamed Aegdyth, Princess of Scotland, **Matilda** and married her 11 November 1100. They have a son born 5 August 1103 and daughter Matilda, born 7 February 1102. King Henry's other titles include: Count of Cotentin, Count of Avranches, Lord of Buckinghamshire, Lord of Gloucestershire.

Lady Bernice. Lady who serves Queen Matilda.

Lady Cecily. Fourth child of Lord Charles of Royal Oaks and the late Lady Rosamonde.

Lady Claire de Clerkx. Lady in service to Queen Matilda. Wife of Roland de Clerkx, Lord of York Downs.

Lady Clarise. Lady in service to Queen Matilda and the daughter of Lord Roland de Clerkx, Lord of York Downs, and the **Lady Claire de Clerkx**.

Lady Cleanthe. Wife of Lord Charles of Royal Oaks and mother of Young Charles.

Lady Estoile de Foret. Younger daughter of **Lord Cai of the Fens** and wife of **Lord William de Foret**.

Lady Margaret. First-born child of late Lord Charles of Royal Oaks and the late Lady Rosamonde.

Lady Margaret de Riviere. Elder daughter of **Lord Cai of the Fens** and wife of **Lord Richard de Rieviere**.

Lady Pensee Wife of **Lord William of Avondale**. Formerly named Maertisa, she is a Saxon widow of a Saxon husband. She has two daughters from that marriage.

Lady Perrine. Lady of the court who serves Queen Matilda.

Lady Rochelle. Lady of the court who serves Queen Matilda.

Lord Baudric of Huntedun. The lord where lives the Saxons **Elbeorht**, her son **Wulf** and his family.

Lord Cai of the Fens. A former squire to King William I of England, who awarded him a knighthood, made him a lord, and gave him an estate.

Lord Charles of Royal Oaks. His estate, which he inherited from this father, lies three days' ride north of Gloucester in Worcestershire. His older sister is the **Lady Margaret.**

Lord Henry de Beaumont, 1st Earl of Warwick. Holds the most lands for the Crown and is the most powerful earl in England. His immediate support of Henry helped to make him king of England.

Lord Richard de Riviere. Holder of an estate in Normandy and one in southwestern England, is the son-in-law of **Lord Cai of the Fens**.

Lord Wilbur. Owns an estate three day's ride north from Lady Margaret's estate.

Lord William of Avondale. A strong supporter of King Henry. He was a widower with two small sons when King Henry married him to the Saxon widow Maertisa. William changed her name to the Norman **Pensee**. William was formerly Lady Margaret's undeclared champion, who wished to marry her.

Lord William de Foret. Holder of an estate in Normandy; son-in-law of **Lord Cai of the Fens**.

Louvel. Knight errant, brother of **Pernel.**

Pernel. Knight errant, brother of **Louvel.**

Prince William Adelin. The son and heir of King Henry and Queen Matilda.

Princess Matilda. The daughter of King Henry and Queen Matilda and their first-born child.

Sir Cyrille. Son of Lord Cai of the Fens. Went to Grand Crusade with his Saxon squire **Alfred**.

Sir Emile. Serves **Lord Wilbur.**

Sir Laurent. Knight landed who serves Lord Montaign of Birchdale. Laurent's's wife is the Lady Liale.

Sir Portier. Lord Wilbur's most trusted knight.

Sir Ricardo de Campo. A knight from the Iberian peninsula who fought with King William I, who awarded de Campo an estate and the management of the King's Inn at an important crossroads.

Sir Roger. Constable of the new castle in Winchester. He moved from the same position in the small castle after it burned. His wife is the Lady Mary.

Lady Margaret's Knights Errant

Sir Claude	**Sir Demetre**
Sir Giraud	**Sir Hughes**
Sir Masselin	**Sir Roulin**
Sir Sauvill	**Sir Verel**

Clergy

Anselm, Archbishop of Canterbury. An important monk and theologian. In England he defended the Church's interests. He was exiled by King William II in 1097 and called back by Henry before he was crowned king. He and King Henry are in disagreement as to how much power the Church will have in England and is again in self exile.

Father Alphonse. Priest who collected tithes for the Church.

Father Joseph. Serves **Lord Baudric of Huntedun.**

Father Gregory. A former advisor **to Lady Margaret.**

Father Manntun. Served Lord William de Warenne. Now resides on de Warenne's former estate and serves **Lady Margaret**. He married **Gytha**, the estate alewife.

Father Robert. Serves **Lord Cai of the Fens**.

William Giffard, Bishop of Winchester.

Others

Cormac mac Cennedig, Scot. He has known Queen Matilda since her birth and had served her brothers, Donald III and Edgar, Kings of Scotland. He now serves Lady Margaret as her seneschal. His wife is **Caitlin**.

Caitlin. Irish. Brought to London to be sold as a slave and bought by Lord Charles as a wedding gift for his bride. She had been the nursemaid to Lady Margaret since her birth. Freed upon the birth of Margaret's first brother, Lord Charles, Caitlin was Lady Margaret's helper when she ran her own estate. Her husband is **Cormac**.

Matilda, Queen of England. Half Scot and half Saxon. Princess of Scotland and sister to King Edgar of Scotland. She was born Aegdyth and renamed Matilda, after King Henry's mother, when she married **King Henry** in 1100 A.D. and became his queen. Henry often called her Aegdyth in private.

Syghelm. Dane. He fights with an axe and has spent his adult life as a mercenary.

Saxons on Lady Margaret's Estate

Hus.:**Felamaere.** Reeve

Wife: **Erwina**

Son: **Ainemaere**

Son: **Denemaere**

Hus.: **Father Manntun**

Wife: **Gytha**

Son: **Linton Younger**

Son: **Lindene**

Dau.:**Goscelyn**

Hus.: **Scirburne.** Farmer

Wife: **Ifig**

Dau.: **Leoma** (see Garwig)

Dau.: **Willa**

Son: **Scirwode**

Hus.: **Rammeg Elder.** Carpenter

Wife: **Hugiet.** Cook's Helper

Son: **Rammeg Younger**

Son: **Rammethan**

Dau.: **Haesel**

Hus.: **Scelfdune.** Farmer

Wife: **Raedaelf**

Son: **Scandy.** Page

Dau.: **Cleva**

Hus.: **Jorgon.** Hostler

Wife: **Dena**

Dau.: **Leah**

Hus.: **Aldcot**. Farmer

Wife: **Beornia**. Cook's Helper

Dau.: **Alura**

Dau.: **Aeda**

Son: **Haelum**

Hus.: **Garwig,** Black smith

Wife: **Leoma** (see Scirburne))

Hus.: **Haraleah.** Farmer

Wife: **Cadda.** Cook's Helper

Son: **Hartun**. Page

Dau.: **Cyne**

Son : **Haraford**

Hus.: **Eadgar,** Miller

Wife: **Daele**

Son: **Eadhard**

Son: **Eadsale**

Son: **Eadwine**

Daug.: **Ertha**

Hus.: **Hloedun,** farmer

Wife: **Berthtilde**

Dau.: **Midryth**

Son: **Hloedulf**

Margaret's Servants/Maids

Daelton. Jorgan's Helper

Duone. Kitchen Worker

Elstan. Serves Lady Margaret

Hopa, Baker

Cleva

Midryth

Haesel

Cyne

Alura

Other Saxons

Elbeorn (deceased)	m.	**Elbeorht**	m.	**Elsworth** (deceased)
Wulf				Aldrich
Alrich				Elbeorht (Beorhti)

Wulf	m.	**Mercia**

children:

Wulf Younger Waerdun Maerwine Waermund

Alfred's Friends:

Arnaud   **Bertrand**

Louvel   **Pernel**

In Newbury:

Fayme. Wife of **Geofroi.**

Geofroi, Sokeman, runs Newbury Inn

Preface

On 5 August 1100, Henry, son of King William the Conqueror, was crowned King of England. When his queen delivered a healthy son on the same date three years later, King Henry considered Prince William's birth not only vital but also the auspicious beginning of a new era in his reign.

Matilda had given Henry what he most needed, and she was certain she was no longer in danger of being replaced. Lady Margaret was happy the royals had an heir, and she believed she was no longer Henry's spare queen. Margaret thought her plan to escape from Henry's clutches was now unnecessary.

Margaret was summoned to Court with the instruction that she bring her marriage clothes. She expects she will be wed to a highly-ranked lord or a baron of the realm. Margaret is shocked when she learns the royals' plan for her future.

1

A Riddle

11 August 1103 A.D.

As Margaret rode beyond her estate, she worried. *What did that evil Lady Claire put into Her Royal Highness's head? Why does she not know I never wanted to replace her? Would she believe me if I told her so? What will the queen do to me when I arrive as the king commanded? Something bad. Something vengeful. Of that I am cert.*

At King Henry's messenger's orders, Lady Margaret had packed and skipped her midday meal. The four king's guardsmen and the messenger hastened Lady Margaret and Sir Masselin eight miles to the King's Inn, near the junction of two royal roads.

No sleeping in royal quarters and dining like one. I will eat in the great room at the women's table, but I will ask to have a room to myself or at least mine own bed. As the king ordered me here, he can pay for it. I will not.

The men supped at their own table and slept a few hours before the messenger awakened Margaret and ordered her to rise. *Two days more. We shall arrive Wednesday, late I hope. I will refuse to seek Her Royal Highness until the next morn. She frets and angers easily when she is tired.* Margaret rose, dressed and descended the two flights of circular stone stairs to the Great Room. After breaking their fasts in haste, the party rode south toward Winchester. Nine miles later, the group broke their travels at a roadside inn after Lady Margaret complained they were driving her too fast for her old gelding. *Am I using Night as an excuse to delay my arrival? Yes. No, his head droops, and his gait is wobbling. I do well to rest him now, for the morrow is an even longer day of riding.* She followed the king's men into the inn yard.

"My lady," said the innkeeper as he bowed, "I am glad at your return and am eager to serve a royal party."

"I look forward to your wife's good cooking, and Night to your stable hands' excellent care. Sir Masselin, please assist my dismount."

The twelfth day in August was dry and hot. By dismounting Night herself or with Masselin's aid, Margaret twice forced the party to stop to water and rest Night. *You tire more easily than I remembered. Old. Twenty-two? Twenty-three? Rest, my friend. I am in no hurry to meet the queen. I fear her.* Margaret remembered the Half Moon Inn was two hours from the city. As she passed the opt gates, she veered left and urged Night across the road.

"Stop not! My lady, we must reach the city this eventide," called a man behind her. As two knights and Masselin followed her into the yard, the messenger and the other two knights, who had already passed the gate, returned.

Ask not. Act like a lord, no, the king. Order. Here he comes.

"YOU! Innkeeper. See you the royal banner of King Henry's messenger and his knights? We are on His Royal Highness's business, and you will perform every task I order." Seated on Night well above the fellow, Margaret scowled at him as if he had already failed her. "Produce your best hostler. I expect excellent care for my steed and excellent meals and wine for ourselves. The king's men will tell you where they want to sleep. I choose the women's room." After hearing the man order a boy to the stables, Margaret untied herself from her riding platform. Climbing down unaided, she landed hard and kicked up dirt. She cupped Night's drooped head in the curve of her arm and stroked his cheek as she cooed, "There, there, boy. You will soon feel better with water and food. You will rest well this night, I promise." Night lifted his weary head toward her and nickered as if he understood.

"My lady, you must not..." began the messenger.

"NO!" I will hear it not. If you push Night for two more hours, he will die on the road. I will not have it! We stay the night. Ride ahead if you will. Night and I sleep here."

"I am at your service, my lady," said a young man who had skidded to her side. His brown hair bobbed into his face. He pulled his forelock and dropped his chin. He was so tall Margaret had to crane her neck to meet his eyes.

"He is Night. Walk him slowly until he cools. Wipe him down with soft cloths. In small portions, give him first water, then a mixture of alfalfa, oats and hay. Make him wait. Let his stomach settle. If he shivers, cover him well. Do not let him founder with too much too soon. When you think him ready, again give him small portions of water then food. Wait until you hear his gut rumbling and add a third time if you think he still hungers. Stay close to him all night and watch. Summon me at once if he acts unwell in any manner."

"Yes, my lady, said the boy as he nodded twice. "As you command."

"Best you do. Your life depends on Night being in good health and well rested in the morn." *Fear in his eyes. Good.* Margaret saw the boy shudder before he took up Night's reins. Speaking softly to the horse, he led Night toward the stables. *Two hours before sundown, good time to stop. Longer to sleep.* Margret turned. "Innkeeper, we will take half the great room and I will sit at mine own table." Margaret gestured over her shoulder and behind. "They will inform you of their desires. We wait here while I count ten. Be ready when we enter." The innkeeper, a man of sallow complexion and middling years and girth, dashed inside. Margaret turned and crossed her arms over her chest. She stared at the men still on their horses. "Messenger, I have something to tell you when you are ready to learn it. Four…five… six…seven…eight…nine…ten." Margaret turned away. As Margaret grasped the door latch, behind her she heard saddles creaking.

Seated alone at a large round table, Margaret ignored those in the other half of the great room. Several mumbled about being forced to share tables or to sup standing while holding bowls. *See them not. Ignore them.* Margaret finished her meal, pushed her soup bowl and bread board toward the table center, and refilled her mug. She looked toward the men's table to see the messenger frowning at her. Margaret cocked her head as if asking a question as she raised the bottle and tilted it as if she was about to pour wine into the air. The messenger took up his mug and stepped to her."

"Sir, if it please you, join me."

After the messenger sat, Margaret filled his mug and set the bottle near him.

"You are a froward girl."

"True." Margaret ignored his insult. "Sir, Night needs rest, as do I. Also, I choose not to face Her Royal Highness in dirty traveling clothes. I have let a house in which to wash and change into suitable clothes before I present myself."

"We sleep but a few hours. The city gates will op to us no matter the hour. You will be quick in your preparations and be at the castle by dawn."

"Sir, have you learned nothing of royals? I approach them not until their bellies are full, and they have drunk at least one goblet of ale or wine. Time it as you will, but I will go not to Her Royal Highness until after she has attended Mass, broken her fast, and is at her ease."

"You are impossible!"

"True again! *I might as well say what he already knows.* I displeased her Royal Highness." Margaret snorted. "More than displeased." Margaret shuddered involuntarily. "I am unwilling to face her until I am at least presentable. I pray she will be in a favorable mood, but I will risk neither my horse nor my life to disturb her morning routine." When the man said nothing, Margaret added, "Please take the rest of the wine for yourself or the others. I am for bed. Knock on the women's door at dawn. I will answer." As she strode toward the stairs, Margaret nodded to Masselin, who had also sat alone at a table with the sacks at his feet. Masselin smiled at her as he nodded in return. *Good man. Glad he came with me. To bed. Not sleepy; what tires me is fear.*

Margaret chose a straw pad on the floor and pulled it nearest to the door. *Do not pretend I have any rank as a girl. Avoid trouble.* She lay with her back to the wall with her sword atop its sheath between her and the room. Even though the sun still streamed into the room through a window slit, Margaret tried to sleep. A single, fat candle with three wicks sat on its own tall table and illumined the darkest corner. Others entered and disturbed Margaret's efforts to nod off. As they prepared for bed and settled, Margaret lowered her lids to slits so she could observe unnoticed a pair who had drawn her attention. A mother and daughter wearing rich fur-trimmed clothes had taken one of the beds. They appeared to be at odds over something. Margaret guessed the girl to be of an age to be married. *Mayhap the contract is already signed. Mayhap she is being taken to her husband's family and wants not to go.* The daughter refused to look at her mother, gave curt one-word answers when spoken to, and insisted on sleeping in her chemise and on the side of the bed toward the room. The room quieted as the candle sputtered and re-settled to a steady burn. The setting sun shifted and lit the room no more.

Margaret was almost asleep when a movement caught her eye. Through slits, Margaret saw the girl slip out of bed and move through shadow toward her. The girl bent and extended her hand. At her last step she reached. In a single, fluid movement, Margaret rose to her knees and grabbed the girl's right wrist. Margaret's right hand held her sword.

"I just wanted to touch it!" yelped the girl.

The girl's mother sat up and begged, "Please God, no! I beg you. Harm her not!"

Other women woke, but moved not from their pads. They stared at the pair frozen in a tableau.

Margaret slowly pulled; the girl struggled to be released. Margaret remained silent until the girl was on her knees before her and trapped. She set her sword on the rushes between them and stared into the girl's eyes.

"You want to touch it?" Margaret asked in a steady, soft voice. In the silence, the girl nodded. *Silly girl, you know not the cost. I will teach you.*

"Before you touch my sword, solve a riddle. What can a woman do that a man cannot?" Margaret pulled the girl's wrist to stop her looking to her mother. "No help. You are clever; figure the answer." She let the girl think for a bit, then she distracted her. "Did your mother teach you every decision comes with a cost?"

"No-o-o."

"Then I will. When you marry, what do you gain?"

"A husband, a new family. An equal or higher rank. A new home…a chance for children." The girl's voice bespoke her confidence in her response.

"What do you lose?"

"I must leave my family," was the girl's immediate reply.

"And?"

The girl furrowed her brow. Margaret answered for her. "Any freedom you had in your own family. Your husband tells you what to do, how to do it and when. He chooses everything, even the names of your children." Her voice was slow and unyielding; Margaret watched the girl's shoulders droop and her brow furrow. "What did I gain in picking up this sword?"

"Your freedom! You go where you want and do what you will. You are equal to any man. I was told you protect the queen. You are important."

"What did I lose?"

"You lost nothing. You got more of everything."

"Wrong!" Margaret was terse. "I lost my womanhood." At the girl's obvious confusion, she explained, "I carry a sword. No man

7

sees me as a woman. No man wants me. Which man will marry a girl who knows sword work? None. No woman will befriend me. I am no longer one of them. They pity me and avoid me. This night no woman spoke to me or even looked my way. I am neither a man nor a woman; I am a thing to everyone."

Shocked, the girl sat back on her heels. Margaret felt a little shocked herself, at so exposing herself, but kept on. *This is secret not.*

"Back to the riddle. What doth a man with a sword?"

"He practices, he fights, he kills."

"Yes. He carries death, and he delivers death."

"What doth a woman carry?"

The girl's eyes lit. "Life!" she exclaimed. "She carries life and brings it forth."

"So the answer to the riddle is…"

"A woman can bring forth a life. She gives birth; a man cannot." The girl grinned at her own cleverness.

"I carry death, so how can I bring forth life? Now do you understand what carrying and using a sword cost me?" At the girl's nod, Margaret continued, "Now, you may touch the sword. Pick it up and hold it if you like. Would I had realized its cost before I had accepted it." Margaret pulled the girl's hand toward the blade.

"No! No! I want it no more!" The girl pulled hard to escape. "Release me! Please!" Margaret let her struggle for a moment before letting go of her. The girl jumped up, turned, saw her mother standing behind her, and fled into her arms. The girl buried her face between her mother's breasts and held on as tightly as her mother did her.

Margaret sat back on her heels. *Upon my soul's redemption, I wish Mother lived and could embrace me like that. I miss you every day, Mother. Always will.* Her heart ached with longing. Even in the room's darkness, Margaret saw the lower part of the woman's face in the candle's dim light. To Margaret, she silently mouthed "I thank you" as she stroked her daughter's hair.

Margaret nodded recognition and lay down. She was cert the others had heard her; she could face them not. *They pity and scorn me. Better think myself alone than to see that.* Margaret closed her eyes. *I chose without knowing the cost. Would that I had.*

At dawn the party passed through Winchester's northwest gate.

Outside Lord Cai's door, his housekeeper reported, "My lady, I regret this house is let and full of men." She pointed left. "The woman the second door up the lane is ready for you with hot water, linens, and a meal."

Margaret thanked her. She walked up the lane with Masselin as they led their horses. "Sir Masselin, please inspect the house and garden to see only women are in it. Will you guard the door while I prepare to meet the queen?"

Masselin handed Margaret his reins, stepped to the door, and knocked. After Masselin confirmed only one women and two girls occupied the house, he reached for the reins Margaret had been holding. Margaret thanked her retainer and stepped through the doorway

2

Audience

13 August

Why do we exit this gate and walk northwest outside the city? Margaret noted the shards of flint cemented into the city walls. *Attackers who try to climb this wall will bloody themselves. Too high to drop from. Shards on the ground. I doubt these walls can be breached but at a gate. The barbican and portcullis stop attacks. No wonder the king lives here. Ah, now I understand. The big castle is on the other side of this wall. The West Gate is closest. Double wall guards too.*

Margaret stood inside the huge double doors of the Great Hall and looked toward the dais. At his ease, King Henry leaned against the back of his throne. The richly attired lord before him was speaking in an earnest tone as he leaned forward. King Henry listened a moment more and then addressed the men surrounding him. He saw her not. A woman of rank approached.

"I am the Lady Perrine, Lady Margaret. I serve you during your stay. Pages, take the satchels to Lady Margaret's room."

Margaret curtsied. "God give you a good day, Lady Perrine. These may go to my room, but the two heavy ones Sir Masselin carries are gifts for the queen."

"They must be inspected and declared safe before you may present them, Lady Margaret." Perrine gave instructions and a page picked up Margaret's satchels. Lady Perrine invited the Lady Margaret to follow as she walked the right-side wall to the far corner where stood men guarding the door to the queen's wing.

The guards inspected the satchels' contents. The first page left with Lady Margaret's satchels; two others each picked up a heavy sack. When the guards forbade Masselin's entrance, he informed his mistress he would await her in the hall.

Behind the Lady Perrine, Margaret climbed the five steps. *What lies below this wooden floor? Might the floor be breached from below? How can this be safe?* "My lady, what lies below?"

"A well. Stored food and arms should this wing need to protect itself." Lady Perrine glanced back. "Worry not, my lady. Below is stone to the middle of the world. No one can breach us from below." When she heard Margaret's "Good!" she smiled.

Tall stands between doorways. I smell the lit candles are beeswax. A great expense.

At that moment, the first of the two women Saxon sentries left the wall and stepped to Lady Margaret. She whispered, "My lady, the royals have changed how to address them. The king and queen are now 'Your Grace.' The king may also be called the more informal 'Sire.' Now the prince and princess are 'Royal Highness.'" She stepped backward to her place.

Surprised to receive help from an unknown Saxon, Margaret whispered, "I thank you."

Margaret stepped past the other doors to catch Lady Perrine as she reached the end door. Lady Perrine knocked softly and was given entrance. She motioned Margaret to follow. Inside the queen's audience room, Margaret indicated the near corner; the pages deposited their sacks and left. Margaret looked to the other end of the room and saw the queen. Dressed in a pale green bliaut with gold linen lining the sleeves, Queen Matilda had slouched with her head lolled to one side as she napped. Her crown was only slightly askew, and she looked like a little girl in the great chair. Nearby, a nurse on a stool watched a cradle. Sunlight from the clerestory windows lit all the room but the queen's chair and the prince's bed.

Near the door stood a party of women, most of whom Margaret knew not. She saw the Lady Claire and gave obeisance to her first. She ignored Lady Claire's scowl and glare. Margaret heard her hiss, "Try not to humiliate yourself."

Margaret chose to ignore the woman's smirk. "God give you a good day, Lady Claire," she replied before she silently curtsied to each of the other ladies. Margaret waited with the women.

"Well, are you coming here or not?" asked the queen with her eyes still closed. Matilda sat upright and stiffened her spine. She tilted her head and glared at Margaret, just as she always did when she was impatient with someone.

Margaret stepped forward until she stood before Queen Matilda's footstool. She curtsied so low her knee touched the rushes. "Your Grace," Margaret spoke softly. She stayed down, so she missed seeing Lady Claire's face sour at her knowing the new royal address. From the corner of her eye, Queen Matilda did see the old woman's expression, but her face remained impassive.

With a wrist movement, the queen motioned and Margaret rose. Matilda smiled. Realizing the queen was glad to see her, Margaret smiled back. Then she frowned. *You look worn and not as rested as you should.*

"What?" demanded Matilda in her Queen of England voice.

Margaret worried. *The king warned me never to tell her she looks tired or worn.* "Your Grace, I will happily leave so you may rest."

"Nonsense. We have much to discuss."

Margaret stood. *First, put things aright. A command is not an invitation, but best I call it so.* "Your Grace, I thank you for your kind invitation bringing me to Court. I am most glad to be in your presence. I hope you were pleased to receive my letter of March last."

Matilda sat forward. "I received no letter." She looked to her ladies. "What became of Lady Margaret's letter?"

Lady Claire answered, "Your Grace, the evening it arrived, I opt it for fear it contained poison. I examined it too close to the flames and it caught fire. I feared telling you."

Liar. Margaret's face revealed her thought. She schooled her expression to be more neutral. "Your Grace, it came from all on my estate and spoke of our gratitude for your, Prince William Adelin's and Princess Matilda's safe removal from the small palace as it burned. It told you we continue to pray for your good health and the wellbeing of everyone in your family and in your care. We wished you well and happy."

Lady Claire had the sense to curtsey and keep her head down as she rose.

Think no more on her; she is not the one to be feared. Margaret pointed. "Your Grace, I gift you four iron locks and keys like the ones which secure your royal rooms at the King's Inn. The locks on your entry door and the one to this room are not big enough and have not the thickness and length of the bolts I present to you and His Grace. To keep your family safe is my intent."

"How came you by them?"

"Your Grace, I have acquired the services of a black smith for the estate His Grace and you so generously bestowed upon me. He is a Gloucester-trained journeyman of some skill."

"I shall present them to His Grace. Thank you, Lady Margaret. Once again, you consider mine and my family's safety."

Margaret glanced toward the cradle.

"You may look at him."

Margaret stepped toward the cradle as his nurse stood and backed away. "He is beautiful," intoned Margaret. "His lips are perfect."

"He looks like his father." The queen spoke the formal words Margaret should have said.

"Indeed," replied Margaret as she tried to recover. "I see His Grace in His Royal Highness's high forehead and his chin."

Margaret returned to the stand before the footstool. She looked into the queen's eyes and saw her pride and possessiveness. *Always smile a little less than the queen.* Margaret folded her hands delicately at her waist and waited.

"I have news, Lady Margaret. A good man has asked for you. The king gave his permission. All that is required is you saying 'yes.'"

Margaret said nothing.

"Would you like to know of him?"

Margaret nodded.

"He is four and twenty years and has returned from the Grand Crusade. He served in the Battle of Antioch. He is so trustworthy, lords sent him to carry messages to Pope Pascal. He received the pope's blessing and a letter of passage. On his way home, he was entrusted to deliver the pope's letters to royal and noble persons. His final delivery was to our king. His Grace says your suitor then gave him service on a matter of importance."

I know how religious you are, so the pope's blessing and trust are very important to you. But I want more than that. "He sounds to be an admirable man, Your Grace. Has he family?"

"A good one. He is a third son, so your marrying him will make him a lord. Your dowry will become his land and coin. Just as you planned when you asked for it."

"May I know his name and family?"

"He said you may not. He insists on the traditional way—even without your father's consent. First sign the marriage contract. Then you meet him." An afterthought, Matilda repeated, "He comes from a good family, I assure you."

A bit of color caught Margaret's eye. Lady Claire had lifted her arm so her long sleeve moved. When Margaret looked left, she saw the Lady Claire silently laughing at her. *She knows something I do not. What?* Margaret saw not the queen follow her head turning. Margaret looked back at the queen. *She withholds something of import.*

"Is there something else you wish to tell me, Your Grace?" *That is as direct as I dare be.*

Queen Matilda paused as if she were counting his good qualities. "Many think he is handsome. He stands a head taller than you and is very strong. He speaks Norman dresses like a Norman and is well-mannered." The queen tried to wait out Margaret, but Margaret stayed silent, expectant. "Oh yes, did I mention? He is Saxon."

16

Lady Claire's laugh of derision filled the room. Margaret grabbed her locks with both hands and pulled them over her face. She dare not lower her head to the queen, but she also dare not display her shock and dismay.

A Saxon! Saxon! Marry a Saxon! Be the lowest-ranked lady in the land. Reviled the rest of my days. Dismissed from Court and never seen again. Never visited by Norman guests. No Norman family take our sons to foster. They are punishing me for asking to sign mine own marriage contract. They will never permit me my third boon. I cannot accept this match. A Saxon. Married to a man from a different people. They demand it. I cannot. A Saxon! Saxon! Better the old knight than this. I might have soon been a widow. Not a Saxon. Please God, not a Saxon. Margaret thought not beyond that word. No other quality mattered more nor was worse.

Margaret heard neither Queen Matilda question the nurse nor her instruction for the nurse to leave until she was called for. Margaret heard not the queen command her ladies to clear the room and to wait well down the hall. She heard not the queen calling her name. Her mind was roiling around one word.

To no avail, Matilda called, "Margaret, Margaret." The girl was lost to her. In her royal, imperious voice, Matilda ordered, "Margaret! Stop!" She kicked her footstool into Margaret's shins.

Margaret's mind jolted back into the world.

"Look at me! Look … at … me," ordered Queen Matilda.

Margaret shook her head once.

"I hear your thinking. You are thinking we are punishing you. We are not."

"Ohyesyouare," replied Margaret all in a word.

"I order you to sit upon the stool. I order you to look at me. Look at me, and I will tell you something only I know."

Margaret landed with a thump. Matilda leaned forward and removed Margaret's hands from her face. She gently brushed Margaret's hair away with one hand and then the other. She wiped away Margaret's tears with her thumbs.

"He asked for you when you had nothing. Do you understand? You had nothing. Not rank, not land, not coin. He begged me to permit him marry you. He was so taken with you he agreed to all my terms. And he said shocking things to me because he wanted you so badly."

That got Margaret's attention. *No one says shocking things to you.*

"Are you ready to hear his true story?"

Have I a choice? No. Agree or face her wroth.

Margaret nodded only because the queen had ordered it.

"This man saw you and was smitten. He spoke with you and immediately came to me to ask for your hand. I informed him everything you wore I had given you. I told him your father had disinherited you. All you had from your mother's estate was an old gelding, a tattered mantle, and a pair of gloves with holes in the fingertips. Do you know what he replied?" the queen asked archly. Margaret stayed frozen. "He smiled so politely. Then he said, 'I will take Margaret on her horse or off it. I will take Margaret wrapped in her mantle or without it. I will take her in the clothes you gave her or naked. I care for nothing but her! I want Margaret!'"

As the queen spoke, Margaret's eyes widened.

"Shocking! Absolutely shocking! He wanted you so badly, he was willing to take you…unclothed! To say that to me! Me!"

Knowing the queen's extreme modesty, Margaret stared at Matilda's shocked expression. She found her voice. "What happened next?" *Not that I care.*

"I asked him what he had to offer you. Did he have a lord, a place, a home, farmland?" The queen took a breath. "He revealed he was uncert his lord still wanted him, if he still had a place. I informed him he needed both—and a house and garden where you could live in comfort. At least one servant for you. I was not about to send you into a life of fieldwork. He promised to return as soon as he had all I required. He swore he and the king were working together. He said he soon would have coin enough to purchase all he needed to gain your hand."

"He only wants for me for my dowry, merchet in Saxon. My lands, goods, chattel, and chest."

The queen leaned back in her chair. "Not so. I repeat. He first asked for you when you had none of that. Say it so I know you hear me."

Do it or face her wroth. "He first asked for me when I had nothing," repeated Margaret in a flat voice. *I doubt that. Does he lie or does she?*

Matilda was tiring, but she thought she spotted a spark in Margaret's eyes. "Margaret, he cares for you. More than I have seen in a man since—since the king wanted me. Margaret, rank only counts when you are in Court. That will be once every year or two or longer. Rank gives you no happiness. Look at Lady Claire. With all her rank, she is the unhappiest woman I know. While she and her lord were at Court, King William, my lord's brother, sat them beside each other at banquets for the pleasure of watching them snub each other. Lord de Clerkx dumped her on the king's brother and fled. Her husband raced to join the Grand Crusade, and no one thinks he will return. Her son and his wife rule her husband's estate in his absence, and they want her not. She has rank but no love, no happiness." The queen took a breath. "She did do you and me one favor."

With only her eyes, Margaret asked what it might be. "She sent you away at Christmas Court without my knowledge or permission. She saved you. No matter what happened to me, you would have been innocent because you were never in my presence."

The queen returned to her persuasive arguments. "The day after our prince was born, this man somehow gained entrance into this well-guarded hall. He knelt beside my bed. I woke to his words. 'Now, may I have Margaret to wed?' The man is still determined to have you. Margaret, he is such a man any woman would want. Intelligent, resourceful, honorable, admired by His Grace. I want you happy every day for the rest of your life." The queen paused. "Well, most days." Margaret showed a small smile. *She admits wives have unhappy times. How many does she? I wonder.* "He will make you happy, my dear; I know he will. You know it not yet, but you two are well suited to each other."

No Norman will have me, not even for land and coin. Margaret voiced her fear. "No Norman wants me. Nor any Norman family."

Matilda gave one nod. "Most Norman men want a wife who is quiet, obedient, invisible. A wife he can command, walk away from and forget. Quiet? Obedient? Invisible? You are none of those. You were not that girl even before you took up the sword." Matilda sighed her tiredness. "Saxons are different, my dear. They expect a woman to have a mind and to speak it. A Saxon wants a partner, not a servant. Normans know it not, but we Saxons have traditions of warrior women, who took up weapons and fought alongside their fathers, brothers, husbands, and sons. We tell their stories and honor their courage. You scare him not. Your suitor admires your courage, your strength. As do I." Queen Matilda paused her argument with a long breath. "He will make you happy, I promise."

"Promise?" Margaret's tone revealed her disbelief.

"He promised me he would make you happy, and I promised him, if he fails, he will answer to me."

"You are marrying me to a Saxon to make that new peoples you called 'Englishmen' when we were in Forest Keep."

"That is what the king thinks. True, you will be among the first to birth such children His Grace calls the English people. I chose him for mine own reasons."

"Why this Saxon?"

The queen willingly repeated herself. "Because I want you happy, and I believe he will make you happy. I am convinced you will be good together. Clever, strong, independent, resourceful. You are a pair."

Margaret looked away and considered. *The king forced Lord Avondale to marry a Saxon, and he is much more powerful than I. If I choose a convent, I am shut out of the world the rest of my life. If I refuse and live a maid, I will always be in danger of being ravaged and having to marry my attacker. I want not Leoma's fate.* Margaret looked toward the cradle. *Go ahead, tell your half-Saxon queen accepting a Saxon is an insult to mine honor. Insult both her and her mother's memory. That will please her not! I am stuck. I am stuck. I know not how to get unstuck.*

"Ask me how I am able to choose your husband," ordered Matilda. Slowly, Margaret looked back to her queen. "The king was so happy I birthed a fine, healthy heir, he said he would give me anything I wanted. Can you guess for what I asked?" In Margaret's silence, the queen answered her own question. "Three boons. First, to choose my own Ladies of the Court. I want younger women, like the Lady Perrine, so I may marry them off. Second, to select your husband—subject to my lord's approval. I asked to save the third boon for later. I know what I want, but His Grace is neither ready to hear it nor can he yet fund it. My lord scowled at me and said, 'You have spent too much time with the Lady Margaret, and she gave you ideas.' Then we laughed together."

Margaret dared to be bold. "Do you like him?" No title, no rank. She asked woman to woman.

Matilda understood why Margaret had been so direct and forgave her slip to equality. "Of course! I like him very much. If I did not, I would have chosen him not."

You are determined, and I know you. I have no choice. I must surrender to your will. She acquiesced slowly, "Well. If you like him. Then I do."

Matilda leaned forward. "I want to hear the words, Margaret. Say them. 'Yes, I choose to marry the man you have selected for me.'" In expectation, Matilda raised her brows and cocked her head.

Margaret stood and set aside the stool. She recalled what her mother had long ago taught her: *'When you are forced, when you have no choice, smile and be gracious as you give in. It pleases him and may give you a slight advantage you may use later.'*

Margaret curtsied and spoke the words Queen Matilda had demanded. "Your Grace, yes, I choose to marry the man you have selected for me."

The queen clapped her hands. "Good!" Then she looked to her son to see if she had awakened him. He slept on.

"The king's scribe is waiting to write your marriage clauses and for you to sign the contract. I have asked someone to sit with you should you have a question. He successfully wrote contracts for his two daughters. He says he is your friend."

22

A friend? Who? I have no friends. Interrupt her not with questions. Let her keep her good mood. I must pretend mine.

"After you sign your marriage contract, return here. Your new lord has gifts for you. The Lady Perrine will show you the way. Now, please ask only the Lady Claire to join me. The others may wait in the hall." Matilda leaned back and closed her eyes.

3

*

Marriage Contract

As Margaret walked the Great Hall toward the entrance doors, she looked for Masselin without success. At the double entry doors, she turned right to cross the room toward a guarded door.

"The entrance to the king's wing," explained Lady Perrine. "His Grace's scribing room is at the top of the stairs. I will wait here."

"Thank you, Lady Perrine."

The guards opt the door for her. With one hand trailing the outer wall to steady her nerves, Margaret climbed a circular tower of stone steps. At the top, she looked down a long hall with doors on each side. Margaret approached the door to her left because it was cracked open, and from the room, bright sunlight streamed across the floor. She knocked.

"Enter," ordered an impatient voice.

Margaret pushed op the door and approached the priest dressed in his traditional black garb; he sat on a stool behind a tall desk top.

Of course, the king's scribe is a priest. They know writing. She curtsied. "Father, I am the…"

"I know who you are, child. Let us be about this. I have much to do."

"Yes, Father." *I deserve not even a glance or smile? Why not?*

The king's scribe lifted his chin and showed his chiseled features, thin lips, and gray eyes. He pointed behind her. Margaret turned. "Lord Cai!" she exclaimed with delight. "I am so glad to see you again." She curtsied.

"And I you, my lady. After the prince's christening, Her Grace asked me to stay to be what assistance I can as you dictate your contract."

His shoulders stoop more. Tired? Hair thinner and skin paler. Please God, let him not be ill or worse. Margaret approached. "She said I would meet a friend." Impetuously, Margaret hugged the old man. "I thank you for staying. I do need your help." *He is too old to be left standing, and I may not sit unless he does.* "Let us each take a stool."

The scribe stated, "Lady Margaret, His Grace gives you this message. 'If she insists on signing her own contact, write only what I just dictated. Tell her she may have anything she likes only if a man signs her contract.'" The scribe picked up a quill and held it ready.

Trapped again! First a Saxon husband. Now I lose my third boon and what I want if I force my will upon His Grace. I fear what he told the scribe. Bad, I am cert. He always makes good his threats. Nothing I can do about it. Drat! All my planning and plotting for naught. They will have their way. I trust them not a bit. Margaret closed her slacked jaw. *Dear God, I pray Sir Cai is an honorable man. I pray he is the friend she says he is.* She spun on her stool until her back was to the scribe. She leaned toward Lord Cai until her shoulder touched his. She whispered, "Lord Cai, will you help me in this matter?"

"Of course," he whispered back.

"Are you willing to challenge the king? To fight for what I want if His Grace balks at my conditions?"

"I am old, my dear, but I am not dead. I still have a fight or two left in me, and well the king knows it."

Margaret nudged his shoulder. "I think it best if we whisper together, then you state the condition. The scribe will want to speak to another man, not a girl."

"Good thinking. What is your first condition?"

"I spotted writing on the pair of parchments on his desk. I would hear what the scribe has already written."

Sir Cai made his request. The scribe translated the Latin to Norman and reported the usual beginnings. The marriage agreement then repeated the features of Margaret's contract with the Crown when she had won her boons. It described the five hides of land and named the 111 pounds the king had given her. Margaret forgot the king had excused her service of five knights' services to the Crown each year, and that the services would be due from her lord after she married. Included were the conditions that the land, goods, and property be returned to the Crown should she die without giving her lord an heir, either male or female. The scribe read the part of the king's agreement to make her husband a lord. He finished with the unknown man's wedding gift to Lady Margaret, a house and property, a virgate of land.

Thirty acres! One fourth a hide. He is a man of substance. A freeman, mayhap? Best I be cert.

Margaret had nodded agreement at each feature the scribe had translated. She leaned in to Lord Cai and whispered.

"Sir Scribe, her first condition is thus: His Grace, Henry, King of England, shall make…you said not his name."

"I will write it, Lord Cai. The Lady Margaret will learn it from Her Grace after the king signs the documents."

"Her husband a free man and a lord with all rights and responsibilities a Norman lord has and to do so before they meet for the Church's blessing of the match. As this contract already makes the marriage, Lady Margaret wants him to be free and a lord before they take the other steps of the ceremony." After the scribe spoke what he had written, Margaret again leaned into Cai. Such was the pattern for the rest of the document. At each condition the scribe recorded on both sheets and read from the one to his left.

"The title of lord shall be hereditary and shall pass down the male line for as long as England rises above the sea. This includes males who are brothers uncles, cousins and all other blood-related males. Three separate times during England's history, the land, goods, property, and chattel may pass to a daughter if no male can inherit. If she produces a legal son, he inherits the title of lord with all its rights and responsibilities and the family line continues. Should she produce not a legal male heir and the male line be gone, all land, goods, property, and chattel revert to the Crown."

I want a gift to increase my lord's standing. Which? Coin or land? Coin is easily given but taken for tithes and taxes and easily spent. Land can yield wealth time after time for as long as our heirs live. Land it is. Margaret leaned and whispered into Lord Cai's ear.

"His Majesty's marriage gift to the couple is land. Lady Margaret's new lord and his heirs may double the land they hold by clearing royal forest land adjacent to their current property, using it for crops, meadows and such. They and their heirs will pay taxes on the products from the land and will never touch king's deer and boar."

"Double!" exclaimed the scribe.

"His Grace did say she may have anything she likes. She likes land. Will King Henry keep his word?"

The scribe shrugged. "He must. But you had best be signing her contract."

"I will," averred Lord Cai. "I will also see each condition is met." As the scribe wrote, Lord Cai whispered to Margaret. At her nod, he spoke his first recommendation. "Any gifts given to Lady Margaret, no matter who gives them to her or what they are, belong to her completely. She may do whatever she wishes with each gift without need of anyone else's permission."

Lord Cai's idea inspired Margaret. She whispered, "Lord Cai, in the contract, I want my lord's gift to me of the house and virgate of land to revert to him at my death should I die before I birth him an heir or if his heir dies before he doth. The king owns all of England, but I will surrender not my lord's gift to the Crown; His Majesty already has enough. I want my lord to have a home should something happen to me or his heir. A landless lord is no lord at all. I refuse to have him sleeping in ditches or being forced to serve another lord in order to have a home."

Lord Cai patted her hand. "You are clever to think of this. You are a good wife to care for your husband's future." He turned to the scribe and added that clause.

"My lord, Her Grace said you wrote your daughters' marriage contracts. What conditions have I forgot? What recommend you?" Lord Cai smiled and spoke his mind. "I agree. Please state them to the scribe." As the scribe wrote, Margaret again whispered to Lord Cai, "What happens next?"

"I sign both documents, then your lord. If the king approves the contract, he marks them and the scribe affixes the royal seal. By law, you are married. The Church blesses the match as a sign of God's recognition of your union But you are not truly wed until he beds you and makes you his."

"At any point, May I halt the match?"

Cai nodded. "As may he. The most common reason for a man is because you prove not to be a virgin."

"Which I am," averred Margaret.

"Good. A man wants to be cert his first-born is his."

Unless she has been King Henry's mistress and is with child when he marries her to another. Her husband may gain land, coin, and favor, but we all know why. Six or seven now? Thank you, God, for keeping him away from me. I will ask my lord permit me to gift Your Church in gratitude for Your protection. Margaret sighed her relief. Then she frowned. *Can the Saxon protect me should the king call for me before the match is sealed? Better to jump from the ramparts and die than that.* The image of flint shards on the wall and flint scraps below flashed in her mind.

The scribe called Lord Cai forth. He made his marks, and the scribe witnessed them. The scribe stood. "You are married as soon as I affix His Majesty's seal to the documents. The Crown keeps a copy. I will send the second one to your lord. I dismiss you."

Lord Cai gestured Margaret to precede him. He informed her his room was down the hall. "My lord, will you do me the honor of attending the blessing ceremony? I want my new lord to meet you." At Lord Cai's positive response, Margaret added, "Thank you, my lord, for all you have done for me. You told me a story about my grandparents; you were kind to me when no one else was, and saw to my writing a good contract. And now this. You truly are a good friend." Margaret curtsied low. Then she smiled at him and kissed his cheek. To her delight, he kissed her cheek in return.

"I like you, Margaret. You have spirit, much like the Margaret I married."

She watched him walk the hall, enter his room and close the door. Margaret saw the scribe take the documents into a room at the end of the hall. She heard King Henry roar, "Five hides! Double! Unheard of!" She also heard a loud, "Only because I must. That girl knows well how to bargain. Glad I am to be rid of her."

At the bottom of the stairs stood the Lady Perrine. Before the pair had taken six steps into the Great Hall, they were met by Sir Masselin, who charged toward them and stood within Margaret's sword range.

"A Saxon!" hissed Masselin. Margaret froze. In full voice, he announced, "You married a Saxon!" Everyone within hearing turned. Lady Perrine slipped away. "You chose a Saxon dog when you could have had any one of eight good Norman knights. You insult your men, your household, your family. No Norman of rank will speak to you again. A Saxon dog will paw you, and you will rise with his fleas. You will birth mongrels. You debase yourself with a Saxon and disgrace our people!" As Masselin opt his mouth to speak more disgust and rage, Margaret exploded.

"ENOUGH! Insult not my lord and me with your insolence. Your pay is in your pocket. Begone!" Masselin glared. Margaret glared back. "The horse you rode belongs to my lord as do your helmet, your jerkin, and your sword. Return them or be punished as a thief."

Masselin yanked off his helmet and threw it at her feet. She stepped not back despite taking a blow to her toes. *I refuse to wince. No matter what I think of my new lord, I will disgrace myself not.* Masselin pulled off his leather jerkin; the metal rings clinked as he threw that down as well. As he unbuckled his sword, he glanced down and saw what Margaret held. Masselin gasped. Her dagger point was an inch from his manhood.

"Insult me again and bleed a horrible death," Margaret hissed in a tight, hard voice. Masselin felt his man parts shrink in their pouch. His love for his lady died. He lowered his sword belt until the sheath tip touched the rushes at his feet. He released the buckle and dropped the sword. "Step around me and leave. I will gut you if ere I see you again."

Still glaring, Masselin stepped back, turned left, and exited the hall through the main doors. Margaret followed him with her eyes. Only then did the men and women of the Court see the blade in her hand. They watched her sheathe her dagger. When she saw them staring, she drew her sword. A woman shrank back and hid behind her husband. Margaret created a wide path by swinging her blade left and right to the rhythm of her walk as she strode toward the queen's door. Silent courtiers gave way. From his stairway entrance, King Henry watched with a fire in his loins and a plan.

4

Introductions

The Saxon sentry whispered "she sleeps" before she opt the door to the queen's chambers. Margaret tiptoed in and nodded to the ladies leaning against the wall. *Glad I am the Lady Claire is on an errand.* One of the women gestured Margaret to her.

She whispered, "She instructed me to braid your hair. Want you to add hair lengths?"

If he likes me as I am, he already knows my chopped locks only touch my shoulder blades. Margaret shook her head, turned to give the woman her back, and sat on the stool. She sighed her pleasure at having her hair brushed. The woman wet her hands from a bowl and smoothed down Margaret's hair before using a bone comb to draw a part from her forehead to her nape. She tied each braid with a thin strip of leather. Margaret stayed seated and as silent as the Ladies of the Court until Queen Matilda awakened.

"I told you to wake me when she arrived."

"My fault, Your Grace." Margaret rose and approached the queen. "They just finished braiding my hair." Margaret curtsied and gazed at the footstool upon which Matilda's feet rested.

"No hair lengths?"

Margaret rose and shook her head.

"Mmm. Make him see you as you really are. Well done." Matilda sat straight, kicked her footstool aside and turned to the table beside her. She reached for two silver goblets and held them toward Margaret. "His Grace's and mine marriage gifts to you and your lord."

"Oh, Your Grace!" gushed Margaret. "They are magnificent!" Margret admired the carvings depicting grapes on vines, which sprang from the foot of each goblet. On one side, a cross in their open center. On the other, a medallion of swirling lines framing other markings. *I recognize the double arches of my name, but what are the lines and swirls on the right goblet?*

"The left goblet is yours and has an "M" for Margaret on it. The right has an "A" for Alfred, your lord."

Alfred? A name I heard never. Who is this Alfred? A very Saxon name for cert.

Goblets in hand, Margaret dipped her knee almost to the floor. "We thank Your Graces for your generous gift. We will drink from them at our wedding dinner. We will use them with pride and pass them to our heirs and report how you both helped us marry."

"You have more gifts. Perrine." The girl stepped forward and took the goblets from Margaret. She set them on the table beside a silver tray, which she picked up and carried to the queen. "Your lord's first gift is this shining fabric. The Church calls it "sericum, from the name of its country. It is rare and valuable." Matilda picked it up, and it waved as if a breeze had brushed past it. "Your lord carried it all the way from from the Holy Land, but comes from a land far east of there. We Normans say 'seire.' Saxons call it sioloc. Yours is this pale blue. He gifted me this cream one and showed me how they wear it in the Holy Land." With that, Matilda removed her small coronet, placed her own seire cloth upon her head, and replaced the circle. She pulled down the coronet with its single jewel on the center peak, and adjusted it so it set straight on her head and over the cloth, which waved across her forehead. The back section flowed over the queen's braids but only covered them to the middle of her back. Matilda picked up the blue seire and held it toward Margaret.

"Light as air. Soft and supple. So shiny." Margaret admired the oval shape she estimated was two feet long. "Who hemmed it with such delicate stitches?"

"They arrived so."

Margaret smiled and nodded. She watched Matilda lift from the tray a bronze circlet with small balls at its open ends. The metal was twisted and bore scratchings of a design Margaret knew not.

"This is Saxon. Passed down and worn by the women in Lord Alfred's family. A woman wears it for a year and a day from her marriage so all know she is a bride. Lord Alfred asks you to wear it to honor his family's custom."

"Your Grace, how may I do so? Others may think it a coronet. I dare not wear it."

"Nonsense, Margaret. I order you to wear it for a year and a day. The Saxons know it. I will explain the custom to the Court. Send to me any Norman who gainsays your wearing it." Matilda softened her tone. "You place it across your forehead with the open end to the back; that makes it adjustable. Lean forward. I will place the cloth and the circlet this first time." Margaret knelt. The queen talked as she worked, "Margaret, you will look lovely so attired, especially since you wore the blue gown I gave you at Forest Keep. The sight of you will take away his breath."

You flatter me because you are in a good mood. Because you got your way.

"Rochelle, fetch my viewer for the Lady Margaret to see herself."

Lady Rochelle offered the queen the small circle of polished silver framed and backed in polished wood; the queen handed it to Margaret. Margaret could see her chin and eyes clearly. To see the circlet and the blue cloth, she held the device away from her and turned her head this way and that. The silver circle caught the sunlight streaming from the windows above and flashed a beam across the room. *How delightful to see clearly how I look. Much better than a stream. How looks he? With a manly beard, not boyish, I pray.* Margaret sucked in her lips to stop her thoughts becoming words. *Is he squinty-eyed like the scribe? Will he smile or does he keep his lips straight and his face a scowl. No matter how vile his looks, I am yoked to him for life.* Margaret returned the viewer to its owner, who held it away from her so the Lady Rochelle could take it back.

Margaret stroked the fabric flowing down her back and felt it more than covered her stubbed braids. *Too fine for every day. Wear it only on Sundays and holy days.*

Queen Matilda caught Margaret's attention with, "Lord Alfred's third gift to you is this ring." In the queen's palm, Margaret saw a gold band with a red stone imbedded in it. "You wear it like me." Matilda put forth her right hand with a jeweled ring on the finger next to the smallest one. "The Church says the blood from this finger goes straight into your heart." Matilda leaned forward and whispered, "May his love encircle your heart all your days."

Margaret blushed. She took the ring and placed it on her finger. *It fits. Not too tight. How could he know?* She watched the queen gesture toward the door and heard, "Send in Lord Alfred."

As the door opt, Margaret's mind raced. *Bound for life to whatever walks through. He owns me now and can do as he wills. I must obey his every wish. Smile and pretend gladness. Blessed Mary, let me faint not!* Margaret turned toward the door and almost collapsed into her curtsey. With one knee on the floor to steady herself, Margaret stared at the rushes and prayed, *Dear God, help me find the right words, do the right things, embarrass myself not nor him. Your will, Oh God, in all things.* She saw a pair of tanned hands turned palms up and fingers gesturing her to take them.

Margaret raised her arms and placed her fingers atop Lord Alfred's. *Warm?* Alfred placed his thumbs over Margaret's fingers and slowly raised his hands. She inhaled a deep breath and moved. *Brown leather boots. Ankle high. Only lightly scuffed. New? Brown chausses cross gartered with leather strips. Shapely legs.* She rose from her knee and stood with her eyes still downward. *Thick thighs. Skip that Part! No over tunic or surcoat in this heat. Green tunic. White shirt. No sword. Brown leather jerkin. Broad chest. Thick neck. Well built. Strong looking. Breathe. Smile.* Margaret saw his chin and firm jaw, his smile, and looked into blue eyes twinkling at her. She blushed. *Not handsome, but manly. Manly enough to have shaved. A nick below his right ear. Blue eyes, bright, merry. Warm smile. High forehead. Smile back.*

"My lady."

In a hush, Margaret murmured, "My lord."

Alfred leaned toward her and whispered, "Glad I am to see you again."

"Has it been long?" she whispered back. *When met we?*

37

"Indeed."

"*Start now. Let the whole room hear.* My lord, I thank you most sincerely for your marvelous gifts. I am greatly pleased to receive the seire from beyond the Holy Land. I am honored to wear something from your family." She lifted her right hand, which he would surrender not. "The ring is lovely and fits perfectly."

"Know you why the stone is red as blood?" he asked above a hush.

"No, my lord," she whispered.

"Just thinking of you makes my blood boil." Alfred squeezed her fingers and then held them tight. He would have put her hands to his heart, but she pulled back and refused to let him draw her closer. *Heart stop beating so fast. Slower. Feel not. Think. Smell I soap. Washed. Hair Norman cut. Deep voice. Not handsome but neither ugly as I feared. Feel a power from him. What is that?*

Margaret blushed almost as crimson as the stone as she glanced about. *I pray no one heard him. Especially her. She looks smug, not shocked. Please her to see this. Deep breath. Now.*

"My lord, may I give you my gift?" Margaret stepped back and pulled her fingers from his with some effort. Alfred nodded. She unbuckled her sword belt and pulled the sheathed blade from her hip. She wound the belt around the sheath and held it in both hands, one on the sword's grip and the other near the tip.

"My Lord Alfred, this sword was given me by the command of Henry, King of England, for me to protect Her Grace, Queen Matilda, because I could go where men could not. I also wore it to protect myself in this world of men. Her Grace is now safe and needs my protection no more." Margaret inhaled deeply and thought, *Might I need this against him? Think not on it. Farewell, my friend.* "I gift this sword to you this day of our marriage to do with as you will. I need it not because I now have you. You are my sword, and I stand within your protection." Margaret handed Alfred the sword, which he took and held at his left side, where his own soon would be.

"My Lady Margaret, protect you I shall. All your days and even until your last breath. You are safe within my protection. Always."

Margret blushed again. *Said "my" hard like he owns me. Small smile. Does his brows lifting mean determination or something else? Protect me? I will await that test. Safe. Not been safe since I was six, that day my father... Oh God, I pray he will be true to his word. Please God, let it be true.* Margaret breathed deeply. Unable to bear his stare, Margaret dropped her eyes to his chin. *Know not what is behind that smile, what means merry eyes. Gladness to see me? Triumph he has me for land and rank?*

At the moment King Henry charged into the room. "My queen! Heard you not the dinner bell? I am famished!" Henry noticed the couple between him and his wife. "Ah, Lord Alfred. She has already gifted you her sword. A woman of her word." He looked past the pair. "I wish to dine now, my queen." Matilda rose; Alfred and Margaret stepped aside. Henry looked at his wife and then at Margaret. "Are you two setting a new fashion? Cloths covering your hair under a coronet and a Saxon marriage circlet?"

Matilda laughed. In a light tone, she reported, "Yes, we are. I wager you, every woman at Court will be wearing something similar within the week."

"If I know them," retorted Henry as he took her arm, "by the morrow. Lord Alfred, the Bishop of Winchester dines between us. Sit at my right."

The place of honor!

"Lady Margaret, you will sit to Her Grace's left. Follow."

Margaret bobbed a curtsey. Alfred raised his left arm; Margaret placed her hand upon his forearm. *After that blood remark, I dare not touch his flesh. What might he say then?* They followed the royals. The queen's ladies trailed.

Shortened his pace to match mine. A thoughtful gesture.

In the hall, Henry called back, "After we dine, I hunt. Lord Alfred, join us."

"Thank you, Your Grace."

Their attentions may gain us no approval from the Court, but they dare not snub us while we are with the royals. He is well-dressed in Norman clothes. Cut his hair, Norman fashion in front, and shaved the back of his head like a knight. Speaks Norman without that hard Saxon rolled rrrr sound. Will he stay pleasant when we are alone? Stay on his good side. Be obedient.

Margaret admired Queen Matilda's golden braids brushing her backside as she walked. She frowned. *Years will pass before my braids are that far from this cloth.*

Alfred saw Margaret's frown. He whispered, "Please smile for the Court."

Fearful, Margaret did as she was told. *Already ordering me. How much worse and how soon? Will my smile ever again be true? Your will, Oh God, in all things.*

Trumpets sounded; the Court stood. The king and queen stepped through the doorway. The party processed down the side of the hall and turned to parade up the center aisle. At the turn, Alfred lifted Margaret's sword toward a page, who raced forward and took it.

"With my things," was all Alfred had time to say before he and Margaret turned into the enter aisle and toward the dais.

5

More Gifts

"Your lord is gifting you with clothes. He asked me to choose the fabrics." Queen Matilda waved her hand, and one of her ladies opt the door. Three well-dressed seamstresses paraded into the room, each carrying four bolts of cloth. The tall, slim one stepped forward and gave silent obeisance to her queen. "The Lady Margaret is to have three linen bliauts with matching mantles and two woolen bliauts with matching mantles. Measure her feet and order three pairs of boots, one plain leather. Dye the other two so they match one outfit for each season." The seamstress nodded and gestured the other two women forward. "For winter, that dark green and that dark blue." Matilda looked at Margaret. "Yes, they will go nicely with your coloring. Now, lighter colors for the rest of summer." Matilda paused. "That pale yellow. The pale red as well." She pointed to a cream-colored bolt and ordered, "Seamstress, that outfit must be completed by the morrow. Lady Margaret, you will sew your wedding rib on the cream-colored bliaut for your church ceremony and Mass. I like that color best."

"Margaret asked, "Your Grace, the banns?"

"Bishop Giffard dispensed with the usual three Sundays and announced the first bann while you were with Lord Cai. The morrow is the second, with Saturday the third announcement. As this is Thursday, you must be ready in two days. No one works on Sunday, and you will be wed the morn after that."

"Yes, Your Grace." *No time to think or run. Has she also ordered a close watch?* "I can be measured in mine own room while you rest," offered Margaret.

"Nonsense, girl. We have yet to determine the length of your sleeves." At Margaret's confused expression, Matilda explained, "At Court, the length of your sleeve bell reflects your lord's rank. You give obeisance to women whose sleeves are longer than yours; you accept obeisance from those whose sleeves are shorter or who have no sleeve bell at all. You nod recognition to any woman whose sleeve bell is the same length as yours, for her lord's rank is the same as your lord's."

Married to a Saxon, I will have the shortest bell in the land.

"I disliked the confusion of ranks at Court, so I adopted this way of marking a woman. Only my sleeves touch the floor with my arms at my side. All others are shorter. My ladies, stand in line longest to shortest sleeve." The queen called forth the Lady Rochelle. She ordered the seamstress measure the woman's sleeve and to make Lady Margaret's two inches shorter.

Barely a bell at all. I will be giving obeisance to every woman in the land save servants. And she thinks I will be happy. Nod agreement.

Let not your face reveal your thought. "Your Grace, I plead with you to recline in your bed. I promise to stay as long as you wish. Please watch from the comfort of your bed."

Matilda moved to the bed and lay on her back atop the coverings. The seamstress was moving about and tying knots in a thick woolen thread as she whispered. "We will do the cream first."

Margaret waited to make her wish known until she was cert Queen Matilda had fallen asleep. *Glad I insisted and she relented. Worn from the birthing and doing too much too soon, she snores.*

"Seamstress," whispered Margaret, "her Grace chose fine bolts for my bliauts and mantles. I wish to change one part. I need but two linen bliauts. Please change the red bolt to plain work cloth, a serviceable wool for winter, laced not in back to fit my body but unlaced and straight from shoulder to hem and with straight sleeves. I cannot work with the bell sleeves she ordered."

The woman whispered back, "Good thinking. You will need it should you get with child."

Margaret blushed as she nodded. "Please remember to have pockets in all the sleeve hems."

"I must keep the sleeves belled, or she will be angry. At home, you may change them as you like. Please continue to stand straight with your arms out. I need finish this string with your measurements. I must have the cream done by the end of the morrow."

"My rib is long enough to band both the bliaut and the mantle. You will give me but a day to sew on my wedding rib."

"We shall work as fast as we can, my lady. After Mass on the morrow, may I see you to fit the cream? If so, I can complete it by sundown."

"Ask a page to find me. We will meet in my bedroom. I want not to disturb Her Grace any more than I must."

The seamstresses tiptoed out of the room. Margaret joined the ladies and stood against the wall. They watched the queen roll left and slumber on. The prince's nurse put him to her breast the moment he squeaked. The Saxon sentry stood between the ladies and the queen with her back against the wall.

Margaret parsed every moment with Alfred. *Very proper. Said the right things to the king. Acted Norman. Hides well among these. He will be good to me until we reach home. No royal protection there. No power either. Only one escape from this marriage. I needs test him. What to reveal?* Margaret clutched her hands before her and began choosing words.

After supping with the royals again on the dais, Lord Alfred and Lady Margaret followed them to the chapel for Vespers. Lord Alfred escorted her to the door of the queen's wing. He smiled at her.

Best I smile back.

"God give you good rest, my lady," he murmured. "I will escort you to chapel in the morn."

Margaret took her arm from atop his and bobbed a curtsey. "Thank you, Lord Alfred. I look forward to it. God give you good rest, my lord." She passed into the hall and turned to watch the door close.

As she approached the female sentry, the Saxon whispered, "My lady, I needs speak with you. May I enter your room?" At Margaret's nod, the woman stepped back to the wall.

Margaret pulled a pale green bliaut from a satchel and unrolled it. She hung it on a nearby peg and tried to smooth the wrinkles. At a knock, she opt the door. The Saxon slipped through and softly closed the door. She pointed to items on a stool in the corner.

"My lady, those blankets are for your use. Beneath your bed is the trapdoor to the stored food chambers for this wing. When you sleep under your bed, I suggest you avoid the cold seeping through its cracks."

"Why should I sleep on the floor? This bed looks soft and comfortable. The appointments are rich."

"Because you will be summoned to leave it. Want you that? A messenger would look upon your empty, untouched bed and think you are with the queen. He might wait a while, but, if you remain silent, he will leave. I tell you true. I am cert he will try this night or the next nights."

"Lord Alfred would take my maidenhead before the church ceremony?"

The woman shook her head. "Her Grace put you next to her rooms thinking you will be safe, but no one is safe when he wants to bed her."

Margaret covered her opt mouth. She nodded her understanding.

"If you bolt the door, he will know you are within, demand entrance and expect you to leave with him. Leaving it unlocked also places you in danger, but then he may wonder if you are with the queen. That may stop him," she added helpfully.

"Thank you for your good advice. God give you a good night." Margaret watched the woman leave. At the click of the door latch, she strode to the stool and took the blankets. On her knees, she assembled a makeshift bed and shoved it between the oak legs and under the bed frame. *When I was a slave at Royal Oaks, I slept on the ground with Cook and Caitlin. This will be no worse.* She blew out the candle and slipped into her hiding place. *Why would he do this to me? I am a good girl. I served him well. Yet he would sully me for his own pleasure. He thinks himself a good king, but he is not a good man. Like Sir Charles. Does she know? How can she smile at him and be pleasant if she does. Blessed Mary, is that what she meant by 'happy most days'? If I fail to protect mine honor, I might bear a royal brat. I could never face her. Better to run into the church for sanctuary than be set aside by a Saxon because I am no virgin.* Too upset to sleep, Margaret held her dagger under the blankets and prayed God to protect her. Finally she closed her eyes.

Later, Margaret awoke to a sound. Only her hand moved as she clutched the dagger beside her. She saw dim light on the floor between her bed and the door. Margaret held her breath.

"The bed is untouched. Where is she? He expects her in his chambers," Margaret heard a deep voice hiss.

"I know not. I saw her enter after Vespers. Mayhap Her Grace called her to her side."

"When she returns, send word at once. I will leave a page outside the outer door."

"Yes, my lord. At once."

The door closed and footsteps faded, but Margaret moved not. *How dare he! He calls himself a king, but he is base to treat women so. I want not his favor nor even his glance. I sought him not for this but for my freedom. I paid for it with honest labor. Now he wants my honor? He shall not have it. I will not be dishonored by such a one as he. Kings may order what they want, but he will not have me!* Again, she prayed to God He let her keep her honor. Much later, dagger still in hand, she closed her eyes.

6

Confessions

After breaking her fast, Lady Margaret dawdled behind Queen Matilda and her ladies until they disappeared through the doorway of the queen's wing. *Glad I caught his eye and mouthed 'talk.' Long strides. Walks with authority. Like a proud Norman. How can I talk with him before others?*

"My lord, thank you for your generous gifts. You clothe me in garments and shoes so I look a very elegant lady." *His eyes do twinkle when he is pleased. Mark that.*

"As you should be. I want everyone to know I care well for you and your appearance."

"Thank you for meeting me. I have things of import to tell you. Yet I know not where we may go for privacy when we must stay where we can be seen."

"Follow me, my lady." Alfred led her well away from the dais and down the Great Hall's long wall until he stood halfway between windows. He put his back to the front of the room. Alfred leaned his left shoulder against the wall.

Margaret stepped to face him with her right shoulder against the wall. *No one can fault us while we stand in full view of everyone and a foot apart.* Margaret looked into Alfred's eyes. *They seem to smile at me like his lips. See I kindness? I pray so.* Unable to bear the force of his stare, she looked toward the servants clearing the long table near them. After they hefted full trays and walked away, Margaret looked back at her lord. *Looking at his chin will unsettle me less.*

"My Lord, you need know things about me before we meet at the church door," she whispered.

Alfred whispered too. "Speak Saxon, Margaret. Few Normans know it and can read not our lips."

Margaret switched to her second language. "I have faults, my lord. And fears."

Be brave. I can do this. I dare not become his wife unless he knows I am willful and can be disobedient. When Alfred said nothing, Margaret looked up. She saw his nod, his serious expression, and took a deep breath. "When I was five, I stopped my father from beating a boy to death. He punished me for embarrassing him, but I cared not because the boy lived. I defied him again when I was six. He broke his promise to teach me to ride, so I jumped man-style on my brother's pony. He pulled me off, and my mother hid me to prevent a beating. Twice I ran into the forest in hopes he would come to find me. He sent others. After that, he never spoke to me unless it was to be unkind."

Margaret stopped while a Norman woman walked close by them. She frowned as she looked their way and continued on.

"Last year, we were attacked as we reached the estate the king gave me for my dowry. They killed a knight and my—our—aleman.

I was angry. Sir Masselin talked of heads on pikes in London, and I ordered the dead to be so treated. Lord Bedwin stated he should be the one to order it done; he told His Grace the idea was his. Also, last summer a ravager attacked one of…our villeins. I took him to Saxon court and plotted against him. I watched him hang." Margaret paused her litany of faults and glanced up. Alfred's expression had changed not. "My lord, I am stubborn and I am willful. When I think I have been wronged, I am vengeful. These are bad qualities in a woman, a wife."

"They are good ones given our times, Lady Margaret. You protected someone weak; you expected a promise to be kept, and you demanded justice when someone was wronged. I see not fault. I see strength."

"You will approve not the next one."

"Try me."

Just saying it is bad enough. This will stop him. Margaret sighed. "I like ordering men. For one year and a half year more, I have acted a little like a lord. Like a lord. I consulted with my men about sentry duties, practicing, and other men's matters. Oh, I said 'please' when I wanted something done or speak 'that is a good idea' when I thought so. I have become accustomed to being in charge. To having my way."

Expecting to be yelled at, Margaret squinted, looked down, and cringed. *He will tell me I am bad. Yell at me.*

"Owning land means each year I give forty days' service to the king, counting not the days to travel where he wants me to serve and the days to return home. Margaret, who will be in charge of our estate when I am absent two or three months every year?"

He sounds too reasonable. Is he following her orders to accept whatever I say until we are wed? Is he being honest? State just what is and see. "My father made his seneschal in charge when he served the second King William. Your seneschal is Cormac mac Cennedig, a Scot."

"The knights may follow him not because he is foreign. Besides, you will really be the one in charge, will you not?"

He knows. Admit it. Margaret nodded without looking up.

"Then our problem is solved. I rule when I am home. You rule when I am not."

Margaret looked up in disbelief. *Smiling?* Shocked, she returned a surprised face.

"I saved the worst for last." When Alfred commented not, Margaret gazed not at his chin but at his chest. "Like you, my father was a third son. My mother, her father's only heir, was his chatelaine. As he declined, she ruled. She grew accustomed to having her way. After Father and Mother wed, she stepped back. For a time they were happy, but Father's ways were unlike Mother's. At first, she objected when he did things she liked not. Then she countermanded him. They fought. To avoid him, she left to midwife women of rank. He punished her by taking Saxon women." Margaret started tearing. "Toward the end, they said dreadful things to hurt each other. They hated each other and made each other miserable." Tears spilled down Margaret's cheeks. "I want not their life. I want not to become like my mother. I want not ..."

"Hush, hush," murmured Alfred as he drew her into his arms and hugged her. *The warmth from him! Steady heart. Strong beats. Comfort.* Margaret felt a melting of the hard knot of fear choking her. He rocked her side to side. *Mother's way of comforting me.* Margaret leaned into that memory and his arms. She turned her head toward the wall. He bend his head close to hers. "That will happen not to us."

"Yes, it will. I am a terrible person." Margaret kept crying despite feeling his lips on her head.

"You are not a terrible person, Margaret. That will happen not to us because we know what not to do. How not to treat each other. Two strong-willed persons will have differences. When you overstep your place, I shall tell you. When you disagree with my decisions, you shall tell me. But we shall do so privately, decide, and then present a single face to the world."

"You shall yell not at me before others? Strike me?" Margaret sniffed back tears.

"No."

Margaret sniffled. "I shall disagree not with you before others."

"You see?" Alfred said cheerfully. "Already we are better than they. We have agreed…"

"Saxon! Unhand that lady!" demanded the foremost of a pair of knights, who had approached them.

Alfred returned to speaking Norman. "We are married, my lords. My lady is crying over a sadness not of her making."

"We do not touch our women before others!" commanded the lord.

"Tsk-tsk. You would let your lady cry and leave her uncomforted. How cold-hearted. Mayhap that is why she chose marry a Saxon instead of one of you."

A single face, he said. Margaret turned her head toward the men accosting Alfred. *Go away! You care not for him nor me, only in your self importance.* With her head still against his chest, she did something her mother had forbade. She stuck out her tongue. *Good. Pleased I am at your shock.* She hid her tongue and closed her lips.

Alfred saw the men's expressions. He heard, "What!"and "Well, I never!"

He watched the men spin on their heels and stride away.

Margaret sniffed back her nose's stuffiness. "Thank you, my lord."

"Are we done with crying?'

"Yes. Now I have an offer." Margaret slowly withdrew from Alfred's embrace, but he kept her hands. *Mother, you taught me no one can lie to you when you two are touching. I will feel it immediately. Thank you.* Margaret drew away far enough to see Alfred's face. "Before the church door, the priest will ask me if I go to this marriage willingly. If I say no and dash into the church, God will give me sanctuary. When it is safe, they will take me to a convent. If you no longer want this marriage, I will do that to free you."

Alfred squeezed her hands. "No, Margaret. Please, no. I wed you not for land or coin or title. They are nice, but they are not you. Take it all away; I care not. As long as we are husband and wife, I would live happy in my house on the virgate." Margaret pinked at the truth she felt in his touch and the passion in his voice. "Did not the queen tell you? I asked for you before you had any of it." Margaret nodded. "Then you know I speak true. Promise me you will jump not into the church and leave me alone and bereft. Never to see you. Never to have you to wife. Please promise me."

Margaret stared into his hopeful eyes. *What I see! Dare I risk marriage? I want not to be shut from the world, but what world will he make for me? I still have my running away garments. If I choose to marry, and he is evil, I can still escape.* Margaret took a deep breath, sighed, and whispered. "I promise…to be at the church door on Monday. I promise…to say yes." Margaret felt her heart beat hard at Alfred's warm look. *His eyes! How they draw me in. The Norman world for a man who says he wants me. What a cost! Please God, let it not be too high.*

He squeeze her hands hard. With bright eyes, Alfred replied, "I promise to be there before you, waiting with a glad heart." Then he teased, "I am so glad now I could hug you again." He sighed and added, "But the poor Normans could bear not to see two scandals in the same morn." He released her hands and winked.

Margaret stared back. *What I just said! Trapped by her. Trapped again by mine own words. How he looks at me! Heart, do slow. If only he were not Saxon.*

A page bowed to Alfred before addressing Margaret. "My lady, a seamstress awaits you in your room."

Margaret curtsied. "If you will excuse me, my lord. I needs fit a bliaut for Monday."

Alfred steped back and bowed.

As Margaret walked to the door ahead, she smiled and held high her head. *I tested him, and he passed. He defended me when he need not. Can a man be that good? Or is he acting so until I cannot escape. Am I seeing him aright? Why am I feeling pleased? How shall I act now? Act happy. God willing, someday it may be true.*

7

Preparations

Late Friday night, the seamstress delivered Margaret's cream bliaut and mantle to the queen's guards. The knight carried the items down the hall and was intercepted by the Saxon sentry.

"I will take them for the Lady Margaret and deliver the bundle in the morning. She sleeps in the same chamber with Her Grace, who ordered she be disturbed not." The woman hoped he passed her lie should King Henry again attempt to summon Alfred's bride.

Saturday morning sunlight streamed into the queen's audience chamber as a circle of ladies sewed. Queen Matilda had lent Margaret her second-best needle and invited her to sit with the group. "Thank you, Your Grace. I was so eager to see you again I forgot to pack my needle and scissors."

"No matter, you may use the scissors my ladies share," commented the queen as she worked to smock the top front of a gown for the Princess Matilda. She tied off and snipped the thread with her own scissors. She knotted the bottom of the remaining thread and drew her needle through the fabric. "I am already preparing her Christmastide garment, but she is growing so quickly I will fit not the parts of it to her and stitch it together until Advent."

"Will Prince William's clothing match hers?" asked the Lady Rochelle.

"Prince William will match his father. Black with cloth of gold trim."

"They will look magnificent," commented a lady.

"How came you by the design on your rib?" asked a dark-haired lady whose name Margaret knew not.

"The white petals with its yellow center refer to my name. I used the green line and leaves to flow from one flower to the next. The border stitching is blue because it is my favorite color."

The women chatted, gossiped really, as they sewed. They passed who was speaking to whom and who was not. They repeated what they had heard before Vespers and after this morning's Mass. They speculated the meaning of who met whom and what might be their business. One asked Margaret what food and drink her lord would serve the Court at their marriage dinner. Margaret gasped, for she knew nothing of the custom. *I pray he knows. He was not at Mass in the chapel. How do I reach him in time to prepare today? What might it cost? Are they trying to spend my dowry to nothing?*

"As the Lady Margaret knows not our custom, Lord Alfred and I made the arrangements," reported Queen Matilda. She set her work in her lap and looked up at Margaret. "When a lord and lady marry in Winchester, after the Church's blessing and the Mass, they provide a meal and dine with the Court. You will be seated with His Grace and me."

Margaret nodded, the relief evident in her expression. "My lord and I are grateful for your attentions, Your Grace. I am cert you chose well because you know what the Court likes best. You do us more honor than we deserve."

"His Grace and I are well pleased to see Norman and Saxon join. We will have our new English people sooner with each match we arrange."

The queen's words warned the three girls in their group they might next be married to a Saxon. The Lady Bernice changed the subject, and the other ladies eagerly joined in. When the queen excused herself, she took a lady with her into her inner chamber.

"Chamber pot," whispered the lady beside Margaret.

Seeking the whereabouts of her nemesis, Margaret commented, "I saw not the Lady Claire yester nor today."

"The queen sent her home while you were with the king's scribe and Lord Cai," reported the Lady Bernice.

"Oh." *I pray I am not the cause of her dismissal. These ladies will hate me for it.*

"The Lady Claire was chatelaine for the palace and led the Court for King William Rufus. After the queen married the king, the queen arrived at Court. The Lady Claire kept her power. Her Grace tried to reduce her influence, but Lady Claire plotted. Finally, the queen gave in. With the prince's birth, the queen has all the power she desires. She used how Lady Claire treated you as her excuse for dismissing the woman, but we knew it was coming. The Lady Claire overstepped her place too many times. Step lightly, Lady Margaret, as do we," continued the Lady Bernice. "You are in her favor now, but for how long you and we shall remain so or what will bring one of us down, none of us knows."

When the queen returned, the Lady Perrine was speaking of the fine weather with others joining in, so Queen Matilda knew they had been talking about her. She also knew whom to ask later to learn what they had said. By midday the sun was too high to see their stitches in the shadows of the room, so they stopped and waited for the dinner bell to ring in the Great Hall.

By the end of the day, Margaret had sewn her marriage rib around the neck and sleeves of her gown. She had chosen to trim the neck and the arm slits of the matching mantle rather than the hem of her gown. *The trim will show I am married even when I wear it over my bliaut.* Margaret spread her marriage clothes on the bed. *Should he op the door, he will see this and think I am not here.* She left to return the needle and the ladies' scissors before Vespers.

"Margaret, know you the custom of a mother and daughter sleeping together her last night at home?" Margaret shook her head. "Like you, my mother died before my marriage, so I had no one," said Matilda. "If you like, I shall replace your mother Sunday night."

"Happily will I sleep on a pallet beside your bed, Your Grace." *Stay cheerful.*

Matilda smiled. "My bed is wide enough. We will pretend we are in Forest Keep and sleep together as we did then. We will pretend we are mother and daughter. You ask for my advice, and I tell you how to be a good wife."

Margaret's eyes filled. *Only this night under my bed and I am safe.* Too moved to speak, Margaret's knee touched the floor as she curtsied. Matilda thought Margaret's wet eyes were tears of gratitude.

Again, Margaret slept hidden under her unmade bed with her dagger in hand. The Saxon sentinel shook her head at King Henry's emissary, who turned back without inspecting Margaret's room. Margaret slept but lightly and woke every time she turned. Her ears told her she was still safe. Near dawn, she fell into a deep sleep.

Sunday was special for Queen Matilda. As ten days had passed since Prince William's birth, the queen could again attend services. Her ladies helped her bathe and don new, clean garments, She presented herself at the chapel door on the castle grounds. Her confessor blessed her, sprinkled holy water over her, and declared her clean again and re-churched. King Henry escorted her inside and all those behind her attended Mass with the royals. *Where is he? Why is he not at Mass? Has he promised to meet me and now abandons me? I dare ask none, but where is he?*

On Sundays, all Christendom spent the day as the Church ordered. Mass, breaking one's fast just ahead of noon, and a day of visiting, resting, or prayer. The Church forbade hunting, gaming, gambling or any form of entertainment or work. The second meal was soup followed by a Vespers longer than the weekday ones. Then to bed at sundown as usual.

Matilda rocked her son to sleep and placed him in his cradle. The nurse lay in a cot beside him. Matilda disappeared into the inner room, where Margaret helped her undress. She brushed the queen's unbraided hair as it glimmered gold in the candlelight.

"I admire your honesty in not asking for added hair. Someday your daughter will brush your hair when it is this long. I never can seem to get mine to my ankles like other women. I have combed in oils and other things, but it thins and breaks at my knees no matter how hard I try."

"No one else has your golden color. It shines and glimmers behind you even in braids."

"You are kind to say so, Margaret."

Margaret crawled into the bed first, so the queen might leave more easily in the night. *She no longer needs me on the outer side to protect her.* "Your Grace, what must I do to be a good wife?"

Matilda was long with her list. She paused after each to give Margaret a moment to put it to memory. "Walk behind your lord, one step to his left and two steps behind. Never impede his sword or his sword arm. Always support him before others. Never correct him. Ask questions like 'How will you?' 'Might you consider?' and 'What think you of?' to turn his mind in a direction you want him to go, but never force it. Compliment him when he doth well, but only honestly. Men hate falsehoods and flattery. Feed him his favorite foods but at odd times, so he thinks you do it to please him. Then he may not suspect when you feed it to him when you need him in a good mood or when you want something. Occasionally, watch him at horse or weapons practice and admire his skills. Never cry when he leaves, but it is acceptable to tell him you will be forlorn without him and to look sad as he departs. Badger him not with questions. Listen to his words and observe his actions to learn his thinking. Laugh when he jokes. Raise his children to respect him, to honor him, and to obey him at all times." Matilda thought a moment before she finished with, "Saxons like kissing and hugging, so be generous with those. Sometimes surprise him and kiss him first. But only when you are private."

"Yes, Your Grace. I shall remember everything you told me." When Margaret heard no more, she dared to ask, "What of wifing? I know nothing of men, not their desires and … and parts."

"I will tell you nought. That is Lord Alfred's office. Leave it to him to instruct you. God give you good rest and a happy marriage day, Margaret."

"God give you a good night, Your Grace." *She is not hiding anything; she is just too modest to speak of being bedded. What is it like? Pleasant I hope.* Margaret closed her eyes.

8

Church Day

17 August 1103

Margaret woke with a jolt and looked to the clerestory windows. The blackness was lightening. She saw a woman's dark shape standing beyond the bed. She gestured Margaret forward. *Not if it is to the king.* She saw the queen was curled and facing her. Margaret crept past Matilda's feet and left the bed.

"Your lord ordered a bathe for you. I am to attend you and dress you for church," the Saxon servant whispered.

"Where is His Grace?"

"In his bed with another."

Margaret nodded and followed her with her bliaut and girdle over her left arm and her shoes in hand. At the door, she pulled out her dagger. *No tricks. I will cut him. I will scream.* The servant opt the door and walked through. Margaret crept to the opening and searched left, right, and down the hall. She looked back to see the female sentry standing behind her. She pointed to her and pantomimed closing the door. Margaret rushed through her doorway with her blade slashing left and right. She halted. Her room was empty save for the girl in front of a wooden tub.

"No tricks, my lady. The guard will give alarm." She stood beside two buckets, one full of hot water, one half-full of cool.

Margaret gazed at a large tub lined with wide linen strips draped over the edges. *Much higher than a horse trough. Linen? No splinters. Mayhap I can sit instead of instead of kneel.* She turned and shut the door.

"If you kneel and place your head over the edge, I will wash your hair before you bathe, my lady."

The girl said nothing about Margaret holding her dagger while she was on her knees facing the door as the girl wet, soaped and rinsed her hair. Margaret knelt back to have her hair toweled and wrap in a clean linen. Margaret lay her dagger on the rushes and stepped into the tub. *Oh-h-h, almost hot. Just right.* Margaret knelt to bathe all but her back. *With such a tub, this is a luxury I would have a bathe every week. I would order one large enough for me to sit and high enough the water would be at my neck. I doubt I will ever be rich enough to have one.* After she finished, the girl washed Margaret's back. Wrapped in a clean blanket, Margaret sat on the stool while the girl finished her hair with another linen.

"I will braid it damp so it stays together longer."

Where is he? I have seen him not since Friday Vespers. Was he avoiding me because he is angry about our private talk? Is it some Saxon custom to stay apart between contract and church? He is Saxon. She is Saxon. Might I ask her? No, appear not ignorant. The sentry who warned me about the king is one too. Did they help me because I am his wife? Should I ask him? No. Observe and wait for him to talk. Follow the queen's advice. Remember to smile. Smile all day no matter what.

Margaret smiled and thanked the girl for her service. When Margaret dressed, the girl tightened the laces at her back so the gown fit close to her body and displayed her high breasts and small waist. Margaret admired her wedding rib on her sleeves.

As the first church bells announced the day, Margaret stepped into the Great Hall. Lord Cai, dressed in fine garments of green and brown, pushed himself off a bench and approached. Margaret wore her head cloth and bridal wreath. She had fastened her mantle at her neck but had lain the front panels over each shoulder. The mantle hem gently waved as she walked toward Lord Cai.

"You look lovely, my lady. The king sent me to escort you."

"God's good morrow to you, Lord Cai. I am honored you do so." *He is so kind. A good man.*

With her hand upon his forearm, Lord Cai escorted the bride toward and out the double doors. They turned left, strode through the barbican, and stepped onto High Street. Margaret blinked at the bright summer sun still rising in front of them. The street was lined with Saxons, who pulled forelocks and curtsied as Margaret passed. They followed the pair. Margaret heard murmuring behind her but looked only ahead. They proceeded east until they turned right down Great Minster Street and then left; they walked over a grassy area to the approach the Cathedral. Their growing entourage followed. Margaret admired the new building with its stones glimmering as the sun rose behind it. *Magnificent. Three doors on this west side with the high one in the middle. No one but a bishop uses that door.*

Lord Cai turned left and around the building as he reminded Margaret, "No ceremonies but God's in His church. Marriage blessings, baptisms, and funerals are at the south door. Today we enter from there to stand behind the king, who stands before the choir."

Tell him not I already know this. Embarrass him not. Margaret only nodded and smiled a bit more.

Lord Cai and Margaret turned the corner and saw courtiers standing about. They parted to make an aisle as the bride approached. Bishop Giffard, stood outside the closed south door. Altar boys flanked him, one holding a silver bowl and the other a small book. Margaret spotted Alfred standing the to bishop's left and lowered her eyes to watch her feet moving. *A man of his word. He stands so straight. Wearing dark blue and black. I like his broad shoulders, but he grins too broadly. How embarrassing! Only a modest smile.*

Lord Cai stopped ten feet from Margaret's groom. From behind came a loud disturbance. The courtiers parted wider, and Lord Cai moved them left. In rode King Henry with four knights' escort. Margaret's eyes narrowed. *Haughty, but I stopped you. Hide my thoughts. Smile.* Margaret opt her eyes wide and smiled. *Thirty-five now? Still black-haired. Still strong, imposing. He thinks himself handsome.* Margaret kept smiling. The king dismounted with a sword in a scabbard in his left hand and threw his reins to a courtier, who grabbed them and led the horse away. Hoping to see Roussel, Giraud, or Cachier, Margaret looked toward his knights, but recognized none of them. *I wish I could see them again.*

"Time to make a Saxon a lord!" roared King Henry. The Saxon crowd behind him shouted, "Huzzah!" The courtiers remained silent.

"Kneel, Alfred." After Alfred did so a bit awkwardly, King Henry drew his sword and held it over the man's head. "Do you swear to Almighty God you will faithfully serve Him who made you, His Church who leads you, and His priests who guide you?"

"I so swear."

"Do you swear to serve your king, defend his lands, obey his laws and live honorably all the days of your life?"

"I so swear."

"Do you swear to defend the weak, aid the poor, and in all things do what is right, honorable, and just?"

"I so swear."

"I declare you to be worthy to live in my realm, serve me, hold my lands, pay tithes and taxes, protect my people and have all the responsibilities, rights and privileges of a lord of England." With the flat of his sword, King Henry touched Alfred's right and left shoulders. "Rise, Lord Alfred. Accept this sword as a symbol of your rank. As you arm yourself, remember those whom you have sworn to serve and to protect with this blade and your honor." The king waited for Lord Alfred to don the sword. King Henry clasped right wrists with him and slapped him on the shoulder. He turned Lord Alfred to the crowd and called out. "Greet Lord Alfred. He is now one of us."

The courtiers' applause was barely polite. The Saxons' was thunderous. He grins. Saxons, I thank you. King Henry waved Lady Margaret toward himself. Lord Cai lowered his arm, and Margaret walked to the king. She accepted his arm and let him lead her to her husband.

Bishop Giffard raised his hand for silence. "Lady Margaret, did you make this match of your own free will without pressure from anyone and without any reservations?"

"Yes, I did." *No running inside now.*

"Did you, Lord Alfred, make this match of your own free will without pressure from anyone and without any reservations?

"Yes, I did."

"This marriage is valid in the eyes of God and is as everlasting as is his Church. Let all witnesses say "Aye." King Henry did so, and the crowd followed. Bishop Giffard instructed the couple to kneel. He raised his right hand over them and took the small book in his left. After the bishop had read the blessing in Latin, he translated the Latin to Norman and repeated it in Saxon.

"Let us pray to the Lord for Alfred and Margaret,
who come to God's altar at the beginning of their married life.
May they always be united in Christian love for each other.
Jesus teaches us this union may never be divided as a sign
of the perpetual marriage between the Christ and his Church.

Lord, give your blessing to Alfred, your son,
so he may be a faithful husband and a good father.
Bless him with heirs and children who honor him.
May he honor his wife and love her
as Jesus the Christ loves his bride, the Church.

Lord, give your blessing to Margaret, your daughter,
so she may be a good wife and mother,
caring for her home, being faithful to her husband,
and obeying his good will.
Give her the grace of love and peace.

May they live to serve God and to obey His Church.
May they see their children's children and live to old age.
Father, grant, as they come together to your table on earth,
they may one day have the joy of sharing your feast in Heaven.
We ask all this be Your will through Jesus the Christ, our Lord.
Amen."

Bishop Giffard took handfuls of blessed water from the silver bowl the altar boy standing beside him held and sprinkled it over first Alfred and then Margaret. "This holy water is your blessing from God. Please rise and face each other. The peace of God be with you for the peace you seek between you in your marriage. Alfred and Margaret, seal your union with the kiss of peace."

Margaret froze. *Not on the cheek like a brother. Lips together. Where goes my nose?* Alfred stepped forward until he almost touched her body with his. Margaret lifted her head to meet his warm gaze. He tilted his head right. Margaret tilted her head the same direction, read his expression, and switched to tilt to her right. She held her breath. Alfred leaned in and pressed his lips to hers. *Soft. Warm. Nice.* Alfred pulled three inches from her face. In Saxon, he whispered, "Thaes hal, wif."

In Saxon, Margaret replied, "Thaes hal, husband." She blushed and smiled back. Lord Alfred stepped away and offered his left arm; Margaret placed her hand upon his forearm.

"Enter God's church to start your marriage with the Mass, which was ordained by Our Lord through Jesus the Christ," instructed the bishop. He turned to the door behind him. An altar boy held the door op for all who entered: Bishop Giffard, King Henry, his knights, Lord Alfred and Lady Margaret, and those of the Court. The Saxons turned away to enter through left door at the west end of the cathedral.

That was not so hard. Pray he is good to me. Pray I anger him not and learn his ways quickly. Pray for a good life together. Pray for decorum when the ladies put me to bed, and the men push him into my—our room.

After Mass, King Henry and his men left the cathedral first, followed by his knights. The courtiers, all Norman, pointedly made their way down the center aisle immediately after the knights to force Lord Alfred and Lady Margaret to wait. The couple knew they ranked lowest in the opinion of the Court. They kept their smiles and waited for everyone else to exit the right-side door at the west end of the church. The Saxons waited for the married couple to pass.

Become accustomed. A favor from the royals matters not to them. Wait for him to move first and follow as she said.

Outside the cathedral, Saxons stood in clumps behind the couple and followed them at a respectful distance. Alfred and Margaret turned right on Great Minster Street to reach High Street. Everyone felt hooves pounding the ground behind them. Saxons looked back, shouted warning, and scattered.

Margaret turned toward Alfred just as a steed raced to separate them. The force of the horse's blow knocked down Alfred, but Margaret fell against a horse behind her. Someone threw a blanket over her head, hoisted her, and tossed her upward to the second horseman. He grabbed her, threw her over his saddle and held her tight. The knight dashed up Great Minster Street and turned right as Alfred struggled under the first horse's belly. He scrambled away and stood in time to see the knight who had almost trampled him riding up the street.

"Where is she?"

"The knights took her," yelled one Saxon. "East on High Street," called another.

"My horse!" shouted Alfred as he raced across the meadow. The Saxon, who had thrown the blanket over Lady Margaret and had lifted her to be taken, followed Lord Alfred and grabbed his arm.

"Stop, my lord. I know how to find her." He shrank back when Alfred drew his sword.

Alfred grabbed the Saxon's tunic and yanked the man to him. "Tell me or die!"

9

A Wild Ride

Despite someone's hand on her neck holding Margaret against the horse, she struggled against her captor. He slapped her backside hard, grabbed her hips, and pulled until her left hip was against his belly. Through the blanket encasing her, Margaret heard, "Fall and you die." She heard the horse's hooves on a wooden bridge. It turned left.

Right on High Street. Over the bridge. Through East Gate. Now north. Why?

The horseman rode on, splashing through a stream turning left for a time and then turning right again. Margaret memorized sounds and turns as she formed a mental map of where she was being taken. *Best way to work my way back after I escape.* Margaret gasped and attempted deep breaths, but the tight blanket almost closed her nose. Her belly hurt from being bounced on the horse. The horse slowed to a walk. The smoothness of its gate told her they were on a road, but to where she could not guess. After what seemed forever to Margaret, the horse stopped. Instead of releasing her, the horseman bent close to her head.

"Listen well, Lady Margaret. If you want not to be ravaged by your lord's enemies, do as I instruct. In the forest to your right, you will see a path. Follow it. Each time it splits follow what I tell you." The man paused. "Right, left, over a narrow stream, left, and left again. Stop in a clearing with a wide stream just beyond it. Stay hidden. Your lord will meet you there. Now repeat the path." The man heard Margaret's muffled correct response. "After I set you down, count ten before you remove the blanket. That will protect me. Drag it behind you to hide your trail until you are well into the forest. Remember, let no one but your lord find you. Do you agree to this?" At Margaret's muffled "yes" and head nod, the man released his grip on her. He grabbed her under her armpits and lowered her until she felt her toes touch the ground. He released her.

"Count ten!" he yelled.

Margaret heard the horse's hooves pound away and become faint.

… eight… nine… ten.

Margaret pulled off the blanket and sucked in deep breaths. She looked down the road she had come and up the road her attacker had taken. *No one. Nothing but a dirt road between bushes beyond the small ditches and forest beyond that. No path across the road. Where am I? Where is my seire and circlet?* Margaret searched the blanket folds until she found them. *Cloth still clean. Circlet undamaged.* She stuffed the seire between her breasts and pushed the circlet on her head. Margaret spotted hoof prints in the dirt. *Disturb them not or they will know where he released me.* Margaret gathered in the blanket, draped its corner over her footprints and stepped backward. *This works!* She looked behind her and angled off the road edge, down the ditch, and to the path. Before she turned toward the forest, she folded the blanket into a strip narrower than the path. *Break not branches and reveal my path.* She turned to walk forward but kept pulling the blanket behind her. *Did Alfred arrange this because he knows someone wants to harm me? If I am dead, he loses everything. Question not. Walk.* At the first junction, Margaret took the right path. *Ten more steps and I will pull up the blanket. If it breaks brush, I can be followed.* She looked around and saw only forest and the narrow animal path ahead. *Deer path? Boar? Listen and be watchful; boar are dangerous.*

At the next juncture she stepped left. Soon she jumped a narrow stream bed. *Just a trickle. Now left again.* When the path split, she stayed to the left. *The quiet is lovely. I smell flowers.* Margaret stopped at the edge of a clearing filled with bright sunlight but no shade. *Birds sing, so no one is tramping through the forest. Unless they are hiding and waiting for me to show myself.* To cert she was alone, she stayed in the shadows and waited. *A camp? Ring of rocks beneath a spit, a pile of wood. Chopped tree trunks for seats.* She leaned forward and looked right. *A lean-to? Who leaves behind bedding?* When she saw no motion, heard no noice, she tiptoed left over twigs and dead leaves. At a fallen trunk, she folded the blanket and set it upon the log. Margaret removed her mantle, folded it, and placed it on the blanket. *Too hot to wear.* She sat next to the mantle.

Margaret stared at the lean-to opposite her. *Roof slants toward the tree it rests against. Sides and back are closely woven withies. Sun darkened and old. This place has been used for years. Linens? Who leaves behind valuable linens and blankets? Why?* From within the shadows of the forest around the camp, Margaret smelled flowers, heard buzzing and saw birds hopping from branch to branch. *No breeze. The summer feels so hot.* After a time, Margaret decided to loose her lacings. She reached behind her and undid the bow. Because she could only pull at the first few lacings, she only released her waist and half her back from the tight bindings. *Bound inside my bliaut with no relief unless a maid helps me. A fashion I like not. Better a looser garment belted.* She pulled out her seire and smoothed it against her leg. Birds went silent. Margaret froze.

From opposite the way Margaret had come, she spotted a shadow cautiously approach the clearing's edge. Beside a tree, the shadow drew his sword, and boldly strode to the center of the camp. Alfred turned in a circle as if he expected to be attacked. When he faced Margaret, he stopped and peered into the trees. He looked about before instructing her to silence by holding his pointing finger to his lips before gesturing her forward.

Margaret set her seire on her mantle and it took up with the blanket and stepped out of the forest. With his sword still in hand, Alfred approached and whispered, "Only you?" At her nod, Alfred took her hand and led her toward the trees to Margaret's right. Margaret concentrated on her feet as the couple wended their way. A deer path led to a meadow fragrant with many-colored blooms. Still holding his wife's hand, Alfred stood at the edge of the grasses; Margaret stood behind. When the birds resumed their noises and songs, Alfred led her around the edge of the meadow to the shady side. He reached for the blanket and shook it out before laying it on the grass.

Alfred took Margaret's things from her arm and dropped them beside the blanket. Still silent, he walked Margaret to the blanket's center. "Remove your boots, pull up your skirts and lie on your back." *And reveal my body! Why? Ask not. Obey.* Margaret did so. She watched Alfred toe his heels to step out of his boots. Margaret looked away as he pulled his tunic and shirt over his head.

"We are not fully wed until I bed you. We may have been followed. This must be done now." He looked away and toward the trees. "I am sorry it must be done quickly, but it must. Close your eyes, Margaret."

He raised her skirts above her waist and parted her legs. The weight of his body hurt her sore stomach, but she had no time to react. *A sword! The pain! He has pierced my body with a sword! God save me from this death!* Each thrust stabbed her body and pierced her heart. *A shade of Hell. Hell and the smell of his sweat and horse. His weight hurts my breasts. Oh God, is this how I die?* He shuddered, stopped moving, and withdrew. He knelt beside her, lifted her heels, and moved them together. Alfred lowered her skirts and draped her mantle over her. Margaret felt wetness between her thighs as shame washed over her. Her heart went cold, and she shuddered.

"Oh, Margaret. I wanted this to be pleasant. Next time. I promise next time it will be." She turned her head away from him and spoke not. "Stay here. I must pace our area to be cert we are alone. If you hear fighting, follow me not. Hide in the forest and live."

Eyes still shut so hard her forehead wrinkled, Margaret nodded, rolled to her side, and clutched her knees to herself. *Caitlin lied. She spoke of love and pleasures. Being married is no pleasure. Only pain. Oh, the pain of it. That is why Her Grace refused to speak of this. How can women smile at their lords when they know they must face this? Do this whenever he demands. I want not marriage. I want death. Dearest God, save me from this world. Let me bleed to death. Take me now.*

Shadows lengthened and covered half the meadow before Alfred returned. He said Margaret's name as he approached. When she reacted not, he thought her asleep. Alfred donned his garments and lay down behind her. Margaret had heard him. Now she felt him curl himself against her back, felt his arm around her waist and his breath on the back of her neck. *Move not, speak not. God, please make me dead.*

Alfred gently shook her. "Margaret, wake. We are alone and safe. Do you not hunger? Someone left us food." He shook her again and called her name.

Margaret stirred and sat up with her back to Alfred. She nodded, reached for her mantle and seire at her knees and clutched them as she stood. Still silent, she slipped into her boots and kept her eyes to the ground. At her first step, she stopped the groan of pain welling within her. Every step hurt her inner thighs, her woman parts. *I am damaged for life.* When Alfred grasped her hand she forced herself to let him keep it. She swallowed her pain as he led her across the meadow. To her, the grass and flowers looked gray. *Soon they will be dead. My heart, my soul is as gray as these. Please let me die as well.*

Alfred stopped. "Look up."

Margaret spotted a large, dark bag hanging among the tree branches. She saw Alfred reach for the rope above them. When he pulled it and the bag moved, she stepped back. Alfred caught the bag.

"I feel two bottles and a haunch of meat. Follow me; I will warm you with a small fire."

Margaret did as she was bid. At the fire pit, she stood behind him. She saw him remove two flints and a wad of wool from the bag, knock the stones together over some of the fibers and push the small fire under the sticks and twigs he had found leaning together inside the stone circle.

A need rose in her body, urgent, demanding. "May I step into the trees? I have need."

"Go not far."

"No, my lord."

Alfred turned to speak, but he saw only Margaret's back as she strode down the path from which he had come. He saw her turn right and disappear into the bushes. He stood, shook the blanket Margaret's captors had used, and settled it on the ground before the fire pit. At hearing Margaret's shriek, he dashed to her. Alfred found her crouched with her mantle splayed about her. He grabbed her shoulders to stop her from falling over.

"I cannot! Cannot! It burns so. Burns. Yet I must. I must!"

"Come with me," commanded Alfred as he pulled her to stand. With his arm about her shoulders, Alfred took her out of the bushes and down the path. At a stream's edge, Alfred talked as he worked. "Step into it. Kneel facing upstream. The water will take away your piss and cool your flesh," he said as he removed Margaret's mantle, threw it over a bush. She froze when he unfastened her girdle and hung it over a limb. When he removed her boots, Margaret was so unsteady she had to put her hands on his shoulders to remain upright. Alfred set her boots aside. "Raise your arms." With both hands, Alfred grasped Margaret's bliaut and chemise as one and pulled them over her head. He pushed her forward. "Go. I will guard."

Margaret stepped into the stream; its coolness roused her. When she toed a sandy spot, she faced upstream and knelt. Margaret relieved herself. Alfred heard a small sigh. The tension in Margaret's back, hips, and thighs eased. She sat back on her heels and sighed again. *I could stay in this coolness forever.* Margaret swirled her hands at her hips, and the water cooled both them and her fevered thoughts.

She splashed water over her breasts and stomach again and again. She turned away and twice lifted a handful of water to her lips and drank. Finally she splashed water on her face and hid behind her hands. *Cry not. Cry not or you will anger him.* She heard Alfred call her name. She relieved herself again. Then she released her face and stood. She ignored his smile as she stepped out of the stream.

"A water nymph. Young and perfect you are."

Margaret ignored his remark and gave him her back as she slipped into her boots. He draped her mantle over her, and she hid herself inside it.

"Supper awaits us." Alfred lifted her things from the branches and draped them over his left arm. With his sword in his right hand, he turned and led the way.

He takes my clothes because he plans to attack me again. This time naked. Dare I fight him?

Alfred hung her clothes over the lean-to roof before turning and kneeling to the left of the food bag beside the blanket. He patted the spot to his left. "Please sit here."

Margaret picked up her seire to place it atop her garments before she slowly approached the fire. She slipped her hands through the arm slits, tucked her mantle under her knees, and knelt to his right. When he did not grab her, she pushed her arms out as far as her elbows and sat back on her heels. *You will not surprise me again. I will fight to keep my cover.*

Alfred offered Margaret the opt bottle, and she sipped wine. *Not bitter. Good quality. He spared not cost.* Then she drank and set the bottle between them. Margaret watched Alfred place a haunch of smoked beef on s dinner board. He cut a slice, poked it with the tip of his dagger and offered her first bite. Margaret took the meat.

She nibbled at it as she looked sideways and watched Alfred cut a piece for himself. When her portion was small enough, she pushed the rest into her mouth and chewed. After Alfred took his drink and set down the bottle between them, Margaret picked it up and drank again. Thus they dined, eating silently as each took a turn at meat and wine.

With a head shake, Margaret refused a bite of meat. Alfred finished it before he offered her the wine, which she also refused. Alfred drank, re-corked the bottle and set it aside. He shoved the board and remaining chunk of beef inside the bag.

The shadows inch toward the fire pit. Dark coming. Too soon.

"Time for bed," he murmured. He stood and offered her his hand. When she did not take it, he added, "I am going to put you in the bed and finish cleaning up. This night I will be sleeping fireside."

Margaret took a deep breath and accepted his help to rise. *That is a bad start. Do what I must. Be strong.* She faced him and shook her head. She said, "We are married. I want us to sleep in the same bed."

Alfred nodded agreement even though the tightness he heard in her voice told him she meant it not. "Would you like to wear your shift to bed?" he offered.

"Yes, thank you." *Mayhap he means not to attack me now, but after I sleep a while.*

At the lean-to, Margaret turned her back to Alfred and pulled the chemise from inside her bliaut. She heard, "Allow me," as Alfred removed her mantle and held it between them high enough he could not see over it. Margaret donned her undergarment. *At least he knows something of modesty.*

As Margaret knelt to crawl under the wool blanket and between linen sheets, Alfred draped her mantle with her bliaut. Alfred watched her lie on her side to face out, pull the blanket under her chin and tightly grasp them. He nodded at her message and turned away.

Margaret watched Alfred return to the fire, kneel, and poke the low flames with a stick. *Strange, he would provide down pillows and fine bedding in such a place as this. But I will pay for it, I know I will.* Her eyes filled, spilled, and wet the pillow cloth.

If he looks back, he will know. Best I turn to the back wall.

Alfred heard the covers rustle. He turned not, but rather uncorked the bottle and finished it. He left the bottle fireside, pulled close the drawstrings of the food bag, and left to hang it high in a tree far from the clearing so as not to draw wild animals to them. He stopped at the clearing edge and listened. He heard a distance owl hoot, other night sounds, and soft crying.

Alfred tiptoed to the lean-to, and toed the heels of his boots. He lay his sword upon its sheath on the ground where he could grab it while abed. He crawled between the the sheets and over a bed of soft evergreen boughs under the lower sheet. He lay beside his wife. Margaret sniffed back tears and froze. Alfred slowly rolled Margaret to him. He lifted her head and put his left arm under it. Moonlight revealed her wide, fear-filled, wet eyes.

"Oh, Margaret, this is not the wedding day I had planned. I am sorry it went ever so amiss, that you were taken from me, that I hurt you. Go ahead. Cry it all out. I can bear it."

Margaret let loose a sob that tore at Alfred's heart. He pulled her to him and held her as she sobbed into his chest and soaked his shirt. Alfred stroked her head and back and kissed her hair as he repeated, "I am sorry, my love. So sorry. So sorry." He continued to stroke her hair for a long time. When Margaret's wailing subsided, Alfred again spoke.

"The morrow will be a better day, I promise. We will begin anew. I promise a better day." Alfred offered her his sleeve; Margaret wiped her eyes and nose. Without looking at Alfred, she rolled to face the wall.

"God give a good rest, Margaret." At her throaty, "and you," Alfred turned to lay on his back. He pulled the blanket over himself and stared at the ceiling of woven evergreen boughs. Alfred moved not until he heard his wife's soft, regular breathing.

From sound asleep, Alfred sat upright and grabbed his sword. He released his grip when he realized Margaret's rolling back and forth on her side had awakened him. "No, no. Stop, please stop," she moaned as she thrashed. Ashamed, Alfred froze. He vacillated between leaving her to her night terror or waking her. He feared her blame, her hatred for his ill treatment of her. He wondered if he should have explained himself before they slept. When Margaret stopped without waking, he lay back and pondered how to keep the morrow as good as he had promised.

10

Second Day

Margaret roused from slumber at the smells of rabbit cooking and wood burning. She rolled to her back and spotted bits of sunlight through evergreens atop the lean-to's wooden frame. *Their scent is both sweet and piney. Fresh laid. That is why I saw him not before the church. He was preparing this place.* She rolled again and saw Alfred's shirtless back as he turned the spit. She sat up and frowned as she stretched. *Why are your back and arms blackened and bruised? That band around your middle bespeaks you have broke your ribs. What have you been doing?* Margaret pushed tendrils and loose strands back into her hair. *I must redo my braids.* She inhaled. *Eat. No, stream first. Before I burst.*

She dipped her head to step outside the abode, slipped into her boots, and straightened her back and chemise. *Too dirty a place for my bliaut, but this hides me not. I must don the mantle and flap it to cool me as needed.* She spotted his dagger on one side of him and his unsheathed sword on the other. *Startle him not.*

"God give you a good day, my lord."

Alfred turned and gave her a broad smile. "Alfred. When we are alone, use my name. Please say 'Alfred.' I like 'Husband' as well."

"Alfred."

"Thank you." Still smiling, Alfred patted the blanket spot to his left.

Margaret knelt and rested her hands on her knees. "Are we speaking Saxon today?"

"Norman when others are within hearing. We shall always speak Saxon to each other when we are alone."

"May I ask why?"

"Saxon has more words of love and affection, happiness and merriment. Better suited between husband and wife."

Start this day following. "Good." She watched him remove the spit and lean it against one of its uprights. "You are shirtless."

Alfred looked askance as he answered, "It needed washing." Margaret blushed. He added, "Drying on a bush." He pointed, "These must cool or we burn our fingers and mouths."

Keep him talking and away from the bed. "I need the stream again ... Alfred."

He slipped his dagger into its sheath, stood, and offered his hand, which she took. Alfred took up his sword. With his blade held forward, he led the way.

If we are attacked, I shall need my dagger as well. Best I wear my girdle. After the stream, she thought in Saxon.

At the path's end, Alfred stepped aside, gallantly bowed, and waved her forward.

Margaret put her hand to her mantle clasp. "Please turn your back."

Alfred shook his head. Still smiling broadly, he reported, "Husband's privilege. I may see you naked." He cocked his head as if expecting a retort; she gave him none. He watched his wife unclasp her cover and drape it over a bush, slip out of her boots, and pull her chemise over her head. He forced himself not to reach for her. Margaret quickly stepped into the stream to stop his being able to do so.

She shivered as she knelt. *Not yet sun-warmed. No pain this time.* She only splashed her face before standing and returning to her garments. She pulled her chemise down her wet skin and swirled her mantle around herself before fixing the broach a little lower than her neck. "Alfred, have you broke your ribs?" He nodded. *Mayhap he will treat me better if I am kind.* "If you permit me, I shall dip that strip of cloth into the water and rewrap you. Its coldness may soothe you."

"I thank you for thinking of my need." With that, he lifted his sword above his head and raised his left arm skyward.

Margaret found the tucked-in end at his waist. "If you will turn as I unroll, this will go faster." He turned once and stopped while facing her. After rolling the strip close to his body, Margaret asked him to turn again.

Alfred shook his head. "Reach around me."

Margaret rolled her eyes at him and glared. At his smirk, she cocked her head and sighed in frustration. He moved not. Margaret was forced to stand toe to toe with him and to briefly touch chests as she reached behind him for the growing wad. Margaret stepped back and around him. Kneeling at the stream's edge, she swished the rolled linen in the water as she plotted. *You may have started this game, but I shall end it my way.* She squeezed out much of the water before standing. She approached Alfred and spoke in a quiet, reasonable tone. "Alfred, I cannot reach around you and position this wetness to

83

your best advantage unless you keep your arms up and turn when I ask." He nodded. "Also, I must pat down the cloth against your skin; tell me if I hurt you. I want to be gentle." Alfred did as he was told, and Margaret began under his left arm. She patted the cloth across his front. "If you take deep breaths now, this will fall anon. Please breath normally." Alfred flinched the first time she patted his back. Chagrined at causing him pain, Margaret forgave him for his game playing and apologized before proceeding. She only patted to set the cloth where his skin was not bruised. As she worked, Margaret commented, "I smell herbs. I know not who helped you."

"A Saxon healer from among the castle servants."

She guessed if she worded her next comment well, she would learn more. "Someone broke your ribs."

"A lord and his knight."

"And you fought them."

"If I had, by right they would have killed me. Any Saxon who even touches a Norman dies. The law. I could only take the beating."

"But the king had signed the contract. You were also a knight and could defend yourself."

"Not so. Not until I received my sword and bedded you to make our marriage fully legal."

To protect yourself, you took my maidenhead with no care for my pain. If they found us before he... I could hate him for that. I dare not. I must let that pass or my face will reveal my disgust. Be careful with him. She finished the last round and tucked the end under his right arm.

Act relieved and sound so. "I am grateful you survived."

"I was on the ground curled to protect my innards as they were kicking me when Sir Roger, the king's constable, stopped them." Alfred looked over her head as if he were seeing, reliving the scene.

"Sir Roger said, "Kill him if you like, but do not expect your family to be alive when you return home.""

Alfred sighed. "They stopped. Then he said, 'Look into the shadows. Saxons are watching. He is one of them. What you do to him, they will do to your heirs, mayhap your whole family. Three years ago, remember? The Saxons killed their lord and his family after their lord raped a girl and then killed her and her family when she reported him to the estate priest. The whole lot of them have disappeared, and we have yet to find them. There are ten times more of them than us, and they care more for honor than their lives. It is their Saxon way.' He ended with, 'Do what you will, but I want my family to live.' He said loudly, as if to the watchers, 'I will watch not this murder. I am party to it not.' I heard him walk away. They each kicked me one more time. They left me to die." Alfred snorted his derision. "They know not how hardy we are."

"The Saxons took you in and nursed you. That is why I saw you not until yester morn." At his nod, Margaret hugged his left arm despite wetting part of her mantle at being so close. "I shall pray for Sir Roger and his family. He is a good man."

"You may not remember my saying how sorry I was I hurt you when we lay in the meadow. I say it again, Margaret. I am so sorry I had to rush our first union. My plans were so much better than that. You deserve so much. I will do better. I promise you we will be better together." Alfred bent and kissed the top of her head. He held his sword downward as he hugged her shoulder and held her for a moment. When Margaret withdrew and look up at him, she saw sympathy in his eyes and heard, "Our breakfast is cool now."

Margaret stepped aside and followed. *Contract, church, bedding. I thought those hard. Not so. The hard part will be living together. I must learn his ways, be obedient, and follow Her Grace's advice. Badger him not with questions. Observe. Step lightly. Learn what he thinks from his deeds. I thought marriage was going to be a good thing. Now I know better. As dangerous it might have been to remain single, it is just as dangerous to be wed. I must be careful every moment.*

At the lean-to, Margaret donned her girdle. The couple ate in companionable silence. Margaret lifted her arm to toss a bone toward the trees.

"No. I must take the bones far from here and bury them if I am to snare more for the morrow. Also, we want not boar sniffing nearby and finding us." Margaret handed him the bone, which he placed on the corner of the blanket. The pile grew as they finished their meal. Alfred stood, gathered the bones, and walked west into the trees. When he returned, he found Margaret seated on the stub of an old tree trunk with her mantle wrapped around her. Only her head, hands and boots showed. Alfred picked up the blanket and disappeared toward the stream. When he returned, he draped the blanket over a bush.

He washed the bone corner. A careful man. Margaret's face colored as she looked at his half-covered chest and broad shoulders. *Please wear your shirt. You unsettle me.*

Alfred walked to the lean-to and placed his clean shirt atop Margaret's bliaut. As he approached his wife, he watched her bounce off the stump and stand beside it at attention as if she awaited an order. Alfred stopped four feet from her.

Distract him. "What is this place?"

"A wedding bower." Alfred watched her face show confusion as she glanced about. "An hunter's campsite remade. An old Saxon custom. The husband makes and fills a place in the woods. After they wed, they run away and hide. Villagers seek them. If they find them, the couple must return. If they are found not, they may stay away as long as they wish." Alfred smirked. "I have been told some stay so long, she returns fat with child."

"When prepared you this?"

"I did not. After I was attacked, I suspect Saxon friends arranged your capture and outfitted this place. I am sorry you missed the fine wedding dinner I had arranged."

"I hate Court. I am not welcome. They say mean things of me."

"I, too, like it not. Yet, we must return to show the royals we are well. Then we shall go home as soon as possible."

Margaret looked down the path as if she wished to run away and seek a place to hide.

"I will not attack. I will not surprise you. Please sit." Alfred waited. When she stayed seated, he said, "Ask what you will."

His face says he is done with questions. Stop asking. Margaret returned his favor. "Ask what you will."

"Why are you wearing your girdle?"

"Should we be attacked, I needs stand at your back, dagger in hand, to protect or warn you against someone coming at you from behind."

Margaret looked up at hearing Alfred chuckle. "Glad I am you will be at my back." Then he added, "God help the man who comes against you." Alfred's face turned serious. "Do you hate me?"

Margaret shook her head. "No."

"Why are you afraid of me?"

In the silence, Margaret again looked down and considered how to say it. Be yourself. Honest. When she looked up, Alfred's face was a mask. "No one told me anything of being a wife." Margaret looked at her boots. "That it hurts. That it will always hurt."

"Oh, Margaret, not so, not so. Your maidenhead was a locked door, but I had no time to op it gently, make it pleasant for you. I thought us followed. To protect us, I had to act fast and break it down. Now, if any man so much as touches your littlest finger, by right, I can kill him. And I will," Alfred averred. "You may be sore this day, but the hurting is over, never to return. I so swear."

Do you swear to put me in a false ease?

Alfred approached his wife. He sat cross-legged at her feet, lifted her chin so she had to meet his gaze, and held her face in his hands. With his thumbs, he gently brushed away the tears in the corners of her eyes. "Margaret, we needs become accustomed to each other. I know a pleasant way. We can start right here. Shall we try?" After Margaret gave a tentative nod, Alfred cheerfully said, "Good!"

He stood and stepped back. "My turn to sit on the stump." The couple switched places. "Margaret, please take one step back. Face me. You kiss me anywhere you like but only below my neck, only on my flesh, only once in each place. You may tell me to move a part," he extended his right arm as an example, "to reach a place, and I will do so."

Margaret's eyes narrowed. "How many times?"

Alfred paused to consider. "Five. You may move clothing but kisses only touch flesh," he added. Alfred rested his hands on his knees and closed his eyes.

Expecting him to grab her, Margaret waited until she was cert he would move not. She walked around him. *Shoulder, hand, back. Need two more.* As she searched, she appraised him. *Thick neck, broad shoulders, well-muscled. His right arm a bit larger, more muscular than his left. Even that looks strong. Small scars under the bruises on his arms and back. Glad he is clothed from the waist down.* She circled him a second time as she chose the final pair of places. She started at top of his left shoulder.

"Margaret, that is only a maiden's peck. A kiss lasts longer. If you want that to count, you must do more."

Margaret again dipped her head and pursed her lips. This time she tasted salty sweat as she mentally counted to five. She lifted her head and heard, "That was a kiss. I am going to be silent now and enjoy this."

"Right arm out, please." Margaret kissed his forearm. Alfred slowly returned his arm to its place. "Left hand out, please." She kissed the back of his hand and watched him smile as he replaced that too. Margaret walked behind him and knelt. *Dare I do what Mother did to my wounds when I was a child? Why not.* With two fingers, she lifted the bandage at his waist, leaned in and kissed his exposed bruise. She heard him inhale and his breath whoosh out.

"You are a wicked woman!"

Torturing him will be my revenge. "No talking."

Alfred heard her smile and smirked.

Margaret stood and came around his right side. She leaned forward as far as she dared and kissed his chest above his bandaging. Then she blew gently on his flesh before she straightened. *Why did I do that?* Margaret returned to her spot before she looked his way. *That is no smile. A leer with a straight mouth of determination. What have I done? He shall change his mind and grab me.*

Alfred stood, stepped aside, and bowed as he waved her forward. "My lady." He took her place. "Margaret, you are swathed in a cocoon. Please loosen your mantle, so I may reach your arms and such."

Margaret cocked her head and lowered her lids until her eyes were slits of disbelief.

"I shall do no more than you did."

Margaret stood, tossed the fronts of the mantle over each shoulder and sat. She placed her hands on her thighs, but she kept her knees and feet together. She closed her eyes and tried to breathe normally. The first thing she felt was her chemise being lifted from her legs. Then she felt the weight of the cloth above her knees. She held her breath. Alfred kissed her right knee, but he lingered in his kiss much longer than had she. Margaret felt the cloth lifted from her knees and lowered against her legs. *True to his word. He touched me not.* Her senses heightened, and her breathing became shallow and faster.

"Left hand to right shoulder please."

Margaret felt his warmth as he kissed her left elbow. Her knee and elbow tingled. She felt his head under her chin as he kissed her left forearm. When he moved away, she lowered her arm. *The sun is too warm. What is happening to me? I tingle all over and he is not even done. I want to cry. No, I want to laugh. I feel summer heat.*

"Right hand out, please."

Where Alfred kissed her forearm grew hot.

"Now place your right hand palm up."

Margaret anticipated he would kiss her palm. She felt his chin brush her palm as he kissed the inside of her wrist and lingered again. *Mary, Mother of God! I knew not to have such a sensitive place on me! All this tingling and trouble breathing. Is this desire? What do I do with it?*

"Left elbow on your leg, hand up and fingers separated."

. I pray this is the last. I can bear no more. Margaret could not help her smile. *The tip of my littlest finger. And he licked it as he left it. No more. Please no more. I am hot all over.*

"Margaret, op your eyes, please. Shall we start the above-the-neck version?" Margaret vigorously shook her head. "We will always end the same. Please stand. I am going to bring you into my arms and kiss you."

"The kiss of peace?"

"The kiss of husband and wife. Put your arms around my neck." Alfred lowered his head and Margaret correctly tilted hers. She was unready for the sweetness in his kiss growing into passion. She tightened her arms around his neck. She felt him from her mouth to her toes. He flicked his tongue into her mouth, held her even tighter and lifted her until she stood tiptoe and unbalanced. They swayed together. Margaret's mind went blank; she felt hot.

Alfred released her mouth, but kept her within his arms. He let her drop her head to his chest as he swayed side to side. "Now you know why we always start with kisses—and end with them too. The next time we are together, we shall be abed. There you may kiss me wherever you like and as much as you want, as I shall kiss you. Tonight, we shall do the middle part too."

Dear God. More of this and something else as well!

When Alfred finally released Margaret, she plopped hard on the stump and took deep breaths.

What would you like to do now?" he asked.

"I need a nap."

Alfred roared. Margaret jumped up and dashed for the lean-to.

Later, Margaret rolled to look outward. *Calm now. Stay calm.* Alfred had drooped his head as he sat on the stump in the center of the clearing. *Guarding, he slept not. Two days. What kind thing to do?*

"Alfred, if you would like a turn to rest, I shall sit there and keep watch. I shall call out warning if need be."

"I would like to rest. Only if you promise to wake me at any unusual sound."

Margaret nodded as she walked toward him. Alfred stood, took her hand and kissed her cheek. "Just for a short while. I thank you," he added.

Margaret smiled in hopes to cover her blush as she took his place. She drew her dagger and placed it blade up with the handle end on her right thigh. She looked behind herself and then swept the camp with her eyes. She watched Alfred place his sword on its sheath, lie down, and leave a hand on the hilt. Alfred closed his eyes. *I suspect he will stay awake for fear of attack. Who wants him dead?* She answered her own question. *Any Norman who hates Saxons, who wants not to share lordship with one. Kill me as one defiled as Masselin claimed. Kill us and leave us for animals to devour. No witnesses. Just disappeared.*

Margaret soon felt too warm in the sun, but she dared not move. *He sleeps now. Wake him not.* She heard occasional bird calls, the hum of small flying things' wings, leaves rustling. A bee buzzed into the clearing in search of a flower, flew about, and left again. Peaceful forest sounds soothed her, and she relaxed.

What think I of him? He charmed the queen; he is trying to charm me. He said the right things at my test, spoke against that lord and his knight. Suspect words. Margaret counseled herself as she watched. *Look to his actions to learn who he is.*

The sun's bottom touched the tree tops as Alfred slept on. The first soft sound seemed far away, and Margaret turned her head to stare down the path to the stream. The sound repeated; Margaret recognized it. "Nit. Nit." Silence. "Nit. Nit." At the clearing's edge, the doe appeared and froze as did the fawns behind her. *Born this spring. Too big for fawns. Kids now.* Margaret looked toward Alfred and saw his eyes were opt. She smiled at him and gave a tiny shrug. At Margaret's movements, the doe turned and bolted into the trees with her kids behind her.

"Doze on," she whispered. "All is well. Too early to eat." Alfred closed his eyes.

11

Second Night

Again on her knees to Alfred's left, Margaret, watched her husband eat less this eve than he had last. She noticed the beef haunch was much reduced and followed his lead. *Have we enough for the morrow? After we break our fasts, must we return to Winchester and face the king? I prefer we send a message and go home.* Margaret sighed. *Not in charge. He will do as he wills.*

"What is wrong?"

Best I tell him now. Mother said a man gets less angry when his stomach is working.

"You were beaten because of what I did. For that I am sorry, my... Alfred."

"What did you? When?"

Too late to stop now. "That day we stood against the wall. You talked of a joined face against others. When the men accosted you,

I turned my face from the wall." Margaret coughed her nervousness. "I stuck out my tongue at them."

"Margaret!" Alfred was aghast. "Never! Never do that again! It is such a grave deed they could have challenged and killed me."

"Why is it so bad?"

"Because it is an incredibly filthy insult."

"Once I stuck my tongue out at my brother Charles," Margaret admitted. "Mother slapped my face and ordered me never to do that again. She never said why. What means it?"

"That, I shall never reveal. Just never, never do it again, for any reason. I want not to have to kill a man over it." Alfred looked away. A moment later, he added, "Margaret, I instruct you—no, order you—never to permit any of our children to use that insult. Do as your mother did. Slap them across the face. If they are small enough, take them over your knee and spank them hard. Then send them to me. They must never do it again. Do you understand?"

"Yes, Alfred. I shall do as you say." *Never ask again. Behave.* She chewed her last bite.

"While your deed was disgusting, it is not why they beat me. They wanted me dead so I did not meet you at the church. A warning to the king to give you to a Norman. After Sir Roger stopped them, the lord kicked me and swore my first-born would be Norman, or they would kill you too. Margaret, you are not at fault for my beating." He accepted her nod before he looked away. "And I will avenge it."

They heard a small screech and a distant whooshing. Margaret jumped up. Her mantle flowed as she drew her dagger and rounded the fire pit to face the noise.

Alfred stood as he reassured her, "Just a rabbit. They screech like that as they die. Likely a hawk taking it to its nest. What were you going to do?"

94

Margaret stared into the trees as she replied, "Protect you if someone came from behind."

Alfred rounded the pit and faced his bride. "My warrior wife." Alfred smiled at her and gave her a quick peck on her lips. "You kneel on the blanket. I shall return the meat to the tree and look about."

Margaret watched Alfred leave, sword out. She stayed standing, blade in hand. Even though she knew Alfred's direction, she heard him not. She listened hard at forest sounds, the highest leaves still rustling a bit, birds making their final calls of the day and then quieting. *Nothing untoward.* She turned toward Alfred when he came out of the shadows and the trees. Margaret returned his smile and replaced her dagger. She looked toward the lean-to and frowned. *Now will he take me again? Will he hurt me again?*

Alfred read her face and slowed his walk. "Let us return to the blanket."

Margaret knelt before the dying embers and stared at them to avoid her husband. She felt him sit behind her and saw his legs extended on either side, trapping her.

"Move not. There is something I desired to do all day." Margaret froze. She felt him hold the ends of her braids in his hands.

"I am the only one who will ever again see your beautiful unbound hair." He leaned forward and kissed her nape. He murmured, "Another husband's privilege, Margaret. Only I play with your hair."

Margaret felt him untie her right braid and slowly separate its parts. Alfred finger-combed her hair until it was loosed and its waves flowed through his fingers.

So private a deed. As if he is touching my heart. Margaret swallowed her emotions and forced herself to breathe slowly.

Alfred did the same to her left braid. He smiled at hearing her sigh, seeing her shoulders loosen. He gathered her wavy, warm brown locks into his hands and sniffed. "Smells good," he commented. Then he finger-combed her hair and played with its waves. He continued until Margaret relaxed and leaned heavily on her heels.

"Margaret, should my snares be empty in the morn, we must finish the beef and be on our way before dawn. If I snare more rabbits, we stay. We shall have but one meal and have nothing to break our fasts after our third day." Alfred waited for her response. "What are you thinking?"

"I am praying."

"For what?"

"For rabbits in your snares," she quipped. *Why said I that? I am in trouble again! Think before I speak.*

Alfred chuckled as he hugged her. "As am I." With hands on her waist, Alfred lifted his wife and set her on his right thigh. He lifted her legs and placed them over his left thigh.

Margaret leaned her head against his chest. *Cannot kiss me here.* She felt something press against her thigh. He kissed the top of her head. *Now it begins. Blessed Mary, Mother of God, help me through this.* He stroked her arm. Margaret's breaths came fast. At Alfred's whisper of "deep breaths," she inhaled deeply and slowly released it.

"We do nothing now but enjoy each other's company."

When Margaret was cert he was keeping his word, she relaxed. *Thank you, Blessed Mary.* She flinched not when he again stroked her arm.

"While I walk the area, ready for bed. Sleep if you wish."

Margaret crawled from Alfred's lap, stood, and headed for the bushes. Alfred walked the opposite way. With her mantle on the lean-to post, Margaret doffed her boots and socks before she crawled under the linen sheet and blanket. *Now he will come at me, and I must bear whatever he does. God, is husbanding Your punishment for what Eve did in the garden?* Margaret's cheeks soon were wet. She quickly wiped her face when she heard Alfred approaching and rolled toward the tree. Alfred crawled into bed, faced outward, and gave their coverings a short tug to gain some. Margaret froze to let him take as much as he wanted. When Margaret felt him move not and heard his breathing slow, she relaxed, then dozed. Because they were back to back, she slept.

Alfred surveyed the area until full dark. Hearing no strange night sounds, he decided to risk their safety. He shifted to his back without disturbing Margaret and felt for his sword still beside him. Alfred slowly rolled to his bride. She woke to find herself on her side and in his arms. She froze. *I must permit it. Keep my arm down my side to protect me. Will never sleep this way.* He released her and rolled her to her back. Alfred stayed on his side and did nothing more. Margaret dozed. Alfred caressed her waist. Margaret's eyes popped before she shut them tight. He stopped. So tired and warn by fears, Margaret drifted off. Again, Alfred moved. When next she woke, Alfred stopped and lifted his hand.

She knew not how long she had slept, but the night sky still sparkled with stars when she finally opt her eyes. Margaret felt his arm in the space between them and alongside her body. Her mind drifted away. She woke to feel him caressing her hip. She sighed in resignation and fought him not. He lifted his hand, and she soon again slept. Later, Margaret roused to warmth beside her and Alfred's face over hers. He caressed her inner thighs as he kissed her deeply. Soon he did other pleasurable things. He was careful, unhurried, and patient. Languor overtook her. When he was cert Margaret relaxed, he husbanded her without hurting her. Margaret responded not. Fear froze her. Alfred rolled to his back, looked out, and pulled her to his side.

No pain! Yet heat *down there. Warmed me. Now it fades. What is this?* She shivered. "Cold," she whispered.

"Your skin is hot. Night air is cool." Alfred covered them. Margaret snuggled into his warmth. *Like this part.* She fell into a deep sleep.

At dawn's first glimmer, Margaret woke to find herself still snuggled against Alfred. She rolled away and relented when he pulled her back to him. He looked out before he, too, closed his eyes. They slept on.

Chirping birds woke not Margaret; Alfred did when he lifted himself to his elbow beside her. Margaret tucked her head to his chest, but he would have none of it. His forefinger lifted her chin. His lips met hers. Alfred repeated husbanding Margaret. She laid still. When he rolled away and held her close, her thought surprised her. *Again he hurt me not.* She pondered *Same fire. Same warmth.* Margaret sighed. *That was… not bad.*

12

To Winchester

Wednesday, 19 August

Alfred rose before dawn and left Margaret to her own needs. They met fireside, she wrapped in her mantle, he holding empty snare strings and the food bag.

"The hawk likely scared them off. Best we finish what we have and return."

Margaret nodded. *This early the water is too cold for a bathe, but I needs wash after last night.* "After we eat, may I have a quick wash by the stream? I can use the bed blanket to dry myself." Still standing, they ate their few bites and sipped the last of the second bottle. Neither was in a mood to talk. As the pre-dawn light colored the sky, Margaret grabbed the blanket from the lean-to and marched to the stream.

"Please, I beg you. For my sake, just this once, turn away and let me do what I must." After Alfred silently did so, Margaret soaked a blanket end, rang it out, and cleansed herself, rinsed the corner, and used another corner to dry her body. "Done," she announced as she strode passed him. Back at camp she draped the blanket over the front of the hut and crawled inside. *Best not have him see me naked and start something.* Margaret donned her chemise and bliaut. *He will have to tighten my laces. Drat! I hate this fashion, but I must be properly dressed at Court—as if I had a maid and had just left the queen's hall.* As Margaret turned on her knees, she twisted the bottom linen. On the ground under it, she spotted a bit of white. She picked up the small, flat square and sniffed it. *It cannot be!*

Just then, Alfred announced, "I must return this bag to the tree. Come out."

Margaret stuffed the soap chip into her sleeve pocket and tucked the linen end under the pile of evergreen boughs. She pushed the blanket aside and stood. "Alfred, before you go, please tighten my laces." She turned her back and held her hair against the back of her head. Margaret's husband laced her and kissed her nape and her shoulder.

"I am sorry to leave here, my dear one."

"I shall braid my hair and be ready when you return," said Margaret, hoping he would go no further. She worked quickly. *Why would she order this camp? Did she have me taken because she knew of the danger to us? She is half Saxon and may know this old custom. Mayhap she hates me not. Mayhap she wanted us to experience our first night together alone. No, Her Grace would not do all that. This is his doing. Likely, he asked to borrow nice things, and she consented.* Margaret donned her mantle and replaced her head cloth and brass circlet. She looked about to memorize the place. *A rough start here, yet not so bad last night. May each day be better between us. Oh God, Your will in all things.*

Alfred returned, picked up the blanket upon which they had wed, folded it, and draped it over his left arm. At Margaret's question, he replied, "No, leave it. Whoever made this camp will want their things back. We shall return the way I came," he added as he led. Margaret followed his hops from rock to rock as they crossed the stream. *The birds stop their dawn warbling until after we pass,* she thought as they wended their way up a narrow deer path. Before they left the trees, Alfred waved her to stay back. He cautiously approached the road ahead before standing at its edge and looking up and down it. *Best I don my seire and wreath now.* He waved her forward, and into the faint morning light.

Alfred handed her the blanket. "I will walk the road side. If you hear anyone coming, dash into the forest and hide. No matter what happens, do not come out unless I call for you."

Margaret stepped to his left. "Why keep you this blanket?"

"For sentiment. We lay together on it in the meadow. It bears the stain of your maidenhead." He watched her blush. "We will not wash it for a long time."

"That will do no good. Anyone you show the stain can say you nicked yourself to prove an untruth. You cannot prove my worth with it."

"I can swear you were a virgin."

Those who choose not to believe will still gossip. Gossip the king had me first. Say I am a loose women you wed for my wealth. Saying so will only anger him. "Yes, Alfred, you can." They walked briskly in the morning coolness. *Best I say it now.* "Alfred, thank you for having me taken away, for our time alone, for the lovely camp."

"I did not do it. I thought you had arranged it so we might share the Saxon custom of running into the forest to be alone. Though I worried you provided not enough food." He added, "I am glad for our time together. I am only sorry you missed the fine meal I had planned."

"I am cert the Court enjoyed every bite and ordered more wine at your expense. They are a dreadful lot."

"I agree," replied Alfred. He grabbed her arm and held her still. He pointed; she dashed into the trees and crouched behind a large bush.

From the way they had come rumbled a long wagon drawn by two donkeys.

"My lord," called the driver. "I am taking hay to Winchester. If you would ride, I am proud to share my seat." When he saw Alfred looking behind him, he added, "No one on the road this early. I hurry because I want to be home before dark."

"I accept your kind offer. My lady shall share your perch. I shall walk." At Alfred's call, Margaret appeared. Alfred held her hand as she stepped on the wheel hub and climbed aboard.

"God give you a good morrow, kind sir."

"God give you a good morrow, my lady."

Two miles later, the Saxon pulled hard on the reins and the donkeys brayed their disapproval. Alfred reached for Margaret as she jumped down. The sounds of hooves on the dirt road grew louder. Together, they headed into the forest and hid. The wagon driver backed his wagon and moved forward over their tracks just as four knights rode up and surrounded him. Their horses masked the rest of the couple's tracks.

"Who have you seen on this road?" demanded a knight.

The driver pulled his forelock and looked down. "No one, sir."

"We seek a Saxon who thinks he is a lord and his lady. Where are they? Look at me. Lie and you die."

"Good my lord, the only Saxons I saw were walking into a field four miles back." The man pointed behind himself.

"Where are you bound?"

"To the castle, my lord. Thrice each week I haul hay for His Grace's horses."

"Check it," order the same knight. The others drew their swords and plunged them into the hay pile. Without a word, the knights paired and rode on.

Margaret looked at her husband. He barely shook his head. He whispered, "They are watching." The pair saw the man urge his donkeys forward and disappear. Alfred held them in their hiding place. Suddenly, a knight dashed after the wagon. When he returned, he was walking his horse and checking both sides of the road for tracks. Margaret held her breath and looked down. *If I look his way, he may see my face. Then we are dead. I want to reach for my dagger, but I dare not move. Please, God, keep us safe. Please let us live until we are among witnesses to our deaths, if that be Your will.* Margaret continued praying until Alfred touched her shoulder. She pointed behind them and he nodded. Margaret crept behind another bush and relieved herself. After she returned, Alfred did the same. The sun had fully risen before they crept from their hiding place. Alfred held Margaret's hand as they strode down the road.

They had walked a mile when they again spotted the hay wagon. When they reached it, the driver smiled down at the pair.

"Seems my beasts suddenly refused to move without you," he chimed.

Margaret climbed aboard. "You are kind to await us. A dangerous thing to do, lie to a Norman."

"My lady, we Saxons are practiced at it. When we know their desires, we tell them what they want to hear." He flicked his reins, and they moved toward Winchester. After a time and through trees, Alfred and Margaret spotted the top stones of the northwest gate. The driver stopped, and Margaret climbed down. Before she could express her thanks for his help, he surprised them with, "Lord Alfred, congratulations on your wedding. We have been on the roads on some errand or another since you wed. I am honored to be the one to find you. Once you are within the walls, you will be among friends." He pulled his forelock as he said, "My lady, we Saxons wish you well and happy." He announced, "I am for the west gate. I have seen no one on the road but four knights." He turned down a narrow road to his right and disappeared.

Margaret saw Alfred enjoyed her shocked look. She closed her mouth and furrowed her brow. "Know you him?"

Alfred shook his head. "He offered not his name; I asked it not. If anyone inquires, I can swear I walked the whole way back. My lady, I hunger and thirst. Mayhap we can find a food stall ere we report to the castle." He lifted his left arm; Margaret placed her hand on it. Together they approached the city gate. They ignored the gaping guards on the wall and at the barbican. They entered Winchester as if they were returning from a leisurely morning stroll.

13

Court

Within their first dozen steps past the barbican, the street filled. Men stood outside their doors to visit. Children dashed about as they played. Women stepped outside to sweep dirt into the street.

Witnesses. Margaret smiled and nodded to a pair of women looking her way. A man approached. Alfred stopped, dropped her hand and gave a single shake of his head. Margaret halted as Alfred stepped forward to meet the stranger. Margaret watched Alfred look straight ahead as the man whispered into his ear. He nodded his head once and listened more. He spoke a few quiet words Margaret heard not. When he lifted his left arm, Margaret approached and replaced her hand upon it. The man had disappeared. A few steps more, and a woman offered Alfred two sticks of cooked meat; her son offered two mugs of ale. The couple stood in the middle of the street as they ate and drank. They dropped the sticks into empty mugs and returned them to the boy. His mother had already returned to her shop.

Saxons and their strange ways. Will I ever understand them? How knew they we were entering this way? What did that man tell Alfred? Oh, how I shall hate appearing at Court. I will look down, follow Alfred and speak not. I pray Her Grace calls not for me. I pray we are permitted to leave for home at once. We will be murdered in our bed if we are forced to sleep in the Great Hall. Swords through the bed drapes in the middle of the night. She shuddered and prayed as she walked toward the imposing wall surrounding the castle.

From the double doors, Margaret spotted King Henry on his throne with men standing on the floor before him; she looked at her shoes. *Dusty. No help for it.* Alfred spoke to the king's seneschal and took them to the right.

Quiet, calm, dignified, pure keeps a lady steadfast and sure. Margaret repeated the phrase her mother had taught her. When Margaret heard Lord Alfred announced, she followed him. *One step to the left and two steps behind.* Cold with fear, she clutched the folded blanket that hid her forearms and hands.

"Where have you been, Lord Alfred!"

"Your Grace, when my wife was taken, I searched for her and found her in a hunting camp in the forest. Late as it was, I decided to spend the night. I married a virgin, and now she is my wife good and true. We tarried in that pleasant place."

He remembered! Margaret's eyes snapped op then quickly resumed a serious face.

As Alfred responded, members of the Court strolled in. Word had passed, and the room fast filled.

"Pleasant!" roared Henry. "You bed a lady of rank on dirt! You kept her from her friends at Court on her special day. You insult us!"

"Your Grace, I swear she slept on a soft bed, between fine linens and under a new blanket. My lady lay her head on a down pillow. We dined on beef and good wine. We walked the forest paths and smelled flowers in small meadows. I treat my lady well, for I hold her in high regard."

"You had her taken," accused King Henry, "and you soothed our consciences with a rich meal in hopes we would follow you not. You made this place of hiding and took her there."

"Your Grace, I know not who snatched her from me. I only followed. I prepared not that pleasant resting place, only found it."

"Then your lady arranged it all."

"She says she did not."

Henry stared at Margaret. Alfred feared his silence. "I warned you about her. Not only has she a dangerous temper, she is too clever by half again. She dissembles not, but she only answers how you ask. Word your questions carefully, Lord Alfred. I will demonstrate. Lady Margaret, know you who took you away?"

"Your Grace, I do not," Margaret replied from behind her husband. She bobbed a curtsey without looking up.

"Had you ever met him?"

"No, Your Grace."

"Seen his face?"

"No, Your Grace."

Henry leaned back in his throne. "Lady Margaret, know you who created the camp your lord speaks of?"

"No, Your Grace."

"Do you suspect someone who did so?"

Drat! I moved not. He can barely see me. How did I give myself away? What knows he? How do answer I?

"You see, Lord Alfred, she knows not but she doth suspect. Step forward, Lady Margaret. Look at me. Answer."

Margaret looked to Alfred, who gave a nod without looking back. Margaret stepped to Alfred's side. "Your Grace, to suspect someone with no proof might ruin an innocent person's reputation. I am most reluctant to do so." Margaret closed the king's mouth by quickly adding, "I am most willing to whisper my thinking into your ear. Only to you, oh mighty king; only you determine the worth of my words."

"Lord Alfred, take your wife's dagger."

Without looking away from King Henry, Margaret handed her dagger, handle first, to Alfred. A tiny change in her expression was involuntary.

"Lady Margaret, hand him all your weapons."

Margaret hid not her smirk from the king. It did surprise Alfred. She dropped the blanket away from them, pushed her mantle back from her shoulders, and crouched. From each boot, she pulled a full-tanged, handless, short knife, sharp and deadly. She stood and extended her hands for the king to see them. She looked at Alfred and shrugged before she handed over each blade, one at a time.

"Your proof, Lord Alfred, how dangerous she truly is. Have you any other weapons, Lady Margaret?"

"Just my fingernails, Your Grace, but I pared them short before the church ceremony; they can harm you not."

"Approach. I will hear your whispers."

Without looking Alfred's way, Margaret stepped left and approached the dais.

Members of the Court stepped forward, or moved sideways in hopes they would read her lips.

Look at him not. Keep him innocent. Risk my life, not his. Oh God, Your will in all things. Margaret took the steps and knelt beside Henry's throne with her back to the Court. *This way no one may read my lips.* She whispered, "Your Grace, the camp was outfitted by someone who had the authority to provide it with a generous bag of food, with linen sheets, a new wool blanket and two down-filled pillows. Under the bed of evergreen boughs, I found this." Margaret reached into her sleeve, withdrew the sliver of rose-scented soap, and slipped it into the king's hand.

Henry put his fingers to his nose, sniffed, and dropped the item into a pocket. He grabbed Margaret by the throat and pulled her off her knees. Margaret gasped for air and tried to pull away. Her arms flailed; one struck Henry's arm to no avail. She heard "Unhand my lady!" and swords singing as they left their sheaths and men's angry voices. Margaret struggled to see the disturbance behind her as she went light-headed. *Faint and I die.* King Henry hissed his command into her ear before he dropped her, and she fell hard on her knees. Margaret gasped, coughed, and gasped again and again. She dropped her face to her knees and clutched her throat to protect it.

"Lord Alfred, you may take your lady home."

"Your Grace, may we leave anon?"

"You may."

Alfred had learned well. He added, "May we take all our things with us?" After the king's assent, Alfred asked, "May we also take all our men with us?" Alfred's stress of "all" told Henry that Alfred knew whom he held in his donjon. King Henry nodded.

Alfred picked up the blanket and approached the dais. He spoke Margaret's name, and she crawled to him. He draped the blanket over her and took her in his arms. Carrying his wife, Alfred backed three steps, nodded to King Henry, and turned. He carried Margaret through the crowd, out the double doors, and toward his four new knights. Alfred set Margaret down. When her knees gave way, he grabbed her and held her against his chest.

Margaret rasped, "I am sorry."

"Silence until we are alone."

Margaret gratefully obeyed. *My throat. My voice. Will I ever speak again?* She heard not his whispered instructions. Two men departed to follow Alfred's orders. The other two escorted Alfred and his wife as they crossed the grounds and walked out the barbican.

Long after midday, Henry appeared in Queen Matilda's quarters. He stepped to the cradle and picked up his son. He turned to the room and ordered, "Begone!" After everyone left and the nurse closed the door, Henry took his heir to a chair next to his wife's. He pulled the soap sliver out of his pocket and dropped it into Matilda's lap. Matilda left it there.

"You might have informed me."

Matilda knew better than to accuse her husband of ignorance or worse, indifference, so she just stated facts. "Lord Wilbur and his knight beat Alfred, tried to kick him to death. That is why he was so pale and stiff at the church door. Sir Roger stopped them. Before the ceremony, they vowed to ravage Lady Margaret so his first-born would be Norman. I was not about to permit that."

Henry looked away to hide how he had plotted to have Margaret even though she was one door from his wife. Never did he admit he was lustful, wrong, misinformed, or negligent.

"Henry, if you still want Normans and Saxons to marry and birth children to create your new English people, this couple can help you. They need our support to survive. They already have my favor. Have you considered giving them yours?"

"I doubled their land holdings. Is that not enough?"

"The Court and Norman nobility need different proofs. Social acceptance. Even favor. Please consider it."

"I well know you Saxons. What will your lot do to Wilbur?"

"A happy accident the day of the church ceremony. His youngest son was climbing a tree, fell, and broke his sword arm. We had no part in that." Matilda smiled. "As Alfred lived and Margaret stayed a virgin, no one will die." She continued, "His family sickened. Tossed their food and shit their brains." Henry smiled. "Bad butter they say because the next morning all his milch cows were dead. The Saxons were ordered to burn them for fear of disease." Matilda paused and leaned against her chair back. "Of course, Lord Wilbur may suffer sorry events for several months. His Saxons have grievances. They will stop when they will. Worry not, Henry, Wilbur is too dull-witted to realize the source of his ill fortune."

"I will do nothing for him. In 1101, he gave my brother men and coin and came against me. He withdrew when he saw Robert losing; I could not follow him. I have yet to catch him breaking the law. When he does, I will use my Royal Court against him." Henry stood and handed Prince William to his mother. He looked down at his wife and son. "If he kills a Saxon, inform me. That will be enough to bring him under my power. Legally, of course."

Matilda watched Henry leave. She prayed her husband would consider her idea and help the pairing she had made. Matilda cooed at her son as he awakened, hungry as usual. She called for his nurse.

The princess's nurse also arrived with her charge well fed and ready for her daily visit. Princess Matilda's nurse held tight to the toddler until the heir was in his nurse's arms. Then she released Princess Matilda to crawl into her mother's lap.

14

Homeward

Two miles north of Winchester, at the Half Moon Inn, Margaret supped in silence beside her husband at a table separate from others. *Are we traveling slowly because of me? What is in the wagon he rented?* She chewed and swallowed another bit of carrot even as her throat continued to object to everything but liquid. Margaret closed her eyes as she swallowed. *I must stay until he releases me.* She placed her spoon on the table, and lifted the wooden bowl to drink the last of the broth. A clump of vegetables and bits of meat were all that remained.

"God give you a good rest, my lady." Alfred's voice was toneless, his face impassive.

Margaret whispered, "And you, my lord."

They stood, and Alfred escorted her to the bottom of the stairs. With her hand trailing the wall to steady herself, Margaret climbed them. *The lady with the two maids will take the best bed. I know not who else will want the other. Best I take a pad and find a corner.* Even before she closed the door, a voiced accosted her.

'You are the one who married that Saxon!" The woman of highest rank was already sitting on the best bed. "You should not be sleeping with decent women."

"His Grace, King Henry, says otherwise," retorted Margaret through her pain. *I dare speak no more. Be a sheep and all the old goats in the land will attack me. Young ones too.*

"Well, he is not here and I am. You sleep in that corner by the chamber chair." The haughty woman snorted her derision, and the others looked away.

From the pile beside the door, Margaret grabbed a sleeping pad, strode across the room, and took the place where she had been ordered. She sat with her back against the wall with her dagger in her lap. She smiled not at the women who crowded together to be away from her. *Not staying. I know her kind. She will wait until she thinks me asleep. After she uses the piss pot, she will accidentally kick the chair so it falls over and spills the pot's contents on me.* The room soon darkened with the sunset. The women settled. Just before the candle nub sputtered out for the night, Margaret stood, stepped over sleeping women, and silently unlatched the door. She slipped through and closed it without anyone inside stirring.

At the bottom of the stairs, she looked for Alfred among the men sleeping in the great room. The innkeeper's son, who sat in a chair at the main door, watched her.

"Where is Lord Alfred?"

He whispered back, "In the yard." At her gesture, the young man stood and opt the door. He waited not for her to leave the covered porch before he re-latched it.

Margaret turned right. In the moonlight, she spotted Alfred leaning against the wagon as it rested next to the massive barn. As she approached, she heard him murmuring, talking to someone inside the wagon.

"What are you doing here? Go inside," Alfred ordered.

"I cannot. No place to sleep in the women's room. I left to look for you. I thought I might sleep in the wagon. Guarded, if you will it." By the time she had finished her half truths, she stood beside him and stared into his face. *I dare not look inside the wagon without his permission. What if he brings a woman with us?*

He glared at her for a moment before he said, "Say hello to your friend."

Margaret looked. "Elstan? What are you doing here? Why is your back…" She saw dark stripes all the way to the blanket over his backside. "Who whipped you?"

"He left the estate as soon as he learned of our marriage. He brought with him two horses for my use. He was walking them when he was spotted by two Norman knights. They accused him of riding. He said he was not."

"Elstan!"

'They remembered him standing at the back of the hall during your Christmastide visit to Court. They said you four had ridden out of town before they could charge and execute him. They took him to the king because Elstan claimed they needed to see him on a horse to kill him. The king sided with the knights and ruled Elstan guilty; but, as they only assumed he was ahorse and had not seen him, he would not order Elstan beheaded." Margaret gasped. "Elstan said the king ordered, 'Take him to the donjon and see he never sits on a horse or anywhere else again.' They whipped him from nape to knees and hung him standing so he healed unable to bend for the rest of his life. For as long as he lives. They smeared offal in his wounds, and he is fevered."

"My lord! The fault is all mine. I forgot the law and permitted him come with us."

"No. He knew the law and chose to disobey it."

"I want not it to cost him his life. I know something of festers and healing. With your permission, I would like to help him, save him." Margaret searched Alfred's face for a sign. "Please, my lord. Please, may I try?"

Alfred sighed before he replied, "If Elstan agrees." He added, "He needs to know whatever you do will hurt him."

"Elstan, have I your permission to try to save you? Even if it hurts?" After Margaret heard his muffled, "Yes," she announced her conditions. "Elstan, you must swear a holy oath that you will never, within sight of a Norman, bend at your waist or sit. Not ever. If they learn we healed you, they will kill you and punish us. You must let them think they have won. Swear you will never bend or sit when or where any Norman may see you, or we three die."

Elstan clearly stated, "I will never, never reveal I can bend or sit. I will never do so in public or in private where a Norman might see I can. As God is my witness, I swear upon my immortal soul."

"Good." Margaret turned to Alfred, "May I have your supervision and advice? Also, I need your help." Margaret stood close and looked into Alfred's questioning eyes. "I need someone to cover his manhood, for his modesty and mine. Also, this moonlight is not enough. I need a light, so I may examine the damage." Margaret stepped away. *He is going for something. Mayhap he is not so angry with me after all.*

Margaret gazed into the night sky. *The moon is but a crescent, and its light hides stars far around it. When I look the opposite way I see the holes in the floor of heaven. Such beautiful light. Mother, are you looking down on me? Do you approve what I am about to do?* When called, Margaret returned to the wagon. There stood two of Alfred's knights, holding lit, pitch-covered rag balls atop thick branches, a servant boy, and Alfred.

"Boy, we need a pail of hot water, a clean sheet, and later a pot of honey."

The boy nodded and disappeared around the back of the inn.

"Sirs, I am sorry. I know not your names." They gave them. "Sir Louvel, Sir Pernel, thank you for rising to help our Saxon. I need the end of the wagon dropped, so I may climb in." Margaret almost swooned at the stench of the infection. After she knelt next to Elstan, she asked, "Please raise your lights so I may see him." She forced herself to start at his back. She touched him not, but carefully examined the stripes of jagged skin edges, pockets of pus, swollen flesh, and dried blood. Elstan's buttocks and the backs of his thighs were more wounds than undamaged skin. "I count twelve lashes. A whip? At least seven on his backside." The boy returned with a pail and a sheet.

"My lord, I needs tear this sheeting. Will you pay its cost?" At his nod, she asked him to help her cut it into rags and two long cloths. "I need to wet his wounds to soften them, clean off the blood, and draw the poison from his flesh," she explained.

Elstan sighed as she placed the warm, wet cloth over him to soften the scabs. Hours later, Elstan's wounds had been washed, cleaned of pus and dirt, and slathered with honey. Margaret laid a clean portion of sheet over him and covered him with the blanket, which had already had seen many uses. She rinsed and dried her hands before informing the servant they would be keeping the honey pot for future use. She asked Louvel and Pernel to wait and motioned Alfred to follow her around the corner of the barn.

"Elstan needs broth for strength and ale to replace the blood he lost. Also, if he ever expects to bend or sit, we must truss him in a manner most painful."

"Why are you still whispering?"

"I fear my voice is damaged, so I am protecting it for as long as possible before I try to speak."

"What said you to the king? What said he to you?"

In faint moonlight, Margaret stood on tiptoe so Alfred could better look into her eyes and know the truth. "His Majesty commanded, 'Say nothing, answer no one, refer to it never. If you do not remain silent all your days, I will cut out your tongue and unman your lord.' Alfred, I beg you, never ask me again. This is all I may say and only to you. One day the king will demand you tell him if you asked. Please repeat my words so we both may be safe."

Alfred nodded.

"What was the disturbance behind me? I heard swords drawn."

"I called, 'Unhand my lady' and reached for my blade."

Now Margaret was aghast. "They might have killed you!"

"Not so. I only withdrew it three inches." At her frown, Alfred explained, "Showing three inches is a warning, six inches is a challenge, and withdrawing it fully means fight to the death."

Margaret grabbed Alfred's shirt. "You could have been killed!"

Alfred pulled her into himself and kissed her hard. After he released her, he smirked, "How encouraging. You want me not dead." Margaret opt her mouth to retort, decided against it, and clamped her mouth shut. "How do we truss Elstan?"

Margaret explained. "Wine to get him drunk before we do it and a rag in his mouth to mute his screams. Bind his knees to his chest to stretch his skin as it heals."

"Round the corner so my men see you. Stay there."

Margaret noted the other two knights had replaced Louvel and Pernel. Soon she saw the boy return and one knight shift Elstan to his side and raise his shoulders so he might sip the drinks the other knight offered. Alfred returned with rope. He spoke to Elstan and called Margaret. She supervised placing cloth strips behind Elstan's neck and knees before they wound the rope around him as she suggested. The men pulled the rope tightly together and drew Elstan's knees to his chest. At Elstan's first scream, Margaret spun away and put her head against the barn wall. She covered her ears as tears streamed down her cheeks. Elstan's screams stopped when he fainted, but Margaret's tears did not. *Men make cruel laws, stupid ones, and are pleased to enforce them. Why cannot Saxons ride horses? They are men too. Elstan, you deserved not this. You are a good man, just impulsive, foolish. You meant to help me and look what they did to you. Oh, Elstan, I am sorry, so sorry.*

Alfred turned her into his arms and held her close. "Shh, shh. The worst is over. Elstan is both drunk and asleep. Even if he never sits, your plan will enable him to bend. Now his fever needs to break. Let us pray for that." Margaret stopped crying and sniffed back her stuffy nose. "You are tired and hungry. I have arranged we eat first. Look up. The sky is lightening. By dawn we will have broken our fasts and be on our way."

Margaret snaked her arms about Alfred's waist and hugged her thanks. With her cheek still against his chest, she whispered, "Alfred,

I am tired, so very tired. Elstan is trussed. Think you it proper if I lay in the wagon and rest while we travel?"

"Yes."

A sudden scream sounded from inside the inn. A ruckus ensued with loud voices making accusations and demands. They heard a female sobbing. Margaret pulled back and smiled at Alfred's confused expression. "Just as I predicted. In the dark, the haughty one spilled the chamber pot over a woman she believed was me. Poor thing." Margaret meant it. "They hate us. I fear we will only be safe at home." She dared a direct question. "Do you trust the knights with us?"

"Yes. Their mothers are Saxon, fathers Norman. As Normans consider the father to be all, they were permitted to train as squires. These became knights errant, but finding work is hard for them because of their parentage. Louvel and Pernel offered they are brothers. Mayhap their parents wed. Not politic to ask."

"If you trust them, then do I."

Alfred smiled at her. "Our food must be ready. We eat and depart before those women come down." As they walked to the inn door, Alfred kept her hand until he reached for the latch. Margaret followed him into the great room.

Midday, the party stopped beside the road. Alfred called Margaret's name; she sat up and rubbed her eyes. Night, who had been tied to the back of the wagon, neighed his greeting. Margaret climbed out of the wagon to hug Night, stroke his cheek, and assure him she still loved him and would soon ride him again. She stood beside the wagon. "Elstan, are you awake? What may I do for you?" When she heard no response, she called, "My lord, Elstan is silent. I fear for him."

Alfred examined his villein and reported, "No food has made the wine potent. He is still drunk asleep. His fever is the same. That is my worry. Also, blood on the bottom half of the sheet from trussing him."

"If you will make him modest, I will tend him." Margaret asked Sir Pernel to take the rags she handed him to find a stream and soak them. She placed a wet cloth on Elstan's forehead. She re-cleaned two places still festering on his back and re-cleaned his lower back to his knees before reapplying honey and covering him. Elstan stirred not.

"Come eat," ordered Alfred. As she ate bread and cheese and drank from Alfred's ale bag, he asked, "What know you of the next inn?"

"The Lion and Swan is well run, good people. They know me from two other visits. I know not how they will receive a sick Saxon. If he stays in the wagon, will he need guarding?" At Alfred's nod, she added, "I know not if they have a room for a wedded couple, or if we shall be separated."

"I shall send a man ahead to announce our arrival and our needs. I shall walk you into the trees." After Margaret had met her needs, Alfred stood between her and the group. "Why wear you knives in your boots?"

Knew he would ask. Glad I prepared an answer. "Last year, Leoma, a Saxon maid on our estate, was attacked and ravaged. Living a maid in a household with knights and in a world of men who might want me for my wealth, I feared for my honor. In secret, I asked my smith, our smith, to forge them. Our hostler Jorgon made me boots with an inner lining and cut slits between the layers. Until the king asked, only they knew I was so armed."

"You used them not against me in the forest."

Margaret shrugged. "You are my husband." *As long as you stare at me, I shall stare back at you. Will you return them?*

Alfred's face changed. "Swear a holy oath to God you shall never use them against me or our children." After she did so, he pulled them from his cloak pocket and handed them over.

"Thank you. Your enemies are now mine, and I will not always be in your presence." Margaret returned her blades to their hiding places before she followed Alfred back to their party. *That he trusts me this much is a good sign.* As she rode, Margaret turned her face to the breeze to cool her face from the sun's heat.

After they had supped, Alfred escorted Margaret to Elstan, who had just finished a bowl of pottage with Sir Bertrand's help. Alfred introduced him to Margaret. *A full head taller than Alfred and not yet filled out to manhood. Sixteen?* Alfred dismissed him to his supper and watched Margaret feel Elstan's forehead, shoulder, and knees.

"You are still fevered. I made you a drink of musk mallow and periwinkle to lower your fever and St. John's wort for your bruises. My mother used to say, 'If it tastes bad, it will do you good.' Trust me, hold your nose before you swallow." Alfred held Elstan upright; Margaret handed him the mug. After Elstan drank the potion, he made faces and noisy objections about the bitterness of the concoction. "Sleep now. I will make you another potion in the morn." Margaret turned. "Alfred, your drink of St. John's wort is next."

"Untie me."

Margaret looked to Elstan and shook her head. "Not if you want to bend or sit. You are not healed enough. You will stiffen again and be as bad as you were. Just before we reach home, we will untie you so no one knows how serious are your wounds. Then you may decide, tied all day or all night until you can sit. You will be weeks at pulling your knees to your chest many times a day to grow limber."

"She is right, young man," added Alfred. "First, you must lose your fever. Your wounds must stop bleeding every time you move before you can remain untied. I have seen like injuries before. Hurry your healing, and what we have already done will fail you."

The next eventide Alfred pushed his half-empty bowl to the center of the table and glared at his tasteless bread round and weak ale. "You might have told me."

"The Rooster's Nest is not known for its food. I had hoped it would be better this time. My lord, two miles south of the King's Inn and ten miles from home is an inn roadside of the hamlet called Newbury. We will reach either place by Saturday eve and be forced to stay Sunday. I thought you should know of both."

"What recommend you?"

"The King's Inn is richly appointed but very costly. I know not the inn's name at Newbury nor its condition, having only ridden past it. I know not upon whose land it sits, who owns it, or if they will accept Elstan. Also, with everyone harvesting, not many may be traveling, so I am uncert how full either will be. I leave you to choose."

Saturday eventide, they were well met by the Newbury Inn's keeper. *The man's whole family stands to greet us. I wonder what Arnaud said of us and how well he bargained.*

"Welcome Lord Alfred! We are honored to accommodate you for as long as you wish. I am Geofroi; my wife is Fayme, and these our children. We are a small place but clean. Fayme is a good cook, so you will eat well. Mostly we serve those of modest means."

Too small and simple for the ranked who want the King's Inn. Face having less. I am a Saxon's lady.

"You are our sole guests. Please enter and enjoy our ale while we finish preparing your supper. If it please you, we have cherries from the southwest. A rare treat."

"It pleases us well," said Alfred as he dismounted and helped Margaret. "I have a sick villein in the wagon. After we sup, my lady will need supplies to aid him."

Fayme looked over the wagon edge. "What happened?"

Margaret whispered, "He rode a horse." *Speak no opinion for fear someone sends my words to Court.* "His Grace let him live, but he was lashed."

"Why is he trussed up like that?"

"In the hope he will be able to bend a little after his skin heals."

"We have wine to ease his suffering. I have herbs that aid healing, and I can make a salve for his wounds. I can also make a drink to help his fever."

"That is most kind of you, Fayme. I thought I needs wait until we reach home, but starting now will help him greatly. May I help by grinding the herbs?" In the kitchen shed, the women worked together while Fayme's daughters cleaned the dish ware and shed before they soaked the grains for the morrow's pottage. *Good people. I would rather stay with these Saxons than with the highly ranked ones in King's Inn. I hope Alfred chooses them again.*

After Vespers, dark was fast arriving when Margaret climbed the stairs to the women's room. *One bed. Glad I need not share it. Who would be knocking?* "Who are you?"

"Alfred. Mayhap you have heard of me?" he teased.

Margaret slid the door's bolt and stepped back.

Alfred entered and halted at seeing her dagger in hand. "You trust no one." At Margaret's head shake, he said, "Good. Neither do I." As Alfred closed and bolted the door, he reported, "One guards the gate. One sits on the top step. The others shall change in the night." Margaret replaced her blade. He added, "Geofroi said we may share this room."

Margaret teased back with a sigh, "I thought I was going to have the bed all to myself."

"Not for our lifetime if I can help it." Alfred drew her into his arms. "Two nights away from you is too long. Thaes hal, wif," he whispered.

"Thaes hal, husband." Margaret responded in Saxon as she glanced away, again all shyness and reserve.

She turned her back to him as she doffed her boots and removed her bliaut. As she stepped to the bed, she heard, "Chemise also." Margaret crossed her arms, bent, grasped her hem, pulled the chemise inside out, and flung it from her. She dashed into the bed and pulled the sheet under her chin. When Alfred began undressing she closed her eyes.

Alfred covered his lower self with a corner of the sheet. His kisses explored her exposed parts: neck, ear, cheek, mouth, as his fingers atop the sheet explored what Margaret hid beneath. He kissed her hands clutching the cloth over rise of her breasts.

Is this to be every night?

Margaret's husband eased her toward husbanding. He slipped his hand under the sheet and touched. *Resign myself to this.* Alfred thought her sigh was acceptance and did more.

Much later, spent, warm, and held, Margaret snuggled against Alfred. *I do like the warmth of him.* Alfred positioned Margaret so her head lay on his shoulder. *Strong steady heart.* She felt him kiss her head; she let Alfred entwine their legs. Later, she stirred. "Alfred, I cannot sleep curled together like this. I am not rejecting you, just rolling over and using mine own pillow."

After Margaret settled herself, Alfred pulled the sheet over them, drew her close, and draped his arm over her. He snuggled against her back, matching her curves and bending his knees so he touched her from back to toes as he breathed into her hair. *Too warm to be this close. I am going to like this more on a cold night. For now, let him be.*

15

Sunday in Newbury

Margaret awakened to church bells ordering the world to rise, opt her eyes, and saw a glimmer of predawn light in the window slit. She rolled to her back. Looking right, she saw Alfred's back and debated calling him. Instead she rolled and lightly kissed his bare shoulder. "Alfred?"

"Do that again and we shall miss Mass." Alfred bolted upright and pushed himself to the edge of the bed. He leaned over for his loin cloth, stood and quickly wrapped himself. He stepped to Margaret's clothes and dropped them at the end of the bed before he walked away and gave her his back as he finished dressing. When he turned around, Alfred saw Margaret dressed, on her knees, and pushing stray locks into her hair. He gestured and said, "Off the bed. You are too tempting." In an offhand manner, Alfred informed her, "I remember the Church's dictum. No kissing, no touching, no husbanding on Sundays." As he belted his sword, he listed, "Not during Lent. Not during Advent. They say not on holy days too, but there are too many of those. A hundred or more. I know not about Normans, but we Saxons ignore that part of the ruling. When would we beget our children?"

Margaret blushed, climbed off the bed, and pushed down her clothes.

As she reached for her seire cloth and circlet, she heard, "Margaret, test your voice." She curtsied and said aloud, "God give a good day, Alfred." She added, "It is still a little sore. I will use it lightly this day. It should be fine on the morrow."

"Good. We will leave before dawn and be home for a later-than-midday feast."

"You ordered one?"

"Before we supped, I sent word of our arrival. I added we had missed our wedding dinner."

"I suspect they already know, given how successfully Saxons communicate, even though they may not live their estates. Is my circlet straight?" Informed that it was, Margaret nodded she was ready. The bells again rang to call the faithful.

Alfred, Margaret, and their four knights filled the front of the small church. About two dozen families crowded behind them. After Mass, rank dictated the couple leave first. Margaret took a step away as Alfred complimented the priest on his fine sermon of how God wants us to treat strangers. The couple walked in silence as they returned to the inn to break their fasts.

As they ate, Geofroi stood beside their table and answered Alfred's question. "My lord, we have one church, one inn, and two mills on the north edge of the village on the River Kennet. We grind grain for several estates. Our lord is rich enough to give this village a plough for every two families. We have twelve ploughs."

"How came this town to be?"

"My lady, the King's Inn made us. Workers needed bread and places to live as they built it. Our lord built this village, sent his villeins here and assigned cropland. After the inn was done, our lord permitted us to stay. The millers and I are sokemen. The rest are villeins moved from his two estates." Geofroi puffed his chest with pride. "Including all the fields around us, Newbury is about five hundred acres."

"A good-sized village," said Alfred.

After Geofroi left, Margaret whispered, "Our estate is six hundred acres."

"Soon we will clear forest and be big enough to gain royal permission to be a town. What have we?"

"One small mill on a stream, a black smith, but no inn."

Alfred pushed his bowl away and took up his ale. Sitting with her hands in her lap, Margaret watched him thinking. *He is already planing for a bigger mill or two and an inn. Might he want to take charge of Lord Warwick's inn three miles from our lane? I hope not. Old, decrepit and smelly. Need Alfred have his overlord's approval for any of it? To which of King Henry's barons doth he answer? Dare I ask?*

"My lord, I have a question." At his nod, she again whispered, "Every lord answers to a baron. Did His Grace assign you?"

"Warwick. I assume because we share border with him. I needs protect it."

Warwick! The most powerful baron in the realm. He helped Henry become king. What an honor! How that must have shocked the Court. Mayhap he favors Alfred more than he displayed three days ago. Mayhap he let Elstan live because of his favor. "Now I have two more. May I see how Elstan fares? Aiding the sick and injured is permitted on Sundays." At Alfred's nod, she also asked, "May I nap until the heat of the day declines?"

"For a time, but I shall wake you. I want to see their mills before we sup." Alfred grinned at his wife. "I will set a guard at your door. He will, of course, also guard you against me."

He likes to tease, thought Margaret as she climbed the stairs. *I needs become better at it.*

As they supped on chicken stew, bread and butter, they visited. Margaret reported Elstan's fever had abated a little, and he felt stronger. He was eating. Alfred talked about finding a river near their borders so they could clear land that direction and build a mill on it like the ones they had seen. Margaret told Alfred about Warwick's dilapidated inn. She informed Alfred she had named the estate Mine, and Alfred laughed heartily. She explained he needed to give their estate its permanent name before he rode past the marker stones. He said he would have one on the morrow. At the church bells, they left for Vespers and then to their room.

"I leave you here, my dear. I will walk for a time after I order our meal ready so we may leave before dawn. Ten miles is a long way. Before I return, I will also see to our villein and instruct our knights about the morrow."

In deep night, Margaret need not op her eyes to know Alfred was caressing her body, trying to stir her passion. She heard a whispered "Happy Monday" before he kissed her ear, licked its folds, and softly blew his warm breath into it. He caressed her body. When he placed his hand on her womanhood, she gasped. Heat raced from her ear to her loins. Her eyes opt wide in surprise as Alfred continued his questing.

Margaret slowly returned to the world in a warm afterglow. Snuggled into Alfred's arms, she felt his muscles relax and his breathing slow. *He is as spent as I. Better each time. Caitlin might be right. Being husbanded can be pleasant.* Before she slept she thought, *I dare not return home without first washing. They shall smell what we did and mock me.*

At a knock, Margaret woke. Alfred was already rolling over her. On the floor and crouched, sword in hand.

"My lord, the food is ready."

"Thank you, Arnaud." Alfred stood, stepped to the table, and struck two flints together over the candle wick.

"Alfred, I needs wash."

"As do I. He stepped aside and flourished his arm toward the table top with its pitcher of water, a bowl and a stack of small cloths. "I brought them up last night."

"You are kind to think of my need. You first. I will stay abed until you leave. After I dress, I must braid my hair."

As Alfred worked, he talked. "Yes, you must. When I saw you sleeping so peacefully with your hair splayed on your pillow, I needed walk the yard again until more than half the night was over. I wanted not to have to confess to our priest the moment we arrived." He rinsed his hands before he wet a cloth and started with his face, neck, armpits, and proceeded to his feet. He took a fresh cloth to dry himself. "Wear your best clothes, for we go directly to the feast." He donned his loincloth and braies before he dropped to one knee. "I have something for you," he announced as he rummaged through his satchel. He stood and approached the bed with one hand behind him. "Left wrist, please." Margaret pulled her arm from under the sheet and extended it. Alfred slipped a bracelet over her hand.

"Gold?"

He grinned at her surprise. "And garnets, the same stones as your ring."

"It is so beautiful." She turned it to examine the ring of square stones set in the band. "It has the same designs around the stones as my ring."

"A set. They have been in my family for more generations than we remember. It is also a wedding gift, but I wanted you to wear it first on the day we reach home."

He is the first to gift me jewelry. Gold. So costly. So generous. From his family?

"Oh, Alfred, I thank you is not enough." For the first time, Margaret gazed at him with warmth in her eyes.

"Close your eyes! Under the covers!" he ordered. "If you again look at me like that, we will be abed all day, and you shall miss another wedding feast!" Alfred dressed in his wedding clothes and hurried out of the room, satchel in hand.

Margaret picked up a rag and dipped it into the cold water. She chuckled to herself. *Here I stand, naked but for a ring and a bracelet. One way or another, he has surprised me every day. Only one of them was bad; may that happen never again. Let it go. This is a day to enjoy. At home, I have friends.* Margaret washed her face and neck and cleaned the rest of herself. After dressing, she wet her hands and drew them down her locks to tame them. Hair braided, and headgear in place, Margaret floated down the stairs. She smiled warmly at Alfred and took up her bowl. *Fayme's pottage is spiced with … I know it not. Adds good flavor to the grains.* As she finished her pottage, she spotted Geofroi's son taking her satchel out the main door.

16

Wedding Feast

24 August

Alfred stopped at Warwick's inn. While he and Louvel rode into the yard, Margaret turned Night to the wagon. She was pleased to see Elstan untied and lying on his side with his knees toward his chest.

"God, give you a good day, Elstan. How fare you?"

"Much better now that I am no longer bound as if I were about to be skewered for roasting."

Margaret laughed. Then she frowned. "Your fever?"

"Gone. That woman kept making me swallow a bitter drink, but it worked." Elstan paused. "You are right about tying me. Bending hurts, but I am trying to stretch a bit. I have decided tied during the day and relaxed to sleep. May I stay on the guests' platform above the storage rooms at the back of the hall? No one will see me there."

"I can see to you there, but best you ask my lord. I have not the authority. He returns. My lord, Elstan has a question for you."

Margaret returned to the head of column as Alfred arrived at the wagon. *Fayme cared for him well. I must do something for her.*

"Wretched place," announced Alfred as they rode on. "We shall build a bigger, better one. Margaret, reveal not our new men are only half Norman. I leave it to them to speak of it."

Margaret nodded. *I so want to ask why four, but I dare not. Who else besides Masselin abandoned me?*

"Also, we have guests. I invited my mother Elbeorht to visit. My oldest brother Wulf refused to permit her to come alone, so he accompanied her."

Margaret saw Alfred clench his jaw as if he were forcing himself to silence. *Something is amiss in this. Be it his mother or his brother, I needs be careful.*

The party turned up the lane and soon stopped. From behind Alfred, Margaret heard him call out in Saxon and then in Norman, "I name this place Dryhtenton."

Lord town in Saxon. Some day, God willing. A good name. Margaret called the name as Night stepped past the stone as did the knights and even Elstan. They were met at the tree line by cheering boys and girls who ran ahead of the couple as they rode into the east meadow, now full of people and tables. The new knights took the wagon up the lane to the bailey.

Margaret searched the group to the right of the villeins. *Oh, good! Verel and Syghelm stand to the front. Demetre, Claude, Hughes, Roulin. Where are Sauville and Giraud? I pray they are guarding and not gone. His family. Elbeorht is tall like her son and willowy. Hair cut short like all Saxon women and full gray. She looks right into my eyes like an equal even though she is not. Proud stance. For her son or for herself? Beware her pride. Wulf is built more like a gray-haired bear. Shorter than Alfred, stocky with calloused hands. Wonder his age?*

Margaret smiled at her husband as he helped her dismount. She placed her right forearm on his left and strode to the pair in front of the villeins.

"Mother!" Alfred stepped forward to hug her and kiss her cheek. Margaret stayed where he had left her. Alfred turned and gestured her forward. "I present my wife, the Lady Margaret."

Elbeorht gave obeisance; Margaret opt her arms. "Welcome to our home. We are so pleased to see you."

Alfred beamed at their warm embrace.

"I am honored you called for me. May I call you daughter?"

"Please do. My mother is with God, so I am grateful you want to be mother to both of us. We value your wisdom and your counsel."

Alfred drew Margaret's attention to the man before him. "My lady, this is our brother Wulf, who was so kind to accompany our mother here."

Ignore his glare. His refusal to even nod. "Wulf, we are pleased to see you as well." *His "my lady" was as cold and hard as ice on a frozen river. Why?*

"Mother, if you will excuse us, I would like to introduce my lord to his people." Margaret started with Father Manntun and his family, Cormac and Caitlin, their knights and Syghelm. She proceeded by rank to their villeins, starting with Garwig and Leoma then Felamaere and his family. By the time the couple reached the last family, Margaret's stomach was rumbling.

"My lord, the meat is cut and the smells from the tables! I hope you hunger as much as I."

"Indeed," he replied as he led them toward tables laden with platters of roast pork, lamb, chicken, boiled vegetables and bread. Beyond the end table stood a wagon holding ale barrels. The couple were redirected to a wagon at the end of the meadow nearest the lane. With one side removed and a trestle table, the wagon had become a dais. On it were two oak chairs, one armed and the other not.

Oh my, someone remembered the chairs I bought that market day so long ago in… February 1102. How they shine in the sunlight. Someone polished them. On the morrow, they will stand on the dais in our hall just as I planned. I will stitch matching cushions for them.

Alfred stood on a stump, stepped aboard and helped Margaret join him. Father Manntun stood below to speak the blessing and lead the Te Deum. Alfred noted the four new knights standing beyond the crowd and motioned them forward. They lined up before the wagon.

"Father Manntun, Mother, Brother, our knights and our people, I introduce you to the knights errant I brought with us." He pointed to each man and announced his name. He looked to Margaret's knights, but spoke to all. "We expect you to give them the same warm welcome you gave us."

Alfred seated Margaret and took the armed chair. Women served them ale, full platters of meat, wooden bowls of greens and vegetables, rounds of bread, and both butter and a honey pot. Margaret sniffed. *Wonderful smells, but I must wait. Silence, stomach.* Father Manntun led the partiers to the tables, who had lined up by rank, as usual. After Alfred speared a chunk of meat and bit down on it, Margaret did the same. As they ate, they watched the others. The knights sat at two tables with Syghelm, Verel, and Roulin inviting the new men to join them.

The villeins pull their forelocks or curtsey at Elbeorht. Mayhap they are being so respectful to impress her son, noted Margaret as she ate.

Soon Duone arrived at the dais wagon and announced, "I put three barrels of ale on the wagon. They are empty. Gytha told me to ask. Should I fetch more?"

Margaret leaned forward and gently instructed, "Duone, pull your forelock. Then ask, 'My lord, should I fetch more?'"

Duone did so.

"Well done, Duone. What think you? Two or three more barrels?"

Duone thought for a moment. He pulled his forelock again. "My lord, it is hot. I think three more would be better."

"Good thinking, Duone. Please fetch them."

Duone stood a bit taller, beamed at his lord, and pulled his forelock. "My lord." He turned and strode across the lane to the west meadow to get the donkeys.

"You have made a friend for life."

"You told me not about him. Is he the only one?"

"Yes. His aunt is Nearra, our cook. She keeps him in hand, and he lifts, carries, and sculleries. One thing. You must stop him from feeding my dog." Margaret exclaimed, "Ferrant! I forgot him. An Epiphany gift from everyone. They must have tied him in the barn. He will be frantic to see me. May we see him?"

"We finish eating. After my announcement." Alfred looked to see the line had disappeared and only those seeking second helpings were at the food tables. Soon they too were again seated. As Alfred ate, he spoke a loud compliment as he tasted each food. *He is being gracious. Good.* Scandy brought them a second platter of meat, and Alfred ate most of it. Alfred waited for Margaret to finish. He stood and drew Margaret to join him beside the table. The meadow went silent as everyone looked at the couple.

137

Speaking first in Norman and then Saxon, Alfred called out, "We thank you for your warm welcome and this wonderful meal." He looked at Father Manntun before he turned back to the crowd. "God has been good to all of us. We feast on great bounty because of His grace toward us and our labors. On the morrow, we will continue to harvest the bounty Our Lord has bestowed upon us. By our labors, we will be well fed." He pointed to the knights. "We will be safe." He swept his arm over the meadow the villeins filled. "We look forward to years together. We may not be a family, varied in peoples, skills, and talents as we are, yet we are bound together like a family. I am proud to be your lord. May we live together in peace and harmony."

The meadow resounded with applause and "huzzahs." The villeins stood first and the rest followed. The approving noises continued.

Alfred heard Margaret speak quietly. "Well done, my lord. You pulled them together as one. May they stay that way." She beamed at him.

Alfred raised his arm and gestured. Everyone sat. Alfred stood Margaret in front of him. He took Margaret's right hand in his. She heard his voice booming above her head.

Lean not against him or they will think me brazen.

"I have an announcement. " After everyone quieted, he continued. "For a year and again a half year, you have enjoyed my lady's care, concern, and total attention. She devoted all of herself to you." He paused for effect as he raised her right wrist aloft so everyone could see her wedding ring. "Now she is my wife, and you must share her with me. I am willing to share her with you, BUT," Alfred reach behind her and raised her left arm so all could see the bracelet, "everything between her ring and her bracelet is all MINE! The rest I will share with you."

Everyone froze in shock. Silence. Syghelm broke the tension as he roared his laughter. Everyone joined him. Children jumped up and cheered as well, even if they understood not the reason.

Still holding Margaret's arms aloft, Alfred whispered into her ear, "I love you."

Stunned, Margaret spun about to seek his face for truth in his words. Alfred pulled her into his arms and kissed her hard. Margaret dropped her arms on his, froze and returned not his kiss. Behind the embracing couple, everyone but Father Manntun cheered, clapped, and stomped their feet. Wulf yelled, "That is right. Show her who is master." Margaret pulled away and pushed her forehead into his chest.

How could you! I want to slap you for your arrogance. I dare not. Face them not. Do nothing. Say nothing. How could he embarrass me like this!

"My lady wishes to see her dog. When we return, we hope to hear music and see dancing. Let the feasting and party continue. We return anon."

Alfred slipped past Margaret, who refused to move. He jumped down and called, "My lady."

Margaret, red-faced and looking down, accepted his hand and stepped to the stump and then the ground. She let Alfred keep her hand as they walked around the wagon and toward the lane. She objected not when he pulled her shoulder to shoulder as they walked toward the bailey. She said nothing until they were inside the barn.

Margaret yanked her hand from him and turned on him. Her eyes flashed; her face reddened again. "How dare you! How could you embarrass me like that! All mine from here to there. You treat me like property, not a person, not a wife. You did that not for me but for them. To gain their favor."

139

"I just wanted them to know you are mine now, not just theirs. I…"

Margaret cut him off. "Made a fool of yourself. And of me. Kissing me in public! What will people think?"

Alfred shouted back, "That you are my wife! That I love you!"

That stopped her diatribe. From their entrance until that moment, Ferrant had been furiously barking and pulling on his rope until he was almost out of his collar. Now he was on his hind legs growling not to be petted, but to protect his mistress. He understood not the words, but he saw how she stood and heard the tension in his mistress' voice. Ferrant responded with a mind to kill. Margaret looked his way.

"If you release him, he will attack me," warned Alfred.

Mayhap I should let him. Serve you right. No. No temper. Regain control of yourself. A bad start to fight the first day home. He rules. Not I. Begin again.

"You startled me. Surprised me, Alfred. I am sorry I yelled at you. Permit me to quiet him. Then he will be friendly." Margaret went to Ferrant, palms forward. She spoke softly, and her voice soon stopped his furious barking. He pulled not so hard against his rope as he whined to be released. Margaret untied the rope and clutched it as Ferrant jumped against her legs.

Alfred had stepped to Night's stall to greet him. Night neighed his disapproval. Fearing a bite, Alfred kept out of Night's reach as he talked softly to the steed. Margaret led Ferrant to a stool and sat to pet him. Finally, Ferrant stood at her feet to enjoy her soft words and cooing. Once Ferrant had settled, Night pushed his head over his stall gate and nuzzled Alfred, who stroked his cheek.

Margaret looked up and sounded her surprise. "Night usually likes men not. He seems to like you."

"Horses sense feelings. He knows I am not just anybody."

Margaret put her hand on Ferrant's neck. "I think he is calm now. Would you like to approach?"

Alfred had raised his second foot when Ferrant started growling. Margaret hit his side with the flat of her hand. "NO!" she commanded. Alfred finished his second step and froze.

"Mayhap we should wait and try later."

We are alone. Remember, he wants Saxon. "No, Alfred. If we stop, he shall think he has won. He shall attack you whenever he sees you. Please take one step." Ferrant growled again. This time Margaret pulled the rope hard and half choked her dog. "NO!" She grabbed him by the collar and twisted it just tight enough for Ferrant to be very uncomfortable. At her nod, Alfred lifted a foot.

Before Ferrant could react, Margaret yanked and yelled, "DOWN!" She pushed Ferrant into the rushes. "Stay." Without releasing Ferrant, Margaret looked up and smiled at Alfred. In a warm, pleasant voice, she said, "Please stand in front of him, but do not bend down or he will think you are being submissive. Reach for him not; touch him not. I shall hold him still." Alfred's toes were inches before Ferrant's nose. When the dog reacted not, Margaret petted him with her free hand but did not release him.

"Good, Ferrant. You are a good dog. Good boy."

"What next?"

"We shall walk him to the wagon and tie him to a wheel. I shall feed him and leave him in the shade. You give him drink. Watching us being pleasant together shall confuse him. That is good. If you work with us every day, we can teach him you are his master. Ferrant knows he is my dog. If you train him as well, he shall quickly learn he must also obey you. He is very smart."

With a light voice, Alfred asked, "My lady, may I escort you and Ferrant to the meadow?"

In an equally sweet voice, Margaret responded, "Oh, yes, my lord. I am most pleased to rejoin the feast."

Alfred stepped aside, so she could rise. She held Ferrant's rope an inch from his collar, so he was unable to get around her. "He must never walk between us. We are together; he is extra. Always. When we are together, you must go first in or out every door as usual. He shall accept your leading. You, me, then him, and Ferrant will know who is the head of our pack." They left the barn and strolled toward the bailey gate with Margaret to Alfred's left and Ferrant to hers.

"Who taught you so much about training a dog?"

"Cormac and Felamaere. Cormac managed the king of Scotland's dogs and Felamaere the dogs of the traitor who owned this estate before you."

"Us. We own this estate together."

Margaret smiled at her husband. "Thank you, Alfred." *Is that his apology? Accept it, whatever it means. Start not like Mother and Father ended. I must be second, always second. Mother took over Father's rule and look what it cost her.*

Normans and Saxons alike turned to watch the young couple smiling at each other as they returned. Women whispered together how handsome and strong their lord was, how manly his walk. Men smiled to see their lady looking happy. The knights looked impassive; they were not about to approve a man when they knew neither his character nor his fighting abilities.

The couple arrived and stopped in front of the wagon. A choir of girls serenaded them. They moved into a circle and re-sung the carola as they danced in a ring. After they finished, they giggled and ran off. Alfred went for meat; Margaret tied off Ferrant. Margaret put her hands on the meat and picked up a piece and licked it. Only then did she spill the bowl's contents to the ground and watch Ferrant gobble his meal. At Margaret's request, Alfred filled the bowl from his own mug and set the ale before Ferrant. The dog eyed Alfred as he hesitated. At Margaret's word, Ferrant slurped the bowl dry and lay under the wagon for shade. As the young couple tended Ferrant, the villeins moved tables and benches to the edges of the meadow.

"That went well, my lord. I thank you for your help. First, you are the only one to give him drink. When he is sure of you, we take turns feeding him."

"We always touch his food and pretend to take a bite or eat a bite to show him we are in charge of him, not the other way round," concluded Alfred.

"Indeed, my lord. Cormac explained dogs live in a pack. We are his pack. As he was given to me, and I fed him first, he thinks I am the leader. Now he must learn I am second, and he has moved from second to third." Margaret liked Alfred's nod of understanding. Might a *wife train a husband the same way? This is mine; that is yours? This is how I want things done? I must ask Caitlin.* Margaret looked up to see the sun was just above the trees. *This will be over soon. Then what?*

Felamaere called out, "Time for a carola! Married folk only."

Alfred bowed and offered his arm to escort her to the center of meadow. "Know you this dance?"

"No, my lord. I have only danced once. May Day with the other maidens."

"The steps are easy. I will show you."

Assorted villains played a lyre, a bone horn, three reed flutes, and two small drums as they sat together at the edge of the field.

The couples gathered. Felamaere instructed them to stand man to woman to man. Speaking Saxon, he yelled his first dance instruction. "Bow to your parcener!" Then he called out, "Clasp hands!" Margaret held Cormac's; Alfred took up Edwina's. At Felamaere's "Right!" they danced right. Margaret looked at Alfred's feet and quickly learned the steps. Everyone was smiling at the people across from them as they moved in a large circle. When they were again where they had started, Felamaere called, "Left!" and the circle moved that way. Before they reached the starting place, they heard "Right!" Soon they heard "Left!" The tunes' speed increased, and the calls came faster and faster until everyone took but two steps one direction before the other was called. One step left; one step right, faster and faster. The dance ended in a cacophony of musical noise and the dancers laughing at their failed attempts to keep up. Feleamaere called his last instruction, "Kiss!"

Margaret shyly returned Alfred's embrace and kiss. She blushed.

Father and Gytha had stayed seated rather than dance.

"The sun is in the trees and Father Manntun is looking vexed," Alfred noted.

Margaret moved to Alfred's side and placed her hand upon his forearm. "Mayhap walking toward the church will signal the others to follow," she suggested.

With a question in his voice, he called Father Manntun's name. Father said something to Gytha, stood, and hurried to be ahead of the pair. The knights stood and everyone followed by rank.

Will the kitchen staff put away the remains? Who will return the tables to the hall? Not I. Others. Margaret touched her seire's hem. *This day I am a bride. I will chatelaine on the morrow.*

The wedding couple following Father into the church. After Vespers, everyone traipsed behind their lord and lady. Margaret again kept a close hold of Ferrant. The pair strolled through the gate, across the bailey, and up the steps to the Keep. Only Elbeorht and the serving girls followed; Syghelm closed and locked the gate, and stood guard before it. Dusk was fast arriving.

Alfred secured the keep door. The girls curtsied, and bid the adults, "God give you a good rest." Alfred gestured his mother precede them. Elbeorht stopped on the second-floor landing, kissed and hugged Margaret and Alfred. She bid them the same nighttime farewell before entering the guest room. Alfred led the way to the top landing.

"Stay. Guard," she ordered her dog. Alfred stood by the door as Margaret passed, and latched it behind her.

"Why doth this door lack a lock?"

"I thought the bar on the keep door and the guards at the gate sufficient."

Distracted, Margaret wandered the room and noticed not her simples box was gone from its corner. Ferrant started a low whine.

"Not if we are sieged and the bailey lost. I shall order locks on the morrow."

Ferrant gave a bark, to which Margaret responded, "No, Ferrant" and repeated her earlier commands.

Alfred examined the room. "Our carpenter will make what I need to set my sword on my side of the bed and forms for hanging my armor and my clothing. You may keep the pegs you have. Think what more you want, and I shall order it." Alfred knew why she again walked the room. In a soothing voice, Alfred called her name. When she stopped, Alfred asked, "Ferrant slept beside your bed?"

At Margaret's nod, he continued, "I thank you for sending him to the landing. I am accustomed not to dogs being so close unless their Norman owners use them to keep Saxons in their place."

"Ferrant follows me everywhere. He left not my side during my illness of winter last. Soon you two shall get on. Especially if you take him hunting. He loves to hunt rabbits."

"The sun is gone, my dear. Time for bed." For privacy, Alfred gave her his back.

Margaret removed her circlet and seire and placed them on her clothes chest. She toed her boots and shoved them under her mantle, which Haesel and taken from her at the feast. She placed her girdle on the next peg. *Shall I go abed naked? Not this first time home. Keep my chemise. I know not how he will behave.* Margaret doffed her bliaut and hung it over her girdle. "Alfred, which side of the bed do you prefer?"

"The side you are on," he countered. He added kindly, "Take the one you like."

Shall I give him Caitlin's side? Too much like my maiden days. Take Caitlin's side and see if I like it. No matter, really. He shall move the bed so he sleeps facing the door as he did in the forest.

Margaret put her hand on a post and plopped on the edge of the mattress. She screamed.

Alfred spun to see the four posts caving in on themselves, the drape ropes collapsing, and draperies fluttering. Margaret had disappeared. The head and foot boards were caving inward and looked to crush anyone between them. Alfred dashed over and pulled two posts apart. "Escape before it falls on you!" he shouted as he held only part of the bed upright.

Unable to get her footing, Margaret flailed under draperies. She struggled for a hole in the folds until she spotted a bit of stone wall, rolled off the bed, and thudded to the floor. From the other side, she called, "I am out."

Alfred let the mess fall into a pile. He saw Margaret standing on the other side of the jumble of wood, rope, and fabric. "Are you all right?" She nodded as she viewed the mess.

"Someone loosed the ropes holding it together."

Alfred roared, "Who ruined our marriage bed!"

A cacophony of laughter, hoots, and applause beyond the keep gate answered him. Margaret came round the bed to calm her husband; she was surprised to see him smiling. He put his pointing finger to his lips. As if in anger, he roared again, " I want to know who did this to us. Where shall we sleep?" He grinned at the ensuing shouts from below of "On the floor!" Before the revelers left, they shouted other farewells, most ribald and a few too descriptive of how a traditional first night should be spent. Alfred grinned; Margaret blushed.

Alfred strode to the door, opt it, and shouted down the stairs, "I shall behead every one of you girls if any one of you lowers the keep ladder. Only I may do that." He heard "Yes, my lord" five times. He slammed the door before Ferrant snuck between his legs. He turned to his wife. "You need not sleep on rushes; we can make a bed," said Alfred in a soft voice.

Together they wrestled pillows and bedding from the pile. Harder was pulling the mattress out of a hole over the fallen headboard. After they had made their bed, Alfred approached and turned Margaret. He carefully brushed rushes from her back. Silently, he lifted her chemise hem and pulled it over her head. With the chemise draped over his forearm, he lifted the covers for her to crawl under and lay them over her. After stripping, he crawled under the sheet and blanket to lay on his side facing her. In the darkness, they saw only the outlines of the other from a dash of faint moonlight through a window slit.

"Better than the castle. No swords through the drapes in the night."

"Please do not punish them, Alfred. We are fine, and it was only a bit of fun."

"I shall not." He sighed. " I shall miss the stars."

"As shall I."

"I am going to kiss you."

Long day. So tired. Want to sleep.

Pleasant kisses and caresses soon became passionate. Margaret forgot her tiredness. His body atop hers, Alfred rested on his elbows and dipped in for a kiss here, a kiss there.

No hurrying now, no fear of being found. We are safe. I have the rest of our lives to learn this, was Margaret's last thought.

Afterward, they lay on their sides with their legs intertwined. They held each other close and ended with a deep kiss. Alfred rolled to his back, and brought Margaret with him to place her head in the shallow between his shoulder and his chest. Their breathing slowed almost in unison. Thinking Alfred was now sleeping, Margaret slowly and gently extricated herself from his embrace and rolled away. Alfred rolled with her, put his arm about her waist and pulled himself to her body so they curved together as one.

"Sweet dreams, my darling," he whispered as he kissed her shoulder.

17

Betrayal

To stay out of the sun, Margaret walked the bailey edges from the hall toward palisade. *Mother said, "Being sun-colored is fit for a Saxon, not for a lady of rank. Pale skin shows you supervise and labor not."* She walked under the palisade toward her husband and brother. *"Women of rank speak softly, so call them gently. Yelling is only to call danger," Mother declared. I must act proper.* Reaching the palisade walkway almost under the pair, Margaret heard, "The harvest seems to be starting well. I would never roast a pig for Saxons. Bread and ale is good enough. Your course is costly."

"They work hard, Brother, and the meat feeds them noon and night. We get better work and longer when we feed them well."

"You are rich enough to do as you wish," grumbled Wulf. "You are already the richest Saxon in the land. Too bad you had to wed a Norman to get what should be ours."

Trying to soothe his older brother, Alfred once again succumbed to Wolf's persuasive ways. "Worry not, Wulf. We will get back what was ours, one plot at a time if we must."

"Do you love her?"

Alfred looked away. "No. I do what I must to get all this." Alfred fanned his arm wide.

Margaret's heart fell.

"You smile and dote on her as if you care," commented Wulf in an oily voice.

"An act. I need heirs to keep this estate. Letting her think I care will get them sooner. Because she believes, the time will pass swifter. I do what I must," Alfred repeated. "That is all."

Wulf nodded his approval. In a smooth voice, he concluded, "Once you have them, you can dispose of her and wed a good Saxon woman. I guess only half-Saxon heirs need do."

Margaret clapped her hand over her mouth. She turned and fled the way she had come with Ferrant at her heels. When she was before the hall door, she turned and called, "My lord, Brother Wulf, time to break your fasts." Before Alfred could speak, Margaret fled into the hall, leaving the door ajar.

They sat on the dais with Wulf on the end next to Alfred and Elbeorht to Margaret's left. Her face looked to be in a smile as if all was well, but no smile shone in her eyes.

Alfred stood and frowned at those assembled. The knights stopped eating. "We arrived to warm greetings and a wonderful celebration only to end with a loud crash!" The men froze. "If your intention was to impede our night, you were misguided. I know not which of you undid our bed, but I have two punishments for the lot of you. First, immediately after this meal, four of you will return to our floor and retie the bed together, and I mean tightly. Then, you will replace the mattress, make up the bed, fix the draperies, and leave the room as you found it. Your other punishment is this," Alfred smiled. "To thank you for a wonderful night on the floor, a second round of ale for all of you."

When the men saw Alfred's smirk, they smiled, drank their mugs dry and lifted them for the refill. They expressed their thanks, laughed and returned to their meal.

Margaret's face went crimson. She kept her eyes downward to avoid Elbeorht's piercing gaze. The food arrived, but Margaret touched it not.

"Daughter, are you well?"

"I am fine, Mother. How fare you this morn?"

"I seek your forgiveness for borrowing your simples box, which I have left on the visitor's platform behind us."

"Elstan! I forgot him!" Margaret rose, but Alfred put his hand on her arm. She dropped back onto her chair. *Presume not. Ask.* "May I attend Elstan, my lord?"

Elbeorht intervened. "I attended him last night after he supped. I used that excellent salve you made for burns. I am somewhat skilled as a healer, Margaret. With your permission and from the herbs you have, I can make another salve that will soften his skin and help it heal."

"Thank you, Mother, for attending our villein," said Alfred. "You may continue to do so. You do not mind my asking Mother for help, do you, my lady?"

Margaret shook her head and took up her spoon. *I must escape. He lied. He lied. I am living with a liar. I dare not stay, knowing what I heard.* Margaret sipped her ale. Her stomach was so knotted, she could barely swallow. She dipped into her pottage and ate only half a spoonful.

Am I so upset I wet myself? What is sticking my thighs together? Oh. Thank you, God. I am saved!

Margaret leaned right and whispered, "My lord, I have a need. I am for the keep and will return anon." At his nod, she rose, stepped off the dais and left through the back door. She strode purposefully to the keep while she managed a necessary smile or two on the way. *Let no one suspect,* she warned herself. On the first floor, she found only Cleva, whom she motioned to come to her. "Keep what I tell you secret. Find Jorgon. Tell him to saddle Night. You wait with him in the barn." Cleva descended the ladder; Margaret took the stairs. She closed the door, stripped bare, and reached for her courses pail stashed behind her marriage chest. Standing, she washed and dried herself. From the pail, she put one foot through her waistband and pulled up the device. Into the cloth sling between her legs, she layered her courses' cloths and tied the waistband about her. That done, she replaced her boots and garments. *He cares for me not a whit. He will use me and then kill me. Like Father killed Mother. I must escape. Now.*

She looked to be sure the bailey was bare. Margaret crossed a space as empty as her heart. When she was almost at the barn, Haelum came running through the gate. He held out his hand as he called, "My lady, my lady! My hands are clean. May I walk with you?" Margaret silently waved him off, entered the barn, and closed the small door behind her and Ferrant.

Margaret took the reins from Jorgon before she commanded, "Tell no one I left."

"No, my lady."

"Tie Ferrant inside here. Cleva, keep him company and quiet."

Jorgon opt the wide barn door, and Night flew toward the gate. The guards looked astonished to see their lady racing away, but they had no power to stop her. Margaret and Night dashed down the lane. Workers harvesting wheat stopped to watch her.

Into the forest. No one will find me. Go to my bathing place. Fetch my escape clothes. Disappear. Margaret slowed Night as they entered the trees. On a path Night knew, he cantered between the trees as he had so many times before.

Alfred was standing between the dais and the fire pit as he talked with two knights when Haelum flew through the main door. He wove through the departing men. Haelum ran full force into Alfred's legs. Alfred harrumphed and stepped back. He grabbed the boy pummeling his stomach and yelling. Alfred picked up the boy, set him on the nearest bench, slapped his face, and yelled, "Stop!"

Haelum sobbed, "She was crying. She refused my hand. You made her cry! She was crying. She rode away." Haelum flailed at Alfred to no avail. "I hate you! I hate you! You made my lady cry."

As Alfred released Haelum, the boy swung at Alfred and struck his upper arm. He turned and ran down the bench. At the other end, Haelum looked back and yelled, "You are a bad man!" Haelum vowed, "When I get big enough, I am going to kill you!" before he jumped down and disappeared out the front door.

Alfred saw every man in the hall staring at him. "Two knights with me!" he ordered. He strode through them. Outside the barn, he found Jorgon holding his saddled horse.

Hughes and Demetre headed into the barn for their steeds.

"Where?" demanded Alfred as he mounted.

"The guards may have seen her." Jorgon turned back into the barn to assist Lord Alfred's escort.

Alfred shouted, "Where?" as he approached the gate. A guard answered and pointed. Alfred waited not for the others; he raced down the lane and took the forest path to the left.

Margaret dismounted and tied Night to a tree. "Be a good boy, Night. They will care for you well." She patted his neck and kissed his cheek. "Fare thee well, my friend. You cannot go with me. I will miss you. " Night neighed. "Quiet now, boy. He will find you soon enough."

Margaret stepped away and looked about as if she had never been in that clearing before. She pressed her fingers to her forehead to clear her mind. *Think. Which way?* She walked to the tree at the river's edge and leaned against it. She looked around the clearing, frowned, and then smiled. *That way!* Margaret headed for the trees and toward the rotted-out stump, which hid her escape clothes, boots, and knife. Just as she reached the stump, she heard horses approaching. *Drat! Caught. He must not find them. I must find a way. No, make a plan.* Margaret raced back.

Alfred rode into the clearing and pulled his reins so hard his horse skidded to a halt. He glowered at his wife with her back against the gnarled, giant tree beside the river. He dismounted and tied his steed next to Night. Seeing her red eyes stopped him not. With fear in his voice, he yelled, "Running off unescorted is dangerous! What are you about?"

Margaret stood and put out her arms. "Halt! Come no further. You may not touch me."

"You are my wife! I can do anything I want."

Her fury rose. "Such as killing me after I give you heirs?" *I should have remained silent.*

154

Demetre and Hughes barged into the scene. They saw their lord leaning toward their lady while she held out her arms to stop his approach.

Without looking away from his wife, Alfred gestured backwards. "Guard. Out of our sight!"

"And within hearing should you call for help, my lady," called Demetre. The pair turned their horses the way they had come and disappeared.

Dear God, I thank you for my men. "You may not touch me because I am in my courses. You shall become unclean if you do," reasoned Margaret in a calm, quiet voice.

"You make not sense."

"I am in my monthly courses." At his frown, she added, "It means I am not with child."

"Oh-h-h!" He frowned again. "Why unclean?"

"I may not weed, garden, weave, sew, mend, cook, serve food, anything really, when I am in my courses. I cannot be touched. Also, the Church says I am unclean and may not attend Mass, receive communion, or confess until it is over. Then I must wash and receive the Church's blessing before I am clean again."

"Saxon women do all those things all the time, no matter their condition."

"Not so for me. I am Norman."

Alfred stepped back. "Very well. Is that why you ran off?" At her slowly shaking her head, Alfred demanded, "Why?"

Margaret stared hard. *Lie and my face will reveal it. Accuse and he will deny. Speak the truth and watch his eyes.* Margaret's words came out dangerously quiet and flat. "I heard you." She took a deep breath and felt cold inside. "You and your brother. Before I called you to eat." She watched his eyes widen a bit. "I was under the parapet walkway to summon you." She changed her voice with each speech so he would recall which of them had said what. She began with, "Do you love her?" and finished with, "Once you have them, you can dispose of her and wed a good Saxon woman. I guess only half-Saxon heirs need do." *Silence is all you give me because that is all you have.* "You lied to me. From the first moment. You lied to the queen before that." *He will lie and then punish me as he pleases.*

Each stood frozen. Margaret barely breathed.

Alfred's voice was quiet, but full of feeling. "Margaret, you are right. I did lie. Not to you. To Wulf. He is a dangerous man, and he hates you. All Normans but especially you." When she asked not why, Alfred continued. "All my life, from my first memory, he has hit me, destroyed anything I made. Always when no one saw. He made cert I feared him. Ran from him. Yet he would find me alone and hurt me. I knew not why. Because of him, I ran away and was gone six years before they found me." Still Alfred received no response. "Because of you, I now have more than he shall ever have. He wants you dead. Should he have the chance, he would grab you and slit your throat before my eyes." Alfred saw her eyes widen. "Have you noticed how I protect you? If I am not beside you, a knight is between you and him. Should he take one step toward you, they are instructed to kill him. Ask any one of them; he will tell you."

Margaret nodded and called Hughes' and Demtre's names. They dashed into the clearing. They realized the distance between the pair was the same. "Halt. I am fine. I have a question." At their nods, she asked, "What are my lord's instructions regarding his brother Wulf?"

The men looked at each other. As Demetre was older, he spoke. "He sleeps in the barracks with us, but one of us must stay awake to guard him. Should he rise in the night, we are to wake another man. Stop him if he tries to leave the barracks. Tie and gag him should he give us any trouble."

Margaret glanced at Alfred before she spoke. "Hughes, any other instructions?"

"My lord?"

"Tell her." He stared at Margaret as hard as she did at him.

"One man behind him on the dais. One man behind him when he moves. Plus one man between you and him when you are about. If he makes any move, any step toward you, we kill him."

"Is he aware?"

"Oh, yes, my lady. He likes it not one bit. We know he is biding his time. Worry not, my lady. Should he move wrong, he dies."

"Thank you, Demetre. Thank you, Hughes. Please leave us to finish our talk," requested Margaret in a pleasant tone.

Again alone, each wondered who would speak first.

"You have other questions." Margaret nodded. "After Wulf is gone, I will sit with you and answer all your questions. I shall speak the truth, no matter what."

They will be hard ones. You tell a good story, but how can I know the truth? You are a stranger. But I have no choice now. I must return. For a while. "My lord, I am ready to return."

"I have a plan. I escort you home and to the keep. When I am asked why you abide there, I shall say, 'Some Norman custom when a woman is in her courses,' and I say no more. I set a guard on the gate. Wulf crosses not the keep gate, and you are safe. You meet your needs during your time. I shall touch you not. After Wulf and Mother leave, I shall meet you on the keep green and we shall talk."

"That is a good plan." Margaret moved toward Night.

"May I help you mount?" Margaret shook her head. "Wait."

Margaret was shocked to see Alfred drop to all fours beside Night and announce, "I am a stump, a rock." She could not help smiling as she placed her boot on his backside, pulled herself up by the platform edges, and placed her other foot on the wooden platform as she mounted. She watched Alfred turn and stand with his back to her. He mounted and led them down the path. Hughes and Demetre moved aside to let them pass and followed.

Halfway out of the forest, they met a small boy trudging toward them. He ignored Lord Alfred and let him pass. When Margaret was beside him, Haelum pulled his forelock. "My lady, are you well?" Margaret nodded. Hughes's horse sidled, and the boy jumped off the path. He followed them home.

Everyone in the fields stopped work and watched them pass, as did the guards at the gate, and those in the bailey. The knights headed for the barn. Alfred called for Roulin to follow. At the keep gate, Margaret dismounted, passed through, and climbed the ladder. Alfred bent to speak to Roulin, who closed the gate and stood before it. Only then did Alfred take up Night's reins to lead him to the barn.

That night, Margaret again suffered the old night terror of being beaten, but she thrashed and cried out alone. She knew not why she had awakened and was clutching the side rail. She rolled to the middle of the bed and fell back asleep.

18

Taking Control

Margaret awakened to, "Daughter, may I enter?" At hearing her muffled permission, Elbeorht opt the door to see Margaret swinging her legs out of bed and rubbing the sleep from her eyes. Ferrant dashed to her side. Margaret stood and motioned her husband's mother toward the pair of stools on either side of an unlit brazier. She ordered Ferrant out and yelled down the stairs, "Someone tie Ferrant in the barn. I am unclean and may pet him not." She closed the door to him.

"I am glad you napped after you dined. You have had several hard days since you left home."

Margaret gave Elbeorht a wan smile before she nodded.

"I would talk with you about several things and answer any questions you may have." After Elbeorht saw a second pair of nods, she proceeded. "What did your mother tell you about being wedded and bedded?"

159

"Nothing."

Elbeorht looked astonished. "Norman girls go to their weddings knowing nothing about husbanding or how to be a wife!"

In a defensive tone, Margaret replied, "Mother had no time. Right after the contract was signed, she died." She looked away.

Elbeorht reached out and stopped at touching the girl's knee. "Forgive me. I knew she was with God, but I knew not that."

"Of her marriage, I remember anger between them. Mother took me with her to midwife ladies of rank. She was happier, lighter, and freer then."

Elbeorht watched Margaret suck her lips between her teeth to silence herself. She decided to begin again. "I think you ran off because you were disappointed to get your courses. That you are not with child immediately. Almost no bride gets with child the first time she and her husband lie together. Just as they needs become accustomed to what each likes when they love, their bodies need time to adjust to being joined. Ofttimes, a wife gets not with child for months or even for a year after the wedding." Elbeorht shrugged. "Though I admit they beget a child sooner when they like each other and oft spend time trying." Margaret's face colored. Elbeorht softened her tone. "Want you children?"

"Yes."

"May they all be healthy, God willing." When Margaret spoke not, Elbeorht did. "My son and you live on a large estate and can avoid each other all day. You are with company at every meal; you ride escorted wherever you go. The only time you are alone together is bedtime unless you carve out time alone during the day. Just standing together on the parapet walkway as you watch the knights practicing or the villeins working can be enough time for talk. We

Saxons live in one room, work together, and see each other through-out the day. We talk about things as we go. At night, when we lie together, it is for loving or sleeping." Elbeorht stopped and hoped Margaret caught her meaning. "Set a place—these stools are good enough—where you privately discuss and make decisions regarding all outside matters. I suggest you tell him you are done talking, rise, and take his hand. Walk him to bed and do not talk except words of love. You will be surprised how quickly he learns."

"Are you saying we should never talk about estate matters in bed? That behind the draperies, we are only husband and wife, not lord and lady? Am I training him as I did Ferrant?"

"You are training each other. Have you two not already made decisions together?"

"We made one regarding how we shall face the world outside ourselves."

Elbeorht nodded her approval. "I was told the first year after a wedding is challenging because you not only create a joint house-hold, you also create a joined life." Elbeorht frowned. "Just be cert, my new daughter, you get what you want and what you need. Do not give in to his wish or demand if it hurts you. In our Saxon world, husband and wife are partners; Alfred is not your lord to be obeyed."

"Before we met at the church door, he said something like that." *I can refuse him? Not yet though. Wait to see how he treats me after this.*

"Good. I have been fearful his years living with Normans made him too Norman and not enough Saxon."

In her mind, Margaret tucked away a question for Alfred.

"Margaret, I know not if Norman mothers teach their daughters this most important thing. As your mother was unable to tell you, I needs do so. The Church forbids certain actions between husband

and wife. In Confession, they ask not husbands if they have done them; they ask wives. If you ever answer yes to one of them, both your penances shall be severe. His for doing it, and yours for not stopping him."

"How do I stop Alfred when we are abed? He is so forceful."

Elbeorght waited for Margaret to stop blushing at her admission. "After I explain what is forbidden, I shall tell you how to distract or stop him." As Elbeorht described in detail the first forbidden act, Margaret pinked. She turned crimson at hearing the second. She dropped her head and covered her face with her hands while hearing the third.

Oh Dear God, he would do not those things to me! How could he? Why would he even try? They are disgusting! I would never forgive him. Never.

Even though Margaret kept her face covered and her head down, Elbeorht stopped not. She explained in detail how to distract Alfred, how to turn him away from each start he might make, and how to stop him. "Did you hear me?" At Margaret's nodding, Elbeorht asked, "Do you understand?" After another nod, Elbeorht, asked, "Will you remember?"

"How can I forget? The sight of them happening to me are burned in my head! Why am I responsible for stopping him, for any of this? Why not tell him what he must do never?"

"He is a man. Tell him what is forbidden, and he shall want to do it. Not stop until he tries it. Believe me, if you want to be cert Alfred does something, tell him he ought not. I know of one man whose priest punished him by having him walk on his knees from his church to Canterbury Cathedral and back again. His family saw him not for two years. He returned a broken man and never worked again."

The Church orders our lives. Mass every morning, Vespers every evening. When we must fast, what we may not eat. Holy days. Music. Dancing. Stay a virgin or be thrown into a ditch. When and how to marry. Now even how to lie together. It is all powerful. Even in this. Margaret felt a familiar emotion rise in her; quelling rebellious thoughts was hard for her. *Why is the Church all powerful? Did God give them the authority or did they create it themselves? Oh how priests love their power. Even into our beds. Why may we not think for ourselves. Make our own choices? Think no more on it or I might rebel. I dare not. I might lose my soul and be damned to everlasting Hell. Stop thinking. Accept what is. Change our talk.* "How fares Elstan?"

"He is young and healing fast. He is pushing hard to bend enough to sit and is succeeding. I doubt he shall ever be able to bend at his waist to touch his feet. He needs to learn new ways to don his leggings. He shall need someone else to fasten his boots."

"When I served Queen Matilda in Forest Keep before the princess was born, she was guarded by Saxons who were 'El-something.' Elric said they were all cousins. You are Elbeorht and he is Elstan. Are you related?"

Elbeorht shifted on her stool, smiled, and kept her soft tone as she shrugged. "I suspect we are some way or another. I thought not to ask how."

A knock on the door interrupted them. "My lady, I have brought your supper."

Elbeorht stood. "Oh my, I want not to miss mine. Then Vespers and bed. I shall visit you on the morrow, daughter. I bid God give you a good rest." Elbeorht opt the door and let Cleva pass before she took the stairs.

With her tray set on Elbeorht's stool, Margaret ate. She picked up her bowl to slurp the last of the broth and finished her bread and ale. After she placed the tray on the landing, she changed her courses rags and left them to soak overnight. She walked the room as she undid her braids and brushed her hair. *So many things to consider. How do I behave since our confrontation? What say I or not say? I called him a liar. He was dangerously calm. Do not do that again. He explained, but is it truth or more lies? I know him not well enough. The queen said learn his mind from his actions, but I needs ask him questions. Note his words. Learn from the stories he tells. Questions for Alfred. Why does Wulf hate you? No. Know you why Wulf hates you? Why does he hate me? He just met me, and I was polite. How did you come to live among the Normans? Where are Sauville and Giraud? How are my old knights receiving you? Your new knights being received? Best I ask not about knights; I want not him to think I challenge his authority with them.* On she continued until she noticed the window slits were dark. She peered out one and stared at the stars. *Mother, do you see me? I desire your advice how to proceed with this man. Tell me how to live with a man I trust not. I pray for guidance. Please answer me.* Margaret climbed into bed to pray there and sleep if she could. She had the unwelcome thought that her mother would not have been the best guide for dealing with her new husband. *Elbeorht? I cannot talk to her of her son. But if I could… yes, I might trust her.*

Just after the church bells rang a second time, Midryth arrived with Margaret's pottage, bread, and ale. "We are feeding you first. You needs dress, my lady. I suspect you will have visitors after Mass."

"What has gone amiss?"

Without answering, Midryth shrugged and quickly left.

Margaret gobbled her pottage while it was still warm. She dressed and braided her hair. At a hard knock, she jumped up to face the door. Alfred said, "My mother needs your assistance. Please meet her anon in her room. Bring a stool." Margaret waited for Alfred to depart before she donned her circlet, opt the door and took the stairs.

Margaret knew to touch not the latch, so she said, "Mother Elbeorht, I am here."

She was surprised to see Alfred op the door. Still on the landing, she curtsied as she set down the stool, "God give you a good day." At his gesture, she picked up the stool and entered. Elbeorht was seated on the only armed chair in the keep. "Mother, why do you cry? Are you hurt? What has distressed you so?"

"You should not have done it. You … should..not..have..done … it."

Margaret placed her stool near Elbeorht and sat. "My lord should not have done what?"

"Alfred, remember. Also with family." He turned to his mother. "Mother, you know I had to save you for your own good." Margaret turned to Alfred with an unspoken question. "Before dawn, I sent Wulf home."

"He would not have left of his own will. He would have to have been assaulted, tied and gagged. Not for my sake, but for your own revenge on him."

"You are only half right, Mother. They did have to tie and gang him before they put him in the wagon. You shall be his slave no more. Now I have the power and the means to stop him, so I did. You shall spend the rest of your days at your ease. I told you; I have already arranged it."

"I must return. They need me."

"No, Mother, they do not. Wulf uses you for his gain. He wants to work you to death and claim your dowry as payment for keeping you in his house."

This family discord is old. What does he want from me? Remember, one face to the world. Even here with family? Yes. "Mother, I want to hug you, comfort you, but you know I may not. I understand none of this. Please talk to me. What do you in Wulf's house?" Elbeorht still wept.

Behind her, Margaret heard, "She does all the work in the house and garden his wife should be doing. Mother is fifty-four years and should be honored and at her ease, but Wulf orders her like a slave; he is harsh and unkind to her."

She is so old she was alive when the Conquerer invaded! Even twenty years older than King Henry! A long life. This morn she looks her age.

Elbeorght did not dispute it, so Margaret looked to Alfred. "His wife works not?"

"She weaves all day; she is famous for her patterns, for the excellence of her work. Wulf's lord is made rich from her labor, and he pays Wulf well for his wife's extra service. Wulf also demanded to be made a sokeman, and his lord granted it. His wife is glad to have a loom in her own shed in the bailey, to be well fed from their lord's table, and to avoid Wulf. The cost has been my mother's health." In a cold, hard voice, Alfred added, "No more."

"Mother, we would be honored if you would live with us. Alfred and I would like it very much. You have your own room. We can send for your things. Please consider it."

"No, you are a new couple. You needs be alone; I would be in your way."

"Never," vowed Margaret. "If you stay not with us, then what?"

Alfred repeated to Margaret what his mother had already heard. "Her things are already in our small house on my old lord's estate. I am sending Elstan with her for company, for service, and for her help in his healing. She has a servant girl to do whatever she wants, a garden, and a wide forest to find herbs and things for the simples she likes to make." Alfred turned. "Mother, you shall sleep when you will, do what you like, and spend your last years loved and in comfort."

"Without me, his house will fall apart."

Margaret saw Alfred cross his arms over his chest and a stern face.

"Mother, Wulf's house will fall apart not. His wife will work at home and weave two or three days a week. Surely their children are grown and can help."

Elbeorht reminded her son, "When they are together, he treats her badly. Always has."

"After you go to God, you know it shall happen anyway," reasoned Margaret. "Please spend these next years with your family who loves you." Margaret motioned to Alfred and whispered, "Please hug her; I cannot."

Alfred lifted his mother, held her close, and rocked her. Alfred whispered, "I love you, and I will protect you the rest of your days. You will have all the good things you deserve. I love you, Mother."

Margaret teared at seeing how loving he was. *Would he treat me so. Be kind.* She heard a muffled, "I am a little tired." *He has won.*

She watched Alfred guide his mother out the door with, "Let us break our fasts. If you like, I will escort you here, and you may rest." Alfred looked back at Margaret and mouthed, "I thank you." Margaret nodded.

She returned to their room. She rinsed her dirty rags. From behind a chest, she pulled out the wooden rack to hang them. After donning a new set of courses' rags and soaking the used ones, she struck flint and started a small fire in a brazier beside the rack. *One day gone; Mayhap four more before it is over.* Margaret returned to bed to memorize the questions for which she wanted answers.

The next morning, Margaret met Elbeorht before she left for Mass. "Mother, before you leave us for a time, I have a request. Will you return for a visit at Christmastide?" At Elbeorht's, "Of course," Margaret added, "If I should get with child, I would like to you to stay with us my last month and help me with the birthing."

"Of course!" Elbeorht hugged Margaret, who froze.

"Mother, I have made you unclean!"

"Nonsense! While we do not lie with our husbands during our courses, we believe not the Church about the rest of it. Priests! They are taught we are dirty and are to be avoided at all times. Be more Saxon, daughter; it is much more enjoyable." Margaret was shocked speechless.

Later, Margaret stood on a step halfway to the keep gate. She watched Elstan carried from the hall and laid in the back of the wagon. Alfred and Elbeorht followed. Two knights rode out of the barn to escort the wagon. *Giraud! Sauville! You are here! I thank you for staying. Where have you been?* She returned Elbeorht's wave. Alfred helped his mother to the wagon's seat and mounted his steed. The party left. Margaret decided to sit in the bright sunlight and enjoy the day. *I may work not, but I can supervise. I hear knights practicing beyond the palisade. I hear the pigs; Haesel weeds the garden. All know their duties; I need not worry. I wonder who walks and feeds Ferrant?* When the sun became too warm, she returned to the keep.

19

Conversing

Cyne picked up Margaret's dinner tray. "My lady, my lord wishes to meet you on the keep green."

Margaret stood, straightened her clothes, and followed Cyne. She walked down the steps until she stood even with Alfred, who sat in the grass to one side.

"Sit on the other side, so all will see a good space between us." After Margaret did so, he instructed, "Ask away."

"Who are your family?"

"My father was Elsworth, a farmer. My two older brothers are Wulf, who farms our land, and Aldrich, who is a priest on the continent. Then me, my sister Elbeorht—we call her Beorhti—and a younger brother. Beorhti is wed to a black smith, has two sons and is with child."

"How came you to live among Normans?"

"Remember you what I told in the forest about Wulf?" Margaret nodded. "It is a long tale." *The more you tell, the better I will learn your character.* Margaret smiled.

"My younger brother was born when Beorhti was four; I was six. Wulf told me Norman law forbade a Saxon from having more than three sons."

Margaret frowned. *I have heard not such a law.*

"One of us would die. Not him; he was eldest, nor Aldrich because he was studying for the Church. He convinced me either the babe or I would die. Wanting to live, I thought to strangle the babe, but Mother held him so close. Wulf warned me that if Father suggested we go into the forest, he meant to kill me and keep the babe. The way they gushed over him and fussed, I feared for my life. I tried to be good so they would choose me. One supper, Father said that, in the morn, he and I were to go into the forest to find acorns for the pigs. Wulf gave me a look and nodded. After we ate, I said I was going to play with a friend. Instead, I ran into the woods.

"The first night I climbed a tree to avoid boars. I headed north and ran and ran. I ate what I could find, drank when I could, and each night I slept in the crook of a tree. I know not how many days or how far I fled, but I was dirty, hungry, and afraid to be found. One morning, I awoke to being poked. I heard, 'I see a strange bird in a tree. What kind think you it might be?' I was too frightened to speak because he was a Norman yeoman. I feared death. He took me to his lord, who spoke Norman, then Saxon. I stood before him and answered neither my name nor from whence I had come. I stayed silent while he and his wife talked what to do with me. I spotted their son Cyrille. His nurse was flirting with a man. She saw not their dogs run by him and knock him into the fire pit. I ran, pulled him out, and burned my hands putting out his tunic." Alfred displayed his palms and fingers.

"I am so sorry."

"Not I. Their roughness helps me. I never lose a grip on my weapons no matter how hard the fight." Alfred paused. "They declared me dumb-spoke but helpful. I nodded when they asked if I would guard their son. They took me in. Over time, I understood Norman; I practiced speaking it when I was alone. The Easter I was eight, I tried my voice with, 'The Christ is risen, and we are saved. Thanks be to God.' They declared my speaking an Easter miracle. I still pretended I had no family. They made me a page. I learned to squire with Cyrille and squired for him as he trained to be a knight." They were good to me and I loved them."

"Your family look for you not?"

"I thought not. I was twelve when I walked into the hall and saw my father talking with my lord. He had finally heard the rumors about a Saxon squire in the north. I refused to return home. When he asked why not, I told him. He was aghast. My lord swore a holy oath no such law existed. I reported what Wulf had said. I told Father, 'I am Norman now and want not a Saxon's life.' I told my father I thought they loved my baby brother more than they loved me. He told me Mother had lost a babe after Beorhti; that was why she clung so to the boy. Still, I refused to return because of Wulf. My father was heartbroken. He stayed. My lord arranged things. He convinced me to go home for a year and a day. After that, if I wanted to again squire for Cyrille, he would hire me. But two months of each year, I had to live with my parents. I would make a final decision who to be when I was sixteen and a man."

"Oh, Alfred, your poor parents. How they must have suffered thinking you were dead."

"At the time, I hated them for their weakness. For protecting me not from that villain." Alfred saw her shock, looked away and added, "After they reported Wulf's actions to the village, they and everyone else banished him from their company while I was home. After I saw how much Father and Mother and the rest loved me and had missed me, I forgave them."

Poor man, his childhood was as hard as was mine. No, harder. He thought himself unloved. At least I had Mother's love and protection until her death.

"I learned Wulf and Aldrich are my half-brothers. Mother's first husband had been rich and high born. He fought with King Harold and died at Pevensey. You call it Hastings." Alfred spoke to himself. "That is why he hates me. He lost his father, so he wanted me not to have mine." He looked at Margaret. "What think you?"

Margaret's heart went out to him. "I think you have hit upon it. None of this was your fault, Alfred."

"That was then; this is now. I will think on Wulf no more. Next question."

"Why did Sir Cyrille and you join the Grand Crusade?"

Alfred's voice turned hard. "He joined, not I!" He softened his tone. "His father wanted him to go not because his older brother had died, and Cyrille was now my lord's only son. Cyrille insisted God was calling him to serve. I think he wanted the excitement, the adventure. He had no idea the real of it. The journey to the Holy Land was hard. After we arrived, we learned the Saracens had outflanked our fighters in one battle and destroyed their camp. They took horses and everything else after they killed all the squires and workers. The old group demanded everyone receive weapons and learn to fight. The new group disagreed. That is why I was taught sword fighting. Glad I was I never had to use it except in practice. Saracens are mad and dangerous. Their swords are curved and longer than ours. Our armor helps, but they oft win in hand-to-hand fighting. Cyrille got nicked in a practice with another knight. It festered in that heat. He fevered and died."

Margaret thought a quick prayer for the repose of Sir Cyrille's soul. "May I ask another question?" At Alfred's assent, she asked, "Queen Matilda said you met the pope and served him before you returned home. What did you?"

"Lordless, I volunteered to squire a knight sent to the pope with dispatches and booty. Rome is big, beautiful, crowded, and dirty. He chose to stay. I volunteered to carry the pope's letters on my way home. I received coins, a letter of passage, and packets for various leaders. I saw much of the continent. Some places were beautiful, but I longed for home. My last stop was King Henry. I reported the sad news to my lord. Old as he is, he bore it. I think he already knew, but I know not how."

"Have you been in England long?"

"Yes."

Margaret spotted Alura coming around the end of the hall with her supper tray in hand. "I have a few more questions. May we do this again on the morrow?"

"We may, but it must be late. On the morrow, I shall be with the men on the practice field."

"Thank you, Alfred, for a good afternoon. I have missed your company." *I like the surprise on your face. Politic of me to say it.*

They stood and waited for Alura to pass. Alfred bid her farewell and took the steps to the gate. Margaret watched him walking toward the hall. Before Alfred entered, he turned back and nodded at her. Margaret reciprocated and waited for him to disappear before she followed her supper.

I am slept out and bored. This day I shall walk the bailey to see all is well. I think in Saxon these days. Practice Norman, or I may lose it. Margaret stepped into another sunny day and jauntily took the stairs. She admired her well-weeded garden, visited the pig pen. For a time, she watched two men and three women clearing the old grain from the bins, shoveling it into sacks and sewing the sacks shut. Duone returned from the hall to fetch more sacks to store in the hall stalls.

"God give you a good day, Duone."

Duone pulled his forelock. "My lady, are you well now? Aunt Nearra says you shall be back soon."

"A few more days, Duone. Today I am just walking about."

Duone grunted not as he hefted a heavy sack under each arm and headed for the hall.

Margaret strolled to the kitchen and visited over the half door without touching it. Nearra reported all was well. The roast pig would be ready in time. The villeins still had to be stopped from finishing it instead of waiting until the eventide meal. Margaret avoided the barn. *If I go there, Night and Ferrant will want petting. I may not touch them, despite Elbeorht's advice.* She followed her ears and climbed the ladder to the parapet walkway. She watched the villeins harvest a far-off field. Someone spotted her and waved. She waved back. Others turned and waved as well. She waved again before walking toward the gate. The guard put his back to the parapet to let her pass. *All but the guards and the sentries are on the field. They are demonstrating their skill on horse and with the apparatuses. They must thirst in this heat. I wonder what Alfred is saying to Verel.* She spotted Daelton across the bailey and summoned him. He returned with a donkey and cart. Duone rolled a barrel of ale out of the hall and lifted it into the wagon. Two girls piled pottery mugs next to it, and Daelton led the donkey out the bailey. *They see it coming!* She watched Claude point her direction. Verel opt the barrel and dipped mug after mug. Margaret watched the men pass them down the line. Verel and Alfred took the last mugs. As one, the men lifted their drinks to her and yelled, "Our thanks, my lady!" Margaret beamed at them and waved. *He looks at his ease. I see how they visit with him. That is another good sign.* She looked down and saw she had almost no shadow. *Time to return to the keep.*

Well after midday, Haesel called up the keep stairs, "My lady, Lord Alfred is walking this way." Margaret dashed down the stairs, stopped at the door to set her clothes. She descended the ladder and met Alfred at their spot.

"God give you a good day, Margaret."

"And you as well, Alfred."

They sat.

"How fare the new knights?"

"At every task I set, I pair them with one of your men. Given time, I hope all may come to work well together and to a friendliness among themselves."

"Alfred, when did we meet?"

"Ah-h. That is the one question I shall answer not. I want you to recall it yourself, for it was special." At her "But I remember it not!" Alfred replied, "While I shall not tell you, I shall give you hints. Every Sunday you may ask one question to which I can answer 'yes' or 'no.' If you are as clever as King Henry said, you shall remember soon enough. We shall start in two days. Agreed?" He enjoyed her sigh of frustration and accepted her nod. "Any more questions?"

"I heard what Haelum did. One of the girls said you punished him, but said no more." *I may only hint.*

"I ordered him and his parents to the hall and gave him the most severe punishment I could think."

Dear God, please let him not have whipped or beaten Haelum! He can be foolish, but he is a good boy.

Alfred read her face. "Your eyes are so expressive, I read your thoughts in them. I decreed Haelum may not enter the bailey, come near you, speak to you, or reach for your hand. He is dead to you and to me; we see him not. He was devastated and starting crying. Margaret, I cannot have your champions, small or grown, endangering my life. I warned him never to strike me again, or he will die. He is forgiven and may speak to us Michaelmas morn."

"A fair punishment. Though I shall miss him. What mean you by grown champions?"

Alfred looked askance at her. "I am in danger every minute you do not smile at me. They are devoted to you. With whom shall I start? I talked with each man alone. Demetre informed me he will stay to repay you for saving his shield arm. Syghelm rolled his axe handle in his hand as he talked; he said he is staying because he is your special guardian. Each man made clear I am under his judgment until he is cert you are well cared for and happy. Look in the bailey. At least two of them are watching us. Margaret, for my safety, please smile."

Margaret burst out laughing, leaned back, and had to right herself to compose her demeanor. She smiled broadly at Alfred. "Will that do for now?"

"Yes, thank you. Now I may live until the morrow."

Margaret covered her mouth with her hand and laughed into it. Then she turned serious. "I am done with questions. Have you questions for me?"

"How long do courses last?"

"Five, mayhap six days, depending when it arrives."

"How much longer?"

"Three days more, mayhap four."

"Shall you answer me honestly?"

"Yes."

"Do you trust me?" Alfred's question went unanswered. He saw Margaret avoid his stare and look away.

"You said, 'I love you' before everyone. Then you kissed me." Margaret paused. "Not for me but to win the crowd."

Stunned, Alfred replied, "But I meant it."

"I was taught, 'A man will say anything to get you abed, to get what he wants.'"

"Who said that?"

"Mother."

"Such a saying is from a disappointed woman, who speaks her own unhappiness, not a truth for all women." Alfred looked toward the bailey to give her time to think. "Do you agree to give us a chance for our own happiness?"

Margaret gave him a long, hard look. *Do I see a bit of honesty in his eyes? Give him something and see what he does with it.* She whispered, "Yes."

"Why is saying 'I love you' not good enough?"

"Love is not what you say. It is what you do." Margaret watched him looked away.

Alfred thought a bit. "Fair enough. Deeds not words."

The sun was low in the sky and still hot as the pair slipped into silence. "Before I depart to sup, I want you to know an ancient Saxon custom—-no, a law. No man or woman can be forced to wed. If either told anyone he or she was being forced, the whole village rose up against that person's parents to prevent the match. A couple was wed before as many witnesses as possible, family, friends, villagers, who could swear in court the match was freely made. He started with, 'I choose to wed Margaret;' she responded with 'I choose to wed Alfred.' Her parents announced what the bride brought, her dowry. His parents announced their acceptance and reported what they had given the couple. All parties agreed they were satisfied with the match and the terms. Then the witnesses shouted 'You are wed!' and all celebrated with food, drink and dance.

"When the Church came, they wanted us to stand before a priest, but we fought that for almost two hundred years. Only when the Archbishop of Canterbury wrote letters to all priests in the land the words they had to use at every Saxon wedding did we agree to accept the Church blessing the match and making it holy before God.

"The Church still cannot force a Saxon to wed. That is why at the church door we both had to answer 'Yes' to the priest's question, 'Do you make this match of your own free will without pressure from anyone and without any reservations?' I chose you thrice, each time I asked for you and at the church door. You chose me. First, before the queen, who is half Saxon, and also at the church door. We are wed by both ancient Saxon custom and blessed by God's holy Church."

Margaret saw Alfred had turned her way with solemn eyes and his jaw clenched. She gave him a short nod of understanding because she had guessed what he wanted to hear.

"As God is my witness, I have never said to anyone I was forced to wed you. Not even in Confession. I shall never say it. Those words shall never cross my lips, Alfred, I so swear."

"Good." Alfred rose, trod the step near Margaret's feet and stood in the grass before his wife. He leaned forward with his hands clasped behind his back to signal anyone looking their way he was not touching her. He stared into her eyes and whispered, "Now all you need do is stop telling yourself."

When Margaret's eyes widened with shock, Alfred raised his eyebrows and cocked his head. With a sardonic smile, he turned away, strutted down the grassy hill and out the opt motte gate. Margaret closed her lips tight and placed her hand over her mouth.

How knew he? Did my face give me away? My eyes, he said. So that is why I am unable to dissemble. Did the queen tell him what she saw in my eyes? He knows me not well enough to know what I have been think-ing. Does he? Clearly he wants something from me. What assurances must I give him? Assurances I have stopped thinking I am his wife by force? How? Think. First, stop thinking it. Then do something. What? At the rumble of her empty stomach, Margarett's thoughts changed. *Eat. Then to bed. Sleep. Decide later.*

Margaret remained where she sat and waited for the serving girl carrying her tray toward the motte. She shrugged her shoulders to ease her stiff back.

Not true. I was forced. We both know it. How can I convince myself of a lie?

As Alfred's bride waited for her meal, she said softly in Norman, "I chose to marry Alfred."

A forced choice. No. Forget. Say it until I believe it.

"I chose to marry Alfred…I chose to marry Alfred…I chose…"

20

Sunday Visits

Caitlin knocked. "Are you well, my lady?" When she received no answer, she knocked again and commanded, "Margaret, op this door or I shall walk in." The door swung wide, and Margaret gave her old nurse her back as she strode to face the far wall. Caitlin closed the door and settled herself on a stool. She told Margaret's back, "Yester, your girls left your trays before the door; you returned them to the landing barely touched. What is amiss?"

"Did he send you to me?"

"After Mass, he asked me about Norman women's customary behavior during their courses. I confirmed your actions. He commented no one had seen you and you had barely eaten. I volunteered to visit you."

Margaret spoke neither question nor compliment. "Subtle, is he not." Caitlin waited. "I wanted a day to myself." Caitlin spoke not.

She knew her girl would soon fret at the silence. Margaret turned. "Caitlin, does Cormac love you?" Caitlin gave Margaret a smile and a nod. "When knew you it?"

"January. The morning after your fever broke. I touched your forehead and burst into tears. Cormac drew me into his arms and held me. Just held me; he said not a word.

When I stopped, he kissed my forehead and said, 'She will live. Now for you.' He led me to these stools and sat beside me with his arm about my shoulder to hold me up. Cormac gently took charge of me. He gave a girl instructions. He would not let me stop until I had finished all pottage and all the ale. He walked me behind the chamber pot drape and left me. He escorted me to the pallet I had slept on during your illness, tucked me under the coverings, knelt beside me, and kissed me sweetly on my lips. He said, 'Sleep now, my love. I will watch for you.'" Caitlin looked away as if recalling the scene before she whispered, "Hours later when I woke, I opt my eyes and there he was. Sitting on a stool, watching me, smiling. It was not his words. It was in his deeds. I looked into his eyes, and I could finally admit to myself what he had been trying to show me. That he truly loves me." Caitlin sighed. "I remembered what I had taught you. Love is not words; it is deeds. Is that it? You trust not Alfred's claim of love."

"He kissed me in front of everyone. Not for me. To gain their favor."

"We knew that."

Shocked, Margaret's mouth gaped. Caitlin patted the stool beside her. Margaret sat. "After I admitted Cormac loves me, I recalled things he did for me and saw the love in them. Not an imagined love of fancy words and extravagant deeds, but small things. A kind look, a soft word, something helpful. Love is in the little things, my girl." Caitlin added cheerfully, "At home, every time he passes me, he gives me a smile, a touch on my arm; his hand strokes my back. His actions say, 'I love you.' Believe me, Margaret. Such gestures in the day make for a very warm night."

Margaret blushed and looked away.

"This may not be the match you wanted, but you can make it a good one."

"How? We are from different peoples. So different."

"Do as I do. Look for his feelings in small things." Caitlin patted Margaret's knee. "Answer me not. Just think it. Can you recall three things he has done to show you how he feels since the two of you met?"

He held me when I cried. The way he looked at me at the church door. When he took me to the stream. He held my hand as we walked the road. He remembered to tell the Court I had been a virgin. He pulled his sword in warning when the king attacked me.

"More than three."

"Ah! There you have it. A start—if you will accept it." Caitlin waited.

He destroyed our start when he told Wulf he loves me not. Truth or lie? Which is it? I have paced trying to figure it. How practiced in deceit is he? How much of what he said is lies. That he dislikes Wulf is true, but is the story of his childhood truth? Is he back trying to win my favor, get me with child, and then rid himself of me after an heir or two? I could be years in this uncert state. I cannot live this way, ever cautious, ever fearful. My head is a muddle. I cannot see the real story, the real man. I may go mad trying to piece it all together. Oh, that I had run into the cathedral for sanctuary! I have no sanctuary here. Only rags in a tree stump. How long before I can reach them?

183

Caitlin heard Margaret's loud exhale.

Truth or lie. I must know. I want not to live like Mother—nor die like her either. I am forced give him another chance. Again, my freedom is gone, but I will look askance. Not be so easily impressed. Not trust until I am cert. Margaret sighed again.

"Caitlin, you are still the wisest woman I know. I hear right in everything you said." Margaret paused as she silently practiced her words before speaking. "Let us go out into the sunlight. I will sit a time on the keep green. I will wait and hope for him to visit me. Will you tell him where I am?"

"Now who is failing to be subtle?"

Margaret rose and Caitlin followed. She almost hugged Caitlin, so Caitlin hugged her. "Thank you for coming and for your good advice. I will give him a second chance."

"Smart girl. I know not what came between you. I do know in a marriage there is no second chance. Only chance after chance." Caitlin smiled. "I tell you; I see something powerful between you two. Lose it not, my girl, for it may be love."

Margaret and Caitlin stood on opposite sides of the keep steps as they lifted their faces to the sun. "In the keep, I forgot. I hugged you back and made you unclean. I am sorry."

"Nonsense." Caitlin snorted in derision. "I think some woman invented that practice to gain a week of rest each month and to avoid her husband. Likely, some agreeable priest supported her claim, and now women are stuck with it."

"What of the Church's teachings?"

"You know the Church demands control. With having married priests, it wants to control even their desires. Men want not to bed a bleeding woman. That is just being practical, not evil."

"Let Father hear not your saying that!"

"Never. He is married now, and he knows better. Yet he must speak the Church's rulings on this." Caitlin paused before she added, "I wonder if he practices what he preaches?"

Margaret hissed, "Caitlin! Speak not blasphemy!"

Caitlin laughed. "I think I will go into the hall to see if Cormac is there." She took the steps and waved at Margaret when she reached the gate.

Margaret watched the guards ambling the parapet walkway, heard pigs snorting, and watched Caitlin leave the hall door op before she walked across the bailey alone and disappeared out the gate. *Rather warm sunshine than the shadowed, lonely keep.* She drew up her knees, set her elbows on them, and held her head as she considered how she might start their conversation should Alfred come to her. *Now what question was I going to ask him this day? Oh, yes, that will be a good start.*

Alfred stepped out of the hall. He looked around the bailey before he glanced toward the motte. Margaret saw that same sardonic grin of two days before. She stood not until he passed the gate.

"God give you a good day, Alfred," she offered with a shy smile. "And you."

"I hope you shall sit with me a while." She and Alfred retook their former spots on the grass. Margaret noted how stiffly he sat. *Doth his ribs bother him still?* She offered, "Alfred, I am hoping to be at church on the morrow, but I shall not know until I wake." He only nodded. *He is not making this easy. What say I now?* "I am glad Caitlin visited. I have missed her company and good advice."

"What said she?"

"They wed in June. Mostly we talked of how happy she and Cormac are. They are from different peoples, you know." At his nod, Margaret tried again, "She advised me we should start again."

"I thought we had a start, a good one."

"We did," she offered. *Until I heard you with Wulf. What you told Wulf destroyed it. Say it differently.* "Your talk with Wulf damaged it."

"Only if you let him. It would surprise me not if he had spotted you coming our way. See how clever he is. If I lied to him, you would hear me. If I told him the truth, he could have jumped down and slit your throat. You arrived with no knight between you two and expected no treachery. I talked to them about that."

Is this another of his excuses, another set of lies. What if he speaks truth? Did I see it wrong? Mayhap. Say so. "You are right, Alfred. I would not have drawn blade against your brother."

Alfred nodded agreement. "After Mass, I called Seon and Heour on him. I told them he threatened your life, wants you dead. Now they understand why I had him tied and hauled away. "

Margaret saw Alfred clench his jaw. *He wants me to agree.* "Glad I am you did. I liked him not from the moment we met, but I knew not why. That you trust him not is good enough. I count him our enemy and pray we never see him again."

Alfred relaxed his jaw and his back.

"If your ribs hurt still, gladly would I rebind... Sorry, I forgot my state."

Alfred smirked at her. "Margaret, even thinking you might touch me makes my manhood," he sought a mild word, "uncomfortable."

Margaret covered her face and heard Alfred laughing,

"I promise to behave even if I can stop not where my desire goes."

Distract him with my question. Margaret uncovered her face and looked at his shoulder. "It is Sunday, Alfred, and I am allowed a question about our meeting."

"I was hoping you would forget. Go ahead."

"Did I meet you before I met Queen Matilda?"

"No." Alfred glowered at her. "King Henry underestimates you. One question and you eliminate the first fourteen years of your life. If I count aright, you just reduced the time span possible to two years plus two months. I fear you will learn the date before Michaelmas."

Margaret grinned at his back-handed compliment. "That is a whole month away."

Alfred countered, "Next week, the question you ask will reduce the time even more, will it not?"

"You must wait until Sunday next. Your rules, remember," Margaret took her turn to smirk.

Alfred's next words came soft and intimate. "Wife, I have kept my word given you our wedding day. I protect you against Wulf. You kept your word with my mother and presented a joined face to what I wanted done. I have answered every question you asked. I want you to trust me again. Believe I do love you."

Margaret was silent. She started with, "Caitlin said—no, not fair," she admitted. "Mother taught me a grown girl blames no one but herself; she is responsible for her own thoughts, decisions, and deeds. Mother said I must do it if I want to be a woman." She looked at Alfred who stared back. "I listened to Caitlin's advice, but I make my own decisions." She paused and started again. "That we started well, I agree. Except for when you took my maidenhood, you have been gentle, kind and caring. Kind and caring are good, and I want more of them, but I do not know if they are love. Mother said she

187

loved me, yet she lied to me. Every day you are honest with me, I will trust you a little more."

"Done."

"Alfred, I shall be honest with you. I believe something Caitlin said. 'Love is not words. Love is deeds.' I shall know what you feel by how you treat me." Margaret's eyes filled. "I know I am hurting you, and I do not want to. I wish I could touch you so you would feel I do like you." Margaret jumped up and raced up the stairs. She turned at the top and saw Alfred had stood to face her. She saw his cockeyed smile and warmth in his eyes. Sudden tears stung her eyes as Margaret said, "I shall not say it until I mean it. Please say it not again until you are cert you do." She spun on her heel and fled to the keep ladder.

21

A Fresh Start

31 August

Margaret waited at the church door in the dark. She watched the predawn glow light tree tops. Father Mantunn approached from the village and smiled at her. He entered the church and returned with a cup of holy water. Margaret knelt. "Father, I am clean and I ask for the Church's blessing." After she received it, she stood and asked for Confession. Hers was brief; her penance a few prayers. She stepped away to say them and entered the church before the first bell chimed dawn. The villagers arrived before those from the bailey. Those in the doorway saw Margaret standing in her usual place, head down, hands in prayer before her heart. They waited outside.

Alfred walked in, stopped a moment at seeing Margaret, and continued to lead the knights. He stood to the right of the invisible space called the "aisle." Only two feet separated them, but neither looked the other's way. The villeins stood behind the Normans. After

Mass, Alfred followed Father Mantunn outside, as did Margaret, the knights and the Saxons. Margaret approached Alfred and slipped her hand in his.

"What are you doing?"

"Pretending I am Saxon."

Alfred returned her grin. The Saxons warily stepped passed them.

Margaret whispered, "Please follow my lead." At his nod, she extended her left hand and wiggled her fingers. She asked, "Who would like to walk to the village with us?" Chidden stopped and stared, but accepted not her offer.

"They fear me since I punished the boy. They run when they see me."

"We must change that. Smile at the girls. You are handsome enough they might accept."

Alfred did so and extended his arm. Eadgar nodded to his lord as he ushered his two youngest toward the couple. Three-year-old Ertha toddled toward Alfred, who smiled and bent low. At his "Hello," she grabbed her father's tunic and hid. Edgar lifted her. "She likes to be carried and we have spoiled her."

"I want not to frighten her."

"If I may, I will walk beside you. She may take your hand."

"Thank you, Eadgar."

In the meantime, five-year-old Eadwine took Margaret's hand.

"We would like to walk you home," said Margaret. "Would you like that?" At his nod, Margaret looked to Alfred. Still holding hands, the couple strolled. Alfred offered his pointing finger, and Ertha took it and kept it after her father praised her.

"She is a darling. You are fortunate to get a girl after three sons."

Eadgar thanked Alfred for his compliment. From the trailings of Saxons heading home, Goscelyn looked back and giggled at the sight of a tiny hand clutching a large finger and at how funny her lord looked holding his arm as oddly as he did.

This is a good start. Hopefully, on the morrow we will do even better.

At the miller's hut, Margaret and Alfred released the children. The couple stayed a few moments to chat with Eadgar and his wife Daele before departing to break their fasts.

On the way, Margaret explained. "When I arrived, the children were afraid of me. I think I confused them, a woman with a sword. To change that, every day after Mass, I took the hands of two children and chatted with them as I walked them home behind their parents. No child could repeat our hand holding until all the children in the village had a turn. I used it to meet the Saxon families and to create bonds."

"Why do they approach you with, 'I washed my hands' or 'My hands are clean'?"

"They were a starving, filthy lot. Likely to die. Mother taught me washing hands helps keep you healthy, so I only accepted children with clean hands."

Alfred replied. "That is why we have a rag hanging next to a pail of water outside the church door."

"M-m-m."

From the door to the dais, Margaret nodded at those across the fire pit and greeted the knights she passed. Alfred spoke to Midryth, who left.

As they ate, Margaret admitted, "I feel a bit lonely with only the two of us on the dais."

"Who sat with you before?"

Margaret pointed to the empty spots as she named them. "Most days it was Cormac, Sir Roussel, who led the king's men, me, Father and Caitlin."

"Where sat Verel?"

"He chose to lead from below and sat with the men." *Does he permit a leader or is he the only one?*

"They voted Verel to speak for them." Alfred finished his ale. "A good man, I am told."

"They all are, my lord."

"The Saxons say Masselin wanted you to marry him."

"I knew it not. I dismissed him and am glad he is gone."

Alfred chuckled. "I heard how you did so. The Saxons treating me reported Court gossip."

Of course they did.

"Come. We are going riding." As they walked the hall, Alfred stopped. "Sir Verel, we require two knights to ride with us, one former, one new." Named, Demetre and Arnaud stood and followed. Outside, Alfred said, "Knights, we will wait in the yard while you choose and saddle your horses."

"What named you your horse?"

"Garhard."

"Spear brave. A good name for going into battle."

"Thank you." Alfred took the horses' reins from Daelton and handed Night's to his wife.

As Margaret petted Night, he kept turning his head Alfred's way. "Alfred, why does Night look to you?"

"Mayhap he seeks a treat." As he checked his saddle, he glanced over it to his wife. "That is how I won his favor in Winchester. I heard how you value him and his reputation with men." He shrugged. "An apple in the morning and a carrot at night."

"The night you were beaten, you were leaving the barn after giving Night a carrot."

"M-m-m."

"What else know you about me?"

"Time to mount." Alfred stepped around his horse and cupped his hands for her foot. After Margaret mounted and tied herself to the platform, Alfred mounted the dappled gray he had purchased as part of his knighthood equipment. The horses ambled toward the gate, and Demetre and Arnaud caught up.

In the forest clearing, Alfred ordered, "Guard facing outward a hundred yards this direction and that. Return not until I summon you."

"This summer has been a hot one. I am glad to be under the trees and again at my favorite spot." Margaret watched Alfred dismount, tie his horse, and remove two satchels. He placed them against the big tree beside the river before returning for her.

After he tied Night, he raised his arms and held Margaret's waist as she dismounted. Margaret placed her hands upon his shoulders because she knew what was next. She kissed him back. *I chose you. I chose you. I do like your kisses.* Alfred's tongue flicked into her mouth, and her heart jumped. His heart thumped against her breast. He slowly pulled away and released her.

"Later," he promised. "Right now, I have a treat for you."

"Are you not my treat?"

Alfred glowered and pointed at her. "Do not tease! We are not alone, and I am having trouble being good."

Margaret dropped her gaze. "Yes, Alfred." She stood still.

He pulled a pale, linen sheet from a satchel and draped it over the great limb hanging low over the river. Then he pulled out a familiar item.

"That old thing?"

"Today is this blanket's last adventure before I order it washed. If is shrivels or shreds, I shall be sad." Alfred shook out the blanket and set it on a bare spot in the shade. He stood beside it and gazed at Margaret with warm eyes.

How can he stay good if he brought that along? "Are we dining here?" she asked hopefully.

"Yes, but that is not your treat. Margaret, when you lived at home, you oft fled into the forest and bathed in streams and rivers. No more. You are grown, and we have enemies. I cannot have them lying in wait for you to bathe and then take you from me or worse. This day I shall guard you. This is your final forest bathe. Enjoy it." From the satchel, Alfred removed Margaret's hairbrush, her bone comb, and a cube of pine-scented soap, which he set on a corner of their wedding blanket. He stepped away and walked the area, sword in hand. His heart raced at wondering what Margaret might be doing behind him.

He knows my ways before we met. Who told him? Cert not Caitlin. He knows more about me than I him. How? Margaret removed her bridal circlet and took out both braids. Softly humming, she brushed her hair, first gently and then more vigorously. In long reaches, she pulled the brush back from her forehead to the ends. *Never again will you be long enough.* She pulled her locks to one side and measured with her fingers. Remembering the day her father savagely attacked her, she moaned. Then her cheerful nature poked through. *You are longer now than before he cut you. And you will never be short again! I swear.* Tossing her hair from side to side, she smiled and enjoyed the swishing sound her waves and curls made. She threw her hair forward and brushed from her nape past the ends, as if pulling them to be even longer. She shook her mane and ran her fingers through her locks to fluff them. *Now you are halfway down my back. Soon you will be to my waist.*

Margaret dropped her girdle on the blanket and unlaced her bliaut as best she could. She pulled it over her head and lay it on the blanket, stepped out of her boots and removed her socks. She took a deep breath, and lifted her chemise over her head. Tossing it on her bliaut, she picked up the cube. *How knew he of this? The queen, mayhap? He had to have bought it in Winchester. He thinks ahead.* She turned to the river's edge and gingerly stepped into the water. Dipping the rag, she started at her feet and ankles. Stepping into deeper water, next she splashed her face. *This water is cooler than I thought it would be on this hot day. Careful, the river may be deep and run fast.*

Margaret forgot the man leaning against a tree in the shadows. An ache stirred Alfred's insides and nagged his heart. When it flared into his loins, he gasped at the power of his need. Margaret's husband shook his head to throw off his thoughts.

Her humming stopped and was replaced with small splashing noises. The girl's blood played tag with her flesh, rising to the surface and then burying itself to escape. Stepping further into the water, Margaret used the rag to soap and rinse the rest of her and to wiggle her toes in the mud. She rubbed her skin hard, to clean her skin, to discourage impure thoughts, and to prove to herself she was still hardy. She bent over, swished her hair in the water and scooped water over the back of her head. She soaped her locks well. She rinsed her hair twice. As she stood, she flung her head back. Wet hair flew over her head, to behind her, creating an arc of water, which followed. She had forgot she was being watched. Margaret rang water out of her locks by grabbing both sides and twisting her hair. Once more she splashed water all over her body and playfully swirled the water about herself. *Last bathe in the forest. I will miss the smells and sounds, sunlight in the ripples. Oh well. This never was safe. I was just fortunate not to have been caught. Another piece of my girlhood gone.*

Alfred continued to stare as she bent to scoop handfuls of water. He admired her high breasts, pinched waist and flat stomach. Alfred noted how well formed she was and how gracefully she moved. His wife swirled the water and splashed her body again. Alfred felt physical pain at not being able to take her into his arms and express his love with kisses on her naked flesh. He watched her wade ashore and grab the linen sheet. Still at his post, the knight watched as the woman he loved rubbed her hair and herself dry. An errant thought slipped into his mind. He wondered what penance Father might give Margaret for caring for her body, for washing, for being naked. He knew he would confess neither his thoughts and desires nor their deeds. Some things are too private, some memories too precious to give words, he decided.

Draped in a slightly soggy sheet, Margaret fetched her undergarment and her bliaut. She pulled at her laces and let them hang. She fastened her girdle around her waist.

Alfred sucked in his breath as he again thought of her fine figure. He released it to calm himself. With deep, measured breathing, he stared as she pulled on her socks and stepped into her boots. She towel-dried her hair and shook loose her locks. Still standing, she brushed down her hair, parted, and braided it. After she fastened the braids and placed the circlet on her head, she was again a modest Norman lady of rank. Alfred looked around to memorize the site of this most precious memory. *No matter what life brings us, until the day*

I die, she shall always be this beautiful. Shall I ever be able to tell her she is my heart? That I loved her from the moment I saw her? Now this. He waited until the evidence of his desires abated enough for his body to appear normal. He took a deep breath and step out of the shadows. "Our dinner is in the second satchel. I hope you are as hungry as I."

On the blanket, the couple sat cross-legged from each other with only one apple and a little ale remaining in the second flask. Alfred halved the apple, cut the core from each, and balanced one on his knee. He sliced the first half into four wedges and extended his hand. Margaret took one in each hand. They munched. In silence, Alfred repeated his offering before tossing the remains over her head and into the river.

"Thank you, Alfred, for a pleasant day. When I miss my forest bathes, I shall recall this one and smile in remembering it."

"I am loathe to end it, but time we return. We have been gone so long others may think we did saucy things."

Margaret blushed. "Aurnaud and Demetre have eaten not." Margaret stood to fetch the linen sheet she had hung over a nearby bush while Alfred folded the blanket and stuffed it into a satchel after the flasks. Margaret filled the other one with her brush, comb, a sliver of soap and the sheet. *Another sliver of soap. Only this one carries happy memories, not royal intrigue and anger. I shall use it on my face.* Alfred tied a bow at the bottom of her dress lacing before he helped Margaret mount. He tied the satchels back together and laid them over Garhard's flanks. After mounting, he led them down the path and called for their knights.

Margaret watched the horses being led to the barn and missed Alfred receiving a shake of the head from Cook, who stood behind the kitchen half door. "My lady, let us take the walkway to watch the harvesting."

Remember what his mother said about when to talk about estate matters. "My lord, how see you the estate? Is it well run? Is it to your liking?"

"You have done well, my lady. Cormac told me the shambles it was when you arrived. I know how to deal with knights, but squiring taught me nothing of land, crops, harvesting, and such. Felamaere has been most helpful. He explains well. I had but to ask him the why of one thing, and now he includes it in all his answers. Cormac knows everything, including gossip, but I have yet to fully understand the accounts book. He assures me I soon will. With four weeks until Michaelmas, I am cert I will be ready to pay our tithe and taxes."

"I am still surprised all my old knights chose to stay."

"I was cert all would leave. That they stayed proves their love for you. Several, I will not say who, said they were never treated so well when they were in others' services. They admitted they planned to like me not, but your approval of me makes them reconsider."

"Then best I smile at you again." Her quick grin looked forced, but her eyes glinted merrily."

"You like to tease."

"I learned it from you."

They continued to talk of estate matters, with Alfred talking of the villeins in the south field, and Margaret asking about the knights' practices and their skills.

"God give you a good afternoon, my lord, my lady," said Alura from below.

Alfred turned and responded for them both. At the girl's nod, Alfred added, "I have something to show you." Alfred led Margaret up the keep steps and ladder. *Two locks on the keep door, one at my head, and the other at my knees. What else has he ordered?* On the first floor, Midryth, Cleva, Cyne, and Haesel stood in a row. With bright eyes and broad smiles, they bobbed curtseys as the couple passed.

Margaret stopped on the top landing when she spotted a second set of metal rectangles imbedded in the door. Alfred reached around her and opt the door. She stared at the door frame and the door edge. *Bolt holes? Locks? The bed is moved. The whole room. What are those things?* Margaret turned to Alfred and saw him smiling at her.

"I made a few additions. See the tall candle holders on the edges of the room. I thought four enough, but I can order more if you like."

"Fat three-wicked candles for light and use the braziers only for heat. A good idea."

He took her hand, and walked her to the bed. He lifted the coverings and showed her the wooden pieces he ordered added to the side board. "Now I can sleep on my left side to face the door with my sword at hand in these brackets." He pushed on the bedding. "Ropes still tight." At Margaret's frown, Alfred explained, "I told the knights who did this work if they loosed the ropes again, they would get bread and water for a week. When they denied having done it, I told them they could blame the Saxons, but the punishment was the same." He walked her to the next additions. Margaret saw his helmet atop the first item. "This armor tree stores my helmet, mail and other fighting gear. I can keep a lance or two leaning against that side in case I need defend us from here. That tree shall hold my clothes, arms out on top for my outer clothes and shelves for my braies and loin cloths. My boots go on the bottom shelf. What think you?"

"They shall keep your armor and your clothes off the rushes and clean. I have never seen the like."

"In the Holy Land, I saw knights from other countries use these. I liked them so I copied them. We shall sit on stools a while longer. The Rammegs Elder and Younger are still finishing our sitting chairs."

"With arm rests?"

"Not yours. Hugiet was there when I ordered them. She suggested no arms for you. Easier to sew and mend without them."

"She is right. I shall thank her for her good advise."

Alfred leaned toward Margaret and whispered, "I also ordered stools to keep our feet off the floor in winter."

"Such luxury!"

"Oh! And four more pegs for your new clothes." Alfred pointed where Garwig had bored holes in the stone wall and inserted pegs.

Margaret turned to her husband. "And you got all this done this day!"

Alfred puffed his chest. "That is why I hurried not your bathe and lingered over our food."

"You are thoughtful to have made this room so pleasant for us, Alfred."

Alfred gave her a flourish and bow. "Thank you, my lady."

"But I see a problem." At Alfred's frown, she explained. "With the bed so shifted, in the night I might get out, stumble to the wrong corner, and mess the rushes."

Alfred roared at her joke. Through his laughter, he said, "Wife, I shall escort you to the proper corner for as long as necessary."

Margaret lifted her nose. "I think my joking is turned back on me."

"Indeed." Alfred pulled her into his arms and hugged her.

Keep my cheek to his chest or he will start something.

Beyond the door, they heard, "My lord, my lady, we sup anon."

Alfred kissed Margaret's hair and promised, "Later. Food, Vespers and then us." He released her and walked ahead to op the door for her.

Ferrant met them at the keep gate.

"Sit," ordered Alfred. "While you stayed in the keep, I taught him to obey. When he did, I took him hunting and let him have the rabbits he scared out of bushes. You are right, my lady, he is very smart." Alfred lifted his left arm for Margaret. He snapped his fingers at Ferrant. "Right, Ferrant."

At his heel as ordered.

Alfred stopped, as did Ferrant. "Good boy," commended Alfred as he continued.

"Well done, Alfred." *Now we both know who is master.*

That evening, Alfred started a routine. He locked the keep door and ordered Ferrant to guard it. He locked their door before he hung the key on the end arm of his armor rack. He toed his boots to place them on the shelf and draped his socks over their tops to dry them overnight. He doffed all but his loincloth and hung his garments on the clothes rack. Standing on his side of the bed, Alfred set his sword, unwound his loincloth, and hung it over the bed pole at his feet. After brushing stray rushes from his soles, he climbed into bed and leaned on an elbow to watch his wife.

Margaret wandered from one waist-high candle holder to another and touched the wood. *He must have ordered this when we were separated. The Rammegs do fine work, smooth and straight tree trunks. Come pig-killing time, I must order a year's supply of fat candles.* Margaret stood before the new pegs. *I shall remove my bliauts from the trunk and hope hanging shall undo any fold marks.* As she doffed her boots, something nagged at her. *He did this to gain my favor after our fight.* She undid her braids and loosed her locks with her fingers. *All this is a kind deed, but is this a gift or a bribe to make me think again he cares for me? In church, I prayed for guidance. How to answer? Does thinking good of a person help make that person be good or does thinking good of him make a fool of me?* She untied her laces and loosed them. *Remember Mother's advice. He cannot lie to me while I am touching him.* She pulled her bliaut over her head and hung it. *No words.* She doffed her chemise and hung it. *Climb in. I needs learn to enjoy what he is going to do anyway.* She slipped under the covers and rolled to face Alfred.

"Wife, you are…"

Margaret put a finger to his lips and then her mouth against his in a soft kiss.

22

Ordinary Days

In hopes Alfred's happy stomach put him in a good mood, Margaret made her request as he finished breaking his fast.

"My lord, may I speak to our knights about their needs? In the past, I mended their clothes and ordered washing days. Part of my tasks as chatelaine."

"Did you also tend their bruises and wounds?"

"Also my task. Caitlin and I did together. Since her wedding, I have done all the tending. I always did so supervised by others."

"In the hall and in the company of a witness."

"Thank you."

Margaret stood. "Our good knights, since my return, I have been amiss in tending you. If any of you have mending or washing to be done, please pile the mending on the left corner of the dais and the washing on the right. Also, I will send for my simples box should any of you need my assistance. Please do so before you go to the practice field or sentry duty. Thank you." After Alfred left for the practice field, Margaret headed for the kitchen. Everyone stopped work to give obeisance.

"God give you a good day, Cook. Please report what has been done in my absence and what I needs do now." Nearra did so, and Margaret promised she would learn her lord's favored foods and herbs. She called Leoma outside.

"God give you a good day, Leoma. How fare you and Garwig?"

"Well, my lady. We have become a team. I make his bread the night before. I set it to bake before I leave and place the soup pot near the fire. He is a good cook, so I return to a hearty meal. He surprised me with how much he eats," Leoma reported.

Such smiles now! This marriage is a good one. "Smithing is hard, hot work especially in summer."

"Indeed, my lady."

"Will Hopa do? She is a bit young to replace you, but is she ready? Shall I ask for an apprentice wage from my lord or needs I ask for a full wage?"

Leoma smiled at her lady's subtle question. She decided not to report her having missed her courses twice. "An apprentice wage for now."

"I am happy for you and Garwig."

"Thank you, my lady."

Margaret left for the hall; Leoma and Hopa returned to baking. At seeing the piles on the dais, Margaret gasped and gave instructions to op the main, the servants' and the back doors to air the hall. Margaret waited outside the servants' entrance until the girls returned with her simples box, her lap cloth, and her large sewing basket. She approached Sir Hughes, set the simples box on the table, and sat beside him on a bench. Hughes pulled off his shirt. *Well muscled and handsome too. Look away. No down.* He showed her a two-inch cut on his left upper arm, which was red and oozing pus.

"Alura, clean rags, a bowl of boiling-hot water, and the pot of honey from the kitchen, please. Sir Hughes," she chided, "how long were you going to wait before showing this me? Until your whole arm went red? I could not have saved you then."

"I poured ale over it to stop the bleeding after it happened. I thought it worked."

"The only thing worse than ale is pouring water over a wound. Both will make it fester." *Cleva faints at blood; she is no good.* "Alura, help me." Margaret cleansed the wound with a wet rag. Hughes flinched at how hot was the water, but spoke not. Next she slapped a wet square over the cut to draw the pus. "How?"

"I slipped, fell against the pele and got a splinter in my arm. My shirt is in the mending pile. I am wearing Roulin's spare."

Margaret peeled off the square, examined his wound and added another one, not as hot because the water was cooling. She removed that and patted the area dry. "I want to see this every morning. If you fever, find me, even at night. We want not to lose you, Hughes." At his nod, she added, "No practice until I declared you healed. You may guard or sentry, but no fighting." She drizzled honey over the cut, lay a dry square atop it, and wound a strip of clean wool around Hughes's arm before tying it off.

"Yes, my lady." Hughes stood and bowed. "Thank you, my lady. I will see you on the morrow, I promise."

"Tell the others I expect immediately to see every break in their skin, no matter how small. Wounds fast fester in this heat."

Hughes donned Roulin's shirt. "I will, my lady." He stood, bowed, and departed.

Margaret sat on the dais edge. Cleva examined every garment in the washing pile to be cert it needed not a mending its owner had missed. Alura returned and sat beside her mistress. She used Margaret's second-best needle and pinched together straight slits to overstitch. Margaret repaired ragged tears and other difficult ones. *The stench of sweat and whatever else! They hang them to dry overnight and then wear them again and again. Should the harvest be good, we needs provide more clothing for them. Wait to ask until we know our yields.* Cleva took finished items to the washing shed. The pile was high enough to declare the next day a wash day. Before they dined, Margaret had the remaining mending piled outside and washed her hands at the pot scrubbing table outside the kitchen. *I cannot eat with these rank odors on me. I will be at this until we sup. Glad I am the sun still sets late. Are the days already shortening, or am I so busy they race past?*

Walking to the keep from Vespers, Margaret reported sewing all day with more to finish in the morn. Alfred talked of searching the woods to determine in which direction he might clear land. "I found the river our stream flows into. Fortunately, the spot I like for a larger mill is on royal land. When next we ride, I shall show it you." When she commented she would like to view morning practice from the walkway, Alfred said he hoped she would. He had been learning fighting moves from their men. In their room, Margaret examined his garments for tears and found none. She tallied what he had as he stripped and washed.

Margaret looked not his way as she talked. "Alfred, I like you wash each day and smell better than your men. I want to make more braies, shirts and such so you have clean to wear after you wash."

"Good. I would also like a garment to wrap myself in between washing and bed. Unless you like the look of me the way I am."

"I am not looking!"

Alfred laughed.

"I favor your idea. I will make one for myself as well. I do hope a peddler with fabrics soon passes by us."

"On the morrow, I will send word."

Margaret mimicked Alfred's "Good" as she undressed facing her pegs. This night she crawled into bed first. When Alfred arrived, she lay already curled. She murmured, "I am so tired, Alfred. This night I would like only to sleep."

"Then just sleep we shall." Alfred rolled away toward the door and pushed the sheeting to his waist.

Still half asleep, Margaret roused and responded without thinking. She moaned and pushed against him. She arched her back for more. Margaret's lips groped for his mouth. She was swallowed in a kiss so enveloping, she forgot to breathe. She pulled away and gasped. Alfred's kisses tracked the heat of his passion down her neck, between her breasts, and to her waist. *No further Stop him.* Margaret threw a leg over his hip. Together, they moved. Alfred brought her to her first ecstasy.

She clutched him close. *What was that?* He shuddered and pulled her with him as he slipped to his side. As her breathing slowed, Margaret turned her head and felt his ear against her lips. She opt her eyes to see only blackness, felt only him. She relaxed. *Like the kissing before and this holding after, but this… middle part. I tingle inside and out. Did I dream such pleasure? Only the feel of him makes him real. How tell him I liked this.* "Husband," she whispered into his ear. "Is dawn near?" She felt his head shake a slow 'no' against hers. "Good. Again." She tilted her hips to show him she meant it. Their second loving slowly rose to a crescendo. Alfred rolled to his back taking her with him. Margaret lay with her lips against his neck. She kissed him, sighed, and went limp. *This is very good.* Alfred's arm held her tightly against him as his other arm groped for some part of the blanket they had tangled around them. He pulled it over them, and the couple dozed. When Alfred's arms relaxed, Margaret slipped sideways and snuggled against him to keep the warmth between them alive.

At the first ringings of the day, they moaned in unison.

"Would I could stay abed with you all day. Nay, Father would have me walking to the North Wall and back." Alfred rose above her. He again filled her with his seed. "To remind you what awaits you this night," he said as he bent to kiss her breast.

She pushed her husband off, scrambled away, and dashed for the chamber pot with a wetted rag in hand. Cleaned and again fresh, she peeked around the curtain to see Alfred already dressed and pushing a foot into a boot. She ran past him. "Look not until I am clothed. I want not to wait for your return." She liked his chuckling. *A good way to start the day.* She reached for her comb to braid her hair.

Alfred unlocked the door, and Margaret slipped through before he could touch her. *No more excitement. My face.* She schooled her expression to seriousness as she descended the stairs and avoided looking at the girls as she passed them. At the gate, Margaret followed Alfred one step to his left and two behind, with the servant girls following her like ducklings following their mother.

That morning, the young couple set a simple routine. After Mass, they broke their fasts in the hall with their knights before separating to individual duties. Margaret examined and re-bandaged

Hughes before turning to again sewing, supervising the laundry, and weeding her herb garden. Alfred practiced with the knights, hunted, supervised the harvest, or sat with Cormac over estate matters and the accounts book. After they dined, they again separated until they supped and attended Vespers. Margaret reported about her day while they strolled to the keep. He shared his news. They stopped on the second-floor landing for Alfred to finish talking estate matters. Once in their room, Alfred washed himself while Margaret undid her braids and brushed her hair. They met in bed.

23

❧

Rain

5 September

Margaret finished her midday meal and asked, "My lord, think you Father will permit us story telling on Sundays? He has been so much softer and more lenient with penances since he married Gytha."

"I shall ask him for you."

Felamaere dashed through the servants' entrance and stood before the pair. He remembered to look only at Lord Alfred. "My lord, the sky is darkening. Something bad is coming. I fear for the field we started. We have much to lose if rains soak the wheat."

Look straight ahead. Not at him. Let him decide. Speak not unless he asks.

Alfred stood and announced, "Storm coming. Or something worse. If you want not to starve next winter, you will leave your mugs and follow me. I, for one, will eat because I help bring in the crop." Alfred jumped off the front of the dais and strode behind the seated knights to the door. *I noticed he never says please, just orders. I said please, Do women ask permission, but men do not? Is it a man's way or because he is the lord? One face again.* Margaret took the stairs and followed. At her "I too like to eat," every man stood and followed. Felamaere left through the servants' door and rushed to catch his lord.

Those in the hall reached the edge of the field before the villeins looked up and saw them. For a moment, they froze.

"Felamaere, assign tasks. I know scything."

"As do I, my lord," announced Claude. At Alfred's surprised expression, Claude added, "I was not born a knight, my lord. I can sharpen a blade as well as swing one."

"My lord, please relieve Scelfdune. Sir Claude, please sharpen Hoeldun's scythe."

While the men talked, Margaret walked into the field and joined the women gathering chopped stalks, tying off a bunch with a stalk and setting it down. Louvel and Pernel joined the women and held the stalks in their arms, thus omitting a step. They were efficient, fast and soon led the party. Father Mantunn stood at the edge of the field with his arms extended and his face to the sky as he prayed aloud, asking God for time to save the crop. Then he joined the workers. Knights worked in pairs with the women and held out their arms for the bunches to be carried to a wagon. Girls saw how quickly they gathered and copied them. Villeins loaded the wagons. A knight stood beside the pairs of donkeys as he urged them to the lane and into the bailey. Kitchen help met the wagons and unloaded them. A villein flicked his whip and drove the donkeys back for more. When the grain bins filled, they piled the bunches in the center of the barn aisles out of reach of the animals.

The high darkness above them crawled over the edge of the forest toward the field. Wind howled through the trees, flung cold blasts that bunched people's garments and blew astray the last loose stalks. Everyone worked in a frenzy.

The Normans and Saxons followed the last wagon up the lane toward the gate.

To the east, the sky was now only a sliver of light. Darkness seemed poised just above their heads, and wailing winds were upon them. Just as the villeins split from the group, rain fell in spits. Parents grabbed their children and raced for their huts. Felamaere slapped the donkeys and guided them into the animal barn. Duone held the doors open, which slammed together behind the wagon and the boy. Alfred grasped Margaret's arm and rushed her through the gate and across the bailey. By the time they dashed into the hall, the droplets had become a downpour, and they were soaked. Rain poured down the three roof holes over the fire pit and killed the fire below them. Knights rushed inside. They grabbed firewood from stalls to feed what little fire remained. Soon four separate fires blazed. Knights huddled near them as steam rose from their clothes. Alfred and Margaret stood between the dais and the first fire. Margaret bent over and squeezed water from her braids onto the dirt. She was not the only one who sneezed.

"Had I cloak, I would cover you."

Margaret turned her backside toward the fire. "We may be stuck here all night." She looked up. "If so, we can sleep on the guest platform."

He worked, led by example. The men followed him. Margaret turned and watched Alfred walk the hall thanking each man. *They smile and converse. He has won their approval.* Margaret nodded. *He has mine for his actions, but I still know not the truth of his stories.*

As suddenly as the rain struck, it stopped pouring down the roof holes. Several men looked up.

"The sky is graying a bit," noted Bertrand.

Everyone listened.

"The wind has shifted," said one knight. Another added, "Heading to Winchester."

Sir Giraud commented, "If the city is soaked and damaged, I fear someone there did something evil, and God is punishing them all for it."

"What of us?" worried another.

"Someone op the main door and look out. What see you?"

Sauville reported. "My lord, not much sun left. Puddles everywhere. Clotheslines sag with wet clothes. Kitchen door is closed."

"We need a page to inquire if soup is ready," muttered Alfred. At Margaret's, "I will go," Alfred countered, "No, you will not." He called aloud, "Who will inquire about our supper?"

"No need, my lord," said Sauville. "I see light out the top half-door. I will ask about our meal."

One knight opt the supper ale barrel and started filling mugs as they were passed to him. Sir Bertrand brought the first mugs to his lord and lady.

Everyone was surfeited with hot soup, bread, and apples. *I wish we had not to leave this warm hall for the night dampness of going to Vespers.* Margaret sent Cyne ahead to light their braziers and stand guard with a pail of water should a spark fly. Alfred ordered Cleva to fetch his cloak and her mantle. Father Mantunn sent word he recommended everyone care for their health at home;

he dispensed with Vespers this night for a longer sermon at Mass on the morrow.

Thank You, God. Margaret shivered inside her damp bliaut and chemise.

"To bed with you," ordered Alfred as Cleva arrived and handed them their outer garments. Alfred held up Margaret's mantle. He watched her swirl it around her and clutch it tightly to herself rather than use the brooch. He donned his cloak and turn to their men. "Finish the ale barrel if you have not already done so. We thank you for your hard work and for suffering the storm. God give you a good night." Alfred led Margaret off the dais and out the back door. She followed as he guided them around each puddle. "We shall avoid not the mud at the ladder." He sent her up first and held the ladder for the girls, who dashed to the first-floor fireplace. Margaret took the stairs while Alfred pulled up the ladder and secured the door locks.

By the time Alfred locked their door, Margaret had checked the braziers were safe; she was warming her hands over one. She doffed her mantle, undid her braids, and dried her hair with a linen half-sheet. Margaret ignored Alfred's entrance to stretch her bliaut neck over two pegs to give it a better chance to dry. She pulled her soggy chemise from her skin, drew it over her head, and draped it over a stool. Back to the room, Margaret rubbed her skin hard to warm herself before she wound the linen around herself from breasts to knees. Still standing next to a brazier, she looked up to see Alfred leaning against the door staring at her. *His half-smile portends a husbanding, but I am too cold for it.*

"Remind me to ask God to soak you at least once a week."

Margaret harrumphed her distaste and headed for bed. She sat on the sideboard to kick off her boots. She pulled off her socks and dropped them to the rushes before she crawled under the coverings, pulled them over her head, and curled into a tight ball. Alfred draped his wet garments on his racks and about the room. Naked, he crawled into bed. Margaret's cold feed touched his thighs. He rubbed them warm and rubbed one calf and then the other. Margaret unfolded herself a bit. Next he uncrossed her arms from over her breasts and rubbed each arm. He pulled her closer and rubbed her back as he kissed her shoulders, neck, lips. He located the edge of linen and tugged. Margaret sighed. He cared not if it were in resignation or because she was tired. His desire overtook his reason. He kissed the swell of her breasts and pulled the cloth from her body. Alfred caressed and kissed until she relaxed. This night he timed his tongue thrusts into her mouth with his other movements.

Should I try to stop him? Soon she no longer wished to do so.

Sunday Mass was long. Before Communion, Father's sermon started with God's goodness toward them in sparing them from crop loss. Father touched on topic after topic. He ended with, "We caught the edge of a fearful storm. Before God turned His wroth on others, He warned us to behave better. Best we look into our hearts, confess our sins, repent, and better our ways." Father finished the service and dismissed them. Everyone strode home or to the hall under a gray, sunless sky. The cold wind drove them to walk fast, but the mud clinging ankle-high on their footwear made every step an effort.

After they broke their fasts, Margaret gestured to Hughes for inspection. *The scar will be wider in the middle, but not bad.* "The pus is gone and it is healing nicely. One more day of honey on the pad, and I expect all you will need is the winding around it. Wounds heal faster when they are covered. The winding cloth will remind you not to fight."

"How much longer?"

"Five or six days if you bump it not or break it op."

"Thank you, my lady. I wish you a good Sunday." Hughes rejoined the knights.

Nothing more I can do. This grayness and cold make me feel groggy. A nap will while away the day. "Midryth, if my lord asks after me, please tell him I have retired to the keep."

Margaret roused to the smell of her supper. She sat up and saw a tray on the table between the stools and Alfred already seated on his. Margaret pushed her feet into her boots. She stood and shivered. "In this damp, I wish I had a woolen garment like a mantle but with sleeves to wear over my clothes while I am inside. It is a damp cold now, but these stones freeze in winter, and I have seen ice upon them."

"A good idea. I would like one as well. Think you can stitch up a pair before winter?"

As they ate, Margaret considered what she would like. *A collar to warm our necks. Wide sleeves to fit over his shirt and my bliaut.* Margaret crossed her arms over her chest. *Doubled over our hearts and a belt to tie it closed. To our ankles. Yes. Something odd but very warm.*

"I require yards and yards of thick wool cloth and wool thread to make what I am thinking. What mantles and cloaks are made of. Mayhap a bit of fur around the neck if we can bear the cost. Or we can add it later. Yes, I can have them ready. If we have other needs, might you send someone to market day in Reading?"

"Not until after we pay tithe and tax."

Margaret backtracked with, "Ah yes. Good thinking." After she finished eating, Margaret held her mug in both hands and smiled at her husband. "It is Sunday. I have my question ready."

At her smile, Alfred said, "I am ready."

"Did I meet you after I left Forest Keep?"

Alfred's mouth became a hard line before he responded, "Yes." Alfred glowered, "What did you just learn?"

"We met after November 1101 and before August this year." She added, "Worry not, Alfred. I still know it not."

"Glad I am. I like this game and want it to last."

"Until we leave for Vespers, please tell me of your travels to the Holy Land and of your life there. I am in the mood for stories, if it please you."

"I will tell you only the good parts." Alfred began.

I like his smile. His voice soothes me.

That night Margaret again moaned, thrashed, and called out. Alfred drew her into his arms in case she woke in fear. She settled and snuggled into his warmth. He held her until the church bell rang.

24

———— ❧ ————

Finishing the Harvest

While waiting for the crops and the practice field to dry, everyone found other chores. When the knights were not on sentry duty, they cleaned the barracks and their gear, tended their horses, and gamed away the time. Margaret inventoried the storage rooms in the back of the hall. Cormac helped her record what they had and what else she thought they needed. She finished her latest round of mending, supervised the girls cleaning the keep, and consulted Cook about meals.

Villeins arrived to work in teams. They covered the hard dirt floor of the barn aisle with a huge sheet of sailcloth. They flailed the wheat with stout sticks to separate the grain from the stalks. Children stood on the ladder to the loft and passed handfuls of stalks to the boys above to stack for use in the animal stalls.

Winnowing, separating the grains from their husks, took longer. Two handfuls of grain were placed onto a round metal sieve and tossed into the air to rid them of dirt and debris. Finally, they were placed in an iron bushel to be measured and recorded. Finishing five bushels was a good day's work.

On their walk from Sunday Mass to the hall, Margaret was so worried about Giraud's absence she forgot her usual question. "My lord, Giraud has been gone over a fortnight. Should he not have delivered your mother to our small house and have returned by now? I worry for his safety."

"I sent Mother to her new home in the wagon we let in Winchester to carry Elstan. Once Giraud delivers the pair, he will return the wagon to Winchester by the road through Reading. I expect him home by Sunday next." Sauville held the hall door for the couple.

On the dais, Margaret asked, "My lord, I have lost track of the days. What day is this? How soon is Michaelmas?" *Will he understand my concern that we may not be ready?*

Alfred smiled. "This is the thirteenth day of September. We have a fortnight and two days before we needs be ready. Barring another rain, we have time." He leaned toward her and whispered. "You need not be subtle. Ask if you want to know if we shall be ready."

Margaret popped a small bite of pottage into her mouth and swallowed as she pinked. Five days later, Giraud rode to the practice field to report to his lord. When they strode into the hall to dine, Margaret was so glad to see him, she left the dais "Sir Giraud, welcome home. We have missed your good company," she said in a happy tone.

He nodded and replied, "Thank you for your welcome, my lady. I am glad to be home."

Margaret returned to the dais steps, and Giraud sat between Syghelm and Hughes. Alfred paused before starting his pottage to inform Margaret he would tell her Giraud's report after they ate.

Three days later Margaret left the parapet in a happy mood. With *good weather and hard work, we are near finished.* As the couple ate, Cormac appeared inside the main door. *He has the accounts book with him for a reason. I pray it portends increase, not debt.* Dining completed, Margaret sipped her ale and smiled at their men as she waited.

"Good knights, Michaelmas is but a week off. My lady and I have matters to discuss. Thank you for leaving us." Alfred set aside his mug and waited until the hall cleared of men, dish ware, serving girls, and pages. He took the accounts book from Cormac and set it between them. Anticipating he might be needed, Cormac returned to the main door to be out of their hearing but available. "Margaret, I have both good news and small hardships."

"How fares the harvest?"

Alfred smiled and opt the book in the middle. "That is the good news. We have five work days left, plenty of time to finish and inventory the harvest, which is even richer than last year's. Two years of God's grace has made us safe and wealthy. No hunger again this winter and grain to sell when prices rise. The animals are inventoried and all but the horses have increased."

"What be these tic marks under what looks like writing?"

"Each page is a grain so we can compare crops from year to year. I created these pages from your records. See, this page is barley in 1102; 1103 is greater. Each tic is a bushel; ten tics are underlined for easier counting." He pointed to the tics crossed through horizontally. "The spring barley and beans crops are crossed through as we ate them."

He can read and write Norman. If it was permitted, who taught him? "You can read."

"At Cyrille's lessons, I sat beside him. Teaching me was not legal, so I never displayed my learning. Now I can."

Clever too. Margaret nodded. She counted the underlined items and how many sections remained; she smiled.

Alfred turned to the next double page. "The summer rye," he pointed, "and the summer wheat we have yet to finish. You have eaten all of 1102." Then he flipped the rye and wheat pages and explained, "The same with these crops. First we finish the excess. How much of this year's grains we sell shall be easier to determine because we can accurately estimate how much we shall consume before our next harvest. With some saved in case of a bad year," he added.

"I like the method you created. Now we know exactly what we have and which are good and poor years."

"I did the same with our animals," he noted as he showed Margaret the next pages.

"Alfred, you would make an excellent seneschal. What of mistakes?"

"These sheets are parchment. A sharp blade scrapes the error. Then we write the correct amount."

"Have we pages for recording our tithes and taxes?"

"Indeed. Tithes is where our first difficulty lies." At Margaret's frown, Alfred reported, "The error was the priest's, not yours. In 1102, you sent the Bishop of Reading the tithe from the dowry King Henry gave you."

"I, I mean we, have the receipt in the chest under the altar. The priest was upset I had sent it ahead and had proof."

"I saw it. The priest forgot to take the tenth from what the villeins had paid you last year. We still owe that debt. I shall tell them I found it. When I am marked an honest Saxon, we shall have no trouble with the Church."

"Shall the Church claim I deliberately cheated them?"

"I shall not permit them to do so. The error was theirs."

"What do we still owe?"

"Eleven shillings, thruppence. We have it."

There are other withdrawals from the chest. "You said hardships," said Margaret emphasizing the "s" of her last word.

"Cormac told me of your plan to dower each servant girl after her service."

"Midryth! She is the eldest and I forgot!" Margaret sighed. "In spring I was to dower her and permit her to return to her family. I was ill, and the time passed. Is she angry with me?"

"Cormac says not. He asked me to suggest you visit with her."

"I forgot what I promised Midryth; I must ask Cormac. Then I shall speak with her."

"We have two expenses greater than that," Alfred offered.

Margaret folded her hands upon the table and smiled at him. *Best I look not shocked whatever they may be. Most likely, he incurred debts for armor, sword and horse. An un-landed Saxon family would lack such wealth.*

"I bought my mother's freedom."

"Glad I am she escaped Wulf."

Alfred smiled his gratitude at her response. "She did not cost much because she is over fifty and past childbearing. Because her lord knew how much I wanted her, he forced me to pay two pounds instead of one."

"No matter, Alfred. She shall spend the rest of her life in the dignity she deserves." Margaret shrugged. She muttered, "In the dignity all villeins deserve. May they someday be free as well."

"Glad I am you said that, for I bought Elstan's freedom as well."

"Elstan is a villein?"

"In 1101, King Henry asked Lord Baudric for Elstan to guard Queen Matilda and you at Forest Keep. He was to return home after the princess's birth, but he went with you."

"He is a runaway?"

"Yes. Lord Baudric asked not for Elstan's return because you were in the king's favor. After we wed, Lord Baudric declared Elstan had run off and announced him outside the law. I paid for Elstan to save his life." At Margaret raising her eyebrows in a silent question, Alfred revealed, "Ten pounds."

Margaret choked back her words. *Ten pounds! Oh, my dowry! We are paupered!* In a soft voice, Margaret said, "My lord, Elstan served me well. Glad I am you saved him, but I understand not why so much."

"He is valuable, young and strong. Could wed and produce more villeins. I am sorry, Margaret."

"Have we any coins left?"

"Not much after we pay our debts. Next week, we owe all our workers for the year. We also owe eight knights and Syghelm a total of twenty-one and a half pounds and our four new knights one pound and twelve shillings. The total is twenty-two pounds, twelve shillings." *Almost a quarter of my dowry between Elstan and our knights!* Margaret chocked back her shock. "Next Michaelmas, we will owe each man three pounds, a total of thirty-nine pounds. At this time, we have it not."

I knew knights are costly, but so much! Yet we need every man. Margaret hid not her shock. "That is why we must husband our resources and sell grain."

At Alfred's nod, Margaret added, "We will do what we must. What you decide, I support."

"I ordered a second chest built. There we shall store what we hold for the knights and others. Each month we shall move coins from our chest to the second one for paying estate debts. Alfred was sympathetic. "After tithe and tax, you will still see coins in your chest…and its bottom."

Margaret placed her hand over his. "Our chest. I won it for a husband. I am not sorry."

Alfred lifted his hand and kissed the back of hers. "Margaret, you are an extraordinary woman. The Normans who passed over you were fools." Margaret leaned and rested her head against his arm. Alfred placed his arm around her shoulders and kissed the edge of her forehead. "What next?"

Margaret sighed. "I am for church to thank God for two years of great bounty. I think He knew we were going to need it."

Alfred picked up the book, stood, and took her hand. "I shall fetch two men to guard you and shall escort you. I am for the Rammegs to order another wagon. If all goes well, we shall need a third before spring. Then I have other work to finish before we sup."

Cormac slipped away.

Thinking her dowry gone so upset Margaret she forgot her courses were due. At the church door, Ferrant chose to wait for her rather than follow Alfred. She scratched him under his collar and kiss his forehead. "Sit. Stay," she ordered before she opt the door.

The next day, Margaret dismissed the other girls from the keep and asked Midryth to sit fireside with her. "Midryth, sorry I am I forgot my promise to you. As the eldest of the girls, you trained them well and kept them in hand for longer than the year we agreed. What may I do for you?'

"From the cloth you gifted me, I have my wedding bed linens sewed and saved. I know I am owed tuppence for the year," Midryth said softly, "but I know not what I am owed since then."

"Another pence."

"My lady, the boy I favor is younger than I. If I stay until Easter Sunday next year, he will be older too. Then may I have four pence in all?"

More coins out of our money chest. "You may. Who is he?"

Midryth blushed and looked away. "Ainemaere."

Margaret smiled. "A good choice from a good family. Have your parents talked?'

"Yes, my lady. They are in agreement, but they want us to wait because I am two years older than he is."

"Then I suggest you stay." At Midryth's nod, Margaret added, "Midryth, come Eastertide, should I forget our agreement, please remind me before Easter Sunday."

The girl rose and curtsied. "Thank you, my lady. I shall see to your room now." Midryth turned toward the stairs.

Next year Cleva will be of age. Two girls to dower. Two girls to replace. I must tell Alfred.

25

Michaelmas

On the twenty-seventh day of September and after Mass, Alfred ordered the Saxons to join the Normans in the hall before all broke their fasts.

"Our Michaelmas feast will now be the day before the holy day. On the morrow, we celebrate God's goodness." *A subtle change from my way last year. He has taken charge of everything.* "On Michaelmas, you pay your taxes to us. As this is my first year as your lord, I expect Church and Crown will be at our gate the next day. We will be ready. Father has given us dispensation to cook this day, so I expect the kitchen workers to return to work after they break their fasts. Cook still has much to do, and she requires your help." Alfred repeated himself in Saxon to the nods of the villeins. The Saxons left as he sat for the first of the two Sunday meals.

"My lord, may I ask why we celebrate thus?"

Alfred smirked then smiled. "Pigs eaten, grain baked, and ale drunk cannot be taxed."

Margaret smiled back. "I wish I had thought of that when I led." Alfred nodded at her compliment. "May I offer my assistance in the kitchen? I do so hate sitting when I can help."

"You are our chatelaine and may do as you wish."

On their way home from Vespers, Margaret started her Sunday question with, "Alfred, I forgot to ask last Sunday, but I want to ask now. Did I first meet you after the birth of the Princess Matilda?"

Alfred took several steps and opt the keep gate before he faced her. "No, you did not."

Margaret nodded and followed him up the steps. *After we left Forest Keep and before the princess's birth! Between the end of November and February 7. Only a span of two months and a fortnight! On the road to Winchester or in it? I must think on that time. No, eliminate or confirm on the road first. May I remember by All Saints Day!*

Margaret continued to ruminate. *The Saxon men in Forest Keep were honorable and hard working. Elstan and Elric were always helpful and kind, just like the others. Elborg was good with Night. Oft we laughed with Eldene, who humored with us almost daily. Good men. Alfred is like them. Night likes him. I smile at his teasing. He has been kind. So far he has been true to his word, deeds not declaring feelings. The way he looks at me warms my insides. Not all Norman men are good, nor are all Saxon men evil. I think better of him now and needs smile at him more so he knows.*

The next morn after Mass, everyone broke not their fasts to prepare for the feast. Soon trestles, table boards, and benches festooned the meadow. Jorgon and Daelton brought Margaret's surprise from the barn. They set the flags on their poles at the corners of the meadow and admired how the breeze lifted them for all to see. The long triangles were blue with a gold cross broken with a circle at its intersection. Behind the head table, the cloth was attached to the pole at its top and its bottom. It hung down in the shape of a Norman shield, a rounded top with a long taper to a point.

Margaret approached Alfred. "If you like them not, I will change them."

At seeing Alfred's broad grin, Margaret giggled. "You are allowed to wear the cross because you served in the Grand Crusade, and I wait for your suggestion what to place in the circle. Blue is for good fortune."

Alfred side-hugged her. "I like it well. I shall paint it on my shield."

Margaret beamed at him. "This is a good day I shall long remember."

From the lane, Duone led a donkey hauling a harvest wagon of ale barrels to the meadow. Behind him, others led the wagons laddened with food. Alfred had asked Father and Gytha, Verel, and Felamaere and his wife Erwina to join them at the head table. As everyone was finishing their meals, Alfred whispered in Margaret's ear and then stood. A wave of silence slowly rolled from the head table to meadow's end as everyone stopped visiting and looked to their lord.

"On the morrow, we will pay our debts after we break our fasts. Saxons come to the bailey to pay what you owe us. If need be, we will finish the next day." Alfred paused and looked at his people. "As Father said before the Te Deum, Our Lord has blessed us again with safety and a bountiful harvest. In gratitude to these men, who have kept us safe, I have an announcement. You already know King

Henry awarded us five hides of royal forest. Taking them over will take several years; we start this winter. Saxons will spend the winter days they owe us in labor to clear forest land and claim meadows and access to rivers and streams for our use. The first virgate cleared is mine. The second and third virgates I will split into three ten-acre plots. I, we, will be awarding one plot to any knight who has served this estate for three or more years."

Margaret smiled at her shocked knights and nodded to them her lord spoke true. Every knight straightened his back, and several Saxon men gasped.

"As I am Lord Warwick's vassal, I must seek his permission to do this. Eight of you good men are eligible February next. Before Easter Sunday, I hope to have Lord Warwick's consent. I know not how I will choose each man or if it be by drawing lots, but I do know any knight who wishes to be considered must help us clear and prepare the land in addition to his regular duties. If you gain a plot, you will be a knight landed, able to marry and have a family. My hope is six of you will soon be landed with mayhap three more of you in the future. You will be my vassals, and I will declare you my Corps d'Elite. May our grandchildren make Dryhtenton a town."

The knights stood and repeatedly shouted, "Lord Alfred! Lord Alfred!" The Saxons joined them. Alfred reached for Margaret's hand and drew her up. He twined her arm in his. The pair beamed at their people. After a time, Alfred gestured everyone to sit. "Now we are ready for music, singing, and dancing. Duone, fetch another wagonload of ale!"

As they prepared for bed, Margaret asked, "Think you Lord Warwick shall permit you to award land?"

"I know not. At least our knights know I think well of them and have my favor should Warwick forbid it or demand he approve our choices."

Margaret snuggled into her husband's arms and lay her hand on his chest. "Your mother said never discuss estate matters in bed, but I want to say something." When Alfred spoke not, she continued. "You are right to honor our knights; they are good men all. They deserve your reward because they served me well. The ones who choose land will serve you well and help us to remain strong and safe. Thank you for being so good to them." Margaret kissed his neck.

"Thank you for our emblem. Most Norman knights have white shields and but one mark. With blue and gold, they will know me a long way off."

"May you strike fear into their hearts."

"Do you still fear me?"

Margaret shook her head against his shoulder. Alfred, kissed her hair and slowly drew her over him. Margaret looked askance to lying atop her husband. Alfred whispered, "Permit me to show you a new way."

26

Paying Debts

Wednesday morn, Margaret and Alfred stepped outside church and were talking with Father Manntun when Margaret noticed Haelum standing nearby. *He looks so forlorn.* Margaret drew Alfred aside. "My lord, today is the day after Michaelmas. Someone to your right is looking at you."

"I see him."

"If I bring him to you and he apologizes before everyone, is he forgiven?"

"Yes."

Margaret moved to Haelum, dropped her head and whispered. Haelum nodded and followed her.

Haelum went to one knee and said loudly, "My lord, I beg your forgiveness for my evil words and deeds last month."

"You are forgiven, Haelum. Rise and again be seen."

"Haelum, would you like to take my hand as I walk you to your home?"

"Oh yes, my lady," gushed the boy. Margaret extended her hand, and Haelum jumped to her side to take it. Alfred ordered Ferrant.

"So, Haelum, what have you been doing?" Margaret asked to set the boy at ease. Haelum was soon chattering about his chores during the harvest and the family cat's new litter.

Margaret looked at Alfred and smiled back at him. *He keeps his word. Now if he will only be kind to the boy.*

At Aldcot's door, Alfred asked Haelum, "How old are you?"

"I am in seven years, my lord."

"When you are eight years, would you like to be my page? Come with your lady and me after Mass and help us in the bailey? You would go home each night if you wish it."

"Oh, yes, my lord! Gladly!" Haelum bowed and dashed inside. "Mother, Mother, I get to page for my lady when I am eight!"

Alfred chuckled as he took Margaret's arm and turned them homeward. "You have conquests young and old where ere I go. Should he do well, when he is ten, I shall ask a knight to accept him and teach him to squire."

Margaret hugged his arm. *His word is good. Has a kind heart. I like him so much more every week.*

As Alfred had predicted, the king's shire reeve arrived early Thursday morn. He inspected the accounts book, and Alfred paid the required ten percent of their current wealth in coin. The king's reeve scored both halves of the marking sticks and broke the sticks down the middle to give one side to Alfred as proof he had paid his taxes. He would take the other half to the man in charge of the king's inventories.

Alfred invited the man to join them on the dais for dinner while his workers dined with the knights fireside. Afterward, the reeve collected taxes from the knights and Saxons. The King's reeve finished Friday. After the reeve and his men dined with Lord Alfred and Lady Margaret, they departed for the next estate. Before supper, the Church's party arrived to eat with them and attend Vespers. Father Alphonse asked for the barracks for his party. The knights slept in the hall.

"The Church will neither finish nor leave Saturday eve. They will rest here Sunday at our expense. Mayhap they will finish Monday and leave, but I think not. The party will wait until Tuesday morn. We will be forced to feed them for three days. The priests are punishing me for last year." Margaret continued to fret as she undressed. "I rushed them off to the next estate without much grace. God is punishing me for my greed."

'Then we must be gracious so we are not so marked in the future," said Alfred as he pulled off his boots.

I have missed my courses by a week. Am I late because being husbanded has changed me or does it portend a coming babe? Tell him nothing until I am cert.

Margaret had guessed aright. Before departing Tuesday morn, Father Alphonse had filled his wagons with their grain, took what else was owed in coins, and added what the Saxons had owed. To make cert Father Alphonse left happy, Alfred had gifted him smoked meat, breads, and their barrel full of ale, so they may dine in comfort as they traveled to the next estate.

Before dinner Friday, Alfred left the dais and was deep in serious conversations with the knights who bunched together to hear him. He ate in silence; Margaret matched him. *I feel tired for no reason. Mayhap a nap will refresh me.*

Their meal finished, Margaret reported, "My lord, I am for the keep."

Something has happened, a reason for conversing with his knights in hushed tones. Whatever it is, he wants not anyone see my reaction. Smile. Margaret stood and left by the door between the storage rooms behind the dais.

Later, Margaret pushed her covers to the other side of the bed, rose, and joined Alfred, who sat on one stool with their supper beside him. They ate in silence. Margaret picked up the tray and took it to the landing. She called down the stairs, "Whoever is below, our empty tray is on the landing. Disturb us not." Margaret returned to her stool, folded her hands in her lap, and looked at Alfred with expectation in her eyes and a half-smile.

"Remember you my telling of a beating before we met at the church?" Margaret nodded. "Lord Wilbur and his knight."

"Wilbur is holding a tournament. Each time a knight wins a sword fight, he advances until there are only two. The loser receives three lances. The winner gains a war horse and all its gear. I intend to win."

"A fight to the death?" Margaret whispered.

"Until one calls halt."

"Which you shall not do."

Alfred shook his head, and Margaret did as well. "I like it not, but I know you are going. The best I can do is help you prepare and pray for your safety."

"I expected you to rail against my going. Tell me I am too new a knight, an inexperienced fighter."

Margaret shrugged. "I have seen you on the practice field. You acquit yourself well with our men. What of others whose fight moves you know not?"

"I know how most Normans fight. What they know not is how I fight. Knights from other lands have moves I have shown no one since I learned them in the Holy Land." They heard the bell calling them to Vespers. Alfred stood and fetched their outer garments. "To win is my revenge on Wilbur, and I intend to have it."

Kneeling on her prayer cushion, Margaret heard not Father's prayers and admonitions. *Your will, O God, in all things. I beg You, let him live and not to be injured more than I can heal him. I fear Wilbur will find a way to cheat him. I pray the villain poison him not. I must remind him to take a knight who can cook. Not to drink anything but what he brings.* She continued her prayers until Alfred called her name. She crossed herself, stood, and following him home in silence.

This may be Sunday, but ask not my next question. How we met matters less now. He has much to consider and prepare. Do not vex him with a small matter when he is leaving on a great one.

27

Lordless Days

Monday the sun rose and burned the fog crawling the ground, but clouds soon masked the sun and most of its light. The wind blew not so the ground was still wet from the Sunday rain. Scouring the forest for acorns for the livestock and gathering wood for winter needs wait. Instead, the next three days were a flurry of preparations. Men lashed poles together to form a four-sided tent while women in the village sewed a tent lid to sit atop a center pole and drop over the sides. That completed, the women sewed long strips together for the tent's sides and attached leather straps to tie the tenting to the frame. Men coated the tent with pig fat to waterproof it.

At midday Tuesday, between bites Margaret whispered, "My lord, how many go with you?"

"Two. Pernel swears his brother is a good cook. Verel recommended Sauville. Says he is cunning and ruthless."

"Sauville? He is so quiet and mild-mannered."

Alfred smiled at her. "That makes him the best companion. No one expects it from him. Sauville fights with a cold determination and shall quit not. Verel swears he is deadly; I believe him."

I will ask Cormac about his choices. He will know and stay silent. Stop thinking in Norman. Margaret nodded, "I shall have Cook prepare foods to take with you. How far must you travel?"

"We leave Thursday, travel three days, rest Sunday. The tournament starts Monday or Tuesday. How long it lasts depends how many men attend. I shall send word when I am expected home."

"I shall order smoked meats, flour, and a pot of dough starter. A barrel of ale. What else do you require?"

"I have already told Cook. She is doing all."

"My lord, I shall prepare your clothing and pack the satchels. I shall make a bag of salves, simples, and herb bags for bruises, possible wounds, fever. I shall then feel helpless. What else may I do?"

Alfred dropped his hand below the table and gave her knee a quick squeeze before he returned it to reach for his ale. Behind his mug, he said. "Send me off with such warmth and passion, I leave happy and return eager to again be in your arms."

Margaret lifted her mug and behind it, she replied, "Done. Starting this night." She lightly clinked her mug to his and stared into his eyes as he drank. *May I wife you so well, you stay home and risk not your life on this foolhardy trip. He is Saxon, and all will want him dead. How to stop him?* Margaret finished her ale. *Nay, he fights for his honor. Let him secure it. Send him with a glad heart, pray, and see what God has for us.*

Margaret walked through her days performing her regular duties. She set meals, inspected grain bins with Felamaere, and consulted Cormac regarding what needed be done in preparation for All Souls Day, now less than three weeks away. Margaret kept herself busy to banish worry. True to her word, in the privacy of their room, she was a warm, willing wife. By Wednesday eve, the tent had been completed, admired, and disassembled to be hauled in a harvest wagon filled with food, drink and fighting gear. Margaret had supervised the packing of the wagon before Vespers. That night they slept little. Toward dawn, Margaret drifted off. Startled, she woke herself but knew not why. Alfred held her without revealing she had just suffered another night terror.

Alfred tarried not for a last embrace but bounced off the bed at the bell's first peal. Margaret rolled to her side to watch him dress. *Note him well. I may be a widow within a ten-day. Or worse, bound to a defenseless cripple who can only order my safety, not provide it.* Margaret shook her head. *Think not such evils. Pray for him.*

Alfred looked toward the bed. "Wife, the memory of last night and your warm look this morn shall carry me. Be out of bed ere I lose my resolve."

Margaret rose, dressed, and braided her hair before she set her circlet. She opt her marriage chest and returned with her gift, a band of her wedding rib sewed on a linen strip. *Best I include success in my words or he shall think me mean.* "Alfred, please keep this with you to remember my regard for you. Know I pray for your success and your safe return."

Alfred bowed. "I thank you for your 'regard.'" He stuffed the strip down his shirt and over his heart. "May I have a final private kiss?" Margaret stood on tiptoes to reach her arms around his neck and draw his head to hers. She opt her lips to match his. After he flicked his tongue into her mouth, she flicked hers into his. Alfred held her so tightly she stopped breathing. Margaret withdrew her kiss and whispered into his ear, "Return to me."

"Always." Alfred pulled away to gaze into his beloved's eyes. "I must do this."

"Yes, you must." *Send him off well, like a good Norman wife sending her husband into battle.*

Alfred and Margaret walked out of church toward a full wagon with Louvel driving it and with his horse, and Alfred's tied behind. Sauville sat on his roundsey with Alfred's reins in his hands. The Saxons fanned behind their lord and lady.

Alfred announced, "See to my lady and our lands in my absence. Into your care. I give her safety and well-being. Fail me not."

For them all, Cormac responded, "My lord, we shall so succeed, you will be well pleased upon your return. This we swear." In unison, Norman and Saxon alike repeated Cormac's last sentence.

Alfred kissed Margaret's right hand, and turned to mount. He looked down to see Margaret's warm smile and her curtsey. He turned his roundsey down the lane. Ready to wave should Alfred look back, Margaret kept her smile and raised arm, but Alfred looked not back. After the party disappeared into the trees, everyone else drifted homeward. Margaret instructed Cormac to stand in her stead in the hall and re-entered the church. Ferrant lay in front of the door to guard, leaving the two knights to lean against the building. She knelt on her cushion and prayed until Cormac returned to call her to sup. The next morn the forest was dry, and preparations for winter resumed.

Cormac entered the hall as Margaret finished her pottage. He held the accounts book at his side. "My lady, before your lord returns, I suggest we meet to discuss certain matters in the book."

At Margaret's nod, Cormac took the stairs and sat to her left. He listened as she gave morning instructions to others before asking for those in the hall to leave.

"Not good, is it?"

Cormac shrugged as he dropped his head to the left. "I thought you best know it before your lord returns. You want not to be shocked should he choose to share this information with you. I will start with the best pages," he offered. Cormac turned many pages before he reached the crop reports. "Here is what remains of our harvest after tithe and tax."

Not so much gone as I had feared. "Is it enough to sell some when prices are high in February and March?"

"I believe so. This page records what is left in your chest."

Margaret saw the number and gasped. *We are land rich and coin poor. We have enough to pay Midryth, but little else.* "Cormac, my lord informed me of this situation before he left for the tournament. Thank you for showing it me. Now I am cert how careful I must be."

Cormac softly closed the book. "What else may I do for you, my lady?"

"Are the women rendering pig fat to make soaps and simples?" At Cormac's nod, she added, "Please walk with me to the keep as I fetch my dried flowers for the soaps and herbs for the simples." Before Cormac left her, Margaret again thanked him for his company and added, "Please greet Caitlin for me."

"She is standing by the small pot over there."

Margaret glanced the way he pointed. "Indeed," said Margaret as she walked around the fire and the soap makers.

"Caitlin, how long it has been since I have seen you."

Caitlin curtsied and said, "God give you a good day, my lady."

Margaret sidled to her and hissed, "Never do that again, Caitlin. I count you my equal."

"But they do not. You know I must do this in public, no matter how we treat each other in private."

"Very well. When may I visit you in your home?"

"Send word, and I will send Cormac away."

Margaret nodded and handed over her wooden case of dried herbs. "Please take what you like for the simples you are making. Half for you and half for me?"

"Of course, my lady. I serve the Saxons and you the knights. I think to give you more because knights so oft hurt themselves."

"Whatever you say." Margaret left her. She stood beside the soap makers and crushed dried lavender flowers over a soap-filled wooden box a foot square and four inches deep. A woman stirred the bits into the soap and smoothed the top. Margaret crushed a mixture of wild flowers over other forms. That done, she walked away to let the women pour the remaining mixture into forms. *The plain boxes are washing soap. The lavender is mine, the rest are for my household. Each woman must make a box for her own family. I wonder what Caitlin will put in hers now that she is married.* Margaret smiled to herself. *Cert not all flowers. Cormac would like no to smell like blooms.* The women worked the next day to finish the soaps before they began the candles.

Margaret started hemming two new loincloths for Alfred. Next, she whip-stitched the edges of the two pairs of braies. She placed two pieces edge to edge to sew them together. *Glad I am we spent coin on fabric before Michaelmas. He used so much for the tent, I feared I would lack enough to outfit him well. Two sets of chausses and tunics.* Margaret moved her stool to again sit in sunlight. *Soon I must sew at the keep door. I want all this done before he returns in case the king calls him to service. He must have more clothes should he get wet or be wounded. Think not on that! Alfred is well. He will stay well. God, grand it be so.* Margaret crossed herself and prayed for Alfred. She resumed sewing. *He has already given me enough clothes for two years; I need no more.* Cleva called her to dine.

Monday morning, Margaret inspected the villeins' progress on smoking the pork and beef. *I love the smells of smoking wood and curing meat.* A fire near the building set the wood chips aflame. The men pulled the burning chips from the fire and beat them until they but smoked. They pushed the smoking chips under the smoke house with long-handled rakes. A small boy lay on his stomach to look under the building on stilts to be cert the chips flared not.

"Another week of this, and the meat will be ready for winter, my lady," reported Hloedun.

Cleva arrived with an old soap form filled past brining with sixteen dried soap blocks wrapped in clean rags. Margaret looked up from her stitchery. "Please place the box in my room." Cleva climbed the stairs. *Looks to be enough until next soap-making time. Scented ones into my clothes chest and plain blocks in the corner to dry hard. Another winter task completed.*

The next week, Margaret supervised, sewed and napped, *It is as it was before he came. I am in charge of everything. I work, am reported sentry schedules, order, sew, and more. Yet his absence is a hole. A part of me seems missing. I think of him so oft. Worry about him. Want him home. I remember sweet moments between us. Yearn for more. Snuggling against him after a husbanding. I care for him. Heart, I feel you opening. Is that love?*

Friday, Margaret remembered Caitlin and sent word of her arrival after she dined. She took longer to arrive than she had expected because she stopped to speak to each woman in the village to learn what each was doing to prepare for winter. As was customary, Margaret knocked on the closed door and coughed.

Caitlin opt the door and gave obeisance before welcoming Margaret inside. Margaret closed the door and hugged Caitlin hard. "I have missed you, my friend, and my absence is all my fault. I should have come sooner."

"Nonsense. You are a wife now and busier than ever. You know a chatelaine works harder than a lord. Please sit and tell me your news."

With a smile, Margaret shook her head. "Rather, you tell me yours. I see it in your face," she warned. Margaret took Caitlin's hands in hers. "When?"

"The end of April, I think," revealed Caitlin with a wide grin.

Margaret hugged her. "Six months. Oh Caitlin, I am so happy for you and Cormac. Why did you not tell me sooner? Have you enough meat? Did you sicken at all? How fare you? What may I do for you?"

"Stop. Stop. Sit." Still holding one of Caitlin's hands, Margaret did so. "Like many, I sickened the first few weeks. Soups, meats, and rest helped. Since then I feel well and strong."

"Cormac said nothing, and well you know he likes to talk."

"He wants no gossip until I show or our babe comes alive and kicks me. I am a bit old to be a first-time mother."

"The queen had a healthy princess at twenty-two and you are just a little older than that." At Caitlin's silence, Margaret added, "Of course, being careful is best, so I will say nothing until you do."

Speak not of my missed courses or that they are due this day or on the morrow. Follow her example. After all, I am seventeen in two months and am myself four years too old for a first babe.

"Thank you. Want a bit of gossip? Dena is again with child and due early spring. Again she wants no talk until she is ready."

"She wants a boy. I will continue to respect her desire I stay away from her." Margaret looked away. "After she birthed Leah, she gifted to others the items I sewed for her and added to yours. She knows my stitching, so I cannot do that again. I fear we may never speak again."

"Never is a long time, Margaret. Having another son may heal her over the loss of her first. We shall see. How fare you?"

"I am well. I am sewing more clothes for him should the king call him to duty." Margaret considered what to reveal. "We have set a routine of duties and times to meet. His mother gave helpful advice about how to be a good wife. She said to discuss not estate matters in bed. The queen gave instructions before we met at the church. She said to impede never his sword arm by walking behind and to his left. I am following what I remember."

"You like him." Margaret blushed. "Despite he is Saxon, and you Norman? Despite others hating both of you for mixing your peoples and birthing mixed children?"

"I cannot help their hate. I can only prevent them from hurting us for it." Margaret paused. "I see how he treats others and know he is a good man. He treats me well, but ...

"Want you mine opinion?" At Margaret's nod, Caitlin began. "I know you, girl. I know not how, but I am cert the queen forced you into this marriage. A Saxon lord has no rank among the Norman ones. You had wealth; you wanted rank and got it not. You thought him beneath you. You may think it still, but it is not so. He is a good man and a good match for who you really are, not who you think you must be. Your mother acted above her rank and taught you that falsehood. She thought you should sit even higher than she aimed. Forget her false instruction. Choose to be happy, and you will be so.

Caitlin leaned forward to make her point. "Look not at rank but at the man. He is honest, works hard, and as already gained the support of your men. He is stern as he must be in his dealings with us until all accepted his authority. He is harsh when need be. Haelum. He is generous. How many lords give land to raise the rank of his knights? He buys not their favor; he is planning ahead by years. More estate needs more protection. Landed knights guard well what they own. He challenges Lord Wilbur, so we know he protects his honor. He cares for you; we all see that. Do you? We see you smile at him, yet I see you holding yourself away. Have you let him into your heart?" Margaret shrugged. "Be careful, Margaret. He seeks your favor now, but if you withhold it too long." Caitlin paused to form her warning. "What if he gives up trying? What if he decides to stop caring? How might he treat you then?"

"That is my fear. I also fear what he might do to my heart should I give it."

"Oh, Margaret. All women fear that. Not just you. I feared the same until you intervened between Cormac and me. After we talked, really talked, I knew." Caitlin rose to fetch a drink for her former charge. She handed Margaret the mug and sat. Margaret drank a gulp and clutched the mug in both hands. "I will tell you one more thing, and then you must decide for yourself what you will do." Margaret nodded. "To love someone is a leap of faith. Faith that he returns your love. Faith he will hurt not your heart nor harm you. Faith your life will be better because you trust his love. Heed the queen and his mother, but this is my advice: Men can become what we think of them. Think well of him. Give him honest praise; expect the best of him. A good man can become a better man when he is loved."

"I am trying to use what the queen and you say I should do. I am still learning to be a wife."

"If you want to succeed, do it not from your head, but from your heart." Caitlin waited a moment to ask, " Does he start with kisses and end with holding you? When you wake, does he have an arm around you or a hand on you?" Margaret looked away, blushed, and nodded. "Those are strong signs he cares for you. Accept that and leap."

Wanting to speak no more on it, Margaret switched to a worry. "I have night terrors I remember. Darkness. A monster chasing me. One time I woke myself in the middle of one. I woke from another on the night before my lord left for the tourney. Did I have them before I married him?"

"On occasion," replied Caitlin evasively.

"Did I start this at my marriage?"

"I think you have them after something in the day has frightened you." When Margaret spoke not, Caitlin added, "Since you were twelve." She looked away.

Father's beatings. Even from the grave he haunts me. Is that why I fear men? The image of Alfred holding her flashed in her mind. *Is that why I doubt him when he says he will not strike me?* Margaret teared. She nodded and stood. She hugged Caitlin hard and turned away. Margaret shut the door behind her and strode the village lane with such purpose no one dared approach. As Margaret shut the door to their room, she burst into tears and grabbed a rag to cry into. She doffed her boots and crawled into bed to weep into her pillow. That done, Margaret rolled to her back and stared at the canopy.

Not Norman. Yet he behaved like one at Court before others, at table, with the king. Formal, polite, except when I cried. Then was he his real self, or did he do what he must to keep me? Here he is more at his ease. I see how he works with the knights, how they respond to him in the hall. Verel judges others well, and he appears to like him. With Felemaere, he asked a question rather than pretend to know what he did not. He lets Cormac teach him. Confident, not proud or cocky. Margaret recalled the Norman men she had met, Lord William, the king's men, Sirs Rousel, Cachier, Gailard, others. *He is like them, direct, purposeful, determined. Alfred is more open in showing his feelings. All the Saxons I have known are when they are among themselves. Alfred is like that when he chooses, and he chooses to be like that with me. I wish I had more time with his mother to hear her stories of him. What to do? Keep showing him I like him.* Margaret smiled and hugged herself. *Be warmer, more at my ease. Be more willing in bed. I am starting to like that. Wait for a sign.* Margaret continued ruminating on her marriage, on what she wanted, and how to gain it.

Much later Alura called from behind the door, "My lady, time to sup." Margaret rolled out of bed and poured water from the pitcher into the wooden bowl. *He is dead. He can hurt me never again.* Margaret felt herself in Alfred's arms. *He said he would not strike me. Believe him. I must dab my eyes, or they will see I cried.* She held wet fingers over her lids. Margaret scooped water from the bowl and rinsed her face. She reached for the towel on the table and dried her face before she felt for loose strands to push behind her ears. At the ladder, she patted Ferrant, and watched the dog take the rungs.

At the gate, Syghelm waited. Margaret nodded greeting.

"Are you well, my lady?"

"Yes, Syghlem, I am." *Distract him as we walk.* "How did the knights choose who will escort me each day and sit with me on the dais?"

"After Verel escorted you the day Lord Alfred left, the others demanded a turn. They agreed to meet on the practice field to choose who was next. Verel refused, saying he would not permit them to injure each other. He said, 'God has already chosen the order. First you go by length of service, then by rank, then by age, eldest first.' As this day is the ninth day and mine rank is lowest, this turn is mine. Lord Alfred's new knights start on the morrow with Sir Bertrand. If need be, we start the round again.'"

May you be home before then. Margaret sighed. *I miss you.*

Syghelm stopped at the corner of the hall. "My lady, may I speak?" Margaret nodded. "When someone comes into your life, he fills a space inside your mind, your heart. Oft a space you knew not was empty. When he leaves for a time, that space is empty again, only now you feel it. Oh, you enjoyed those first few days because you were in charge again. But he is still gone, and that empty feeling nags you. You miss him, my lady. I think that is why you cried. Have no fear. We see the way he looks at you. He will return. Worry not about your lord, my lady. Wilbur knows not with whom he is dealing."

What means he by that? Margaret looked away. *Swallow my tears. Hide my fears. Set a merry face.* She smiled and raised her hand; Syghelm offered his forearm. They walked the width of the building, turned the corner, and she entered the hall first. The knights stood and sat not until she had.

Margaret ate in silence for a time. *He was so careful to say not love or even caring. Why knows he so much about my empty feeling? Say not love nor even like.* "Syghelm, how know you about that empty feeling?"

"Once I loved a good woman. After several years together, she died."

"I am sorry." *Ask not her name; let him tell me only what he wishes.* "Is that place empty again?"

"Memories help, but that hole in my heart remains."

"Even if you love again?"

"A new love fills a new place. In time, the ache of losing her has eased, but I will always miss her."

Margaret heard the sadness in Syghelm's voice. *Ask no more.* "Syghem, you are wise and kind. When you are ready, I am pleased to walk to Vespers with you."

Three days later, Felamaere met Margaret on her way to Monday Mass. "My lady, your lord rested this day in the forest. He sends this, 'I expect to sup with you Wednesday.'"

Margaret nodded recognition. For a moment, she placed her hand on Felamaere's forearm, which surprised him that she touched a man. "Thank you, Felamakere, for your good news." She entered the church. She prayed to God asking Him to take away her night terrors. She prayed for Alfred's safe return and smiled to herself at that thought.

28

Return

28 October

Alfred's welcome-home feast was almost ready. Wednesday's midday meal was a substantial soup, bread, cheese, and ale. After dining, Margaret repaired to the keep. She stripped, washed, and dressed. She brushed her hair until it gleamed and drew her comb from forehead to nape. As she braided the right half, she imagined Alfred's return. *The Saxons will line the lane and give obeisance as he passes. The gate guards will freeze and stand tall; the knights will applaud as he enters the bailey. The workers will stand behind them and give obeisance. Outside the hall entrance, I will wait for him to dismount; as he approaches, I will smile, curtsey and say a warm, "Welcome home, my lord."* As Margaret tied her left braid, she continued. *I hope he behaves well and kisses me not before others. Should he try, what to do? Accept his kiss or turn my head and give him my cheek? No, he will think that rejection. Let him do as he wills and be agreeable.* Margaret donned her seire and bridal circlet and looked about the cleaned room. *Everything in its place. Braziers full and new candles on the stands. Flints at the ready. What have I forgot? Oh, yes, op the shutters on the sun side for a bit of warmth.* Margaret did so. As she left the room, she strewed sweet herbs and dried flowers over the new rushes. At the bottom of the stairs, she handed her bag to Cyne with instructions the last girl leaving the keep strew the main floor rushes with scent. In the coolness of the hall, Margaret sat on the edge of the dais with a wool cloth over her lap as she mended Duone's torn sleeve. Haesel stood watch at the entrance door. At the guard's hand wave, Haesel turned. "My lady, the guard signals your lord approaches."

Margaret dropped the tunic and lap cloth into her mending basket and rushed to the doorway. "Place my basket outside the servant's entrance," she ordered as she passed Haesel. Margaret took her place. She looked right and saw the sun's lower edge just above the trees. *Just when he said he would arrive. Did he come straight home sweaty and fight-stained or did he wash first?* Margaret saw Sauville entering the bailey holding high Alfred's banner. She held her breath.

Dear God, You made him so handsome! How straight his back, how wide his grin. His pride means success! Margaret realized he saw only her, and her heart leaped up. Even as Alfred dismounted, he looked not away. She blushed at his unwavering gaze. Just as Margaret had imagined, she curtsied and greeted her husband. She noted his damp hair. *He stands so close, yet he is proper and only takes my hand.*

Alfred raised Margaret's hand and kissed its back. "Glad I am to be home, my lady." Alfred turned her hand over and kissed her palm. He moved his lips. The heat of his kiss upon inside of her wrist raced to her heart and flowed to her toes.

Margaret swallowed hard and whispered, "Alfred, please."

"Later," he promised. Alfred released her hand and stepped back to announce loudly, "Thank you, my lady, ale will be a refreshing end to our journey. I follow you."

Behind the party, Louvel spoke to Jorgon, who loped out of the bailey. Margaret led the party inside. *I hope he likes the new soup I ordered. If it fails, at least Cook has prepared his favorite foods.*

Small herbed balls of bread dough boiled in vegetable broth fit upon their spoons. Margaret beamed at Alfred's "Mmm" after his first bite. As usual, after Margaret brought her bowl to her mouth to swallow the remaining broth. Everyone watched Hartun and Scandy wrestle the serving board with half a roast pig through the door and to the serving table. Margaret sighed her relief the meat had not hit the rushes. Everyone applauded Cook as she entered to carve. Haesel on one side of the hall and Alura on the other served the meat-filled wooden boards. Hartun and Scandy returned from the kitchen and offered Alfred and Margaret the vegetables before they passed bowls of boiled turnips and carrots to the men.

The party consumed most of the second half of pork and all the vegetables. As the men ate, several tried to engage Sauville or Louvel in conversation, but both refused to speak. *Only they know what happened. Alfred cannot boast about his accomplishments; they must tell the story. I wager they have a plan.*

To demonstrate how to eat her new dessert idea, Margaret cut her apple and chose cheese from the board before her and Alfred. She placed the slice upon an apple wedge and bit into them. Alfred followed her example, took one bite, and nodded his approval. The men watched and most tried adding cheese to their apple slices. As the men lingered over the last of their feast, the boys filled their mugs. Sauville nodded to Louvel. They stood and approached the dais.

"My lady, may we tell you of our journey, the tournament, and of our return?" asked Sauville.

"Please tell the hall, for we are all eager to hear it."

The pair faced the knights. Scandy, Hartun, Alura, and Haesel stood by the servants' entrance. Straight-faced, Alfred leaned back and rested his mug on the end of his chair arm. Margaret folded her hands in her lap. *I see not their faces. I wish I were seated with the men.*

Louvel began. "Our journey to the tournament was without event. On the road, we met pilgrims going to south to Canterbury or north to York. We saw wagons going to market or returning home. Everyone treated our lord with respect, but mostly they stared as we passed. We think most knew who he is. Word of a Saxon lord seems to have spread." Louvel looked to his partner.

Sauville began his part with, "We arrived at Lord Wilbur's estate Monday midday. Lord Wilbur's sentries were surprised to see us, but they let us pass. At the edge of the tourney field, we were met by Lord Wilbur's seneschal, who showed shock when he learned Lord Alfred's name. After he assigned us a place to camp, he sent a page scurrying to the bailey beyond. As we were unloading the wagon, a knight charged out the bailey toward us. Everyone in the camps surrounding the field stopped to watch him. His horse reared in front of our lord, but Lord Alfred moved not. 'Begone!' he yelled. 'This tournament is for real knights. You are a false one.' Our lord answered, 'Does Lord Wilbur still fear me? Is that why he wants me gone? Or is it you who fear me and what I can do?' Everyone heard him. The knight put his hand to his sword, as did our lord. 'I fear no man, least of all you.' Lord Alfred said, 'I hope we meet on the field, Sir Portier. Give my regards to Lord Wilbur, if he has the strength to hear it.'

Their men laughed.

Why said he that? Knew he not he set all against him? Of course. Alfred already knew they would be against him. He is not one of them. Attend. Louvel is speaking.

"We set our campsite. Others turned away from us and made a point to camp far from us. We cared not, for that was to our advantage. Tuesday morn, a priest said Mass outdoors. Wilbur and his people sat on platforms. After the service, Lord Wilbur stood and announced the tournament rules had changed. He announced, 'Instead of the first-place and second-place winners receiving gifts, the first-place winner will take all. Each man who competes risks his helmet, armor, and sword. The winner takes it and risks his winnings and his gear when fights another man. I set who fights whom and in what order.'"

"Would that you could have heard the uproar!" reported Sauville. "Words we can report," he looked Margaret's way, "include 'Liar!' 'Cheat!' and 'Unfair to draw us with rewards and then take what is ours!' Many swore oaths and refused to fight. Wilbur got red-faced and roared, 'My tournament! My rules!'"

Sauville continued with, "When the noise quieted, Lord Alfred announced, 'See, Lord Wilbur is afraid. Afraid one of us will defeat Sir Portier and win the tournament. I know not if you can, but I am cert I will do it.' Lord Alfred threw his arms wide and asked, 'Who is cert enough he can win and who brave enough to join me in the attempt?' In the silence, our lord added, "Come now. There must be at least one Norman here who thinks he can defeat a Saxon.'"

He won! How?

Louvel continued the story. "Our lord then said, 'If we are to risk our fighting gear and our honor, then we should set the rules.

If not, Lord Wilbur, we will cross the realm and declare you make false promises. We will shred your reputation.' Other knights promised Wilbur the same fate. Wilbur went pale and relented. 'Set the rules as you will, but it must be by majority. The last winner fights Sir Portier. The tournament starts on the morrow.' Wilbur and his party disappeared into the bailey. Wilbur offered no food or drink, entertainment or feast. Again, he broke custom. I returned to camp and let Sauville and our lord counsel with those who wished to fight. By the end of the day, of the twenty-six knights who had arrived, only our lord and six others set the rules and the fight order."

"What rules?" called out Sir Claude.

Sauville answered. "No man must fight more than twice in a day. A winner may rest for the time he wishes so long as his second fight looks to end before sunset. Fights must stay within the field border and continue until one man yields or cannot fight because he is knocked senseless or is bleeding to death. As the host of the tournament, Lord Wilbur was still required to keep and to care for any man injured badly enough to need attention and time to heal before he could return home. As Lord Wilbur wished, winners gain the loser's fight gear; the winner of the tournament takes all. Plus a war horse, its reins, saddle, and such. Wilbur must surrender those or be labeled a cheat. Finally, the order of fighting was determined by drawing stones out of a pouch. If Portier fights, he must draw as well. No exceptions."

The knights and Syghelm cheered, for they remembered seeing Lord Alfred return wearing his helmet, mail, and sword. Through the noise, Margaret turned and acknowledged, "You have both your revenge and a reputation. Well done, Alfred."

"Wait until you hear how I did it."

As Louvel and Sauville gestured, the men quieted.

"A few knights had left Tuesday before combat began; the rest stayed to watch," reported Louvel. "Wednesday morn, two dark stones among the light; each man drew. The knights fought hard; both were injured and kept fighting. The loser yielded, dropped his possessions on the field, and left to have his squires treat him. We ate while the winner rested. That afternoon knight three smashed knight two so hard on his helmet with his shield that the man dropped and was carried from the field. Before we supped, two sets of knight's gear lay at the field's edge. Some of the knights who had refused to fight accepted Lord Wilbur's hospitality, but the fighters and most of the rest of them refused to dine with Wilbur and ate their own food at their own campfires. Such is how honorable men behave before a knave. Three of them promised to guard the winnings overnight. The watchers kept their word.

"Thursday knight three defeated fighter four, but he lost to knight five. The pile of winnings had doubled. Friday morn, all of Wilbur's men and his Saxons gathered to see the fighting. Portier won the morning battle with knight five. Knight six drew the afternoon battle and lost as well." Louvel, turned to the dais. "My lord, only you know the next part."

Alfred rose. "That night I met with all with but Portier. I went to each tent and told each man the same. Should I win on Friday morning, all the booty I wanted was Portier's and Wilbur's. Gladly would I return their possessions if they would grant me one boon. Should I, in my lifetime, want their assistance, on their honor, they would pledge to come to my aid. Four of the six agreed. Two said they would rather die than owe a Saxon a favor. I immediately returned those four knights' possessions so Wilbur could not have them. I knew if I defeated Portier, Wilbur would challenge me. I was ready for it." Alfred nodded to the pair and sat.

In the silent hall, Sauville took up the story. "Saturday, we had filled the wagon with the tent and our supplies. Lord Wilbur arrived wearing his fighting gear and his sword. Wilbur sat on his platform. He looked smug and took wagers against Lord Alfred. We three had watched and studied Portier. Each of us saw a different weakness. Louvel saw Portier lifted his sword higher when his downstroke is right to left than when he cross stroked left to right. I noticed how his footwork revealed a new direction change and when he thrust forward. Our lord saw even more, but I doubt he will tell us what. Lord Alfred began as if he were afraid with weak parries and tentative thrusts. Portier became cocky. He played with Lord Alfred, and our lord let him. When Portier least expected it, Lord Alfred charged and drove him backward and off the field. We thought Lord Alfred mad when he turned his back on Portier to walk to the center of the field. Angry, Portier charged; Lord Alfred spun around and thrust his sword into Portier's ribs. Only his chainmail saved him. Portier fell back.

Sauville paused. "Remember what you were taught while squiring? Never, never fight in anger. You will make mistakes which may cost you your life."

Louvel reported, "Then the battle was on. Our lord may be a bit shorter and a stone lighter than Portier, but he is in better condition, younger, stronger, and faster. Our lord defeated Portier in the fiercest battle of all. Portier fought well and honorably, but he fought in anger and lost. Portier surrendered his possessions and limped away, sweating and bleeding from his wounds as his squires took him off the field."

Louvel continued. "Wilbur was aghast and roared his fury. Wilbur rose and demanded Lord Alfred fight him. Lord Alfred shouted, 'Not part of the rules, Sir Wilbur. Again, are you trying to cheat an honest knight?' Lord Alfred announced, 'If I lose the fight, you win what is left beside the field and my possessions. If I win, I gain what I have honorably won, and your helmet, mail, the sword you are wearing AND your battle horse.'"

"Lord Wilbur yelled back, 'Not my battle horse!'

"'Done!' yelled Lord Alfred. He had Wilbur on the field. 'I am going to piss. Then we fight,' he said. Our lord walked off the field and took his time." Louvel looked to Sauville.

"You know how it ended. An old man, full of pride and too many meals, thought his power and bluster could make our lord afraid. He was wrong. Lord Alfred's fight was honest; Wilbur tried tricks and cheats no honorable knight would use. After Wilbur lost, he refused to part with his possessions. Over a dozen visiting knights, who had stood aside from the tournament, stormed the field and stripped Wilbur of his gear. They pushed him to the ground and surrounded Lord Alfred. They carried our lord's winnings to our wagon with swords drawn and stood between us and Wilbur's men. Strangely, Wilbur's knights charged not as he had demanded, but helped the old man into his bailey and closed the gates. Our lord saluted and thanked the knights who had aided us, and we left immediately. At some point, Lord Alfred took a forest path. We covered our tracks, walked far into the night and all day Sunday before we rested that night." Sauville turned to the dais, "My Lord Alfred, may I have the honor?"

Alfred smiled as he nodded and placed his left hand on the table beside Margaret's. Without looking her way, he nudged his littlest finger against hers.

Sauville called out. "Jorgon, bring it inside!"

Jorgon stood in the doorway, and was heartily laughed at by all. With an oversized helmet covering his eyes and nose, his dragging chain mail on his left side, while his right hand held high a sheathless long sword, he looked a court jester as he wobbled toward the dais trying to carry all that weight and struggling to see where he was going.

The men stood and applauded their lord as they shouted, "Well done!" and other compliments. Margaret stopped laughing as she placed her hand over her husband's. "Oh, Alfred, what fun you had!" Alfred raised her hand and kiss its back. Margaret blushed. He kept her hand as he stood.

Jorgon placed the sword on the dais floor, pulled the mail forward and piled it there as well. He removed the helmet and placed it atop the mail, bowed to his lord and lady, and stepped back to join the foursome at the servant's door.

Alfred motioned for his men to sit. "Men, when you enter the hall, on the wall you face, you will find mounted Wilbur's helmet and sword. A reminder to all who enter. I disarm my enemies; they will lose their lives if I so will it. Wilbur lost his reputation because he tried to cheat honest knights. Who will follow him now? Be not like him. Keep your honor." Alfred dropped his serious demeanor and finished happily, "Another barrel of ale for all the honorable men in this room." Alfred looked right, "Jorgon, you too. Scandy, Hartun, op that last barrel. Girls, best you leave."

The first pitcher went to the head table. Margaret demurred, "My lord, I think it best I leave. Enjoy this celebration. I shall await you in the keep." She turned and left by the back door. Behind her, a chorus of voices toasted Alfred and started a rousing song about winning and drinking.

29

Holy Days

Margaret rose, washed, dressed, and braided her hair before the first bell. At its sound, she shook her husband, "Alfred, rise for Mass."

"Oh, my head! Not this day."

"What shall I tell Father?"

Alfred groaned again. "Tell him ... Drat! What a penance he shall give me for not setting a good example."

Margaret smiled and moved away. Alfred sat on the side of the bed, groaning and holding his head.

"You are barely bruised."

Alfred glanced up. "This time I could fight back."

"Alfred, your men are proud of you." Margaret added, "I am proud of you as well." She approached. "You not only won the day, you behaved honorably to the losers. Others will speak well of you." She lifted each foot and inserted Alfred's legs into his braies, which she bunched at his knees. After she put on his chausses and fastened his boots, she offered Alfred her hands and assisted him to rise. His garments fell to his ankles. Margaret handed him his loincloth and turned to the clothes tree to fetch his shirt and tunic. She pulled up his braies and tied his belt before she did the same to his chausses. Like a child, Alfred let her put his hands through the sleeves and lift the shirt over his head. Margaret helped him don his tunic and over tunic, and helped him with his sword.

"Stay standing. You want not to return abed," she warned. Instead Alfred lowered his head, and she combed his hair forward. The second bell rang as the couple turned to leave. This morn Margaret unlocked the keep door and handed the key to Alfred, who managed to pocket it.

"Please act rested and sober."

"I know. Head up, shoulders back."

Please fall not from the ladder and crack op your head.

After Mass, Alfred took small spoonfuls of pottage until he was cert his stomach would hold them. "Thank you for tending me. How reached I our bed?"

"Syghelm and Jorgon brought you and helped me put you to bed. Your knights were indisposed." *Now I know you snore when you drink too much. Say it not. He is in no humor for a tease.* Margaret looked down the hall with a smile. *They look as bad as you. Poor sentries, who must labor in their state.* "My lord, do you wish to return to the keep?"

Alfred shook his head. He informed their knights, "No practice this morn." To Margaret he said, "Fetch Cormac."

When Cormac arrived, Margaret gave him her place and left to settle meals with Cook.

Friday the men resumed their morning practice while Margaret assisted Leoma and Hopa in baking for All Souls Eve on October 31. The "soul cakes," as they were called, were palm-sized rounds of honey-sweetened bread dough, either plain or flavored with herbs. A person offered them to their loved ones who had died. They were either fried or baked on a water-soaked wooden slab so the bottoms burned not. *One each for Mother, Father, Grandfather, and Grandmother. Alfred will want three, Elbeorht's first husband, his father, and Sir Cyrille. Best I make more should he need them,* thought Margaret as she worked.

Saturday morn, Rammeg Elder stood on a ladder and used a hand drill to make holes high in the hall wall opposite the main door. Alfred supervised. Rammeg Younger handed his father the hammer and pegs. Alfred handed up Wilbur's helmet to be set between two pegs. Below the helmet, Wilbur's sword also hung on two pegs, one between the guard and the handle and the other holding the blade at an upward angle so it looked ready to strike. Margaret was in the kitchen helping to make Sunday's All Saints Day feast. When she arrived to dine, she looked up.

"My lord, that is a fearsome sight. Might the sword fall and kill someone?"

"See the leather thongs tying the helmet and the sword to their pegs?"

"I do now. Will you speak of them before we dine?"

"They are a silent warning." He turned his head from admiring them to meet Margaret's gaze. "'Challenge me not' they will say to any who enter."

Margaret nodded agreement. *He stands tall, shoulders back, head high. He has back his honor and his pride since that beating. I see it in him. Please God, let him not become haughty.* She accepted his arm and proceeded to the dais.

Before they supped, Father Manntun arrived at the keep carrying a wooden box with a letter tied to its top. Margaret placed her stitchery in the basket beside her on the floor, stood, curtseyed to the priest and her lord. She followed them to the top floor.

"Which do you want first, my lord, the letter or the parcel?"

"The letter," said Alfred as he sat; Margaret stood behind him.

Father set the box on Margaret's stool, slipped the parchment from under the ropes and opt it. He smiled as he read it, and then informed the couple, "The parcel is from Lord Charles of Royal Oaks and his lady. The letter reads, 'To Lord Alfred and Lady Margaret. We are overjoyed to learn your good news. Please accept this gift in honor of your marriage. We hope it finds you well and happy. We are well. Charles Younger is strong and cheerful. We hope he soon sleeps the night. We expect him to be an older brother before Easter next. We have sent letters to Raymond and Cecily reporting your marriage. Please forgive us for being bold. They write us, and we answer with our news and now yours. You both are always welcome here. Please visit as soon as you are able. Your loving brother and sister in Christ and in blood. Lord Charles and Lady Cleanthe of Royal Oaks.'" Father handed the letter to Margaret and the wooden box to Alfred and left. Margaret sat.

Using his dagger, Alfred pried op the top, looked inside and leaned the top against a stool leg. He offered the box's contents to Margaret. She leaned to look within and smiled at seeing fine, cream linen folded around something in the center. Alfred set the box on the small table between them. Together they unfolded the cloth.

Alfred pulled up a pewter candlestick and smiled at his wife. She lifted a fold and held its mate.

Margaret gasped, "Oh Charles, you remembered! How kind you are to part with them." Margaret's eyes teared.

"Remembered what?" asked Alfred as he handed her his.

Unable to speak, Margaret clutched them to her breasts. "A wedding gift to my parents from my mother's father." Margaret placed them in her lap to wipe away her tears, so she could see them clearly. "Mother loved these and used them every Sunday we had candles. They graced the table when King Henry arrived to dine with my father." *I can say 'father' now without it hurting. Mayhap some day I will be able to say his name.* "That was the night I met King Henry. I offered to help Queen Matilda birth a healthy child and gained three boons from him if I succeeded." Margaret looked up into kind blue eyes. "They are a reminder of the day I started my life toward this place." Margaret's eyes sparkled. "Toward you."

"Shall we continue your mother's tradition and use them every Sunday? We could start on the morrow. Auspicious to begin on All Saints Day."

Margaret nodded. She placed the candlesticks on the table next to the box. She sat on his lap, put her arms around him, and kissed his cheek. "You are a good man, Alfred. Remind me to thank Queen Matilda for introducing us." Margaret put her cheek to his.

Discomfited, Alfred muttered. "Thank you. Yes."

Just then Midryth called up the stairs, "Time to sup."

Alfred stood, and Margaret shifted to kiss him full on the mouth. Alfred held her close and explored her mouth with his tongue. "You test my will every moment you are awake and oft walk through my dreams." Alfred set her back from him. "Later."

After Vespers, the villagers began an ancient custom older than the Church that tried to ban it. Despite the Church's teachings, admonitions, and even injunctions, the people refused to abandon Samhain, the end of the harvest and the next day's beginning of the new year. Everyone in the bailey and village set out their soul cakes to feed whom they feared, the dead. This night between years, they returned from the hereafter to trouble the world. To placate the dead, the living offered food and sometimes cups of ale. The living doused all fires and stayed inside. In the morning, missing or half-eaten cakes and dry cups proved the dead had been about in the night. After the first Mass of the new year, families relit their fires.

As Margaret dressed for Mass, she pondered. *Should I tell Alfred I long ago pretended to be Mother's ghost? Then others rode Night about Father's bailey when he did an evil to frighten him to better behavior. Now only Caitlin and Jorgon know it. Not yet. Next Samhain, if we are doing well together.* Margaret nodded to herself. *Yes, Wait. The night before the next Samhain is a better time.*

The first day of November, the Church celebrated All Saints Day. Father Manntun's sermon included prayers for the dead and prayers for those who might still be in Purgatory awaiting Heaven. His list of what each person must do to become one of God's saints included: obey the church, live a righteous life, do good works, pray for the souls of the departed. For each deed, Father gave examples of what to do specific to men, to women, and to children. Father reminded them this holy day was especially blessed because the new year also occurred on a Sunday. Each household feasted as it willed. Margaret beamed her happiness at seeing the lit candles before them as they dined.

Margaret waited until after Vespers to ask her next Sunday question. "Alfred, met we in Winchester before Princess Matilda was birthed?

Alfred sighed. "Yes." He opt the keep gate. He took Margaret's hand to lead her up the steps as the world quickly darkened.

That eliminates the trip from Forest keep to Winchester. How could we meet in Winchester? I was locked in the keep with Queen Matilda during her confinement. I needs confirm what he just said. "In Winchester," repeated Margaret as they reached the ladder.

"In Winchester," he repeated as he held the ladder for her.

"Thank you, Alfred." Margaret climbed. As she waited for Alfred inside the keep door, she thought, *I must remember each day. We arrived near the end of November. Which day? Day twenty, day twenty-one? Two? Good enough.* Margaret bid Ferrant good night and followed Alfred to their room. *To the night before the princess's birth, the seventh day in February. Handsome as he is, I should remember meeting him, but nothing comes to mind. I remember meeting the king's constable, but he is Norman, and we were shut up after that. I did sneak a look at the hall on the princess's christening day, but I remember not if I spoke with anyone. And he said we met in the between time. When? I know. Each of the next Sundays ask for the month. Start with November. Mayhap that will jostle my mind.*

30

A Journey

The next morn, preparations for winter continued. Alfred hunted wolves. He killed, skinned and sent back two pelts to be cleaned and pegged to a barn wall to be scraped and the leather dried. Saxons sought the forest for dead wood for their winter fires. Alfred walked and marked with stakes the first area of forest to be cleared. In late afternoon, Felamaere visited Alfred. Margaret was sewing Epiphany gifts when Alfred found her fireside in the keep. At seeing him, Margaret dropped her sewing and stood. "My lord, Alfred, what is amiss?"

Alfred grabbed her shoulders. "My lord. My lord has sickened. I fear he is dying. We must go to him anon."

"Order the horses. I shall be ready when they are."

Alfred steadied himself and shook his head. "Dark soon. We have enemies and must go in force. We leave at dawn."

Margaret hugged Alfred hard, "I am so sorry, I will order the household and pack." She escorted Alfred back to the hall and asked for two knights.

"Caitlin, please do this for us, for me. I know not how long we will be gone, but you and Cormac can manage, can you not?"

"We can. Given the state of things, with you two gone, we could become targets. I think we should stay in the bailey at night."

"I agree. Take our room. I will order clean linens."

"You said the next two days' menus for the hall are set. After that, I will do that as well."

Margaret hugged Caitlin. "Thank you, my friend." She added, "Your babe. You will not tax yourself with this? You will nap during the day? Promise me."

"I promise. Other than giving orders and sitting on the dais, all I will do is nap and sew. Nothing hard."

"If he thinks it not, ask Felamaere to send for news of any enemies coming our way."

"I will have Cormac do it."

"Thank you." Again, Margaret hugged Caitlin and left to order food for the journey.

Mass was a quick service. Jorgon and Daelton waited outside with the party's horses. *Why is my saddle not on Night? Where is he?* Margaret looked to Alfred.

"Night is too old for the fast riding we must do. This horse is young and gentle enough."

"I shall miss him." After Alfred helped his wife to her seat, she tied herself to it, tightened her scarf, and pulled her mantle close. *How fast can we go in a day? Ask not. At the end of this day, ask how far we got.* Margaret watched Arnaud, Bertrand, Demetre, and Claude mount their horses. *Seven left home should be enough. Are not two sufficient? Ask not why we need four. Count all Normans against us.*

At the road, the party turned east and galloped until they reached the King's Inn. They walked their horses north two miles and galloped two. They switched between riding and walking until they stopped at dusk.

"The bread is good, is it not?"

Alfred sopped up the last of his stew with a chunk. "Yes. Stew is good too. We must remember this inn for our return."

"How far are we?"

"About seventeen miles. Good weather and dry roads helped. That you ride on your platform almost as fast as a man astride helped us. Ahead the paths may not be as easy." Alfred finished his ale and leaned back in his chair. "Late on the morrow, we should reach Oxford."

"What is it?"

"Ancient Saxon hill fort, now a Norman town. Sits where two rivers meet. I shall send Claude ahead to find a place for us."

"Will it become even colder the farther north we go?"

"Most likely, but snow is unusual. I saw it but once in all my years there." Alfred watched Margaret's shoulders droop. "Best you sleep now. We have six more days ahead."

Margaret stood, curtsied to her husband, and took the stairs. In the women's room, she found the innkeeper's youngest sitting on one of the beds with her legs swinging to and fro.

"As commanded by your lord, I have saved this bed for you, my lady." The girl jumped off and curtsied. "It is all yours."

Margaret nodded and watched the girl depart. *Ignore the glares of the women on the floor pads. What did this luxury cost us? Mind it not. Accept his gift and thank him in the morn.*

The next evening's supper was a sumptuous meal of broth, roast pig, boiled vegetables, bread, butter, ale, and apples stewed in honey and dried lavender blooms. Margaret was surfeited, warm, and happy. She looked around the table and thought something kind of each man. "Thank you for your company. Sitting on something that is not moving feels good."

After Alfred started chuckling, the others joined in.

"My lady," began Bertrand, "we like your company because, unlike other women, you talk with us but chatter not. Have you other questions, my lady?"

"I think not. I have learned much from hearing how each of you trained." Margaret looked to Alfred and saw his tiny nod. "If you will excuse me, my lord, knights, I will retire." The men stood and watched her leave. They sat not until her head had disappeared up the stairwell.

"My lord?"

Alfred looked to Demetre. "Five, six days northeast. Before we arrive, we must stay the night in a Saxon hut beside a lake. Something I needs do. That night you will guard us." The four nodded. "On the morrow, who rides ahead?"

Demetre answered, "Claude is senior, but I will go, if he agrees."

"Enjoy yourself."

Alfred announced, "I will take this corner. Please array yourselves accordingly." He stood and moved his chair aside. The men shoved the table and chairs toward the room and rolled into blankets on the floor between their lord and the rest of the travelers in the great room. Alfred's sword was not the only one atop its sheath.

In the morn, Margaret asked not about the fifth man who rode with them, but she worried. *Who is he? Doth Alfred know him? Why is he added? Is he safe?* She noted he seemed of an age to Bertrand and Arnaud. He even looks a bit like them. *Is he a half Norman as well? Why need we him? How safe are we going this far north? Accept not the queen's advice this time. Ask Alfred as soon as possible.*

The next night's stop was a remote inn beyond the road and buried into the forest. The hearth fire was high, the food was good, but only three other men sat at one of the remaining three tables. Alfred left his men behind in the great room as he followed his wife up the steep stairs that clung to the east wall.

A room of our own? Margaret shrugged as she climbed. *Why not? They know I am his wife.* Alfred placed his hand on the small of her back as she opt the door.

I hope the strangers depart before we return to the great room. Their glares at us are evil enough. I want not to see their hatred again. Margaret saw the double bed with its coverings turned down, floor pads in the corner and the single candle on the table beside the bed. She heard the door bar bang into its brackets and turned.

"Who is the new man? Is he trustworthy?" Are we safe?"

"Emile worked with Bertrand two years ago. Says he fights well, is a calm man. On trial only for bed and board until he proves his worth. Keeping him makes a dozen knights."

"I want not to have him behind me."

"Worry not, wife. Demetre and Claude eye him close. Well you know their protection of you." Alfred placed his hands upon her waist and drew her to him. Now are you appeased?"

"Only if Demetre and Claude are."

Alfred kissed her forehead. "Please be willing."

Margaret put her hands on his shoulders and whispered, "I like the ways you make me so."

His kiss was slow, sweet. Margaret clasped her hands around his neck as she returned his sweetness. Alfred hungered for more as she pressed her lips harder to his and her body into him. Naked, they warmed each other, the bedding, and their passion. *No need to hurry. Enjoy.* At each "M-m-m," Alfred repeated his actions. Margaret pulled him atop her. *How to drive him mad?* she wondered. She soon learned what to do and how best to do it. Their loving completed, Margaret and Alfred clung to each other as their bodies cooled. Margaret sighed her pleasure and kissed the part of Alfred nearest her lips. She rolled and curled against his back as he faced the door and felt for his sword. *Once far apart. Now this close. I wondered how a marriage is between a man and a woman. A precious bond knitting us together, me into him, him into me. Caitlin once called this lovemaking. Each time, I feel my heart open more to him and I feel his.* Margaret smiled into the blackness around them. *This is a deed, not words. Is love making its way into my heart? I needs be cert before I say it.* Margaret slumbered. In deep night, Margaret awoke enough to respond to Alfred. Afterward, she told herself *Twice is nice.* She fell back asleep.

The next day felt colder, damp, but it smelled not of rain. The party left the road for a forest trail. Two days later, the party took a trail that wound left and right to avoid wet, boggy places. The ground rose and fell in odd patterns. That night they stopped on a small hillock at a wattle and daub structure beside murky water. The men made their camp. Margaret lifted the door drape and stepped into a hut warmed by a fire ringed with rocks. A pot hung from a tripod over the flames. Margaret sniffed. *A hearty meat and vegetable soup. Must not be an inn nearby. He ordered this from some poor Saxon family. Wonder where they are sleeping this night.* She spotted a double bed against the far wall and a table set for two to her right. In its center, three rounds of bread leaned on a fourth. *Prepared well for us. Why are we so far from the road? How close are we to his lord's estate?*

Alfred entered and dropped their satchels on the bed. He motioned Margaret to take a stool. He ladled soup into wooden bowls and served her. He sat, took up a wooden spoon and gobbled his first bowl. Margaret picked up a round and broke it in half. She pulled out some of the middle and dropped it into her bowl. Alfred copied her and resumed eating. After Alfred emptied his bowl, he stirred the pot and took half the remaining soup.

31

Secrets

Margaret had consumed only half her meal as Alfred finished his. "This lake is very important to us Saxons. It taught an important lesson to the Normans. Want to hear the story?" At Margaret's nod, Alfred continued. "You finish while I tell. After Henry's father invaded, killed our king, and declared himself king, the Normans and their allies overran our land. William the Conqueror apportioned land to his followers. The man given this land arrived with knights. He spoke no Saxon, but he made them understand. They stood in families. When he learned who was their leader, he made that man watch him kill his children and his wife. Then he beheaded him."

Margaret crossed herself and clasped her hands together in a quick prayer for the dead.

"Like many in the land, he ruled by terror. Beat men. Ravaged women. The Saxons planted crops, built a hall, anything he wanted.

To keep himself safe, he kept a girl as his food and drink taster and bedmate. He became complacent, but he stayed cruel. After the first harvest, he and his men feasted in the hall. They woke in the morning alone. In secret, the Saxons had prepared well. The knight found his new estate bare. Every bit of crop, everything in the kitchen the smokehouse and storage sheds. All they had was what they wore, and their horses. The knight sent his men in all directions, but he found nothing. Word spread what had happened, but no Norman found the missing Saxons."

"They went into the lake?"

Alfred nodded. They had built and hidden boats. In one night, they left false tracks on a road, and disappeared." Alfred smiled. "Of course, word reached the Conqueror. The king summoned the knight and his men and banished them. The Saxons returned not. Word spread that God had taken them into heaven and destroyed all the ill-gotten gains of the Normans. Fearing God's same punishment, other Norman lords stopped killing and abusing their Saxons. A year passed. No Saxons. No one wanted the cursed land so it lay fallow."

"Then what happened?" whispered Margaret with awe.

"Two more years passed with the buildings empty and the land weeds. The Normans had learned harming Saxons brings disaster. Spring of the fourth year, a knight passed by. He saw the land had been plowed and crops were inching up. He reported to his lord, who sent word to the king. In summer, a few old men were spotted weeding the fields. Each month more men and then boys appeared. They rebuilt wattle and daub huts, and old women arrived to cook for them. No one disturbed them. No one even dared approach. The Normans believed God was sending back the Saxons a few at a time to see how Normans would treat them.

"Before the harvest, King William sent a lord to claim the land. He had learned Saxon and knew something of our ways. When he harmed not the Saxons, they harvested the fields. After the harvest, the girls and children appeared. The women cleaned the hall. He paid several to cook for him and his knights. The estate prospered, grew, and flourished. The lord is a good man, who has never harmed or killed a Saxon. When his people do wrong, his punishments are just."

"And…"

"The Normans learned to treat their Saxons better; they stopped killing us or starving us. They believe we know how to disappear, that God somehow favors us."

Margaret looked askance at Alfred. "There is more to this story."

"Yes," he smirked. "Normans think these waters are unnatural and will not enter them. They extend many miles north, many miles west, and a few miles east, but it is not a lake. It is a dangerously boggy waterway dotted with earthen hillocks. Step into it and you sink. Normans think it a treacherous lake." Alfred paused and revealed, "We Saxons call it 'the fens.'"

"Sir Cai! Sir Cai of the fens!"

Alfred nodded and Margaret gasped. Just as sudden as her realization, Margaret's eyes narrowed dangerously.

"Is Sir Cai your lord?"

"He is."

Margaret's tone threatened Alfred. "Did you send him to me? In February? After the princess was born?"

"No," averred Alfred. "I did not." Alfred shook his head. "I had told him of you. After he attended the princess's christening, he stayed two meet you." Margaret glowered. Alfred held up his hands and vowed, "I swear! I swear I speak truth."

Margaret stood. "He is ill. Mayhap dying. Oh Alfred, we must go to him at once."

Margaret saw Alfred in a new light. "He is the one who kept you for six years, trained you, made you visit your family." Alfred nodded. *He told the truth. His stories are true.*

"We are less than half a day away; but, first, I must tell you more." Alfred took her hand. "Please sit. You must do something first."

While staring at Alfred, Margaret withdrew her hand from him and sat.

"The fens also hold an ancient secret. There are walkways between some of the islands. We Saxons follow a custom we brought with us centuries ago. Once in a lifetime—but only once—we were permitted to ask the gods for a great boon. In exchange for that boon, we had to offer the gods a great gift."

Margaret froze. *I remember a bloody story about Saxons sacrificing people.* "A human sacrifice?"

"Not humans. Something rare, precious. Something metal."

"A ring? A bracelet? A circlet?"

"Yes, like that. We did it alone, in secret, and by the light of a full moon."

"What said the Church about this?"

"The Church forbade it."

Margaret was shocked by his expression. *They still do it!*

"Now the Church knows nothing of it. We think it has forgot. We believe God sees us and chooses whose wish He shall grant. When a Saxon has a great wish, he goes into the fens and prays to God under a full moon. But we still 'donate' something metal." Alfred shrugged. "The old gods may still be alive." Alfred stood and retrieved something from under the satchels. He placed it on the table and sat.

"You seek a great boon from God and intend to offer the king's sword."

"Not me. You."

"Me?"

"The king gave the sword to you. If you want to ask God for a great wish, donate this."

"I gave it you. It is yours to wish with."

Alfred turned his head from right to left and stopped to face his wife. "I already have what I most want." Alfred's even gaze hid his meaning. "If you have a great wish, I shall gift this back to you. Think, Margaret. If God grants you one thing in your life, for what would you ask?" Alfred stood. "I leave you until it is time. When I return, I shall hear your decision." Alfred stepped outside..

Margaret stared at the sword. *For what might I ask? A long life? No. What if I do, and it is filled with misery and sorrows? A happy life? What if it lasts only a year or two, and I die in childbirth? Dying in childbirth is so common. Healthy children. I could ask for that. What if they are born healthy and then die by some other means? Good children. Good health. A happy marriage. A long marriage. Crops that never fail. What? What?* Margaret pondered possibilities, and fretted she might choose wrong. She imagined the rest of her life with all the successes, troubles, and calamities that might befall her. *Ask for Courage. Faith. Love that lasts a lifetime.* Then she hit upon it. The one thing that could get her through it all, bad or good; the one thing she most wanted, most needed. She loosed a heavy sigh. Margaret lay her arms on the table and set her head upon them. She felt a calmness in her body and peace in her heart. *I know for what to ask.*

When Alfred returned, he thought his wife sleeping. "Margaret?"

Margaret raised her head and smiled at him. "I am ready."

"You must change your clothes into rags. Like a pilgrim to God." From one satchel, he pulled old Saxon clothes he had taken from the rags box and a pair of boots with holes in the soles. "These are also practical. The boards of the walkways are old and often get wet in spring floods. I know not when they last were replaced. Please be careful to break not a board and wet your feet or lose a boot." Alfred turned his back as Margaret changed.

"Done."

Alfred picked up the sword and turned. With both hands, he offered the sheathed blade. "I gift you this sword in its sheath. Do with them what you will." Margaret accepted the sword with both hands. "You must kneel in moonlight above the waters. Release the sheath into the water first. Raise the sword to glint in the moonlight. Think your wish as you slip it into the water. Throw it not. Speak not from the time you step out of the boat until the time you return. Hide the sword at your side as we pass the men. Are you ready?" Margaret nodded. Alfred led. He walked between the men and Margaret. "We go for a walk. You need not come."

The angle of the moon is ahead. I see grasses in the distance and no water.

At the shore, Alfred pulled a boat from beneath the tree boughs that hid it and launched it. The boat scraped against the dry ground, and Margaret looked back, fearful a knight had heard. Alfred launched the front end and held the back against the bank. He held Margaret's hand as she stepped in and sat on the wooden board near the bow. Alfred took the back board, lifted a flat-faced paddle from the bottom and pushed off into the darkness. Alfred's careful dips into the murky water went unheard. He paddled toward a glade of water grasses and pushed through them. No one could see them now.

Margaret shivered at the cold breeze coming at her. *How safe is this thing? The night is black; dark ahead, dark here, but moonlight ahead.* The silence seemed to hug Margaret. She tucked her arms inside her mantle and hunched down to hide from it.

The fog-like wisps shift and dance away. The bow knifes through the grasses that hide us. Mysterious. Good or bad? The boat turned and took a new path. *How knows he where we go? Far ahead grass tops gleam in the light.* As if to show them the way, moonlight danced on the moving water between the man-high grasses. The silence was broken only by an occasional swish of the paddle. Even as they moved, the world seemed to have stopped. Time was no more. She looked up to a million stars with one great swath of stars which looked to be a white wave.

Mother, are you watching me? Mother, please protect me. Inside her mantle, Margaret clutched the sword. *He knows these waters. Around a raised spit of dirt or a forest of grasses. When to follow the water left or right. What else do Saxons know we do not?* Margaret watched the boat slice black water. Suddenly, a thick, black pole appeared beside the boat. Alfred passed it and bumped the bow against a second one. He grabbed the wooden boards between them and held the boat fast. Margaret turned and spotted the first pole now behind Alfred. Hanging between the poles was a string of boards. *Three feet wide? What binds them together? They disappear beyond. Eerie.* Margaret shivered. *Where goes this path?*

Alfred whispered, "We are here. Go with God. I may go not with you. Return safe."

Margaret crossed herself and thought a prayer asking God to accept her act. She pulled up her mantle front to expose the sword on her knees. She handed Alfred the sword and stood. She grabbed the pole and stepped onto the boards, which were inches above the water. *They hold my weight.* Moonlight ahead lit half the strips of wood. Ropes weaved boards together, and thick ropes hung from deep notches in the poles to secure the boards. She clung to the pole as she looked ahead. *Eight, ten feet apart. A walkway. To where?* She reached back, and Alfred put the sword in her hand. She widened her stance against a slight swaying beneath her. Margaret steeled her will and released the pole.

Margaret stepped lightly. With her left hand, she touched the next pole as she reached it. *One, two. three.* Past the third pole the boards angled right. She looked ahead. *This path goes to a great mound. An island! Five poles ahead? Wattle and daub walls on this side. No roof. Dilapidated. Who lived here? When? Grasses almost hide it.* Looking toward the island, she spotted moonlight on the water and splashed across the boards. *That place.*

Margaret reached it and knelt. She looked up. *Beautiful moon, be my light as I do this. I feel the magic. Warmer here. Is it you, God?* She pulled the sheath from the sword. Tip first, she touched the water and paused. She saw small circles in the oily blackness. Margaret slipped the leather-covered boards into the water to her left and watched it silently slide away and disappear. The water smoothed. One hand on the hilt and the other under the flat of the blade, Margaret lifted the sword into the moonlight and to God. It sparkled. She thought, *Oh Lord, I have knelt like this before. To King Henry when I offered to return the sword to him. Now I kneel to You, who made him, who made me. Oh, God, this metal came from deep within the earth You made. I return it to You in all humility and ask you to grant my life's wish.* Margaret kissed the blade and dipped the tip toward the moonlight that streamed to the blackness below. When the blade was half-way gone, she thought her wish as she released her gift. As Alfred had predicted, it slipped away and disappeared to land in muck below. Margaret crossed herself. She stood and blew a kiss to God and to His moon.

Five feet past the turn that led back to the boat, Margaret heard something snap. Her back foot wobbled on a board. The board dropped into the water. She dashed forward. More snapping sounds. The string of boards raced and overtook her. Margaret grabbed the disappearing walkway. In water to her waist, Margaret struggled to pull herself up. Muck sucked at her boots. Her waterlogged clothes dragged her down. Margaret felt herself sinking. She threw her right hand forward and grabbed a board. Right. Left. She pulled herself along the walkway as it disappeared under her weight. She looked up to see a shadowed arm reaching for her. Two more giant grabs and a strong hand grasped her left arm and pulled her to the boat's side. Margaret hung onto the boat's edge.

"Let go!" Alfred sat and leaned back to re-balance the boat before they both drowned. "Give me your other hand!"

"I cannot swim! I dare not!"

"I can. I shall save you. A hand!" Alfred grasped her right wrist and pulled slowly. He shifted as he pulled. "Put a leg over, and I shall have you." Margaret labored under her soaked garments and got her knee over the boat edge. Alfred rolled her into the bottom. Margaret gasped and gasped. "You are safe." Margaret shivered; her teeth chattered. With eyes shut tight, she felt a terror. *Did I blaspheme against God to have done this godless ceremony? Is this His warning to be more faithful? Pray for forgiveness. Then thank Him for letting me live.* She began.

Alfred propelled the boat with strong, swift strokes. He cared not who might hear them as they approached land. Farther from their starting point than he intended, Alfred drove the boat tip onto dirt, jumped out, climbed the landing site, and pulled the boat half out of the water. He pulled Margaret upright and out of the boat. Arms crossed over her chest and shivering, Margaret moved not. Alfred pulled her to himself and held her. When he walked them far enough from the boat, he shouted.

Men came running.

"She fell into the water. Help me get her inside. Someone run ahead. Fire."

Bertrand dashed away. With their arms, Arnaud and Claude made a chair and scooped Margaret into it. Alfred ran beside them and Demetre followed. Sword in hand, Emile stood beside the fire. He sheathed his blade as they approached. Arnaud and Claude entered first and stood Margaret beside a blazing fire. With eyes still shut, her head drooped, she leaned against Alfred, who held her upright.

"Leave a pile of firewood beside the door."

The men left.

Alfred leaned Margaret over the table. "Move not." Margaret's gripped the table edge as her teeth chattered. Alfred ripped and stripped his wife of her rags He wrapped her mantle about her, sat her on a stool ,and pulled her only sock off her blue-mottled, icy foot. With the blanket corner, he wiped her feet dry. and stood her close to the fire. She curled her toes as the hot rocks warmed them. Alfred rubbed her arms, back, backside, legs. Margaret clenched her teeth to stop their chattering. When her husband thought her dry enough, he exchanged the mantle for a woolen blanket. Margaret clutched it to herself. Alfred lay a wolf hide fur side up beside the fire pit. He lay Margaret upon it so she faced the flames. Margaret still shivered as she prayed.

Alfred forced Margaret to surrender the blanket. He lay down with his skin to hers to warm her backside as he draped the dry side of the blanket over them. He whispered, "Turn to me after I warm your backside." Alfred breathed upon her neck.

Margaret stopped praying and returned to the world. She sighed, "Better." After a time, she rolled and buried her head against Alfred's chest. She felt him kiss her head and hold her tight. *Only thought. Reach you.* Margaret believed she had spoken, but she had not. She felt the need of his body, but she was too weak to respond or refuse his desire. Eyes still shut, she turned to the fire and fell asleep.

Margaret felt warmth on her face, opt her eyes, and saw her nose near touched the rocks emanating heat. *Warm. All over.* Alfred had snuggled against her, neck to toes, with his arm over her waist. *Saved me. Cared for me. Stopped desire, Did what I needed. Thought of me first. A sign. He loves me.* She sighed as her heart swelled. *Truly he does.* Alfred rose and knelt beside her to add fat sticks and small logs to the fire. He returned to lie behind her; she felt his skin had cooled. She rolled into his arms so close they shared breath.

He whispered. "I heard. Feared I had lost you."

"I ran to you."

"You fought for your life."

"I knew you would save me." Margaret lifted her head and kissed Alfred full on the mouth. She stretched her arm so her hand could keep his head to her as she increased her fervor. Alfred pulled her even tighter to himself.

"Are you cert?"

Margaret nodded twice. He nibbled here and kissed there. *I choose you.* Margaret gave him her heart, and her body responded. *Love him. No words. Only this.* They expressed their feelings in an intense, shared passion. The ecstasy of their union coursed through her. She kissed his skin again and again and refused to let him roll off her. She hugged his chest tight against hers.

Alfred sighed into her ear. "You are a wild woman. What say you to that?"

I am your wild wife. Margaret wound her legs through his, rolled them to their sides, and snuggled against him. The fire burned to embers. The rocks warmed the sleeping pair.

In deep night, Margaret moaned. Fearing the men would think he was hurting her and charge in, Alfred covered her mouth with his to stop her noises and held her tight to stop her thrashing. Margaret woke and froze.

He whispered, "Who gives you night terrors that you moan and cry out in your sleep?"

"I moan nothing."

Alfred repeated her words, "No. No. Stop, please stop."

Margaret shook her head in denial. Then she whispered, "He is dead."

"Fortunate man!" Alfred repeated, "Who?"

Margaret spoke in halting sentences with great spaces between them. "After Mother died. He cancelled my wedding contract. Named me a slattern. Cut off my hair. Made me his slave." She felt Alfred's chest muscles tighten as he murmured, "He beat you." Margaret made a tiny nod. The she released a sob against his chest.

He hugged his wife and uttered, "Sh-h-h. Sh-h-h, my darling." Into her ear, he promised, "No one will ever hurt you like that again. Upon my life, I swear it."

Margaret wet his chest. Alfred held her and waited patiently until she quieted. Alfred revealed, "Wulf strikes his wife. Once knocked her senseless and deafened an ear." Margaret tried to move, but Alfred refused to release her. "Any man who strikes a woman is weak, a coward, and a bully. He deserves neither her regard nor her love. Fear not, my wife. I shall never strike you. Never." Margaret nodded against his chest. "I feared I was the cause of your terrors. Glad I am not." When Alfred received no response, he continued, "After the first one, I wake you each time as I did this night. Then I distract you."

"Distract me?"

"Guess how." Then he showed her.

As the sun crept to begin its dawn, Margaret, still naked under the blanket stood, wrapped it about her, and waited. Alfred stood and wrapped his loin cloth around himself. He picked up his satchel. "I return anon." His fervent kiss was both a parting and a promise.

After he left, Demetre slipped into the hut. Margaret clutched the blanket closer.

Demetre spotted her mantle draped over a stool to dry. "Why were you in rags? Barefoot? I found the boat. What were you two about?"

Margaret cocked her head and used her most imperious tone. "I was not about to sit in this place in my own clothes. I used their rags. I wanted a walk in the moonlight."

"Did he try to drown you?" Demetre's scowl told her Alfred's fate was at stake.

One word and he dies. "No, Demetre, no. After the boat ride, I was walking and looking at the moon. I stepped off the path and fell in. I lost my boots in the mud. I swear it was an accident. My fault, not his."

"You swear?"

"I swear. The accident was my fault." Margaret looked past Demetre. Alfred stood in the doorway.

"My lord." Demetre turned sideways to pass Alfred.

Alfred stepped inside and rasped, "Tell me, Margaret. Am I going to step outside and be stabbed to death?"

In a volume loud enough to be heard beyond the cloth door, Margaret answered, "Alfred. I told the truth. The accident was my fault. I stepped wrong and fell in. You know I cannot swim. I thank God and you for how fast you moved. Because of you, I am alive." Margaret whispered, "I am grateful to be alive. Thank you, Alfred."

Alfred stepped to her and whispered, "I am grateful you want me alive."

Margaret's eyes sparkled. "Well, for today at least. And mayhap this night."

Alfred swatted her backside. Margaret laughed and opt the blanket invitingly. Alfred threw her a hard look and announced, "I leave you, my lady. My cloak is elsewhere." He spun on his heel and escaped. Behind him, Margaret laughed and laughed. Then she opt her satchel, dressed and re-braided her hair.

At her horse, Margaret stepped into Alfred's cupped hand. She settled onto her seat. Before she tied herself to it, she looked down.

"My lord, would you like witnesses to the promises I made you in the hut?"

As their knights stood behind Alfred, they saw not his confusion.

Alfred furrowed his brow and decided to follow her lead. "Yes, I would."

Margaret looked at their men and opt her arms in a wide gesture. "You are my lord's witnesses." She smiled at Alfred. "From henceforth, I promise to let you walk on the water side of any lake or river.

I promise I will never walk and look at the moon at the same time. I will stand first and then look up. Finally, I promise to let you hold my hand when we walk in the dark or on a path we know not. There. Now you have witnesses. Are you content?"

"I am content."

Margaret kissed the first two fingers of her right hand and touched Alfred's forehead. Alfred drew her hand to his lips and kissed her palm. Margaret blushed. Beyond them, the men smiled.

"Men, I have a request of you. Will you speak not of my watery mishap? I have already heard my lord's lecture and want no others. Not his mother's, nor Lord Cai's." She rolled her eyes, "Oh, what Caitlin would say! Such a lecture from her, Cormac, and everyone at home. Please. I ask of you. May we keep my mishap secret?"

The men looked first to Demetre and then to Claude. Claude spoke first. "I will."

"As will I," promised Demetre.

The other three also promised.

Alfred smiled at his wife and turned. "Thank you, good knights. Mount."

Alfred led the party back to the road. Emile and Demetre rode ahead of the couple.

Without turning his head, Alfred murmured, "Well done, wife."

Without looking at Alfred, Margaret responded, "One face, husband."

32

Lord Cai

Through cold but in bright sunlight, Alfred led Margaret down the road to their little house. Field workers stopped to watch them pass. Children dashed from the village toward them and walked beside their horses as they chattered greetings. Elbeorht and Elstan stood outside and watched them approach. *So tall, so big. Chinking still white. Thatching not yet darkened by time. Top half door op. Oiled skins over small windows on each side. Well built.*

Margaret removed her headscarf and draped it over her shoulders; she watched Alfred dismount to hug his mother and greet Elstan. After they spoke, he returned. "We ride to the bailey in force. Lord Cai's elder daughter thinks she is in charge, and she likes me not."

Single file, Claude and Demetre rode before the couple with Bertrand, Arnaud, and Emile behind. They easily gained entrance, dismounted, and were led into the great hall. The seneschal left to announce their arrival. As they waited, Margaret whispered to Alfred and gained his nod of approval. He walked away to speak to their men.

"My lord Alfred, My lady Margaret, Lord Richard invites you to visit Lord Cai, but asks you stay not long."

Margaret followed Alfred and the seneschal up wide, wooden stairs to a door. They stepped into a short wooden hall and through the doorway of the stone building ahead and again up a set of stairs. As the bailey had been built at the bottom of a hill, the great hall was lower than Lord Cai's keep. The seneschal opt the door to Lord Cai's chambers, and Lord Alfred stepped through first. Candles on tall pillars ringed the room. Tapestries covered the windows, which were shuttered against the cold. The room was overly warm and the air stifling

They put their backs against the wall and looked across the room at the foot of the bed then to its head. Lord Cai's daughters knelt on either side of his bed as their husbands stood behind them. Three boys and a girl stood against a side wall and stared at the new arrivals. Lord Cai's head and shoulders were perched on pillows. Pale-faced, with one hand lying over the other on his chest, he looked already dead. The daughter to his right was murmuring at him.

Margaret inhaled. *Candle wax, body smells, herbs, and that dry smell of death. We are too late.* As her eyes filled her hand sought Alfred's for comfort.

Lord Richard de Riviere, in a fur-lined cloak over his tunic, stood behind his wife. As richly dressed as her spouse, the woman kneeling beside Lord Cai's bed continued to whisper in his ear. De Riviere reached for his wife, stood her up by her shoulders, and whispered into her ear. The woman stiffened and refused to move. Her husband pulled her back. She turned and glared at Alfred. "Upset him not, then begone," she hissed.

Alfred ignored her. Still holding his wife's hand, Alfred approached and knelt before the man who had taken him in when he was six, had raised and trained him, and had supported him as he had sought Margaret's hand. Margaret knelt as well.

"My lord Cai, it is I, your faithful servant Alfred, come to tell you my love."

Without oping his eyes, Cai answered, "You mean say farewell."

His voice is stronger than his body looks. His hand reaches.

Alfred kissed the back of Cai's hand and held it. "That too, my lord."

"Fear not, my Saxon son, we said all the last time we spoke." Cai's chest lifted as he took in more air with effort. The pair waited. "Is she here?"

"Beside you, my lord."

Cai took another deep breath. "Margaret."

Alfred handed over Cai's hand, shifted, and stood. Margaret stayed on her knees as she moved into Alfred's place. She kissed Lord Cai's hand and answered, "Here my Lord Cai. Ready to do your will." Tears spilled down her cheeks, but she kept her voice pleasant, cheerful.

"Are you a happy wife?"

"Yes, my lord." She felt Alfred's hand on her shoulder.

"Good. He deserves you. Worked hard to get you." Cai inhaled another labored breath. "He loves you so, almost as much as I loved my Margaret." He heaved again. "In time, may your love increase."

"Enough."

"Silence, daughter. I still rule this house." Cai sighed.

"You are so like my Margaret. Strong, fierce, brave." Again Cai inhaled. "Reach under my pillow. Take it."

Still holding Cai's hand, Margaret slid her left hand under his pillow. *Metal, Sharp edges.* She clutched the item and slid it out. She opt her hand. *Garnets and diamonds in gold. A diamond at each of the two pointed arches. An "M?" His lady's?*

Someone behind them gasped.

"My lord, what is this?"

"Twenty years married. My gift to her. Alfred, tell her stories of my Margaret. Remind her how alike they are."

"Yes, my lord."

"My lord Cai, you honor me more than I deserve. Know we will pass this down our daughter line and tell them of your great goodness to us. And of your lady."

Cai smiled, turned his head, and opt his eyes. He lifted his hand from Margaret's and caressed her cheek. "Wear it proudly, my dear. You are truly a Margaret."

"Leave!" a woman ordered.

Margaret leaned over the bed edge. She gave Cai's hand a light squeeze and whispered into his ear. "My lord, do you hear me?" At his tiny nod, she continued. "Alfred and I seek your permission to name our second son Cai in your honor. We want him to be as good a man as you are. May we do so?"

Cai squeezed her hand as he nodded.

"We thank you, my lord." Margaret kissed his cheek. "Know you go with our love. We will pray for you every day of our lives."

With effort, Cai pulled her hand; Margaret helped him. He put the back of her hand to his mouth and kissed it with papery lips Tears coursed down Margaret's cheeks as she kissed his cheek a second time. She rested his hand over his left and stood. Margaret gazed lovingly. *Would that you had been my father. I will miss you all my days and love your namesake as much as I love you.* Tears dripped onto her chest.

Alfred put his arm around her shoulders and guided her out of the room. Back in the great hall, Margaret turned into Alfred's chest and wept. Alfred held Margaret close and lowered his head to hers. He pulled his lips into his mouth in an effort to stop his own tears.

"Give it back!" Lord's Cai's elder daughter stood at the bottom of the stairs.

Alfred looked up. "No."

She approached. "I am my mother's namesake. It should be mine." She extended her hand as if expecting to be obeyed.

"Margaret, you have been greedy all your life. If anyone has something nice, you want it. I watched you take things from Cyrille and Estoile. You will not take Lord Cai's gift from my lady."

Margaret pulled away from Alfred far enough for her to raise her arm between them and hand him the brooch. She watch him slip it into his overtunic and saw it slide to his belt. She wiped her cheeks, turned and stood to his left. Tears stopped, Margaret's baleful stare was her first warning.

"I will let him think you have it still. I will tell him not, show it not. But I will have it!"

She called the men in the hall to her. Right hands on their hilts, Alfred's men faced them.

"No, you will not!" announced Lord Richard as he descended the stairs with his left hand on his hilt, a signal of peace.. "Men, step back. Hands off hilts."

When they did so, Alfred issued the same instruction. "Lord Richard," Alfred nodded respectfully with his left hand on his hilt.

"Lord Alfred," responded Lord Richard as he nodded as well. He stood on Alfred's side of the room and faced his wife.

"My lord, that brooch belongs to me."

Lord Richard cocked his head and stared at his wife. "So that is why you have been pestering your dying father with 'Where is it? I want it. It should be mine.' He already gifted you half your mother's jewels, silk fabrics, and fine garments. Well I know you expect to take the other half from Estoile before your father's body is cold." His wife's harrumph stopped him not. "Lord Alfred is right; you are greedy. You will not countermand your father's dying wish." Lord Richard turned his face toward Alfred. "My lord, the brooch belongs to your lady." Richard looked beyond Alfred. "Lady Margaret, before you arrived, Lord Cai spoke very highly of you and said many kind things. But the last was a warming. 'Be careful with her, Richard. She is a dangerous woman.'" Richard smiled at her.

Margaret looked to Alfred. "My lord, have I your permission to speak?" At his nod, she looked to Sir Richard. "Sir Richard, know this. If your lady approaches me or attacks me, I will slit her throat." She put her hand on her dagger hilt and glared at the other Margaret. She turned back to Richard. "Further, my lord. Should she send a man or men against me, I will gut them. Then I will find her and slit her throat. Lord Cai spoke true." Hand still on her dagger, Margaret stared at the other woman without blinking. Stern of expression, she waited for the other Margaret to blink first. She did. Cai's daughter spun on her heel and took the stairs.

Lord Richard nodded. "Lord Alfred."

"Lord Richard," replied Alfred as he dropped his chin. In silence, Alfred signaled his men to follow, took Margaret's elbow, and guided her out the hall doors.

33

The Little House

Margaret entered the log house first. She looked left and saw Elbeorht seated on a high-backed bench perpendicular to the fireplace. A matching settle stood on the other side. Between them, a girl stirred the pot creating the mouthwatering smells of simmering smoked beef and vegetables. The table was already set for supper with a bread round and a full mug at each place.

Elbeorht looked to her servant. "You may go. My daughter has arrived." Elbeorht stood and met Margaret, who curtsied. "No ceremony, my dear. We are family." The women hugged. "How fares he?"

Margaret shook her head. "A day. Mayhap two. I am grateful we arrived in time." To comfort herself, Margaret hugged Elbeorht again. *Warm, loving. She hugs from her heart. Like her son.* "I met his Margaret."

Elbeorht led Margaret to the settle. She harrumphed. "That one! Grasping, greedy, selfish. After she arrived, she sent word I am forbidden to see Lord Cai or send him messages. All I can do now is pray for his swift release." Margaret reported their visit. She told Alfred's mother about the brooch and Lady Margaret's reaction. "That surprises me not. My girl told me a servant spotted her going through his papers. She even sent Father Robert on a false errand so she could search the documents chest under the altar."

"Sacrilege!"

"She seeks his will. If it is favorable to her, she will 'find' it. If it is not, she will destroy it and claim this estate by right of birth." Elbeorht chuckled wickedly. "She shall not find it."

She knows where it is. How so? "I saw another woman by Lord Cai's bed."

"Estoile, his younger daughter. A mouse to Margaret's cat. Hides when she can and always yields to her sister."

Alfred entered followed by Elstan. "I see you two are getting along." The women smiled at him. Alfred looked to his mother. "Have you shown her the features of the place?"

"No, son. As you built it, I thought you would like to show it her."

Margaret stood. "Hello, Elstan."

He pulled his forelock. "My lady. Welcome to your home." He turned to hang his cloak on a peg to the right of the door, crossed his arms and leaned against the wall to watch.

Alfred took her hand and pointed as he talked. He started with the fireplace wall that was rocks from floor to above the thatched roof. "The stones for the fireplace came from the estate. The wall extends into Mother's sleeping room. The stones keep her room warm most of the night."

"I shall move and take the middle one."

"Oh no, Mother. You stay where you are. We shall take the middle room," said Margaret. "What is the middle room for? And the one on the end. Why a door?"

"Another sleeping room. Guests. The end room is tiny, windowless, needs a door to shut away its smells. Mother's simples room for now. Storage. Whatever we need."

Margaret looked up. *Same spaces above. A railing to look down into this large room. Same floor plan.* "Why built you a second floor on the long side of the house?

"The room above Mother's is for daughters. Its ladder is against the wall in her room."

Margaret smiled. "So you will know if they come home late or try to sneak out."

"Exactly. The middle room is for sons. More storage above the simples room."

"I see the boy's ladder is down into this part. They will have more freedom to come and go." *Boys always do.* Margaret looked from fireplace to the opposite wall. "Keeping this place warm in winter will be difficult. How large?"

"Twenty-four feet long and eighteen wide. Necessary for our future family." Alfred leaned in and whispered, "Three boys and three girls?" At seeing Margaret's eyes widen and her cheeks pink, Alfred straightened and laughed heartily. "Eight will fit this table—not counting guests."

"You made that as well?"

"And the beds, the settles, benches, all. I needed to keep busy while I waited for you. What think you of it?'

Margaret beamed at him. "It is a fine house, Alfred. Well-designed and well-filled." She squeezed his hand. "Had we not an estate, I would live here happily all our days."

Alfred beamed with pride.

"If you two lovebirds are done cooing over your nest, I hunger and want to sup." Elstan moved to the table in the center of the east half of the house.

Before Elbeorht could stand, Margaret rushed forward. "Mother, please let me serve. I want to be useful."

They sang Te Deum, sat, and supped as they chatted. Omitting their stop at the fens, Alfred told of their trip. Elstan talked of the harvest and the many sacks of grain stacked in the girls' room. He reported their smoked meat was in the Saxons' smoke house and marked as theirs.

When the men finished, Margaret commented. "Elstan, you sat. You are fully upright and seem to move well."

He bowed to Elbeorht seated beside him. "I have her to thank for it. My lady, my lord's mother completed what you had started. I can also bend and touch my knees. When I do sit, I feel my skin pulling. A good reminder not to do so when Normans are about. I remember my oath. As I can no longer wrap my legs, I wear braies and chausses like a Norman, but I do not cross garter them." He quickly added, "I cover them to below my knees with a tunic, so I look Saxon."

How does he get them on if he can bend no lower? Too personal to ask. "Glad I am to hear it."

After the meal, Margaret cleaned. She washed the spoons and bowls outside on a low table near the southeast corner of the house. She turned and looked toward the bailey on the hill beyond the village. She noted the wooden hallway suspended between the great hall and the motte. *It can be burned or torn down so the stone keep is secure.* She looked around. *This house is well set apart. Far from the village, but not in the forest. Door faces east for the morn's warmth.* She walked around the end of the house and looked down the long wall; she spotted a small window for each sleeping room. *Too small for a person to crawl through. A west wind can cool the house when windows and door are op. Well done, my husband.* Margaret froze. *My husband? When started I thinking that? Have I spoke it? I think not.* Hidden from view, she leaned against the end of the house. *After the fens. Warmed me. Held me as if he were afraid to lose me. All night. Did what I needed, not what he wanted. Had I told Demetre 'yes,' he would have died. Answered without thought. I want him to live.* Margaret shivered. *I want him. I lo…*

Alfred startled her. "Margaret, what are you doing?"

"Thinking."

"Well, think inside. The Devil walks the night, and night air is dangerous." He rubbed her arms. "I shall help you carry the dish ware."

Inside, Margaret reset the table as Alfred walked to his mother and Elstan at the fire. "She was outside thinking. In this cold!"

"Sometimes a woman wants a little time alone. She takes it when she can," offered Elbeorht. She returned the smile Margaret had thrown her in gratitude. "I am for bed." She stood, bid both men a good rest and hugged Alfred. She walked to Margaret and winked. "God give you good rest, my dear."

Margaret wore her chemise to bed.

Naked, Alfred crawled in. He cupped her breast.

"No, Alfred. Your mother."

"Is half deaf. She will hear nothing if you are silent."

She brushed away Alfred's hand. "Elstan."

"In the boys' room. Shh." He kissed her mouth and put his hand lower.

She lifted his hand and held it.

"I want to make our first-born in this bed. In the home I made for us."

Will telling stop him? Nay. Say nothing. Do nothing. Just lie still.

Alfred thought her stiffness a feint. He tried new moves to arouse her. Soon she responded.

He is too skilled. Be honest. I do like his husbanding. How odd it is, this part of marriage. I never thought of it, except in curiosity. In truth, was afraid to think too much of it. Now a natural addition to my life. A comfort? No, something I have learned to enjoy. Margaret reached for him. *Such a closeness!*

At the church bell, Margaret stirred in Alfred's arms and rolled to her back. At his muffled "Mmmm," Margaret threw her hands over her head. "Alfred, wake." She nudged his shoulder with hers. "Only Tuesday. I need a Sunday, a day of rest. Ah-h-h, rest."

Alfred pinched her waist, and she pulled away. Margaret rolled out of bed. "My lord, I shall pretend this is Sunday." She pulled her bliaut off its peg. Dressed and belted herself. She reached for her brush on the small table in the corner, bent over, and brushed her hair forward. Throwing her head back, she brushed down her locks. She turned, expecting to see Alfred up and dressing. Still on his pillow with his arms behind his head, he was smiling at her.

Margaret set down her brush and picked up her bone comb. She parted her hair and drew the ends over her shoulders. "Well? Are you going to rise?"

"I already have."

Margaret rolled her eyes at him. She reached for the cloth that closed their alcove and pushed it along its rope. She stepped around it and closed it. She strode into the big room. Seated at the table, Elbeorht was ready for Mass. "Men!" exclaimed Margaret.

Elbeorht smirked, "We do love them for it!"

"Mother!" Margaret turned away and rapidly braided her hair.

Outside the church door, everyone waited for those from the bailey to arrive. Lord Richard led the party. They entered and stood by rank. Before the altar, the women stepped left and the men right, with Margaret and Alfred behind them. Their knights arranged themselves before Alfred's. Elbeorht stood behind Margaret with other Saxon women beside and behind her. After Mass, they departed as they had come.

Elstan is wise to stand at the very back of the Saxon men. He is not of this estate.

Outside, Lady Estoile stopped to walk with Margaret. Alfred stepped away.

"God give you a good morrow, Lady Margaret."

"God give you a good morrow, my lady. May I ask how fares your father?"

"He no longer takes sips. He sleeps and is hard to rouse." Lady Estoile's voice turned hard. "Unless my sister shakes him and pesters him with questions. She will not leave him and pushes me away, orders us out of the room."

"I am sorry to hear that. If you want my help, I will go with you."

"I am sorry. She gave strict orders neither of you is allowed to enter the bailey."

Glad I am we had the time we did. Poor Alfred. Margaret nodded recognition of the lady's meaning.

"Lady Margaret, I was peeking into the hall from the top of the stairs when you threatened my sister." Estoile's eyes twinkled. "Are you really as dangerous as you pretend?"

"Yes. I am also eager for an excuse to attend her. How much would you care if you were your father's only remaining child?'

Estoile wound her arm through Margaret's as they continued. "Not one bit. After I heard what Richard said, I crated everything father had gifted me. It is already on its way to our ship. She will get none of it. For father's sake, I kept peace between us. No more." Estoile added, "I fear she has father's will and wants all this even though Richard has two sons and two estates. My lord has one, and we have two sons as well. She fears father left this one to my younger son. Or worse, to Lord Alfred."

"I doubt Lord Cai would do such a thing to his family."

"You heard him call your lord his 'Saxon son.' If she destroyed not father's will, we will soon find out."

The women parted with hugs and good wishes. After Lady Estoile turned toward the bailey, Alfred arrived at Margaret's side. "Alfred, we are banned from the castle."

"A knight informed me."

"My fault for doing something I ought not."

"Threatening Margaret? No, my dear. She hates me because her father favors me. She says she fears you to hurt me. It does not." Alfred took her arm. "Shall I tell you how much I enjoyed seeing fear in her eyes when you promised to slit her throat? Mind her not. Lord Cai and I settled matters before I left for Winchester to win you."

"Lady Estoile thinks he left this estate to you."

"He did not. I suspect he left it to Lord William's younger son Edward. A good boy with a good heart. A skilled squire to his brother, who is already a knight. Should he inherit, the first order he will give is to throw his aunt off his lands. He likes Lord Richard, not her."

"Likely he grew seeing how his aunt treats his mother."

"Of that I am cert, for in their youth, I oft watched Margaret treat Estoile badly. Enough of them. After we break our fasts, I shall show you our crop land."

The foursome in the little house were finishing their suppers when the church bell rang. After its usual six rings to call them to Vespers, it kept ringing. Margaret set down her spoon and grasped Alfred's hand. He clutched hers. In silence, she touched her shoulder to his.

34

A Funeral

12 November 1103

The next morn's Mass was followed by a funeral outside the church doors. Father Robert stood before the church's closed doors. For this service, Lord Richard and Lady Margaret stood to the right of the door. Their sons, Richard Younger and Cai, and their daughter stood behind them. To the left stood Lord William and Lady Estoile with their sons, Sir William, Edward and their two daughters. As they were not blood family, Alfred and Margaret stood on the left side a short distance behind Lord William's and Lady Estoile's children.

The girls have their mothers' coloring, sun-colored like Estoile and brown like her sister I wonder if they also have their dispositions. I pray his sons met him at God's gate and welcomed him into Heaven. He was too good a man for Purgatory, but I shall pray for the repose of his soul anyway. Margaret dropped her chin.

After the service, all gathered in the cemetery. Four knights carried Lord Cai's shrouded body on a wide board and set it on the ground beside the gravesite near the cemetery gate. After the priest's words, they lowered Lord Cai with rope, and pulled them up. Each member of his family took a handful of dirt and scattered it atop the shroud. Father Robert said prayers and blessings. The family left, but Margaret, Alfred, Elbeorht, and Elstan remained with the Saxons. Margaret stood close to Alfred, but she held not his hand nor touched him. They watched as four Saxons replaced the dirt and left a small mound to show where Lord Cai rested. One lay a hand-hewn wooden cross on his grave as a temporary marker.

So many memories. Each good. Alfred, I pray you are thinking the same. Good memories, kind deeds. My lord, I remember smiling at you before the king's scribe. You said, "I may be old, my dear, but I am not dead." Oh, Lord Cai, now you are, and I am bereft. Margaret looked at Alfred's bent head. *Sad for you too. What can I do to help you?* As they walked home, Alfred slipped his hand in hers. She squeezed it and walked with his arm against his. *May this help.*

After they broke their fasts, Elstan fetched Father Robert from the castle. By the time they arrived, Alfred had gone into his mother's simples room and come out with a rolled parchment in hand. He smiled at Margaret before he gestured she follow, stepped behind the curtain, and had her watch as he stashed it under her pillow.

Father blessed everyone in the house. They sat, but Alfred chose to sit opposite Father. Elstan leaned against the door. Elbeorht served the men ale. None smiled as they sipped and set down their mugs. Margaret looked on from the closest end of a settle.

"Father Robert, whose man are you?"

"I am God's man, my son."

"And after that?"

"I am Lord Cai's."

"Where is his old will?"

"It should be in the documents chest."

Alfred shook his head.

"You have it? When did you take it?"

"Not I, Father. Someone else took it from the chest under the altar. I do know of Lord Cai's new will."

Father guessed, "You have possession of it."

"I know where it is." Alfred smiled back. "Lord Cai gave me instructions. After his funeral, he wanted his will read. In the great hall. With all his family present. No exceptions. No will reading until they are all there."

"Done."

"Also, he wants present all his knights, all his household staff, his seneschal, and his reeve. His seneschal must bring Lord Cai's accounts book. Can you arrange all this?"

"Immediately. Should someone possesses his former will, I will announce it invalid."

"In addition, my lady and I, Elbeorht and Elstan are also required to attend. Further, I may take in as many of my men as I desire. Can you arrange that?"

"Why?"

"I want not to be murdered nor these three harmed because I have Lord Cai's new will in hand. If I can see them, I can protect them. Besides, they are in his will."

"I drew up a will after his lady died. How recent is this one?"

"August."

"I drew it not."

"Done in Winchester by the king's scribe. His Grace, King Henry, read it and witnessed Lord Cai's signing."

Father showed surprise and quickly masked it. "Then it is without dispute."

"I doubt His Majesty would favor any but this one. May I send Sir Emile with you? He will return to accompany us when all is ready."

Father nodded. He finished his ale and stood. "Lord Cai prepared well, my lord."

Alfred stood. "Indeed, Father. Elstan, please fetch Sir Emile."

Emile followed the priest up the hill. The other four knights stood watch at each corner of the house.

Alfred returned and bolted the door.

"Why did you that?"

"My dear, I would not put it beyond her to burn down this house with the will and us in it. She is that hateful." When Margaret began pacing, Alfred said, "Margaret, please sit."

Margaret joined Elbeorht at her favorite spot. While Elstan and Alfred drank and talked at the table, she whispered, "Mother, when? How?"

Elbeorht stared into the fire and whispered back, "When he first fell ill, he sent for me to treat him. He gave it me before he summoned his family. He knew them well. In my simples basket. No one saw him give it me. Lord Cai knew she would never think a Saxon to have it."

"She must have got out of him he had a new one drawn."

"Near the end, a mind goes in and out. He might have thought he was talking to his wife or to you. He loved you."

Margaret teared.

Three hard knocks on the door. Elstan put his ear to the door. "Emile spoke the password. All is well."

The party formed at the bottom of the hill and walked single file: Claude, Bertrand, Alfred, Margaret, Elbeorht, Elstan, Emile, Demetre, Arnaud. Inside the gate, they paired, with Arnaud trailing.

Margaret was not the only one to look about warily. *Empty but for two guards behind us. I hear the gates close. Planks dropped. I wish I had my sword. No, it is gone forever. Depend on Alfred. And our men.*

The party stepped through the stone hall's wide doorway. A long table had been set in the middle of the large room with a tall fireplace on the long, back wall behind it. In the center of the table sat Father Robert. To his right sat Lord Richard, Lady Margaret and their eldest son. To Father's left sat Lord William, Lady Estoile and their eldest son. Their remaining children stood behind their parents. Both couples' men stood before the fireplace wall. The household staff stood near and up the stairs. On the other side stood Lord Cai's seneschal and reeve.

Father unrolled a parchment on the table and announced, "I have before me the signed will of the late Lord Cai of the Fens dated April 1098. What have you?"

Alfred withdrew a parchment from inside his cloak. "I have the will of the late Lord Cai of the Fens dated 18 August this year."

Right after our ceremony at the church door.

"You forged a false will!" charged Lord Richard's wife.

"It was made while I was not in Winchester, writ by the king's own scribe, read by His Grace, King Henry, and witnessed by him as well. Any old will is void."

"I want to see it," Father held out his hand.

"Father, none of his family may be near it until after it is read. Stand here and you may see it. After you declare it Lord

Cai's valid will, you must read it from here. I trust no one in this room. In my house this very day, you affirmed you are God's man first and Lord Cai's second, so I trust you. Only you." With a nod, Alfred motioned everyone with him to join the seneschal and the reeve. Alfred unrolled the will for Father, who read it with great interest.

The tension! Everyone at the table is stiff and sour-looking. The knights look ready to charge. The Saxons hang back and want no part of a fight. Whose sword is nearest? Dare I trip him and try to take it? I must be ready. No, no. Trust Alfred.

Father looked up and announced, "This will is dated 18 August this year. I see Lord Cai's mark, the king's signature, and his royal seal. Alfred turned the document and slowly fanned it from one side of the hall to the other so all could see what Father had described.

Father whispered, "You know what it states?"

"He told me."

"You have done well, Lord Alfred. He would be proud of you. It is safe with me."

Alfred handed over the parchment and joined his party, but he stood apart with his right hand resting on his belly close to his hilt, ready to unsheathe his sword at whatever might happen next.

Father perused the document. Before he began, he reminded everyone, "As it is written in Latin, I may pause from time to time to translate in my mind before I speak it in Norman." He looked at those at the table. "I swear before God what I speak is what is writ. If you doubt me, you and I will go before King Henry and his ruling will be final. "Every Norman in this hall say 'Before God, I swear to be bound by this will.'" After the Normas did so, Father translated his oath and demand in Saxon, and they swore as well.

316

"I am Lord Cai of the Fens. I have writ other wills, which I now declare void. This will is my newest and best reflects my wishes on the date below. I was born the year of Our Lord 1040 near the Norman town of Dieppe. I arrived in England with King William in 1066. In 1071, King William awarded me the land I now hold. As of June 1103, I am sixty-three years. I have worked hard and have earned all my lands, goods, property, and coin. My mind is sound; my will is strong. I can do as I wish. You will do as I say and accept what I give and take no more. I dispose of all my lands, property, goods, and wealth in the following ways."

Father looked up to see almost everyone leaning forward, hopeful, expectant.

"In gratitude for your years of service to me, I give the following:

Father spoke first in Norman and then translated for the Saxons."To all my household staff, in thanks for your hard work and devotion, I give each of you, separately, one shilling. If you are married or are the children of other household staff, you still receive one shilling of your own, no matter your age."

The Saxons gasped and then applauded. They cried out, "Lord Cai! Lord Cai!" Father let them go on for a short time before raising his hand for silence.

"To my seneschal, Antoine, or whoever is my seneschal at my death, I give two shillings in addition to the pay he is due for the whole month of my death, no matter which day I die.

"To my reeve, Baldhere, or whoever is my reeve at my death, I give two shillings in addition to the pay he is due for the whole month of my death, no matter which day I die.

"To my knights, and household guards, I give three shillings in addition to the pay he is due for the whole month of my death, no matter which day I die."

Father read in silence and reported, "These next gifts are a bit unusual, but I read them as they are written." He ignored several individuals seated at the table glowering at him.

"To Elbeorht, two shillings, for your excellent treatments of me when I needed them. To Elstan, no service due this estate as you are a free man and the land you work for Lord Alfred is free of this estate as well. The document setting all this forth is in the chest under the altar. To the Lady Margaret, married to Lord Alfred, I give my wife's brooch of garnets and diamonds set in gold in the shape of the M of her name. I gifted it her at our twentieth anniversary. She wore it but five years. Lady Margaret, may you wear it with pride for decades and pass it to your favorite daughter. When your lord tells stories about my lady, you will understand how alike you two are and why I gift it to you."

Look not her way. I already know her hate-filled face. Margaret smiled at Father and gave him a small nod. *I got it from your hand, Lord Cai, and will cherish it always.*

Father continued with, "To Lord Alfred, I send you my thanks for all to hear. You did so much for me during my life for which I was grateful every day. Lord Alfred, you know I did the same for you. I now announce whatever I gave to Lord Alfred during my lifetime were gifts. He owes neither me nor this estate. Because I have already gifted you all I want you to have, at this time I give you no more. Lord Alfred receives nothing at this time or ever."

A female voice called, "Good!"

Father glared at Lord Richard's lady and added, "You know how well I love you. May your life be as good as mine has been." Father now looked at those at the table. "The rest of the will is for Lord Cai's family, but he included a sentence of explanation. 'I want all those present to stay to be witnesses to all of my will.' 'To my daughters,

Margaret and Estoile, I give half of their mother's personal belongings to each. Half her jewelry and jewelry cases, half her clothes in her chests, and half the fabrics she left behind. The estate keeps all her other sewing, stitchery, and broidering. "

Father stopped to inform those assembled. "The division of the late Lady Margaret's things has already been completed, and Lady Margaret and Lady Estoile have already taken possession of them." Without ceremony Father finished the will.

"I hereby inform all in attendance, my daughters have good husbands who treat them well. They want for nothing more. My elder daughter, Lady Margaret de Riviere, should have more than Lady Estoile de Foret, which she has already taken. After her mother's death, Margaret left the estate with the pair of pewter candlesticks our first King William gifted us upon our marriage. She has refused to return them. She is no longer a thief because I now give them to her as part of her inheritance as well as the other things I know she took from my estate every visit since then. When Lady Margaret and her family leave after this reading of my will, I instruct all their luggage be inspected to keep any of them from stealing from my heir as well." Father looked not at Lord Cai's elder child.

Her sour face! From the grave, writ and announced, he names her thief and punishes her. Why Lord Richard's smirk? For what she took? At Lord Cai's revenge? Her lost reputation? What is between them?

In the silence, the priest continued. "Seneschal, what debts does Lord Cai's estate owe?"

"Father, other than the normal monthly expenses to his people, none. My Lord Cai is free of all other debt."

"Glad I am to hear it. Now as to who gets the estate." Father rolled the top of the document so he could translate the bottom part. "Lord Richard de Riviere has two estates and two sons. Lord William de Foret has two sons and one estate. I pray I am debt free at my death. If I am not, the person or persons inheriting my estate must pay those debts from the estate. All my other possessions and goods, including lands, property, coin and everything else that is mine, I give to my grandson, Edward, son of Lord William de Foret and my daughter the Lady Estoile."

Richard holds tight her hand and leans. Will he silence her?

"If Edward is a minor child at my death, I direct his father, Lord William de Foret, be his legal guardian and to serve as trustee for the estate until Edward's sixteenth birthday. Further, I instruct Lord William to make Edward a knight immediately upon my death or before his sixteenth birthday if he is not already one. I want him well prepared to defend and to rule my lands and goods. Further, should Edward die before producing an heir, all I have given him and all he had gained goes to his sister Joan and her heirs. Should Joan be dead when Edward dies, my estate goes to Lord William's elder son Sir William, also called William Younger, or to his heirs. At no time, nor in any way, will my daughter Margaret de Riviere, her husband Lord Richard de Riviere, or any of their descendants ever obtain, inherit, purchase, or by another mean acquire my estate or any part of my estate or its future proceeds, land or property."

Edward beamed at Father.

"To my grandson, Edward de Foret, I leave this instruction and a hope. Edward, be as good a man as is your father. I hope I have been a good example of how to rule this estate. Edward, I pray whatever the Good Lord sends your way, you will have the strength to bear it and the wisdom to deal with it well. I wish you happy and successful in your life ahead."

Father ended with, "Below these last words are writ the date 18 August 1103, Lord Cai's sign, the signature of Henry Rex, and the royal seal." He looked up at those seated. "I will keep this document in the chest under the altar. If anyone touches that chest, I will have him or her excommunicated. No one will countermand Lord Cai's last wishes or destroy his document."

Tension has lowered, but I feel it still. Sister against sister. What will their husbands do?

"Antoine, after Lord William takes possession of the estate for his son, please meet with him to give the coins as Lord Cai ordered. Hand him the accounts book now."

After the man did so, Father further ordered, "I will now speak privately to everyone in Lord Cai's family. Their knights must leave. All others depart as well."

Lord Alfred lifted his left arm for Margaret to place her hand. He led her, his mother, their knights, and Elstan out of the hall, through the bailey gates and homeward. Alfred invited the knights to dine in the house with them, and Elbeorht's girl served a generous meal. Afterward, first Elbeorht, then Margaret left the group to nap. Margaret fell asleep to soft murmuring beyond the curtain.

35

❦

Treachery and Trial

That night, Margaret was fast asleep in Alfred's arms when she started awake at him jolting her. Both jumped out of bed.

"Fire! Help! Fire and death! Fire! Fire!" a deep voice yelled from outside the house.

As Alfred grabbed his clothes and dashed past the curtain, Margaret touched the outside wall and looked at the thatched roof. *No fire here.* She smelled faint smoke. *Does she burn the estate in revenge?* She threw her bliaut over her head and jammed her feet into her boots. She flung aside the curtain and saw Alfred had dressed. He and Elstan were at the door.

"Mother, Margaret, bolt this door. Open it only for Elstan or me. Our password is … is 'barley soup.'"

Sword to the fore, Alfred opt the door and looked left and right before disappearing into the dark. Elstan followed, and Margaret locked Elbeorht and herself inside. Cold with fear, she pulled her mantle from its peg and donned it before she joined Elbeorht. "Mother, best you dress should we be forced to leave the house." At Elbeorht's nod, she walked with her to her room. "Fear not, Mother. Alfred is strong, brave, and capable. We shall be safe from whatever it is outside."

God, I gave you my old sword for a wish. Would that I could have it. No. If this be Your first test, I will pass it. My dagger needs be enough.

The women sat at the table on the bench nearest the door to face it; they leaned against the table edge. Both women looked upward at hearing someone on the roof. He shouted, "Lord Alfred! Firebrand coming!" Margaret dashed first for Elbeorht's mantle to hand it her and then for the pail of water always guarding the fireplace should a spark escape. She set it between herself and Elbeorht. As she sat, something slammed against the door. The bars bounced in their metal brackets. Both women stood.

"I shall kill you! I shall kill you all!" roared someone in Saxon.

Again bodies slammed against the door. The women jumped. Margaret heard grunting, threats, men fighting. Elbeorht rushed forward and yelled, "Elred! Elstan! Kill not your brother! Dear God, save them all!"

More men's shouts and curses. Then "We have him!" and "Bind him!"

After hearing more death threats, Margaret heard her husband order, "Gag him!" and heard more struggling. Margaret drew Elbeorht from the door and stepped back until the backs of her knees touched the bench. Still holding Elbeorht's shoulders, Margaret sat them both. Elbeorht dropped her face into her hands and shook her head. The noises and actions beyond the door faded. They waited.

A long time later, night noises replaced the chaos they had heard, first close and then distant. An owl hooted; wind rustled through barren branches. Margaret sighed.

On the other side of the door, Alfred announced, "Margaret, Mother, barley soup."

Margaret rose slowly so as not to startle Elbeorht at prayer. With her lips brushing the door, she asked, "What game played we in the forest?"

"Five kisses."

Margaret lifted and set aside the lower bar first. She stepped back and drew her blade. "Op the door." She saw Alfred with his hands upon his hips.

"My wife!" To Elstan behind him he threw, "Told you she would have blade in hand." Margaret sheathed her dagger. Alfred stepped through the doorway first. Smiling, he leaned forward and whispered, "Thaes hal, Wif!"

"Thaes hal, Husband." Margaret grabbed him about his waist and hugged hard. Alfred hugged back, kissed her forehead, and released her not.

Elstan stepped around the pair to place his arm about Elbeorht as she cried. "All is well. Cry not. No one died."

"Wulf?"

"Bound and stored in the donjon. Lord William will try him in the morn."

"Why a trial?" asked Margaret in a hushed tone.

"He set fire to several roofs in the village. He came to fire this house with us in it. I had stationed a man on our roof as a lookout when I learned Wulf had run from home and knew not where he was." Elstan started walking Elbeorht toward her room. "Sleep now.

325

All is well and we are safe. If you hear noises in the night, fear not. As a precaution, Lord Alfred set a man on the roof and another to guard our barred door."

Behind their curtain, Alfred kissed his wife with a passion built by fears now abating. Undressed and abed, Alfred kissed Margaret hard and was fierce in his lovemaking. Margaret matched his passion. *I might have lost you.*

Spent, Alfred rolled them to their sides and held Margaret close as they fell asleep.

"Margaret. Margaret, wake," hissed Alfred as he rolled her toward him.

"Fire?"

"Night terror." When Margaret groaned, he pulled her into his arms. "You know now why. You know he cannot hurt you. Soon you will have them no more. Why this night?"

Margaret sighed her disbelief. "Caitlin said I oft had one in the night after something scared me during the day."

"The fire?"

After a time, she answered, "The fight. I feared you stabbed or worse."

Alfred kissed her forehead. "I am here. I am whole. We are safe. Close your eyes, my wife. Sleep and I will guard." They held each other all night.

As the great hall filled after Mass, Margaret attended Elbeorht in the house. The women sat on a bench moved beside the doorway. Wrapped in their mantles, each lifted her face to the sun's warmth but kept her eyes closed against the light.

"What did Wulf that he needs be tried?" asked Elbeorght.

"In the village, he set three roofs ablaze as a distraction. His aim was to burn this house and stab to death all who fled it."

"He wants me dead."

"All of us. He claims we ruined his life." Margaret repeated what she had been told. "After Alfred took your things and your dowry away, the next morn Mercia sent Wulf Younger and Waerdun to the fields. When they returned at sunset, she and Waermund were gone. As was her dowry and half Wulf's coins from his chest. Her lord sought her and the boy to no avail. Wulf found all his coins gone to pay the wergeld for his missing wife and son. He also owed his lord more coin to finish the debt. All he had left were his house, its contents, and his plots." Margaret placed her hand over Elbeorht's, which were tightly clutched in her lap. "Mother, Alfred said he was unkind to her all their marriage." Elbeorht nodded recognition of a truth. "With Maerwine married this summer, Mercia had only Waermund to attend. Alfred thinks Mercia took the coins and fled to apprentice Waermund to a stone mason somewhere in the land. He thinks she shall change her name, call herself a widow, and use the remaining coins to dower herself into a convent, never to be seen again." At seeing tears flowing from Elbeorht's clenched lids, she stopped. *Enough. Tell her more only if she asks.*

At the table in the great hall sat Edward, Lord William, and Lord Alfred. A distance before them stood Wulf, legs hobbled and wrists tied behind his back; he wore a torn tunic, a swollen, blackened left eye, and a cut lip. Two large knights held Wulf at his elbows. The same people who had filled the hall the morn before were arrayed in groups around the room.

"What debts owes this man?" asked Lord William.

The first man stepped forward. "He burned my house. The roof fell in and destroyed all within, two beds, a table, five stools, wooden dish ware and cooking items, all our clothing. My wife managed to save the metal pots."

A second Saxon joined him. "My roof was burned. Good neighbors helped me put out the fire, so all I am owed is a new roof. What is wet will dry. Unless my things are ruined by rain before my roof is replaced."

A third man repeated what the second had reported. Each man told what he believed he was owed. Baldhere totaled the amounts and reported to Sir William he was owed three pounds, two shillings. A few in the hall gasped. Alfred swallowed hard.

Sir William asked, "Who will house these families until their roofs are replaced and a hut built and furnished?" After other men from the village volunteered to help their neighbors, Sir William addressed Wulf. "Saxon, what coin have you to pay this debt?"

Wulf spewed a mouthful of spittle toward the table. One knight socked him in the jaw. Wulf crumbled. The second knight pulled taut the rope around Wulf's neck. Wulf stirred not.

Staring at his half-brother, Alfred uttered, "I know he has no coin. On one condition, I will pay or owe his debt."

In the quiet hall, all had heard Alfred.

"The condition?"

"Send or take him off this island, Lord William, and swear you will see he never returns. He is yours to do with as you will. Keep him as your slave or sell him into slavery; I care not."

"Done. You and I will settle this matter in private." Lord William announced, "Take the prisoner to the donjon. Tie him well—and gag him."

As the unconscious man was hauled away, his feet dragged behind him and plowed paths in the rushes. The hall emptied of all but those seated at the table. Elstan waited outside the bailey gates and accompanied Alfred homeward.

"You tell her."

Elstan shook his head. "You are the lord."

"You live with her."

The men repeatedly countered each other as they continued down the lane past the battered village and toward the log house.

36

Departure

A cold wind blew. After Vespers, everyone dashed to their homes and hearth fires.

Alfred explained, "I have farther to go and can ride faster without you. I will not have you sleeping on the ground. After we part ways, I am sending you home the way we came. Demetre, Bertrand, and Arnaud will escort you. I take Claude and Emile with me."

Margaret frowned. "We know not yet how reliable is Emile. You two shall be asleep when he stands guard. Is that wise?"

"This is his test. Worry not, my dear. I shall sleep with one eye op."

Argue not before his mother and Elstan. Margaret nodded.

"We shall sleep the first night in the hut by the lake."

"I promise to go not for a walk."

Alfred smiled at his wife. "The third eve we shall stay with Sir Lothaire and his lady. The other nights we shall be at the inns we used until I must leave you. You should be home the eve three days after that. If weather impedes you an extra day, stay at Newbury Inn. If all goes well with my nephews, I should meet you at home. Cert by the day after you arrive."

Everyone left for bed.

"Alfred, I—"

"Hush. We are making our first-born." Margaret knew better but neither spoke nor hindered her husband.

The next morn the couple dressed. Before they left their room, Alfred pinned Margaret between his splayed hands against the logs. "Soon we must part. Please send me away with a kind word." At her "Now?" he nodded.

Margaret slipped her arms from her sides up Alfred's chest and around his neck. She stood on tiptoe so her lips were almost even with his. "When you left me for the tourney, I feared for your safety and prayed for your return. When you leave me now, I shall do the same. Oh, how I shall miss you, my husband." As Alfred kissed her hard, she thought, *I said it. I meant it.* She felt her nipples harden with desire and pulled back to gaze into his summer eyes. "My eyes will be glad to see you again. Husband, my whole body will show you how much." She grabbed Alfred to her and kissed him as hard as he had her. Time stopped for the pair as they felt each other's hearts beating.

"The church bell rings a second time. I hope you two are at least dressed."

Margaret smirked at Alfred. With a sigh, he released her. Margaret strode through the curtain and smiled at Elstan's holding the door for her and bowing. As she passed, she quipped, "Elstan, you need a wife."

Behind her, both men laughed. She heard, "Indeed I do!" Margaret dashed ahead to join Elbeorht.

Lord Cai's and Lord William's men inspected every corner and every container in the wagons Lord Richard and his party had filled. Baldhere and Antoine affirmed nothing had been taken from the estate. After the party returned from Mass, Lord Richard was handed flagons of ale and a sack of bread and cheese to eat on their journey to their property southeast. The sun hid behind a cloud and peeked out before it again hid. A cold wind whirled around the train and attacked each person's mantle or cloak. At the front of the line of wagons, two men stood close together. Lord William whispered to Lord Richard, who nodded. Lady Margaret and her children looked at no one and said no farewells. She and her daughter entered the litter and dropped the curtains. The boys mounted and followed Lord Richard, who led the column east.

After Mass, Elbeorht's girl served the family at the table; the knights ate standing or seated on the settles before taking satchels to the horses.

"Son, while you saddle the horses, I shall talk with Margaret."

"Yes, Mother."

"Alone."

"Yes," agreed Elstan. The men stood.

"Only a short visit." On the other side of the table, Alfred bent and kissed his mother's forehead. "I love you, son."

With her eyes, Margaret followed the men. *They walk alike. They walk alike!*

"You do care for him."

Margaret returned her gaze to Elbeorht. *Nod or she will think ill of me.*

Elbeorght gestured broadly. "My son built all this for you. He wanted to give you a good life. The king's gifts to you shocked him, and he thought you lost to him." At Margaret's nod, Elbeorght added, "I know Normans say 'I am fond of you,' but we are more direct. We say, 'I love you.' I hope you know he does. In January, Alfred was half mad with worry when he learned you were so ill. I threatened to tie him to a tree in the forest. Only my argument that, should he go to you to tell you he loves you and wanted you to live, it would bring him death. That gave him pause. I warned him after King Henry executed him, the king would have a clear field to you. He agreed to stay home only if I would help him should he needs rescue you."

Good God! He was willing to risk his life to say those words to me. When he did say them, I told him I believed him not. How cruel he must think me.

Elbeorght waited but received no response. "He went to Lord Cai for advice. Cai locked Alfred in a room and released him not until my son vowed he would not go to you."

"King Henry would have punished Alfred if he had."

"More likely beheaded him for wanting a Norman wife. Tell me, daughter, how many courses have you missed?"

What? I said nothing of it. Margaret blushed. "Two. How know you?"

"I am a healer. You are six weeks with child, but you have told him not."

"How know you that?"

Elbeorht smiled. "I know my son. He would not have permitted you ride a horse, much less journey on one. Is that why you told him not?"

"I am seventeen next month. Old for a first time. I want to be cert I keep it."

"No riding after this journey. Cert not after your third month."

"Yes, Mother." Margaret smiled, "If I had told him now, he would leave me not to attend his nephews. I know he must do that to ease his mind over Wulf, so I wait. I decided not to tell him. I shall wait until he realizes I am with child."

Elbeorht threw back her head in laughter. While still chuckling, she smiled at Margaret and took her hand. "My dear girl. The babe shall come alive and be kicking you before he figures it. He is more likely to complain you are growing fat from eating too much."

Margaret grinned at that thought. "I am glad I have told him not. He needs to help Wulf's sons. I can see myself home."

Elbeorht turned serious and announced, "Margaret, you may still be wearing a bride's circlet, but you have just become a wife." At seeing Margaret's confusion, she added, "A bride thinks first of herself, what she wants, what she needs. He must attend her. A wife chooses when to put her husband first, to do what he needs, to support his plans instead of her own." Elbeorht leaned across the table and took Margaret's other hand as well. "I am proud of you for becoming a wife so soon. Some women never do."

Margaret beamed at Elbeorht's compliments. "Thank you, Mother. Remember your promise. After Eastertide, come live with us. Our babe is due June for cert, likely the first fortnight."

"I shall. Now off with you. The earlier you start, the slower you may go. Rest as much as you can on your way, daughter. Send word when you are home safe." With loving looks toward each other, the women stood, hugged, and donned mantles. Before Margaret turned her horse toward the road, Elbeorht lifted her hand and said, "Go with God. My prayers go with each of you."

"And mine," added Elstan. Both stood before their door and waved until the party disappeared down the lane.

The next morn, Lord William sent Lady Estoile and his daughters to Normandy under the care of his eldest, Sir William. Gagged, trussed, and under a blanket, Wulf traveled in the last wagon.

Away from the column, Lord William spoke to his most trustworthy man. "He starts fires. He will burn anything ours he can. I will not endanger my family; I refuse to foist him on an unsuspecting buyer. When my family sleeps, take him to the deck for air. If anyone asks, say he stumbled and fell overboard." Lord Willam thought a moment. "Better, say he jumped to his death rather than be enslaved."

The knight nodded.

37

Separate Paths

14 November, Saturday

Alfred's and Margaret's party ate their midday food as their horses walked so as to reach the hut by the lake well before dark. Because the family had not yet vacated the site, Margaret met them, husband, wife, two daughters. She insisted they sup and sleep in their home; they insisted the couple take the bed. Claude reported the sentinels would guard. The family curled together on the floor on the other side of the fire pit. Fully dressed, Margaret slept curled against Alfred with her arm over his waist. He slept with his unsheathed sword on the bed beside him as he faced the door and the family.

Despite it being Sunday, Alfred sought not a church. The party skirted the end of the fens and turned southwest. Again, their only protection lay within a ramshackle inn, this one by a stream near the road. Alfred ordered the innkeeper provide as many freshly caught rabbits as possible for a ha-penny each. Taking turns, the knights guarded the couple's room and the palisade gate, which twisted on its hinges and was easily breached. No one slept well because they trusted neither the place nor its keeper.

Before dark the next day, the group arrived at Sir Lothaire's large house. After having been refused hospitality by Lord Montaign of Birchdale and sent to seek shelter elsewhere, Alfred grumbled, "Birchdale refused us the hospitality owed travelers. I will show him no courtesy by informing him we are on his lands."

Outside, Sir Lothaire welcomed the party with a stiff air. With two small children clutching her skirts, Lady Lieale stood in the doorway and out of the wind to wave everyone inside. Arnaud helped Lady Margaret dismount. She dashed toward the heat pouring out of the doorway.

"My lady, let us greet each other fireside." They disappeared.

Alfred dismounted and handed Sir Lothaire ropes tying four rabbits together. "I count your taking us in fulfills the bargain we made at the tourney. Please accept these in thanks for your kind hospitality."

"My Saxons informed me you would be here this day. I suppose you will never reveal how you do that." When Alfred spoke not, Lothaire replied, "I thought not. Men join us. No camping. This night we all sup together and sleep inside." Informed they would first tend their horses in his barn, Sir Lothaire replied, "We hold our meal until you arrive. Please hurry; the children hunger." After they had supped, the evening was a pleasant one of story telling and singing.

While the women took the little ones to bed, Lothaire's son asked, "Is it true you are Saxon? The only Saxon lord in the realm?"

"Yes, Fabien, true."

"You look and talk like a Norman. How is that?"

"I lived in a Norman household for many years."

"May I ask how met you Father?"

"We met at Lord Wilbur's tourney."

"Enough. Sit fireside, son."

Alfred spoke quietly to his host, "If you want Fabien fostered and trained, I will do it. Bring him before Lent or after Eastertide."

"I thank you." Lothaire's wan smile told Alfred his offer was declined.

Alfred stared into the fire. He knew the knight's soft refusal was because he was Saxon and not ranked. Being trained by a Saxon would cost Fabien a good future. Alfred suspected no Normans would foster his sons and frowned at thinking he might have to train them himself. He worried his heir even knighted, might be rejected. Alfred took Lothaire's cheerfulness to be his pleasure that his obligation to Alfred was so easily dismissed and completed out of sight of others. Alfred's shoulders slumped.

Lothaire's eldest son eyed Emile's blade, and the knight let him place his hand on its hilt. "I am old enough to squire," said the ten-year-old, "but our lord will take me not, so his knights refused me as well."

"You will find a place soon." Emile placed his hand on the boy's shoulder and squeezed. Everyone settled for the night.

The group continued and spent the next night at an inn south of the newly built town of Northampton with its new castle above the river. The city gates were complete and guarded, an illusion of safety. The city's north walls were only foundations with piles of nearby stones yet to be cemented into place. Alfred had determined the established inn with its high palisade and sturdy gate was safer than town. Margaret slept in the women's room, and Alfred in the great hall with his men arrayed between him and Normans of rank.

Wednesday

The morning of the fifth day of travel started with Mass and breaking their fasts. *Glad I am we spoke our farewell before we started. The great room and yard are so public.* Alfred lifted Margaret to her riding platform. She smiled at him. He stood close, grasped her ankles as she tied herself to the platform, and softly looked up to meet her gaze.

"Remember all I said. A hard day's ride south to Oxford. Two more days to home." She nodded. "I am two days northwest, hopefully a half-day to attend my nephews, then three, mayhap four, days to home."

Margaret leaned down and squeezed the hand he offered. "Remember our farewell in the little house. I shall miss you, my lord."

Alfred mounted and led the men through the gate. He, Claude and Emile turned left. Demetre turned right with Margaret, Arnaud, and Bertrand following him.

Margaret reached the Oxford inn, enjoyed a hearty supper and spent the night in the luxury of a bed in the women's room. *He gave me coins; I pray he needs them not. Pray for him first.*

Halfway to Lord Baudric's estate, Alfred and his men camped beside the road

Thursday

Hours before dawn, Margaret started at a hiss in the dark. A soft voice called her name twice and asked she follow. In the hall, she spotted a lit candle on a small wooden plate on the floor. She picked it up and saw the face of the girl who had served their meal.

"My lady, dreadful news. Saxon carried."

Please God, not Alfred.

"Three miles beyond the south gate eight men lie in wait for you. A Lord Wilbur paid them to kill your lord and capture you."

They know not Alfred is elsewhere. Ransom me for the armor? If they kill me, Alfred loses his land and becomes a lord in name only. "Are you cert?" she whispered.

The girl nodded. "Saxons lie not to their own. One overheard them last night at an inn a day's ride away. She sent word immediately. What may I do for you?"

The girl tiptoed into the women's room and returned with Margaret's things. In the hall, she helped Margaret lace her bliaut and held high the candle plate while Margaret braided her hair. She picked up the satchels and led Margaret down the back stairs into the kitchen. She took satchels to the men outside as the cook handed Margaret a cup of hot broth. By the time she finished it, Demetre had entered the kitchen and whispered, "We leave by the west gate as soon as it ops. They say a Saxon will meet us in the forest to tell us how far west we must go before we can turn south. They say they will watch the men for us, but I know not how."

"Neither do I. I pray our trust is well placed. We must ready ourselves for anything." *Lord, is this another test of my wish? So be it.*

The cook handed Demetre four sacks of food. The pair exited the kitchen door to the back yard and slipped unseen around the building. They met Arnaud and Bertrand, who handed them their horse's reins. Led by a stable boy, they walked winding lanes. The sounds of the horses clopping on the stone streets rang in their ears. *Let everyone be so asleep none wakes and throws op a shutter to see us.* At a turn, the boy whispered to Demetre and retreated. Margaret peeked around the corner and saw the city's west gate. They leaned against a shop wall and prayed to remain unseen.

Margaret concluded her prayers for success with a question. *What are you teaching me, Oh God?*

When they heard the portcullis lift, they mounted. A wagonload of wood rumbled toward them as they turned the corner. Demetre led and looked to be at his ease as his steed approached the gate. He smiled and waved to the guards as if their party were on a stroll. They rode west until they were both out of sight and out of the hearing of any men on the city wall.

Just then a young man with a sheep's wool wrapped around his broad shoulders stepped from behind a tree and gestured them toward him. "The path is narrow and the branches low. Please lead your horses."

"Why north?" demanded Demetre.

"North. then east, then well south of the city. First, ride east until another Saxon stops you. You were seen heading west. They know you must go south to reach home. They will follow the road seeking where you should have turned south. When you do turn south, you will be miles east of them. Tis a longer way, but safer. They will know not where you are." The man's smile was wicked. "If asked, Saxons know to report you are still ahead of them." He turned to Margaret, and his face softened. "Worry not, my lady, you are under our protection. We cannot fight them, but we can lie and delay them." He stepped off the path and waved them onward with, "Go with God."

My Lord, are You teaching me to trust Saxons? Do You ask me to trust men I know not? Is this my lesson?

At a junction a thin Saxon boy of eight or nine years slipped from behind a tree, pointed east, and disappeared. So faint were the morning noises of the city, they seemed but whispers. At a juncture of three paths, they spotted a girl, wearing a rough woolen tabbard and worn boots. She appeared to be searching the bushes for berries. As they approached she turned, smiled at them, and pointed to the south path that led around the east side of Oxford.

When the weak sun caste no shadow, Demetre raised his hand for those behind him to halt. He drew his sword and walked his horse toward four Saxons standing in the middle of intersecting roads.

They pulled their forelocks, "My lord, we must report the men have guessed you travel east of Oxford, back tracked, and are heading this way. They are already only half a day behind you." The couples looked beyond the knight and gave obeisance to Lady Margaret. Margaret approached, but she kept her horse behind Demetre's.

"What plan you?"

"My lady, we have a circle of stones and a lit fire over there to let them think you only rode this far and camped the night. They will think you go not far in a day. We need you to dismount and leave tracks around the fire pit area and tie your horses to trees." He pointed where. "After they drop offal, mount and take the road west. Ride until you reach the hot meal and hay awaiting you. We shall brush clean all roads and disappear. They may stop or not. They must separate to follow each road to find your trail. They will waste time to regather, or only be two or three who follow you."

The party dismounted, drank from their flasks, and ate from their bags. They dropped crumbs and bits of cheese before they remounted. Margaret looked back and saw tendrils of smoke rising through bare branches. Behind them, a woman walked backward as she swung a large leafless branch from side to side to brush the dirt road smooth.

They smelled the campsite before they saw it. A faint breeze announced a meat stew awaited them. They came upon a sight not to be believed, a dozen men and women ready to serve. Men led the horses to the stream left of the road. Bertrand inspected the area to the right. He looked into the two pots hanging from tripods over smokeless fires before he walked to look as far into the forest he could in the coming dark. He inspected the empty hand carts. He walked across the road and found each horse's reins tied to a peg in the ground beside a pile of hay and tended by a man who had unsaddled his charge as the horse happily munched.

Margaret and the other two stepped off the road to sit on stools around a lit fire pit. They accepted mugs of ale, drank them dry, and set them on the ground to accept a bowl of stew. A woman with a tray offered bread already chunked. Bertrand joined the others, sat, and reported what he had seen before he accepted his mug and food. Margaret finished her bowl and set it in her lap to pick up her mug. The woman, who seemed to be the one in charge, arrived and refilled it.

"Thank you. We needed food and drink, water and hay."

"We are happy to help you, my lady. We have blankets for you to roll into. The pottage will be ready before dawn. You may set a guard, but so shall we. A mile in each direction. No one will sneak to you in the night."

"Why give us all this help?"

The woman smiled and replied, "My lady, that is a question best asked of your lord." She curtsied and departed.

This day we knew not our path. How did Alfred know which way we need go or where we would stop? Ask him I shall. I am too tired to think on it now.

A woman approached with four folded blankets in her arms. She offered the pile first to Lady Margaret, who took the top one. Bertrand took one, stood, and placed it on his stool.

"I will take first watch and use it later," he offered.

"I will take the second," said Demetre as he reached for a blanket.

Arnaud stood, took accepted a blanket, and thanked the woman.

Margaret chose to sleep with a cart wheel at her back. After setting down the blanket, she lay on it and pulled it around herself until only her face showed. On her side, she watched the Saxons fill bowls and stand or sit on the stools as they ate.

I am trusting more, My Lord. The men and the women. Saxons. They have guided us, protected us, and fed us. Now they guard us. Trust them. Your lesson, Oh Lord, is a good one. After two deep breaths, Margaret was asleep.

Before dark this day, Lord Alfred announced himself to Lord Baudric of Huntdun. They supped, and Lord Baudric dismissed the others on the dais to learn Alfred's reason for coming.

Friday

At the end of Mass the next morn, Father Joseph announced all Saxons need report to the great hall, no exceptions. On the dais, Father sat on one side of Lord Baudric; Alfred sat on the other. At both ends, two knights stood at the bottom of the steps; each door was guarded. The Saxons filed in. Clustered into family groups, they looked about nervously. Lord Baudric introduced Lord Alfred of

Dryhtenton. Lord Alfred reported all Wulf had done since he had run off and of his trial. After Alfred reported Wulf's punishment, he briefly let the Saxons talk among themselves. He called for Wulf's sons to step forward.

The first man, appeared to be in his mid twenties. Tall, well-muscled and proud in his demeanor, Wulf's first-born swaggered as he approached the dais. He bowed not, gave only the tiniest nod, and barely touched his forelock. The younger man who followed him was just as tall and well-muscled, but his demeanor was more respectful in giving a proper head bow and forelock pull. He stood behind and to the side of his elder brother and dropped his gaze to the rushes.

"Wulf Younger, Waerdun, I am now the head of our family."

"I refuse to obey you," announced Wulf Younger.

Alfred ignored his declaration. Alfred knew the answer before he asked, "Wulf Younger, have you a wife?"

"No."

"Any prospects for one?"

"No."

From behind the front groups, a man announced, "Not likely. He is too much like his father. No man wants his daughter ill-treated as Mercia had been."

"If you never wed, your father's line dies. I want that not. Waerdun, do you wish to wed?"

Waerdon straightened and looked directly at his uncle. In a firm voice, he answered. "I do, my lord, but a second son has no land."

"As the head of our family, I can remedy that," Alfred told him. "Wulf Younger, your father owns two plots. Choose one."

"By right of birth, both are mine," sneered the young man, "and the house and everything in it." Wulf Younger puffed out his chest and glared at Lord Alfred as if he was about to challenge him.

"No longer. As a lord and the head of our family, I decide. With Lord Baudric's permission, I award Waerdun one plot in the hope some good family will permit him to wed. Waerdun, I wish you to wed, to become a father with a healthy family, and to have a good life. Wulf Younger, as the first-born, the house and all in it remain yours. If you choose not a plot, Waerdun chooses first."

"I want the bigger one west of the village," was Wulf Younger's swift reply.

"So be it. Waerdun, I award you the plot by the river. It may flood some springs, but that only enriches the soil and gives you better crops."

Lord Baudric spoke next. "Both of you now owe the remainder of your father's debt. I make it in proportion to the size of the land each of you now own. My seneschal will figure your portion and tell you it. You owe at least a fourth of the debt every Michaelmas. You each have ten months until your first payment is due. Wulf Younger. I will have not another Saxon like your father. You will bother not Waerdun, his wife, their children, her family, none of them. If you harm them or their crops, destroy anything that is theirs, or displease me in any way, I will give all you have to Waerdun and his heirs. I will send you to the coast and sell you into slavery." Lord Baudric addressed the room. "I charge every Saxon to report any threat or misdeed Wulf Younger makes to any person from this day to the day he dies. I will have peace in my village, in my fields, everywhere."

As Lord Baudric spoke, Alfred perused the Saxons. He spotted a girl pulling her father's hand to draw his shoulder to her as she spoke into his ear. She gestured toward Waerdun and kept talking. When the lord finished his speech, Alfred coughed softly and whispered, "I wish to speak again." At Lord Baudric's nod, Alfred addressed the hall. "If any Saxon girl favors Waerdun, and her parents agree they would be a good match, I would like to meet you. Know I dine and depart, so wait not. Wulf Younger, Waerdun, stay when your lord dismisses the others."

The hall emptied of all but the knights and five Saxons. With arms across his chest and his hands tucked under his armpits, Wulf Younger stood with one hip slung out. Waerdun took two steps away from his brother. From behind him, Waerdun heard his name spoken. He turned to a slim, brown-haired girl with bright eyes. He smiled broadly and extended his hand. She stepped forward and took it. The pair beamed at each other; her parents stood behind them.

"Wulf Younger, henceforth you may keep the name Wulf Younger or you may drop Younger and just be called Wulf. Choose."

"Wulf."

"From your looks and behavior, I predict you will remain as proud and troublesome as is your father. Beware you do not end as he did, reviled and a slave. Remember you life will only be as good as you are. I dismiss you." Alfred watched Wulf stomp out the doorway.

Alfred smiled. "Waerdun, who is she?"

Now standing tall and confident, Waerdun pulled his forelock, first at his lord and then to his uncle. In a strong voice, Waerdun replied, "She is Aelf, my lords. We have been friends all our lives. She is a second daughter." When Waerdon gave the girl a loving look, Aelf beamed at him and squeezed his hand. He introduced her parents.

"Are you two agreeable to this match?"

The pair, both gray-haired and of equal height, nodded to both lords before giving the couple beside them a broad, happy smile. "We are, my lord," said her father.

"Then I am agreeable. Lord Baudric, have they your approval?"

"They are an honorable family, hardworking and honest. She is a good girl. Yes." He paused a moment, "You may have a plot in the village for a hut and a garden."

Alfred was pleased to see how brightly shone the couple's faces. "Thank you, my lord." To Waerdun and Aelf, s Alfred announced, "To help you build your hut, to fill it, and to start your life together, I give you a wedding gift of two shillings."

Five jaws dropped.

"I thank you, my lord! I thank you! We thank you!" gushed Waerdun.

"Werdun, Aelf, call me Uncle. We are family."

"Thank you, Uncle!" sang the couple in unison.

Father reported he would announce their first wedding banns after Sunday's Mass. Lord Baudric dismissed them and ordered dinner served. Alfred noted Waerdun and Aelf still held hands as they followed her parents out the door.

"My lord, I have only one shilling with me. I give it you now and will send the other by a knight after I return home."

"Lord Alfred, you are an honorable man—too generous—but honorable. I take your shilling and will add one of mine own to give them on their wedding day should yours not arrive on time. I trust you to send it." Lord Baudric lifted the full goblet a page had set before him. He waited for Father Joesph and Alfred to take up theirs. "To peace on our estates," he toasted before he drank.

"To peace," repeated the other two.

The hall filled and dinner served. Between the broth and meat courses, Lord Baudric turned to Alfred. "You are the first Saxon lord in the realm. Before I met you, I thought you a mistake. Now I see the man you are. Sorry I am my father permitted Lord Cai to buy your freedom. You would have been an excellent leader for my Saxons." Alfred only smiled. Lord Baudric accepted his board of meat and boiled vegetables. "But then, I suspect my father saw something special in you and knew you were too big for such a small life. Already, you have accomplished much." After the men swallowed their first mouthfuls, Lord Baudric continued, "I heard rumors of Lord Wilbur's tourney. Tell me of it."

Before dawn, a woman stood a distance from Margaret and spoke her name. Margaret flung the blanket from her and sat with dagger in hand pointed toward the voice.

"Sir Arnaud warned me not to startle you, my lady. Your pottage is ready."

Margaret stood and shook her mantle to settle it about her. She stepped to the nearest tripod and accepted a bowl. As she chewed, she looked about.

Half the camp already packed. Stools in the carts. Across the road, the hay is gone. I see two of the horses still at the stream and the other two are being saddled. Poor Night. Too old for this journey. We could never have ridden fast had I been on you. Need to ride fast again this day. Which way? How safe? Your will, Oh God, in all things.

Margaret handed her bowl to one woman and asked another to accompany her into the forest. Before a bush still clutching a few leaves, the woman stood facing the road while Margaret crouched behind the bush. Her need met, Margaret stood and walked to a different bush and performed the same service for the Saxon. By the time she returned, Arnaud and Bertrand were already on their horses. Demetre cupped his hands for Margaret to mount. As she tied herself to the platform, Demetre talked.

"We ride west until we meet another helper. There we learn which is better, more west or south. We must keep a half day's ride between them and us." He mounted.

Margaret looked toward the Saxons. In the quiet of the night and with two dying fires, she saw only shadows. She turned her horse and kicked it forward to stop before two men. "Saxons, we are grateful for your generous help. We pray you are safe as you return home. Know you are in our prayers. God go with you."

As they turned their horses, they heard the Saxons' soft, "God go with you."

An echo. She followed Bertrand. As soon as it was light enough to see the road, they trotted for a time, walked for a time, and kept switching the pace as they rode west. *To gallop seems faster, but it also wears our horses. If they have no strength left, we needs stop. Then we are easily caught. And dead. In these woods, I could have hidden well. Been the wild woman of the forest and away from the king and the world. I could still have had my sword with me. Hidden, of course. Now I needs depend on others for my safety. God, did I decide aright?*

Saturday

As the sky lightened, Emile roused Claude and his lord. They munched bread as they saddled their horses. Last step was to add the bits to their mounts' mouths, throw the reins over their heads and remove the neck ropes tying them to trees.

"We have a long way. Mayhap this day and at least two more. We stop only if we pass an inn. Eat as we rest our horses. Then continue. I have few coins left, so we may be able to do so only once. Husband your supplies."

"My lord, my stomach well knows I have traveled hungry before," reported Emile.

"When we reach home, I am cert your lady will have a feast ready and hot when we ride into the bailey," said Claude as he mounted.

"I will order my mind tell that to my growling stomach," retorted Alfred with a laugh.

The men continued south.

Mid morning, while trotting their horses, Bertrand raised his hand and the group stopped. A tow-haired boy of eight or nine stood on a sturdy branch with arms hugging the tree trunk. He waved.

"My lady, you have done well. I expected you not until midday. Keep traveling west. You will cross two well-traveled roads. Hide and wait if you must so no Norman sees you cross. The first road is the busy one that goes north and south east of the Oxford. The second goes into the city. Saxons will tarry in each place. If your followers stop at the first road, they shall be told you took it. If they continue west, at the second road, a Saxon will report you went into the city to buy fresh horses and give the name of a stable Norman-owned but Saxon manned. They shall tell your followers you bought fresh, strong horses and inquired the fastest way to leave town for the east road. Continue west of Oxford where someone shall direct you when to turn south. God go with you."

"Boy," called Demetre from behind the others, "only boys of ten can begin squire training. Gain your freedom or send word to Sir Demetre to Lord Alfred's estate you want your freedom. If I can gain it for you, I will train you myself. Your reward for the bravery you show us this day."

The boy pulled his forelock. "I am Acleah, Sir Demetre. If my mother permits it, you will hear my name again. Go with God, my lady and good knights." Acleah saluted Demetre as he passed.

Before they reached the crossing, the group came to a low place in the road flanked by marshes. Tall felled trees lay beside the road with their dirt-filled roots sticking out. Standing beside the trees, several Saxon men pulled their forelocks as the party passed. Arnaud looked back and stopped to see the Saxons lift each tree by its branches and drag it across the road at an odd angle. A man on either side of the road knocked down a small dam. Brown water rushed to make the muddy, tree-covered road impassable. Two of the Saxons waved at the knight before they disappeared

Margaret also had looked back. *They are much more cunning than we Normans think them. The falls look natural. I wager they also cover their tracks to hide their part. Such a network. Normans have only messengers or parchments, but they have a system unseen. Likely through the whole country. That is how Alfred knows me so well; they told him. I would asked about their system, but I know they would look dumb and pretend not to understand me. We think we rule them, but we know them not. Amazing!*

At both crossings, Lady Margaret and her men hid in roadside ditches. At the first road, a man pulled tall brown weeds from the ditches and threw them into a hand cart for kindling. He oft looked up and down the road. When he signaled, they galloped across. He followed, stopped in the middle of the road, and turned over the cart to halt and distract travelers who might look toward Margaret's party before they disappeared around a bend. As it was market day in Oxford, the second road was filled more with those entering the city than leaving. Beside the road, two boys tossed a ball to each other as they watched both directions at the same time without appearing to do so. This time, Margaret waited not as long. Both boys raised a hand shoulder high and yelled, "My turn!" Again, the party raced across the road and kept galloping until they were out of sight.

Seven miles past Oxford, a hand cart stood beside the road only half-filled with kindling. Two men stepped out of the trees and waved. As they approached with sticks in their arms, Arnaud urged his horse forward so he stood between Margaret and the men. The men nodded recognition of his protection and stopped. The shorter of the two gave the party its last instructions.

"My lady, you are more than two days from home because this way is longer. You will arrive through the trees behind the north side of your bailey. This route is unknown to most and is safest for you. It winds, and paths that look good will take you nowhere, while paths that look to go in the wrong direction soon turn to your advantage." He showed them a marker. "Please remember to remove these as you pass."

The taller man warned, "My lady, beware. The closer you are to home, the greater your danger. They seek you still and seem more desperate every morn. They know your destination and may be in the forest alongside a road or inside the forest waiting for you to arrive. Go with God, my lady." The shorter man echoed him. They pulled their forelocks and jointly pointed to their right. Behind her, Margaret heard branches clatter into the cart. Bertrand followed a path into the ditch and the tall, dry grasses that bordered the forest. At the first turn, he spotted two sticks on the ground pointing the direction they should go. He dismounted, and tossed them off the path. Exhausted horses and humans stopped a mile into the forest. The humans watered their horses.

"Drink water and die." Margaret repeated her mother's dictum and was pleased the men drank not.

"Barely wet your lips and use your tongue to roll a bit of ale in your mouth before you swallow," instructed Demetre.

Margaret did so and re-corked her flask. She jiggled it. *So little remaining, yet it must last two more days.* She threw the strap over her neck and pushed the flask to hang behind her.

She led her horse and followed Demetre away from the stream. Soon he examined another intersection of paths. He picked up the sticks and tossed them off the path, which they then took. A dozen yards later he said, "Over here," and entered a small copse. He tied his horse to a tree. It lowered its head and grabbed the few dry grasses at its feet. The other three followed Demetre's example. The sun, almost done setting, sent faint shards below.

Margaret looked for a tree sturdy enough to lean against for the night. She sat against one and the cold ground immediately pierced her mantle and cooled her backside. She tightened her scarf and clutched her mantle around her.

"No fire means we could freeze in this cold. Arnaud, Bertrand, sit on either side of her to give her some warmth. I stand first guard."

Margaret yawned, closed her eyes and dropped her chin.

"My lady, my lady. Wake. Wake! You must rise and walk about to warm yourself."

"Tired."

"Raise your head. We are standing you upright." Strong arms helped Margaret. She opt her eyes and found the trees were only slightly blacker than the night.

Someone to her left had his arm about her shoulders. "Left. Right. Left. Right. Keep walking."

Margaret did as she was told. "I am awake. I am awake."

"Almost," came that same voice.

Margaret deeply inhaled cold air and swooshed it out. 'Now I am awake. Thank you, Bertrand, for your help. Why do this?"

"Sleep too long in this cold, and your heart slows then stops. You are dead and your body freezes."

"Sir Bertrand, what call you those frozen things that hang from a roof?"

"Icicles, my lady."

"Walking in a circle, Margaret retorted, "I want not to become an icicle."

Bertrand chuckled. "Now I am cert you are awake. Walk a bit more and return to your tree. We will wake you once more before dawn."

I want my bed. After this, a little ice on the stones is nothing.

Sunday

Before Alfred and his men broke camp, the wind picked up and blew cold and moist. They smelled the coming rain and looked west. Emile rekindled the fire. Claude searched for more fuel; Emile soon joined him. With his sword, Alfred hacked thin limbs from nearby evergreen trees. To form a lean-to, Alfred pulled two saplings toward each other and lashed them together with his belt. He leaned the boughs against them and threw his mantle on top.

"You need that, my lord."

"If the rain freezes, Emile, my mantle will stop it dripping on us through the boughs. Bring in the horse blankets to keep them dry."

Claude grabbed a long, thick stick and dragged it in a curve to make a ditch to drain water around the lean-to's high side. Fortunately, the wind changed and blew against the back of the lean-to instead of through its sides. The men crawled inside and sat side by side with their backs to the lean-to's back wall. Under their raised knees lay the stack of wood. They wrapped their arms around their knees to hold them close under the saddle blankets they had draped over themselves. A sudden gust announced the storm's arrival, and the water struck hard. Outside, a horse whinnied his displeasure at being soaked.

Bertrand looked north. "I see a band of darkness. Rain. I pray it turns not south. We have no protection."

Because the forest was an ancient one, its canopy was high above them. Branches started above their heads, even when they were ahorse. A few bushes lived here and there. Dead leaves covered the

357

ground. They rode over the flat, smooth paths, and walked over the rocky and root-strewn sections. Occasionally turning east or west to follow their path south, they traveled all day.

These trees are ancient. For cert, older than the Norman time here. Mayhap even longer than when Saxons arrived. I feel their age. I envy their silence, their solitude. They will be here long after we are dead. We matter not to them. What matters to me? Staying alive. Alfred, Our babe. Loving my family and friends. Home.

I am not alone! Even at my worst times, I had Caitlin and Jorgon. Here I have loyal men protecting me and much to live for.

Margaret felt her heart warm and her will strengthen. To keep herself moving, Margaret thought each step a word. *Left. Right. Left. Right. I am brave. I am strong. Lift my feet. Lift my feet.* She blindly followed the man in front of her, tried to ignore the cold, and forced herself to think only her chant. Depending on her watchful men, Margaret paid no attention where her feet took her.

At every open place the group paused. They sought grasses for the horses and talked. At one stop, Margaret took Demetre aside. As their horses nibbled a few bites of dead grass, Margaret said, "Sir Demetre, I am more grateful that I can say you stayed after my marriage. This trip is more than repayment for my healing your shield arm. I want you to stay with us, but because you desire it, not because you feel obligation."

"Serving you is not obligation, my lady. True, at first, I stayed to thank you. Now I stay because I want land, a wife, children, no more wandering. Most men want that. Lord Alfred's announcement at Michaelmas gives me hope I can gain it. For that future, gladly will I fell trees and grub roots." Demetre averred, "I can be a knight and a farmer as well."

Margaret nodded. "Good." *I wish I could tell him he deserves it, but presume not. What if Alfred thinks otherwise? Remember Mother and Father. She interfered with his running the estate; they fought, and she lost his love.* Margaret recalled the talk she and Alfred had about that very matter. *I must accept my lot as a woman, but I do wish the world was different. I can only pray for it. A sorry consolation.*

The group re-formed, mounted, and continued. As they rode, Margaret prayed and reminded herself to be grateful. *Thank you, God, for giving us more smooth paths than rocky ones. Riding is easier.*

Dark came fast under the canopy. Margaret wrapped her mantle close before she sat between two thick roots and leaned against the giant oak. She rested a gloved hand atop a root, felt its gnarled surface, and looked to where it buried itself into the earth. *Must dig deep to keep this great tree standing. Mother, they reburied your body in the forest. Do tree roots now hug your body? Does this root touch another which touches another and another until it reaches you. If I touch this root and send my love, will your body feel it? Have my prayers released you from Purgatory? Are you already in Heaven? God in Heaven, please let her in. Look down on me, Mother. I need your protection as well.* Margaret closed her eyes and prayed herself to sleep.

Monday

Alfred had freed his belt from the saplings. He was donning it and his sword when a Saxon appeared at the tree line across the road. At a soft whistle, Emile whirled as he drew his blade at the sound behind him.

"Halt, Emile. He is a friend." Alfred strode to the young man, who stepped back into the shadows. Alfred waited for the password that the message was a truth.

"Sir Portier and seven of Wilbur's men think you are together. They chase your lady to murder you both."

"Followed you my orders?"

"Every step since you left her. Saturday near dark, she left the road west of Oxford. Now she goes south through the forest to your bailey. Should be home by dark this day. They expect her."

"Portier?"

"Well east of her. On the road toward Newbury. At King's Inn, they will turn west to your estate. We told them you two ride ahead of them."

"Tell all they did well."

The man disappeared.

Albert whirled. "Wilbur is chasing my lady! Mount!"

38

※

Dryhtenton

Mass was delayed because Felamaere had called Father to leave the church. When Father Manntun returned, he sprinted through the congregation. "Verel, Jorgon, outside." Father turned the altar's corners and began Mass even before he reached the cross at the center of the table. He clipped his words, raced through the steps, and omitted the sermon. Father rushed Holy Communion, the end of the service, and strode for the door without giving his customary blessing.

Outside church, Feleamare talked as the three men sprinted to the bailey.

"Jorgon, saddle six knights' horses. Have them ready near the gate. Sir Verel, we must talk in private before everyone arrives."

Seeing who approached at a run, Roulin and Sauville stared into the trees expecting an enemy to charge. Jorgan dashed toward the stables.

"Sir Verel, Lady Margaret and three knights are trying to reach home before Lord Wilbur's men capture her."

"I know you Saxons relay messages; I care not how. Tell it me. You may have missed its meaning."

Felamaere shook his head. "I know the meaning."

"The words." Verel blinked not.

Felamaere relented. "'She plus three toward morning sun. Guard edges. Protect circle and road.' You guard our borders. We meet her and get her inside the bailey."

"Where?"

"From northwest. Through forest paths. Oft too thick or too rocky for riding. Walkers can pass."

"Not enough knights."

"Boys behind the palisade watching all directions? You take the road and lane?"

Verel nodded and strode toward the barracks for his armor.

Father ordered the congregants to remain in church and to stand facing the door. From outside the church, he faced them. "Enemies approach. Soon they will be upon us. Knights, Verel will instruct you; he is in the bailey. Kitchen staff, to your posts; we need food. Saxons, carry food to share and sleeping gear only. Leave your animals. Men, settle your families within the bailey in whatever inside spot you can find. Then report to Felamaere in the bailey. We need your older boys as watchmen. Daelton, hitch donkeys to a wagon and take it to the alehouse. Help Linton and Lindene load ale barrels and take them into the bailey. If we are not yet attacked, make a second trip. I guard the church. He raised his right hand. "God forgives you anything you do to save ourselves. Go with God, my children. MOVE!" He stepped aside.

The knights raced up the lane and the Saxons into the village. Armored, armed, silent, determined men left their barracks. Excited horses whinnied as their riders mounted. Roulin yelled, "Clear the lane!" to the few Saxons already approaching the bailey. The knights raced down the lane. At the road, Pernel and Louvel rode right. Louvel stopped at fifty yards and Pernel at one hundred yards from the lane entrance. Hughes and Giraud rode left the same distances. On either side of the lane's entrance, Verel and Sauville held the middle.

The Saxons locked the gate behind the first wagon of ale, and three men helped Daelton and Gytha's sons place the barrels against the hall walls. Roulin allowed them to attempt a second trip, but the gate was locked against them. As the broad-shouldered knight perused the distant trees from his post, he glanced down at Daelton. Wearing a gray tabbard over his clothes, the boy flicked a whip above the donkey's head, as the boys fetched more ale.

While the Saxons gathered, Felamaere drew Rammeg Elder to one side; they whispered and nodded before they rejoined the group. Felamaere separated the men and boys. "Boys, we have too few knights to guard all our border. Stand on the walkway to make a ring of watchers. Stand far apart, yet so you can still be seen by the other boys or Sir Roulin. If you spot any danger, hide behind the poles and call out 'Danger!' and what you see, like 'Danger! Three knights riding from the east.' The rest of you pass the message to Sir Roulin. Ignore what you hear inside the bailey. Look outward for knights or for a hail of arrows. Right arms raised, safe. Left arms raised, danger. Our lives depend on you being reliable. Keep us safe. Go with God."

After the boys climbed the ladders to arrange themselves around the bailey walls, Felemaere drew the men close and whispered his plan. While everyone nodded agreement, a few argued Felamaere's life was too valuable to endanger by having him joining them.

"I am one of you, not above you. Let the man with the most children stay to manage the bailey."

"Wilfrith," said the men in unison.

"Op the gate," called Roulin.

The Saxon party exited and jumped off the lane, half to the right and half left. Rammeg Elder headed for his home to fetch the long bow and arrows hidden in the roof's thatching. Garwig followed the knights to be their messenger. Wilfrith and Daelton shut the gate and dropped the bars onto their brackets behind the second load of ale. With the gate secured, Wilfrith turned to securing the bailey. He ordered everyone to throw water on all the thatched roofs against possible flaming arrows. The weather and water were so cold, the Saxons saw their breathes and blew on their fingers to keep them limber.

The sun was halfway to casting no shadow when the party was still so deep in the forest all they saw ahead were more trees and another hill blocking their view. Margaret was exhausted, but she plodded on. The group knew not Wilbur's men were on a road almost eight miles east of them or that their Saxons were already in the forest ahead of them.

Past midday, Wilbur's men came in sight of the King's Inn. They walked their horses, turned west and walked past the massive structure. A dozen bowmen with arrows in their notches watched the rough-looking party. They noted the leader and the end man were well-attired, with good swords and stalwart horses. The middle six were a sorry lot with stubbled faces, mismatched clothes, and swords without scabbards. The men waved and kept walking their horses until they were out of sight.

"We must catch them in the next eight miles or they will be home. Before sunset, we will know success or failure. Ride hard," ordered Portier.

Arnaud heard faint noises not of the forest. He stopped and raised his arm. He signaled they mount. Demetre helped Margaret mount before he did. He joined Arnaud. Both heard rustling dead leaves. Bertrand protected Margaret's back.

Frantically searching an escape route, Margaret looked through the trees on either side of her. *Dare I run away when we are attacked? Should I stay among them for protection? Oh, to have a sword!*

A head popped into sight. With both hands, he waved broadly at having found the foursome. Heads far apart from each other appeared left and right of him. All Saxon. The men waved the party forward.

"We are so glad to see you, good sirs," said Hloetun. "God give you a good day, my lady."

"That He does, given He has brought you to us."

"What are you about?" asked Demetre.

"Wilbur's men are on the road riding fast for our lane. They think you are ahead of them and want to catch you before you reach the bailey. Knights stay them; we get you inside. We marked the fastest way to ride out of here and into the bailey." Hloetun smiled as he waved them forward. "Follow the Saxons."

Arnaud and Demetre rode over the hill the way Hloetun had pointed and found a smooth path. Margaret and Bertrand followed as the knights turned at each Saxon they met. Halfway to the fields, Margaret nodded at Felamaere, who smiled at her. *We ride toward the sun.* The horses alternately trotted and walked until the party could see through the trees. The guides and other Saxon searchers followed the horses.

"Good sirs, please stop." Aldcot stepped out of the trees to examine the forest to his right and the fields ahead. He raised his right arm. A boy on the palisade raised his right arm. Aldcot turned. "Good sirs, he sees or hears no one. Ride fast. We know not how close are Wilbur's men or where. They may be coming through the trees from the east."

The men drew their swords. Without looking back, Demetre counseled, "My lady, no matter what happens, reach the bailey. Leave the rest to us."

Margaret checked the leather strap around her waist. She clutched the reins. *Please, God… No. Your will, Oh Lord, in all things. I will do my best. My life and their's are Yours.*

Demestre kneed his horse hard; three followed. The horses plunged through the few remaining trees and raced across stubbled fields, throwing up clods of earth behind them. *I cannot see them coming through the trees behind me.* She craned her neck.

"Fear not, my lady!" called Bertrand. "I guard your back."

Would that I could protect myself. Grateful for their aid. Think not. Ride hard.

The foursome raced toward the bailey's north curve. As they rounded the palisade now curving west, in the distance they spotted the lane and then the gate.

No men! Only boys on the wall with right arms raised.

Behind Demetre, Arnaud's horse stumbled and Margaret jerked her reins to bring her horse to its right. Arnaud regained control, and the pair ran side by side. Because the lane slanted upward to the gate, Demetre aimed for a spot beyond the gate where a horse could safely jump onto the roadway. He stopped his horse and gestured forward with his left arm. Arnaud slowed, and Margaret's horse took the lane. Wilfrith and Jorgon opt the gate and Margaret flew through. *Home! Home! Safe!* Margaret collapsed onto her horse's neck. The men closed and barred the gate.

Demetre stayed by the gate as Arnaud patrolled the tree line east and guarded the Saxons running for the bailey. Bertrand stopped to guard the Saxons as they ran single file around the west side of the bailey and alongside the dry moat toward the gate. At Roulin's call, the bailey gate again opt, and the Saxons disappeared inside. Demetre headed down the lane, and the other two followed him.

Jorgon held the reins at the horse's drooped head as Cormac untied Margaret and helped her dismount. He ordered Ferrant away. All thought of fighting fled, she crumbled against Cormac, who called for aid. Caitlin left the hall, saw their mistress, and asked two women to join her. Ferrant barked his worry. Raeddaelf and Ifig each took a side to guide Margaret toward the motte as Caitlin led. Margaret whispered, "thirst," and her knees buckled again. Duone appeared, and without speaking, picked up Margaret and carried her to the motte, through the gate, and up the stairs. Ferrant followed. Duone set down Margaret, who placed both hands on the ladder and one foot on the bottom rung but was too exhausted to take the next step. Duone grabbed her around her waist and one-armed carried her to the top. The women looked on in horror at how the ladder bowed. Duone disappeared through the doorway; Caitlin pushed Ferrant aside, and the women scurried to follow Margaret's helper.

Cleva announced, "He carried her up the stairs. Midryth is with them."

"Fetch ale and bread," instructed Caitlin. "Women, with me."

In the top room, Caitlin saw Margaret seated on a stool with Duone behind her, holding her shoulders to keep her upright. Midryth was turning down the bedding.

"Thank you, Duone; you did well. Our lady will thank you when she feels better. Go now."

Raedaelf and Ifig took Duone's place. He left, and Ferrant entered. Six months with child, Caitlin feared bending and lifting, so she just gave instructions. "Midryth, hand me a chemise from the chest and a drying cloth. Women, remove her mantle. Midryth, turn your back. Stand her and strip her of those sweaty garments and dry her with this." Margaret shivered but was too spent to cover her breasts with her hands. Caitlin handed over the chemise and picked up the top blanket from the bed. The women worked together to put the chemise on Margaret. Once Caitlin had wrapped the blanket around Margaret, the women re-sat their lady on the stool. Raedaelf stood behind her and held her upright. Caitlin continued. "Midryth, bring the ale and bread when it arrives. My lady, my lady, op your eyes and tell us what you need."

"Drink. Warmth. Sleep." Margaret opt her eyes and gave a wan smile. "Caitlin."

She closed her eyes and sighed, "Like old days."

"Yes, my lady. Sip this." Caitlin put a mug to Margaret's lips; she downed it and half emptied the second mugful. "Tired."

The women put Margaret to bed and piled blankets and a wolf fur atop her.

"Caitlin, stay."

Margaret shifted from her back to her side and placed a hand under her pillow to warm it. With her eyes still shut, she curled her knees toward her chest and placed her other hand over her belly. Standing bedside, Caitlin stroked her hair and made soothing noises. Still pale skinned and blue-eyed, Caitlin's body had changed from girl to woman, and the bump of her babe made her look even more comely and feminine. The redness of Caitlin's hair still shown in sunlight, even in the double braids she wore as a wife.

"If I lose our babe. Find Wilbur. Kill him myself." Margaret pulled her covers to her eyebrows..

Shocked, Caitlin said in a low voice, "Fear not, child of my heart, you will keep your babe. Sleep now. All will be well in the morn." She stayed bedside, stroking Margaret's half-covered head until her girl slept. Ferrant lay at the foot of the bed with his face to the door. To watch over Margaret, Caitlin sat on a stool beside a brazier. Cormac arrived with her food. As she ate, he insisted she sleep in the hall with him. Cleva promised the girls would take turns all night and took her place.

With the sun setting before them, eight knights created a dust cloud as they raced toward their quarry. Verel and Sauville charged forward to stand beside Hughes and Giraud to fully block the road. Louvel and Pernel shifted to guard the lane. All six knights looked formidable in their helmets, armor, and with swords poised. The attackers stopped before drawn swords and hard faces. Seeing the wall of men before them, those behind Portier glanced at each other and stayed behind him.

"Too late! They are already home. Turn back," barked Verel.

"Where is your lord?" sneered the man at the back of the group.

"Behind you. With men on both sides of the road. Draw blades and meet them."

Hughes noted the front man glaring at him and guessed his name. "Recognize your helmet, do you, Sir Portier? Your blade is behind me."

Portier looked beyond the men to see Pernel pointed his own sword at him. Just then, Demetre rode between Pernel and Louvel and approached. Hughes whispered Demetre's name to Verel.

Verel sounded enraged. "Demetre, I told you to stay hidden with the others!"

"Worry not, the others are still hidden. I want to see whose armor I am wearing." Demetre turned his horse so Portier could see what he had lost. "I do look handsome, do I not, Portier?" preened Demetre.

"What others?" asked a man in the middle of the pack as he looked about.

"Why have they your arms and armor?" asked the man beside the other as he looked behind himself.

"Know you of Lord Albert of Drytentun, the man who won Lord Wilbur's tourney last month? Winner took all. He defeated Portier and got his goods. Your Lord Wilbur fought and lost his goods as well. Were you not there to see it?"

"We chase Lord Wilbur's lady, who ran away with his guest. We are charged with killing him and returning her," revealed the man, who wore his own metal-ringed fighting vest and rode just behind Portier.

Verel looked askance as if at a fool. "You chased the Saxon, Lord Alfred of Drytentun, and his lady as they journeyed home from a visit. For cert, you have heard of her. Lady Margaret is the woman who was attacked on her way home two years ago, had her attackers beheaded, and set their heads on poles. Look behind us. The poles stand ready to serve should you prove foolish." Verel gave the men time to look past him before he added, "Your Lord Wilbur has already lost his honor. Now he thinks he will regain his armor. Tell me at least one of you has heard these stories."

"I have," said a tall man whose helmet was only leather. He repeated what he had heard about the tourney and ended with, "I am not one of Wilbur's men. He hired most of us to fetch his straying wife. I want none of this. I will risk not my life for metal fairly won." He raised both hands shoulder high. "I draw no blade in this fight. I am leaving." He turned his horse halfway round.

"Halt!" ordered Portier. "That horse and your blade are lent. Take them with you, and I will hang you for a thief."

Six men dismounted; they slowly drew their blades with their left hands or switched their blades to their left hands and dropped them.

"Take them," said the third man. "But I surrender not my half pay for I gave chase as Wilbur demanded."

The others loudly agreed. Wilbur's mercenaries walked past Wilbur's second man and toward the King's Inn. Portier ordered Wilbur's remaining knight to hand the loose reins to him. That done, the other man dismounted to pick up the swords, tied them together behind his saddle, and remounted. With his nose in the air, Portier turned and walked away with horses trailing behind him. His companion followed. No one spoke until Wilbur's men disappeared the way they had come.

"Well played, Demetre."

"I lied not, Verel. Arnaud and Bertrand are in the lane."

"You three walk well behind them for a mile or two, but be home by dark. Demetre, you take the others to ride the east tree line, should all this prove a trick. I guard the lane entrance."

Garwig saluted Demetre and the others as they passed him. He decided he was not needed and returned to the bailey. Rammeg Elder slipped through the forest to the back of the village. He hid the long bow and metal-tipped war arrows within the thatching of his hut. He ran to the gate and slipped through. Refusing to answer Roulin's questions about his actions, Rammeg sought Felamaere.

"They needed me not. Six knights dismounted and dropped swords. As they walked off, I ran home. No one saw me."

"Good. Had you shot, the law would have killed you. You are a brave man, Rammeg." Felamaere sought confirmation. "It is the only one on the estate?"

Rammeg nodded. "My father's. He taught me to form them."

"I cannot force you, but I want you burn the bow and shafts and bury the points in the forest. You know the law. If anyone ever finds you with that forbidden weapon, you will die. I want you alive."

Rammeg nodded only his understanding, not his agreement.

They heard Roulin report, "Four knights returning. They ride the east line of trees."

"I will tell Cormac," called Felamaere. He and Rammeg headed for the hall.

39

Arrival

In the trees on the other side of the road someone coughed. Half hidden behind an evergreen tree, the boy dressed in brown from neck to toes almost disappeared against the dead leaves on the forest floor. On his side of the road, Alfred turned and smiled. Fireside, Claude and Emile jumped awake with swords in hand as their blankets fell to their feet.

"God give you a good morrow, Sir Claude, Sir Emile. A Saxon for me." Alfred chuckled as he crossed the road. He warned, "You may enjoy making Normans jump, but beware. Someday one might kill you for it."

"All is well, my lord. She is home. Sunday late. At your lane, your men stopped Portier. The mercenaries abandoned him. No blood, no death."

"You sound disappointed."

"Not for you and your lady. For no Normans dying." The messenger sighed. "Mayhap another time."

Alfred handed the short, tousled-haired boy a coin and watched him disappear. He returned to his men. "My lady is safe and home. Pack. We dine in Oxford. Then one more night on the road, before we sup at home."

As Caitlin had instructed, Midryth refused Father Manntun entering the keep. Margaret slept on. She missed the Saxons returning home with their goods, attending Mass, breaking their fasts. Alura brought a dinner tray from the hall. Cyne ate and arrived to exchanged places with Cleva.

The sun faded behind the tree tops when Margaret rolled to her back. She stirred and stretched her legs before she opt her eyes. Margaret smiled at the canopy. *Our room. Where is he?* She pulled the blanket off her nose and stopped at her throat. Still drowsy, she pulled her hands back under her coverings. *Cold.* She prayed for Alfred's safety. Ferrant stood with his nose over the bed frame, but Margaret had already closed her eyes. Cyne slipped downstairs and returned with a small pot of hot broth.

At a sound, she asked, "Caitlin?"

"Cyne, my lady. Shall I fetch her for you?"

"No. When is it?"

"Monday, my lady. You arrived Sunday before sunset. You slept a day since."

Margaret sniffed. "Broth?"

"Yes, my lady. May I serve you?"

"Keep it warm." Margaret rolled to her side and sat up. She pushed away the fur and wrapped the top blanket about her. She padded behind the curtain. Upon her return, she sat on the stool beside a braziers and petted Ferrant. "You are a good boy." Cleva extended the mug, and Margaret warmed her hands on its sides as she cautiously sipped the steaming brew. Next, Alura carried in a bowl of pottage. Margaret finished that as well.

"My lady, Felamaere waits below with a message."

"I will have my boots and mantle."

Felamaere stood in the doorway. Margaret pushed a hand through an arm slit and motioned him forward. "Felamaere, God give you a good Monday, what is left of it."

"You as well, my lady." Felamaere stepped into the room and pulled his forelock. "A message, my lady. Your lord knows of your safe arrival. He dined in Oxford midday and replenished his supplies. Likely, he will camp on the road this night. On the morrow, we expect him home to sup."

Margaret smiled. "Then best we sup at midday and dine well for his return." Margaret furrowed her brow. "I promised my lord's mother I would inform her when I safely reached home. Will you send the message for me?" Felemaere agreed. "Shall it soon be Advent?"

"Yes, my lady. Sunday is the first day."

"Fasting again. Best we dine well at my lord's return and feast the next day as well. Meat and more meat while we can. Will you inform Cook for me?"

"I am honored to do so." Felamaere noted how her shoulders drooped. "My lady, may I suggest you return to bed? Your journey was hard, and I fear you tire still. Sleep again until the morrow. I will have your supper delivered, and the girls will keep it hot should you wake."

"Vespers."

Felamaere smiled. "If you must confess riding on Sunday and missing Mass this morn, you may as well stay abed and confess missing Vespers as well."

Margaret smiled at their reeve. "I like the way you think. Please send a girl to help me."

"God give you a good night, my lady. Sleep well." Felamaere backed to the doorway, and left.

Margaret looked down beside her. "Boy, you are loyal, and I love you for it." Margaret petted Ferrant and bid him stay with her. He licked her hand. She doffed her mantle and boots to return to bed. *Oh Lord, I have learned Your lesson. Trust in Your plan, though I know it not. Ask or lean on others, but depend on You. Your will, O Lord, in all things.* Margaret lay back and pulled her covers to her chin as she waited.

In the morning, with scarf tied tight and mantle clutched close, Margaret waited outside the church in the pre-dawn glimmer. She breathed into her hunched shoulder, and her breath turned into frost on the cloth. Sir Hughes and Sir Louvel stood behind her.

"Father, will you hear my confession before Mass, so I may partake of Communion and thank Our Lord for His goodness?"

Father unlocked the door, Sir Hughes entered and returned. He nodded, and Father and Margaret stepped inside. After Father heard her confession, he said, "Clearly, God loves you. Despite your missing Mass two Sundays in a row, He got you safely home. Not your fault. I can do nothing about those who chased you on a holy day, but I will speak to Lord Alfred about choosing to travel on one."

Margaret stayed at the back of the church to complete her penance. *Father was kind to forgive easily and require so little. Marriage has softened him. Has it softened me?* Before anyone else arrived, Margaret had completed her prayers and had stepped to her place.

After Mass, Margaret asked Caitlin and Cormac to the hall. She waited until they were almost finished with their pottage before she asked for Cormac's report. Cormac began with Sunday morning. He finished with the Saxons returning home after Mass Monday morn.

"Cormac, you and Felamaere did well."

"Thank you, my lady. If you will excuse me, I needs speak with Verel."

After Cormac left the dais, Caitlin leaned and whispered, "I know your secret. When is it due?"

"I told you nothing."

"You mumbled it as I stayed bedside after your return."

Margaret screwed up her face trying to decide what to say. She shrugged. "The first fortnight in June." When she saw Caitlin finger-counting on her thigh, she added. "Three months on my birth date." Margaret yawned. "Tell my lord nothing. I want him to figure it himself." Caitlin barked a laugh. "Not funny."

Caitlin turned serious. "Promise me you will leave Wilbur to your lord." When Margaret shook her head, Caitlin placed her hand over Margaret's. "No longer may you ride, dash through the countryside, or pick up a sword. Trust me, should you lose this babe, Lord Alfred will kill him."

Margaret thought. She nodded, and murmured, "I expect he will." *Must see Verel. Dine then sleep. Have the girls wake me. No, I want not to be abed when he arrives.* "Stay if you wish. I wait for him in the hall."

Caitlin kept Margaret company until Cormac looked her way. She descended the steps and followed Cormac out the main door. Margaret called for Scandy, who fetched her sewing basket from the keep. While she waited, she asked Verel to sit with her and report.

Afterward, she sewed for Alfred. Before they dined, Margaret invited Bertrand and Arnaud to sit on her side of the dais. She looked not at the empty armed chair to her right. They told her they had been born in England. The men reported being trained by their fathers and being sent out as mercenaries when their fathers died.

"My lord said he knew of you before he engaged your services."

Bertrand looked at his friend before he turned back to their lady. "We met him at Lord Cai's estate years ago when he squired Sir Cyrille. Lord Cai engaged us not. Truth is, my lady, we sought him in Winchester after your contract. We brought Pernel and Louvel with us."

'Sir Arnaud?"

"All true, my lady. You should know we four had Norman fathers—and Saxon mothers." Both men held their breaths.

"I know. May I suggest you not tell the other men. As knights can only make other knights, they know your fathers were Norman. Norman men speak not of their women, so they will not think to ask you about your mothers. Should they do so, I suggest you evade them."

"Thank you, my lady," said the men in unison. They stepped down to join the other men.

Cook arrived to discuss the morrow's feast. Margaret moved to the end of a bench and took up her sewing with Ferrant at her feet. As Margaret waited, Hartun kept her end of the pit's fire high, so she could see her work. At a man's shout, Margaret dropped a braies in the basket and handed it to Hartun to remove. Margaret pushed down her skirt. She touched her circlet and made cert her braids were behind her. Her heart hammered in her chest as she stood.

The main door banged op. The knights on Margaret's side of

the fire backed to the stalls. Alfred took no note of the helmet and sword high on the wall before him. He turned his head and body as one and looked down the hall. Straight faced, he took long strides.

Margaret smiled her welcome. When Alfred was halfway to her, she curtseyed while holding his gaze with hers. "We are glad you are home, my lord."

By the time she had risen, he was upon her. Alfred grabbed her waist and pulled her to him. He hugged her tightly and lifted her off her feet. Margaret grabbed his arms to steady herself. He set her down, swooped, and kissed her hard. Margarett pulled away to take a breath. He kissed her again, and she put her arms around his neck, pulled him in, and matched his fervor. They forgot they were alone not.

The knights looked away and talked quietly in pairs and threes. The serving girls and Hartun slipped out the kitchen door; Scandy waited beside the ale barrel with his eyes to the floor. After the pair parted, Alfred put his hand to Margaret's cheek.

"Thaes hal, wif."

She whispered, "Thaes hal, husband." The lovers returned to the world and looked around to see they were almost alone.

"Scandy, send for our meal." Margaret led the way to the dais.

When Alfred reached his place, he announced, "Glad we are to be among you."

The hall turned and applauded his arrival as if they had just seen him. "Lord Cai of the Fens died with his family around him. My lady and I visited him before he went to God. We will miss our dear friend all our days." Alfred paused. "Please find a place among you for Sir Emile, whom I engaged during our journey. I have other news, but it will wait for the morrow."

They sat. Margaret whispered, "The morrow's midday we feast too."

Scandy opt the door for the girls carrying the first course.

After Vespers, Alfred spoke to Father before he gave Margaret his arm. They walked in twilight up the lane trailed by the knights and their household. Knights turned toward the hall. Sir Claude closed the keep gate behind the girls as Alfred and Margaret led. At the doorway, Alfred locked the keep door after the servants.

Hughes was last to enter the hall. He looked at the keep and swore, "By the Christ's blood, I want a wife."

Ahead of him, Syghelm heard. His heart ached but he spoke not.

While Alfred secured the keep door and bid the girls, "God give you a good night," Margaret took the stairs, hung her mantle, returned from that corner to stand between the bed and the door. She watched Alfred enter, lock their door, and toss his cloak toward his clothes tree. *He missed; I care not.* When he turned, she took a step to him and opt her mouth.

"Not a word," said Alfred as he enfolded Margaret into his arms.

40

News

Margaret woke to Alfred curled against her back with his arm over her shoulder. Eyes still closed, she added to her mental list of the times since their talks on the keep steps Alfred had done a kindness. With each memory she added, her heart warmed to him. At recalling his return from the tourney, seeing only her, his kisses, she admitted, *For me, not for show. Not possession. Glad to see me. I kissed him back. I care for him.* That thought pleased her. *I am more than land and rank to him.* She smiled to herself. *Yester's homecoming. My heart pounded at his return. He was all I saw, all he wanted was me.* Knowing how they were together, Margaret liked her thoughts. *I am his wife. Wife and partner. I meant everything I did last night. I love… not yet. Not even think it until I have answers. What is his real name? Why did Saxons help me? When met we?* She thought Sunday's question. *It will eliminate market day.* She lifted Alfred's hand and kissed his palm, the inside of his wrist.

"Did the church bell ring?" came his sleepy voice. At her "No," Alfred placed his hand on her shoulder to roll her to her back. As he climbed atop her, Margaret lifted her head to kiss him. *I do. I know I do, but I shall speak it not until I have answers.*

After Mass and a meal, Alfred left the dais to speak to knights. Margaret saw Cook about the feast before returning to the keep fireplace and her sewing. The feast was meat-based broth with herbed balls of boiled bread dough, platters of warmed smoked pork, bowls of boiled vegetables and bread. Ale flowed. While the servants cleared the tables, Alfred began the stories. He spoke well of Lord Cai and his family. He reported Lord Cai's death and funeral. He omitted how the fire started in the village and stressed how unified was the effort to contain it. He painted a friendlier parting than was true and made the first few days of riding sound pleasant. He summarized his ride home in a single sentence. Honeyed, stewed apples arrived.

Well done. You omitted the lake, all the negative parts at Lord Cai's estate, and Wulf's part in the fire. I suspect your journey home was also not as pleasant as you portrayed it. I will speak not. What might the men say about the Saxon help we received?

Sir Demetre stood and reported Margaret's journey home. He reported all efforts, all decisions, all actions using "we." He said nothing of meeting Saxons or of receiving aid. *I wager Alfred swore them to secrecy. Only, he, I, and they will ever know the truth. Why is he hiding their part? Ask him that as well.*

Dessert finished and bowls removed, everyone looked eager to hear Sir Verel's version of all that had happened at home. *Verel should be a story teller. He has enthralled us. He raises and lowers his voice; he pauses and gestures. He tells a fine tale of courage and heroism. He even praised the villagers for their part. I feel as though I had been standing on the walkway seeing it all unfold. Well done, Verel.*

Alfred stood. "I have an ending for all this. Want you to hear it?"

A chorus of "Yes," "Tell us," and What happened?" rose.

"Sir Claude, Sir Emile, and I sat roadside the last night when two walkers approached. They asked to share our fire, and we shared our meal for a story. They told a sad tale of a great lord lying to them, of chasing that lie, and of being defeated." Alfred gestured to the men, "Well you know their tale." He waited for the talk to stop. "In the morn, the mercenaries asked if I might need two knights' services for the winter or longer. They swore they were brave and good fighters." He stopped until the laughter subsided. "I looked down at them from Garhard and said most kindly, 'I am Lord Alfred of Dryhtenton. The woman you chased is my lady. Were I to bring you home, my lady would greet you, feed you, and order your throats slit in the night. If you want to live, seek your winter home elsewhere.' We turned and rode away. Of course, I knew my lady need do nothing. When any one of you had heard their story, you would have done the deed without our lady having to ask."

Laughter, applause, and foot stomping ensued, much to Alfred's pleasure. He raised his brows at Margaret in a silent question. She confirmed he spoke aright with a firm nod. The men laughed even harder at seeing their exchange. As the hall quieted, Alfred called for another round of ale and sat. Margaret only smiled.

You want others to believe I am still dangerous, bloodthirsty. You know me well. You also know them. Margaret looked for Syghelm, whom she found on the left side of the fire well down the table. They exchanged knowing looks. Alfred saw it but said nothing. *I am tired and want a nap. One more thing and I leave.* Margaret whispered to Alfred for his approval.

Margaret stood and the hall quieted. "Sir Demetre, Sir Bertrand, Sir Arnaud, I was so sure of your protection and skills, I never thought of wanting a sword." *A small lie I must confess, but worth the price.* "I thank you for escorting me home." Margaret saw others slap them on their backs and congratulate them. "I thank all of you for your courage, your cunning, and your protection." She waited for the hall to quiet. "My lord, I have news. Will you join me while I give it?" Alfred stood. "I am sorry to report King Henry will soon be sad."

"Sad, my lady?"

"King Henry thinks he has the best knights in the land. When he hears the stories of our men, he will be sad and jealous. King Henry will know what we know." She lifted her mug as did Alfred. "A toast, my lord." She shouted, "To our knights, the best in all England!" Alfred repeated her words. They clinked mugs together and drank. Thunderous applause and foot-stomping followed. The couple beamed at each other. Margaret set down her mug; Lord Alfred lifted her hand to his lips and kissed its back. Margaret blushed. The noise continued. She waved, picked up her mantle, and took the stairs. As she left the hall by the back door, she heard Alfred call for another round of ale.

The next day, Father joined them in breaking their fasts. He set two small parchments neatly folded and wax-sealed before Lord Alfred. *Please God, let them not be from King Henry or Lord Warwick commanding his service. I want him home for Christmastide.* Margaret ate lightly and glanced oft at the packets. After the bowls had been removed, Father reported, "My lord, in your absence these two arrived but from where I know not."

"You may read them."

He is the only one who can. Seeking permission and granting it is only false politeness and formality. Does Alfred read as well as he figures and wants no one but Cormac and me to know? If he can, we cannot be tricked or cheated.

Father opt the first, read, and announced, "This one is from Normandy; she calls you sister?"

"Cecily, the youngest of the four of us." At noting Father's frown, she added, "She is being fostered there." *Tell no more details than necessary.*

Father read aloud, "Sister, Charles shared the news of your marriage to Lord Alfred in his letter to Lord Guilbert. I add my congratulations to our brother's. I am having Masses said in honor of your marriage and paying the offering myself from the coins I have earned here. Lord Guilbert, Lady Cornelie, Alard, and Leetice have been very kind to me. I have lived with them for a year and three months. Lady Cornelie's way of teaching me to chatelaine is like mother's. At first, I had to do a task perfectly without complaint each day for three weeks before I moved to another household duty. I confess I made a rough beginning. I hated cleaning piss pots, and doing laundry was not much better.

When I reached kitchen and serving duties, Lady Cornelie kindly reduced the time to two weeks for each task. For a year, I have sat an hour each day with Leetice while we broider. Even though Leetice is younger than I am, she was a much better sewer than I, but Lady Cornelie says I am now as skilled as she. I spend an hour each day and sit with Leetice beside Lady Cornelie as we do the estate accounts book, record in it, and keep the estate diary. My lady says I am ready to be a chatelaine, to be married. Shall I shock you? You are reading mine own hand. I now read and write as a proper Norman lady of rank should."

Margaret noted Father's shocked expression. She smiled at watching him squint at the writing and turn the parchment over as if expecting to see Cecily hiding behind it and then turn the document to the writing side and glare at it. She looked away to hide her silent laughter. Father continued in a bemused tone.

"I have learned so much. Until I came here, I had no idea how hard our servants worked, how difficult are their days, and how much a smile, a thank you, or even a nod from me can brighten their day. I will never be short or unkind to servants again."

While under the watchful eye of Lady Cornelie. I wager she reads your letters so you said that to impress the lady you are reformed. Has your proud nature truly changed?

My other good news is that I have improved enough to have a whole set of new garments for Christmastide. I will be joining my lady at her luncheon table, which Leetice is still too young to do. She says she has friends who want to meet me. I do so want to make my lady proud of me.

I thought so. You expect to be presented as a prospective bride for one of her friends' sons. With your ability to charm, you will do well.

"Leetice's riding master taught me to ride. Alard escorts Leetice and me when we ride, so I am well supervised. My life is so much happier here. I am ever so grateful to Charles for sending me to his lovely wife's mother. I understand why he chose Cleanthe. Now I look toward making a good match too and to having a good life, God willing. Know you are in my prayers and of my love for you. Your loving sister in Christ, Cecily."

Throughout the reading, Margaret sat with her hands folded in her lap. Her polite smile had slowly turned into a wide grin.

"You look happy for her, my lady."

"I am, my lord. Cecily learned well. I have high hopes for her. Father, will you say Masses for my sister and the family fostering her? I will write them after they are said."

Alfred handed Father the second letter.

Father read that missive with a smile. "My Lord Alfred and my dear sister, Lady Margaret. Charles wrote me of your marriage. I pray for both of you that Our Blessed Lord gives you a happy marriage, a healthy heir, and other healthy children. As I had predicted, I spent a year working in the kitchens, scrubbing floors, and emptying piss pots. I learned humility and the importance of padding my knees while scrubbing."

Margaret's smile became a chuckle. "Forgive me, Father. I love his gentle humor."

Father continued with, "All the while, I thanked God for leading me to Cluny. I talk with scholars, the abbot has taken an interest in me, and I am now in the scribing room. When I am not at prayer, I assist by preparing goose quill pens and mixing inks. My fingers are now dyed more colors than Joseph's coat, if you remember that story from the Bible. After a few more months here, the Abbot will move me to the best station. I am delighted and grateful, for I will be reading texts and histories and be his student. May God grant you be as happy in your life together as I am in mine. Remember me in your prayers. The brother who always loved you best, Father Raymond."

"My lady, if you desire to write your brother anon, you have my permission. I have matters to attend."

Father left to fetch parchment, quill, and ink. Alone on the dais, Margaret picked up Raymond's letter, kissed the words, and hugged the sheet to her breast. *Oh brother, I am so happy for you. You can be happy for me because I am becoming so. I must choose my words carefully, so he will know it without my saying so. First, I shall ask Father to read it again.*

Alfred was on the practice field despite gray skies and drizzle. Those not on patrol or gate duty joined him. The men were eager to learn the fight moves Alfred had used in the tourney. After Father left, Caitlin arrived to inform Margaret everyone but her husband knew of the coming babe and had sworn secrecy, even the knights. Cormac had accompanied her but kept to the main door. When Margaret asked him if he had anything she needed to know, he stepped to the other end of the fire pit and reported four barrels of salted, dried fish for the hall had arrived.

Margaret groaned and shook her head. "Fish, fish, and fish. God grants us meat on Sundays so we tire not of fish. Oh Lord, I think You planned not well." Caitlin and Cormac chuckled. "How many for the village?"

"Six, my lady. If it is not enough, they needs fish the streams."

"The cost?"

He told her and added, "I ordered them weeks ago to get the best cost. Also, I gained the promise our order would come from the first ship. Let others pay highesr prices and be uncert when their orders will arrive."

"As usual, you did well, Cormac. Be cert to point that out to my lord. This is his first Advent here."

Cormac looked to Caitlin; she shrugged her ignorance at why their lady stated the obvious.

Margaret yawned. "I will wait here ere we dine. Please join us. I like not sitting on the dais without company. Then I am for the keep and a nap."

Cormac wandered back down the pit to sit beside a knight returning from patrol. Margaret reported the contents of the letters. Caitlin was reserved in her comments about Cecily and warm in her praise of Raymond. The women chatted.

Margaret whispered a shocked, "Even Gytha?"

Caitlin enjoyed Margaret's surprise. "I am March, Leoma is April, Gytha is May. You will be the latest at June. I am cert Willa is not yet with child, but I know she wants to join the group. We three are happy for you." She watched Margaret shake her head and smile at the same time. "Remember the saying? 'A heavy harvest is followed by healthy children.'"

"God has shown us favor indeed. Fine weather, good harvests. Happy marriages?" At Caitlin's agreement, Margaret finished with, "Now new life." Margaret grasped both Caitlin's hands. "I am tired, but not sick. Think you my babe is safe?"

"Remember how much water comes before the babe. It lives in a bubble. While you bounced around on your horse, it swayed safe from all of it. Worry not, my dear. It goes as God wills it. He chose when Lord Cai would die. He knew your lord would take you with him. He knew you would ride. Mayhap this was a test of your faith?"

"Which I will pass. Your will, Oh Lord, in all things, especially this." Margaret folded her hands in silent prayer, and Caitlin joined her.

After Vespers, Margaret was too tired to accost Alfred with her question. She was abed before him and already asleep when he crawled under the coverings. At his tap on her shoulder, she stirred not. Alfred rolled away and wondered why she was oft so tired.

41

Revelations

Friday, after Vespers, Margaret watched Alfred lock their door. *I gave him three days at home. He has practiced and tended the estate. This day he searched the forest for a place to clear trees. Now, or I shall lose him to his projects.* Margaret arranged the stools near a brazier. *His face shall be in the light.*

"Alfred, I would talk with you." She pointed to his stool. After he sat, she stood and pulled her stool to sit knees to knees to him. *If I think he lies, I can touch him and know.*

"What is this about?"

Margaret blinked so she could keep her eyes op should he stare and refuse to answer. "Who are you?"

"I am your husband," he replied as he relaxed his shoulders.

"Pretty—and obvious. Who are you that Saxons I know not aided me on my journey home: fed us, guarded us, gave us directions, watched from the trees as we passed, and did other things I saw not?"

"You know we Saxons work together, send messages, give warnings. Before we separated, I asked them to look after you." He glanced away.

An evasion. "What words said you?"

"Three." When she blinked not, moved not, he added, "'Beorgan min wif.'"

They did protect me. "Who are you that they obeyed you with such vigor?"

Alfred reached and placed his hands upon her knees. "The man who loves you and keeps you safe. Margaret…"

You shall not distract me. Margaret lifted his hands and put them on his own knees. "Your name is not Alfred."

"It is."

Margaret shook her head. "The night of the fire, you were fighting Wulf outside our door. Your mother cried out, 'Elred, Elstan, kill not your brother.' At first, I thought she misspoke, but no." Alfred sat as straight and stiff as his wife. "I noted Elstan never sat at table on the same side as you, so I saw you but one at a time." Alfred shrugged, but Margaret continued. "Later, I noticed you and Elstan walk alike. I realized you resemble each other. In the house, I walked apart from you three and watched. You forgot I was there. I saw familiarity and ease among you, the kind seen in families."

Alfred shrugged. "Recall you my story of running away? When I was found, I told Lord Cai my name was Alfred, so I would not be found by my family or my lord."

"Why 'Alfred'?"

"The name is close to mine own. Alfred was famous, King of the West Saxons. Not that any Norman would know of him. We remember him."

Did you so name yourself because you want to be a king too? "When was the other Alfred king?"

"Two hundred years ago."

Too long ago to matter? Oh God, may it be so. Margaret nodded, "Then what shall I call you?"

"Alfred is my name in the Norman world. I want it kept that way. I prefer you use it as well."

Put him at his ease. Ask the easier questions first.

"Did you send Elstan with me to this estate when I left Winchester?"

"I suggested he offer his service. You accepted."

Margaret sucked in a deep breath. *So we did meet there! I know the question for Sunday. Did Elstan introduce us? Have you been keeping watch on me since we met?*

"Did he report my doings to you?"

"Yes."

"Sent you messages to my Saxons before I arrived here in 1102?" Alfred nodded. "What words?"

Alfred smiled at her wording. "Beorgan min wif."

He thought me already his wife? You were cert we would wed. How much power have you? Why?

"How long have I been under your protection?"

"Since the morn after I met you." He watched Margaret lean back in shock.

Watched over. Guarded. Never in real danger? Neither from my Saxons nor my knights whom they watched. Safe and knew it not. All that worry. So many fears for naught. He must be very important to be able to order and be obeyed like that. I know why. When he asked for me the first time, the queen gave her permission. She is half Saxon and ordered it through him. She is with Henry on his plan for marriages between peoples.

"Are we done? I am for bed." He moved as if to rise.

"Not yet, Alfred. We have one more matter." Margaret began, "Two years and half again, I was hidden with Queen Matilda in a place called Forest Keep. She was carrying the princess."

"I know the tale."

Margaret continued as if he had not interrupted her. *I shall not be stopped.* "The Saxons guarding her were 'El-s,' Elric, Elstan, Elborg and such. Elric told me they were cousins from the same clan. You and your family are El-s. Are you related to Elric?"

"We are cousins."

"From the same Saxon clan?"

His eyes narrowed. "In the same clan."

Margaret pounced. "Elric also revealed he was a cousin to the queen. That makes Elstan and you related to her as well. Alfred, tell me what I already know. How are you related to Queen Matilda?" She leaned forward a lightly touched his knees.

Alfred glared at Margaret who returned an even gaze; he knew she would not relent. Staring at his wife, he paused between each word. "My mother and her mother are," he stopped, then finished with, "sisters."

"She married me into her own FAMILY!"

"I told you she likes you." Alfred smiled at shocking her. "After the Normans invaded, the wise men counsel decided, 'one princess known, the others hidden.' Mother is the last princess from the old days."

Margaret stared into the brazier. *The queen's mother was Saxon royalty, Elbeorht too.* "I thought our Saxons curtsied or pulled their forelocks each time she passed to impress you, gain your favor. They did so because she is royal." To Margaret, Alfred became a stranger. "That means you are at least a prince. Elstan as well."

"The whole clan is princes and princesses."

"How can that be?"

"Shall you hear why?" At her nod, he revealed, "For centuries, clans chose their kings. The Saxon king over them all was elected as well. Our high kings only came from the king clan, and all men in the clan were eligible. Kingship never passed father to son like the Normans. It could pass from the old king to his uncle then the uncle's brother, a cousin, a son. The wise men counsel, a man from each clan, met to elect our new high king and advise him. If a princess wanted her sons to be eligible, she married within the clan. Men married outside the clan to bring in new blood. With permission, of course."

"Does Queen Matilda have a Saxon name?"

"Henry renamed her when they wed." He decided to trust her. "To Normans her name was Aegdyth. Her full name is Athelaegdyth."

"Aethel?"

Alfred smiled, pleased she knew not the meaning. "'Noble' in Saxon and shows she is from the king clan."

"In all my life, I have heard not any Saxon use that word."

"No Norman would. No Saxon dares say it even now. We use 'El' to tell Saxons who know us not who we are. "

"They obey all El-s."

"Yes."

Margaret looked downward. *Two realms? The Saxons rule their realm inside the Norman one, who know it not. Saxons pretend ignorance to force Normans to learn Saxon; they carry messages in secret, guard each other, more. A Saxon prince can become their king.*

She looked up. "Are the Saxons preparing to take back their country?" *Please, God, let him not be their leader.*

"Not possible. Before the first King William arrived, we lost men defeating the Norse king's invasion. Then King Harold and his army raced south and fought King William's invasion. Our king died in the battle your people call Hastings. We lost many fighters, including Mother's first husband. Ten years later, a third of our people had been killed, starved to death, or forced to flee to the continent. Finally, we were conquered. The Saxon laws from that time to this forbid us weapons, training, horses. We have not the men, the arms, or the means."

Please, God, let it remain so. "All the Athels now hide," surmised Margaret. Fear struck her heart and voice. She whispered, "If King Henry learns you still exist, he will kill you all."

"For the dozen years his older brother ruled, Henry traveled the land, learned our language and ways, made friends. Somehow he learned about us. He knows who we are."

"He will kill you! He will kill me because I wed you! I will lose…" Margaret teetered off her perch.

Alfred grabbed her and pulled her into his arms. He re-sat, and placed her on his lap. Margaret sagged against him. "Hush…hush. We shall die not. Henry knows who I am. Matilda told him." As Margaret rested her chin on his shoulder, an image of a braid down a man's back flashed in her mind. She drew back in surprise, but it disappeared. *What was that?* She placed her cheek against Alfred's shoulder. He blew in her face so she would take a breath and faint not.

"King Henry worries not. He thinks you the second most-loyal woman in his realm."

"Hah! Not after he near strangled me to death."

"To whom are you loyal?"

Margaret looked into Alfred's eyes. "To you. To all on our estate. To our…lives." She kissed him so he would feel she spoke true. Their passion surprised them both. They parted and smiled at each other with loving hearts.

Safe. Safe at last. As long as he lives and mayhap beyond.

In a casual voice, he asked, "Did I remember to tell you King Henry offered me two pounds to wed you?" At Margaret's shocked, "I am worth but two pounds!" Alfred chuckled. "While I served the king, he asked how I would use my pay. Knowing not my eye for you, he suggested I wed and offered me two pounds to choose a Norman girl." "After he signed the contract, I reminded him of his offer. He ordered me paid. You see, wedding you earned me coin."

Margaret felt his chest heaving. In irritation, she slapped it with the flat of her hand for his laughing at her expense. "You are a strange man to shock me and then laugh. Not funny." Margaret grew suspicious. "How much coin have you?"

"Enough. The king paid me well for my service. Then Lord Cai gifted me all my knighthood gear, Garhard, and coin. He said it was my share of inheritance as his adopted son. He wanted me named not in his will, so his daughters or their husbands could not take me to court and charge me with influencing him in his old age so they could take back his gift."

"I heard not you pay tithe or tax on any of it."

"Both Church and crown assumed all we possessed was recorded in our accounts book. That I came to you a pauper, and your dowry paid for my gear and horse. I keep my coins separate from the chest. A stash for bad times. I copied you, my dear, and answered only what they asked. Had they asked me if I had my own wealth, I would have answered honestly and paid. No man likes to pay tithe and tax. Both Church and crown already have more than enough. Next year, should they think to ask, I will pay; but not until they ask."

Margaret snorted but spoke not.

"You are sagging again. Why are you so tired?"

Memories of her life as a servant to her father flashed in her mind. *Those days are over. Let them go.* "The journey home." She added, "In truth, I have slept poorly for years. Caitlin says I am now sleeping the lost sleep of past times until I reach Sunday last." She yawned. "I have you and your locked doors, so I no longer startle at the smallest sound." Margaret jumped up. "I am for bed."

Margaret pulled her laces as she walked to the pegs and hung her bliaut. Bedside, she toed her boot heels. In chemise and socks, she crawled beneath the covers and curled on her side. By the time Alfred stripped and placed his sword in the brackets on his side of the bed, his wife was sound asleep.

After Vespers the next evening, Margaret sat wrapped in the cosy outer garment she now called a "room mantle." When Alfred had finished polishing his sword, she asked her question softly. "Last eventide you mentioned you needs gain permission for us to wed. From the men in your clan?"

"No, from the wise men counsel who elected the high king and advised him. Well, not all of them. Just the three I met in secret in the forest."

"Did you know them?" *Was one of them from this estate? Might you tell me?*

"I never saw them. They sent word by Saxon. I went to the spot they chose and found a cloth. A voice instructed me to cover my eyes and sit. They asked me questions. I heard them whispering. They gave me permission to seek you."

"Questions?"

"They know who you are. I convinced them it was to our advantage to have a Saxon or two wed a Norman. Elric and Aurore were the first. I wanted us to be next. I put forth my wedding you, a woman of rank, might prove beneficial to all of us. They wanted assurances you could be trusted should you learn about us. They desire the return of the old days when we ruled. We young men know those days are gone, but those old men still dream to be in power again. I told them what they wanted to hear so they would agree to let us wed."

A Saxon prince, royal in the days before the Conqueror. Had we not arrived, he might have been a king or the high king. I see it in his bearing. Please God, let his being a lord be enough. If he is a prince, am I now a princess? She asked.

He looked up. "No, my dear, you are not. You must be born to it." His tone lifted when he added, "Our daughters, 'Aethelbeorht,' and 'Aethelrosamonde,' will be princesses, and our sons, 'Aethelalfred' and 'Aethelcai,' will be princes. We must keep secret the 'Aethel' and use only the 'El' for Saxons." Alfred grinned. "Though I suspect we two are famous enough that all Saxons will know our heirs, and we shall need it not."

"You are planning two of each?"

"I am hoping for six of whichever God chooses to give us." Alfred stood, walked to the bed, and placed his sword in its brackets. He extended his hand, "Wife, if we are to get six babes, best we be about making one right now."

Margaret laughed and walked into this arms. Afterward, more than satisfied and happy about it, she sighed her pleasure and snuggled into Alfred's embrace. *Methinks I shall be sad when it comes alive and we must stop.*

"My dear, you sleep too much and move too little these days." Alfred placed his hand on her belly. "You are a bit thick in your middle. I would like you to fast well this Advent and regain your slimness."

Margaret stopped smiling. "The morrow is the first Sunday of Advent and meat. I should like to enjoy the day. After that, it is fish for the next six days. On fasting days, I shall eat less, Alfred. Shall that do?"

"I suppose it must. Mayhap eating meat will strengthen you enough so you stay awake a whole day, and you do more."

"I expect so. God give you a good night, Alfred."

Alfred yawned. "He already has."

They slept.

42

Advent Begins

29 November

"No. No. It is Sunday." Margaret reminded Alfred when he moved to caress her body; the church bell rang for the first time. Margaret rolled away and crawled out of bed. She shivered against the cold and reached for her room mantle. She slipped into her boots. *I forgot to remove my socks. Oh, well. I shall wear them this week anyway.* Seeing no ember in the nearest brazier, she filled each with kindling and sticks. She lit a taper from a candle, blew out the candle and stepped to the nearest brazier to start a small fire. She warmed her hands as Alfred stirred.

Margaret reached into her clothes chest and picked up her jewelry. *The ring, bracelet and circlet match. They look old. He could not have afforded his knighthood gear and these as well.* From whence came they? She slipped on her ring and bracelet and held the circlet in both hands. Margaret waited until Alfred had dried his face.

"Alfred, my gold things are very old. Are they from your mother?"

"Yes. Her first husband was wealthy. After the invasion succeeded, she buried all their wealth in the forest. These are the first from the stash. She and I decided to gift you with things a few at a time over the years. Better they be worn by you than found and taken by some Norman. That way they stay in the family, and our daughters will be well dowered."

Margaret placed her seire on her head and set it with the bridal circlet. She recalled hearing Saxon words from her days as a servant. *Wita, sage, wise. Witan, know. Gemot, group, counsel. He said wise men counsel. Almost the same. Wise men. Witan. Witangemot?* Margaret turned to her husband, who was belting his braies. "Alfred, the men you spoke with in the forest to gain permission to wed me. Were they called witangemot?"

Alfred dashed across the room and clapped his hand over her mouth. "Never, NEVER say that word again. That word WILL get us killed." Margaret's eyes widened. Alfred saw her fear. With his hand still over her mouth, he explained, "The first King William, the conqueror, thought he had killed them all. He knew not we replaced them. His son William knew nothing of them. King Henry thinks they are long dead. Should he learn they still exist, he would torture anyone he suspects knows one. Even you. He would kill us until they were all found and executed most horribly. We Saxons helped make Henry king. He fears we might unmake him." At Margaret's double nod, he released her. "You must understand. Years ago, they decided if we fought the Normans, most likely we would lose. If we won, our forces would be fewer, and the Norse would invade us again and destroy us. They ruled we would be better under Norman rule than under Norse. We do nothing to unsettle Henry, for it would mean death to our way of life. We do what he asks; he permits us to live our way."

"I give my oath to God and to you. I shall never say that word again or any parts of it."

Alfred hugged her hard. "Say you shall never teach those words to our children, nor to anyone."

"I swear I shall not."

Still holding his wife tight, Alfred admitted, "Margaret, only you could have known each word, combined them, and figured its true meaning. The king is wrong; your are not too clever by half, you are too clever by way too much." Alfred pulled away far enough to look into her face. "One other thing, my dear one, you must keep Henry believing you are most loyal to him, even more loyal to him than to me. He thinks me loyal, but he is cert you will report to him any hint I am not. He must remain thinking you will inform him."

"Are you loyal to Henry?" *If he is not, need I guard my heart?*

Alfred smiled. "Yes, Margaret, I am. I have no desire to be king. I want to rule only your heart and this estate. I already have all I desire—except for an heir plus as many other children as God grants us." Alfred teased. "I intend to make as many babes as I can."

Margaret hugged her husband as hard as she could. *I feel it. He told the truth!* She kissed him her relief. *Thank You, God, thank You.*

The church bell rang a second time. They dressed hurriedly and raced down the stairs. Alfred unlocked the keep door and descended first. With long strides they crossed the bailey as the girls followed. Beyond the gate, they spotted everyone waiting for them outside the church. Their breaths made winter smoke, and they stomped their feet to keep them warm. Father frowned at the couple's tardy entrance. The church filled, and the service began. By rote, Margaret stood and knelt at the proper times and made the correct responses. Father saw an occasional nod and a small smile during his sermon about the meaning of Advent and what each of them should be doing and praying during this first week. Through it all, Margaret's mind was elsewhere.

For us to be safe, Henry must be safe. For us to stay alive, he must live. Saxons know that. Alfred knows it. Now I do. Henry arranged us for his own reasons. I pray we have his support. How show we him our loyalty? Follow his laws. Commend him to our Saxons. Do as he asks. I needs be glad should he call us to Court. Be cheerful, happy to be in his presence. He does like that. See to Henry's good will toward us. Margaret realized not she nodded.

What of Alfred? If I want him gone, all I needs do is betray him. Lakeside I could have. I have the power again. Before we wed, she said love is more important than rank. Poor Lady Claire. If I want not to risk her kind of life, I must forego rank. She is right. He is as good a man as she said. Over and over, I have seen he cares for me. I do care for him. What of our babe? Abandon it to a Saxon woman for rank? Throw away all I already have in the hope of rank? Normans wanted me not before. They hate me now. No. No. Stay where I am. Alfred cares for me, protects me. Keep my babe. Live the life we have started. Now I know all. Most. Enough. When did I choose him? Not pretend for the queen, for myself. Margaret smiled. *Fireside in the hut. When he warmed me and quelled his desire. Mother said rank and wealth are all. She was wrong. We have enough wealth. Do I really want rank?* Margaret paused her thinking. *Not mother's advice. Ask my heart. What do I really want?* She sighed. *A good life with a man who cares for me. I have him. This place. These people. Quiet, not Court. I choose Alfred and this babe.* Margaret smiled to herself. *All his babes. This life. We can have a good life together.*

Already started. He does love me. Say it. I do love him. Margaret felt her whole body warm. *Stop smiling or Father will ask questions.*

Margaret nodded to Father as if in agreement and returned to thought. *Matilda is half-Saxon and is her husband's link into the Saxon world. Am I Alfred's link into the Norman world? Even if they hate us? Is that how he convinced them to grant their permission? Never think on it again. It matters not. She said he wanted me when I had nothing. Asked for me the next day. Winchester for cert, but when? Elstan accompanied me not when I marketed. Ask if Elstan was present when we met. If yes, we met in the small castle. One, mayhap two more questions, and I shall win the game. By Christmastide for cert.* She looked up. *Finally, Mass is over.* She looked across the aisle. *I choose you and our life together.*

At the door, Margaret hooked her arm into Alfred's. "My lord, was Elstan with us when we first met?"

Eyes on the path, Alfred answered, "Yes."

Now all I needs do is remember the days I was with Elstan in the small castle. She hugged his arm close to her to body all the way to the hall.

Sunday's dinner was a merry one. After the servants cleared the tables, and Alfred called for another round of ale, Margaret requested songs and stories. She stopped every yawn and forced herself to stay despite her tiredness. She laughed and clapped her appreciation for every knight's contribution. She smiled broadly at Syghelm's tale of a battle he had fought near Athens, even as she wondered how far away was the place. When supper finally arrived, she started to enjoy the soup, changed her mind, and excused herself. Margaret refused Alfred's escorting her to the kitchen privy shed and took Alura with her. Upon returning, Alura removed her lady's bowl. Margaret finished her bread and ale. After Vespers, Margaret went straight to bed and slumbered deeply.

Before Monday's church bells, Alfred tried to rouse her and failed. He had to shake her hard to wake her for Mass. After breaking her fast, Margaret excused herself and returned to bed.

Alfred canceled practice for the day and called for Cormac and the accounts book. Before they began, Cormac asked, "May I be so bold as to ask how fares your lady?"

Alfred shook his head and complained, "I understand her not. Since her return, she sleeps almost daily. She has been eating so much that she is losing her waist. I asked her to fast, but she just ate a heaping bowl of pottage. I am cert she has returned to bed."

Cormac glanced away as he carefully chose his words. "My lord, her journey was hard, and she hungered. Mayhap she is eating more for the lost meals." Cormac paused and added, "I heard she left the hall at supper; her stomach tossed the soup. Afterward, she ordered Cook to stop preparing rabbit or including it at any meal until she says otherwise."

"Why would she do that? She loves rabbit, stewed or spitted."

"Women sometimes lose taste for a food. For now, my Caitlin eats not onions. When she smelled them on my breath, she lost her stomach." Cormac sighed dramatically. "I must forego onions until after the babe arrives. She can abide them not." Cormac looked at Alfred in hopes his lord had understood his hint. He decided he must add another. "That was before she started getting a thick middle, and she told me the news."

"Mean you, my lady…" Alfred turned his head and used his hand to mask his cheek and mouth so knights in the hall could read not his lips.

"My lord, I said nothing. She would have my head if she learns I said even this little."

"Why?"

"Your lady wants you to figure it yourself with no help from any of us."

"How know you this?"

"Caitlin figured it. Your lady then commanded me to order silence on the matter to all on the estate."

"Who else knows?"

"Now that you know—everyone."

"Everyone?!"

Cormac smiled. "Caitlin, Leoma, and Gytha formed a group of sewers of small garments and piss slings. We husbands noticed when your lady stopped one day and joined them." Cormac shrugged, "We men talk." Alfred moved to stand, and Cormac stopped him with a hand on his lord's arm. "My lord, may I suggest you stay? Dealing with the accounts book and my leaving will save me with both women." When Alfred sat, Cormac added, "May I make another suggestion, my lord?" Alfred nodded. "My lord, when you wake her for dinner, I suggest you figure it then. On your own. Or wait until until the end of her next nap." Cormac shrugged and decided to tell more. "May I share a secret? I stopped husbanding my wife after our babe came alive and kicked her. I am now a … a cloistered monk … until after she births our babe."

"I know almost nothing of babes. When I arrived, Lord Cai's lady was done birthing. I was oblivious before Mother birthed my younger brother." Worried it was already too late, Alfred asked, "How soon must I become a monk?"

"About the middle of the fourth month, mayhap a bit sooner. Depending on if she knows when … it happened."

Alfred nodded. "Best we do the accounts book. After you leave, I will wake her to dine."

"Thank you, my lord, I like my neck as it is." Cormac opt the book and began his report.

With stealth, Alfred climbed the keep ladder. He opt the door and startled Margaret and three girls. Each jumped up, hid something behind her, and stood in a line before three baskets on the floor. Sleeping close to the fire, Ferrant only looked up and replaced his muzzle on his forepaws. "My lady, what are you about?"

"My lord. Epiphany is in five weeks. We are sewing."

"Oh-h. Girls to the hall." Alfred kept his eyes on his wife as the girls scurried past him, grabbed their mantles from the pegs, and left. "Is sewing why you say you 'nap' each day?"

"Most days, Alfred. The first few after my return I slept. Now I sew. Though I started a month ago, I have much yet to do."

"What are you making?"

Margaret dropped her sewing in the basket behind her and walked toward the peg holding her mantle. "Last Epiphany, Caitlin and I sewed a shirt for each knight. Because they now purchase cloth and hire village women to sew their garments, this year I am sewing a different surprise." Margaret swirled the garment about her. "You are kind to come for me, Alfred."

"I came for a kiss before we dine." The couple embraced, and Alfred pulled her close. Margaret stood tiptoe and tilted her head the other way for a second kiss.

"A fine way to start a meal," teased Margaret as she drew back. Ferrant rose and followed the couple down the ladder and walked beside Alfred. On the path to the hall, she looked up. "How gray the sky. I smell rain."

Alfred agreed. "A page shall fetch our greased skins should it begin while we are in the hall."

After they dined, Alfred offered to accompany Margaret to her nap. "A lovely idea, my lord, but I shall be at my stitchery until we sup. Mayhap another day. My lord, we invited your mother for Christmastide. Elstan as well. I hope you remembered to send for them. Ferrant, stay." Margaret accepted her rain skin from Scandy and exited the back door.

After Vespers, the rain spit its last drops on the thatching above the keep's top room, and Margaret snuggled into Alfred's arms. "Alfred, if I am a princess not, why are the Saxons so good to me?"

"Saxons respect you because you show them respect. You have never called any of us a 'Saxon dog' like other Normans. They obey you because you have always protected them, from the time you saved Jorgon's life to the justice you demanded for Leoma's loss. They love you because you love them. You earned their honor by yourself." Alfred paused. "They shall welcome our little princes and princesses into the Aethel clan and be good to them." He placed his hand on her belly. "Starting with this one."

"Who told you?"

Alfred kissed her temple. "No one. At first, I thought you had your courses when I was gone to the tourney. Then I forgot to ask. You sew, but you also nap. Last eve, you tossed rabbit stew, most unusual. You said you shall fast but ate a large bowl of pottage this morn. You are...not as thin as you have been. I guessed."

Margaret smiled to herself. *Such careful wording.* "Alfred, no more riding, not even if the royals summon me."

"When did we make it?"

"Before you left for the tourney."

"Why did you tell me not?"

"At my age, first I feared losing it. Then I decided I wanted you to figure it for yourself."

"When?"

"I think the first fortnight in June. I shall be seventeen next month, old for this being my first. I need rest and good food."

"You are not old, but I do want you careful."

"Alfred, after Epiphany and before Lent, it will kick me to tell me it has come alive. Then no more may you be knocking at its door."

Alfred burst out laughing as he hugged his wife. "My dear, never I have heard living apart so apt described."

"Do you agree?"

"Of course. You are doing all the work of carrying and birthing. My part is to live chaste while I wait." He felt her back stiffen and her muscles tighten. "I waited for you so long. Fear not, my darling, I know how to be faithful."

"You might chase another to ease your waiting."

"And lose you? Never!"

43

An Invitation

The next day, Alfred ordered dinner delayed after the ale was poured. At his request, Father Manntun and Gytha, Cormac and Caitlin, and Felamaere and Erwina had joined them on the dais. Everyone in the bailey but the gate guards stood behind seated knights. Father blessed the day, the month, and all present before he led the Te Deum. Only Alfred remained standing.

"This first day of December is important for what it begins." He nodded to Father. "Every day we will give Our Lord thanks for His protection and goodness, especially in this month. We are in Advent to celebrate the birth of the Christ, whom God sent and whom we await because He saved us all." He nodded to Cormac and Felamaere. "We give thanks to Cormac and Felamaere for their leadership and their hard work, and we thank the labors of all our Saxons. Winter soon starts, and we will eat well." He smiled at Margaret. "We

celebrate my bride's birth a fortnight from this date on the third
Sunday of Advent. By that day, she will be three months carrying
our firstborn, mayhap our heir. God is good indeed." Alfred gestured
with one hand and lifted his mug with the other. After Margaret, the
knights again stood, Alfred raised his glass. "To God Our Father, all
glory. To Jesus the Christ, all gratitude. To the Holy Spirit, all praise."
He emptied his mug first.

Everyone drank, the ranked sat, and the Saxons left. On the dais,
Alfred accepted the mens' congratulations, and Margaret received
the women's good wishes. Three girls filled soup bowls; the pages
and the other two girls delivered them.

"That went well," whispered Gytha, seated to Margaret's left.

"Everyone looks pleased they no longer need guard a
secret."

"No, my lady, pleased you look happy. For a time after you
returned, we worried."

I am happy. She surprised herself. She smiled and nodded to
Gytha before she took up her bowl. She glanced right and saw Alfred
smiling at her. *Happy to be so cared for. With child. Cosseted even more
now. Happy I wed him. How shall I tell him? When?* She leaned back
a bit, looked past Gytha's back and grinned at Caitlin.

The meal finished, Father shocked the hall with a gift. His song
would not be of God nor of Church, but from inspiration.. He began
with,

"Lovely Lady Margaret tells us something new.
After a hard start here, she is the fifth to wed.
Now carrying a babe, she joins more than a few.
When comes spring, healthy babes will be due."

He finished his song with a second verse about proud fathers and was loudly applauded. Both Alfred and Margaret thanked him. Margaret commented to Gytha, "Church song is so proscribed in tones and rhyme, I knew not how rich and warm is his voice nor how skilled his versing."

"I encourage him to sing. When he sings at home, my heart warms to him even more."

That is how he won you! Wanted a family more than ale and comfort. He is more a man for it. Glad I kept him. He just proved himself again. I need not speak for him; he has already won Alfred's approval.

Margaret lay in bed on her back with both hands over her babe. *You, we, are safe with him. I do love him. I shall tell him before Midnight Mass. A Christmastide gift.* Margaret rolled to her side. With a full stomach, she was fast asleep.

Late morning four days later, a royal messenger and his guards arrived. Alfred ordered the usual diners to assemble in the hall. *Keep this false smile no matter what I hear. Likely a command to guard over Christmastide. God keep him safe, I beg You.* The messenger stood before the dais and bowed. "Lord Alfred of Dryhtenton, Henry, King of England, Count of Cotentin and Avranches, and Lord of Buckinghamshire and Gloucestershire, and his Queen Matilda, cordially invite you and your lady to Christmas Court in Winchester." Margaret's face remained frozen. "You are to arrive by noon the twenty-fourth day to dine with their graces. Your room in the castle awaits you. The Lady Perrine will serve your lady. Expect to stay past Epiphany."

"Sir Walter, thank you for delivering their graces' most kind invitation. Please reply, 'Your Grace, King Henry, Your Grace, Queen Matilda, we are greatly honored to be included in such an important

413

time as Christmastide. We hurry to your sides and gladly stay with you for as long as you desire our presence. We prepare anon and depart as soon as we are able. We are at your disposal now and always.'"

"Well said, my lord."

He is surprised Alfred not only speaks perfect Norman but that he also knows how to reply to a royal command. Dear God, please save me from this. Think, think. I must figure how to avoid this trip.

"Sir Walter, we invite you and your men to dine with us. You would honor us greatly. Stay as long as you desire. We are eager for your company and any news you would like to share."

"Thank you, Lord Alfred, for the meal. Then we must depart to extend the next invitation."

Margaret nodded to the Scandy and Hartun. They gave each man a mug. Scandy fetched a pitcher and met Margaret at the dais stairs.

They know not the Saxon custom he taught me, but I must perform this courtesy perfectly. Thus I honor Alfred, our estate, and myself.

Margaret approached the long table fireside. She murmured Sir Walter's name as she poured his drink and asked for each guard's as she poured his. She stopped at the end of the dais and accepted the second pitcher. She refilled each man's mug before she handed the pitcher back to Scandy, who took her place. Seated, she smiled at their guests. While the pages served the soup, she reported each knight's name so Alfred could speak to them as if he knew them. The messenger and his men ate hurriedly and departed. Alfred and several knights escorted them to their horses, now watered and rested. They stood in the gate opening and waved as the group disappeared into the trees.

Demetre commented. "Two days ride to the next estate. They wanted not to stay."

Alfred countered. "Likely, they ride hard to the King's Inn to rest on Sunday. I am not sorry."

Inside the hall, Margaret asked of Sir Roulin, "Please inform my lord I am in the keep. I hope I will see him there before we sup." She accepted her scarf and mantle from Haesel and left by the back door. When Alfred returned, Sir Roulin delivered the message and left for sentry duty.

Too upset to rest, Margaret stitched all afternoon. As she sat in the firelight on the first floor, she considered her arguments. *He comes not because he knows my mind. I must convince him. My traveling at this time is unsafe. My age. I cannot ride. On the road, Wilbur will send an army against us. Staying in the castle endangers both our lives and the one not yet alive. We expect his mother and Elstan. We will not go abed until this matter is settled.* She sucked in her lips so she would mutter not. In silence, Midryth, Alura, and Cleva worked beside her.

At supper time, Hartun came for the group. Alfred met her in the hall on the dais. He extended his hand to assist Margaret's taking the stairs. Without speaking, she accepted his hand and took her place. They ate in silence and their men followed them.

After Vespers, Alfred announced, "I am for the hall for a time."

"Stay as long as you like. I shall wait for you to discuss the royal command. We must have a joined face before Mass."

"The king's invitation is not a matter for discussion."

"Oh, but it is, my lord. It is, and we shall have it."

Hearing her determination, Alfred stopped and faced Margaret. "You shall be led not?"

"Not without our hearing each other."

415

"Then best we settle this now." Alfred continued to the gate, the steps, the ladder. He closed the keep door, but locked it not. "Girls, I am for the hall soon. Guard until I return." He closed the room door and kept his cloak.

Margaret placed the stools as she had before, poked the coals and added a few sticks to the braziers. She doffed her scarf and mantle and hung them.

"I will take the stool with my back to unlocked door so you may see it." Alfred took the other stool and gave his wife a hard stare. "Alfred, I know you are obliged to attend Christmas Court. As his vassal, you must obey his command even when it is dressed as an invitation. I plead ill health, and I desire to stay home. Surely you have the skill to convince them of your wisdom in permitting me remain here."

"You know not why you must attend. With a growing heir and a healthy daughter, they declared themselves a happy family. They announced this Christmastide honors families. Every invited man must appear with his wife and children. To arrive without you would be an insult and a grave mistake. Further, they are putting several of us on display to show marriages between Norman and Saxon can be happy. Already, Elric, Aurore, and their son journey to Winchester. Lord Avondale and his family are invited. That messenger passed our lane twice since our return. He waited to deliver his message to us last in hopes we fail to arrive and incur royal wrath. We shall not."

"You agree we are disliked and not wanted."

"Which is why we shall disappoint them, arrive on time, and be the happily wed couple the royals want to see."

"The Normans hate us and gladly would drive daggers into our backs."

"True. We will take knights with us and show no fear. The Saxons shall help us guard our backs."

"I can no longer ride, so I am bound at home."

"Your Epiphany gift was to be a litter. It is already half built; it shall be ready at our departure."

"At seventeen and three months with child, my traveling shall endanger our coming babe. Mayhap cause me to lose it."

"The litter shall sway gently between two roundseys; it shall rock you as softly as if you are a babe yourself."

"You and our knights need the roundseys to ride. You have not all the animals you need. All that wood and I will be too heavy a load."

"I agree. In the morn, I shall send two men to Reading to purchase two more."

Frustrated at being thwarted, Margaret stood, rounded the stool, and paced before her husband well out of his reach. "The moment we are on the road far enough from here, Wilbur shall attack. This time an army shall overcome our men and kill us all."

"Not possible. Wilbur is banished. Portier and a few others left with him. The other men refused to leave England and left his service. The king paid them until Eastertide. They shall not endanger his good will. We shall not be attacked."

Shocked, Margaret stopped and faced her husband. "What did you to him?"

"Nothing. He did it to himself. In the year of Our Lord 1101, he plotted with de Belleme and the king's brother Robert. He gave men, arms, and coin for Robert to overthrow Henry, but stayed in the background. Henry has been waiting for Wilbur to break a law so he could destroy him for his past treachery."

"I was in Forest Keep with Queen Matilda when that happened."

"Also, before Henry became king, he agreed to return to the good laws of our old King Edward the Confessor and those of his father. Made and signed a document called the Charter of Liberties."

"I have heard those words but I know it not."

"Wilbur broke three if its laws: no going to war with another lord or baron without the king's written permission; no attacking or harming the women and children of an enemy; and no chasing, fighting, or attacking on the king's roads. Wilbur went to war with me, and his men chased you on the roads." Alfred made a wicked chuckle of pleasure. "Saxons reported Wilbur's misdeeds, and Henry's shire reeve and knights were at Wilbur's gate to arrest him even before Portier returned home."

"You are cert Wilbur is gone?"

"Henry could have beheaded him, but he did worse. The king stripped Wilbur of his lands, goods, and property except his personal possessions. Henry banished Wilbur, his family, and their heirs for eternity. A warning to any who had sided with Belleme or his brother that Henry remembers and will punish them. Legally, of course."

Margaret sat in defeat. "All well and good for King Henry, but now we lack the time to plan. Every place in Winchester is already let. Every inn between here and there is already filled because other invited families have already ordered rooms or are already on the roads."

Alfred smirked. "Now, Margaret, well you know by now we Saxons. When the king announced Christmastide, I received word. A home in Winchester awaits us, and we have places saved for us at every inn between here and there."

"What of your mother's visit?"

"Expecting our royal summons, I canceled it. She understands."

Margaret was incredulous. "You knew the invitation was coming?" At Alfred's nod, her heart sunk. Then Margaret's eyes lit. "We have not the coin for the journey. The chest is almost empty, and we have the winter to face. We lack the means to travel. We must stay home."

"Remember? Before we wed, I gave service to King Henry, and he paid me well. Also, Lord Cai was most generous to me. I have coin enough for this trip and more. Remember, the Church's priest and the king's reeve assumed I had nothing of mine own. Their loss. I still have most of it. We can afford this journey."

Margaret sprang from her stool. "I cannot leave here. They shall kill me! You will be landless, a lord in name only."

"No one shall kill you."

Margaret teared and cried out. "Yes, they shall!"

Alfred leaned forward and grabbed Margaret's hands. "Look at me, Margaret." He pulled her hands to force her. "Wilbur is gone. There is no one else who wants you dead."

Tears streaming down her cheeks as she stood before him. "Yes, there are! The poisoners. For revenge."

"What talk is this?"

"Poisoners sickened the queen, and she lost her first babe. I told the king of them. I helped the queen birth the princess. They gave me land and coin for dowry. The poisoners remain unknown and free. Should I go to the castle, they will poison me in revenge for thwarting them. If you force me to go, they shall poison me, and I shall die." Margaret gasped for air and cried out, "I... shall... die!"

Alfred stood and enfolded her into his arms. "Hush. Hush. It is not so. The poisoners are dead." Margaret shook her head against Alfred's chest." Alfred placed his hands on her cheeks and held her face so she saw him. "The man who poisoned Queen Matilda fled to the continent. Henry sent men after him. Before he died, poisoned most likely, he must have revealed the other plotters. Henry's men returned after the princess was born, after you left Winchester. Before the queen conceived Henry's heir, three other men in our country died, all ranked. One of a broken neck from a supposed fall from a horse, one in his sleep, the third in a hunting accident. Believe me, Margaret. No one, no one who has ever harmed Henry or his own lives. Wilbur is the first to live only because Henry is using him as a warning to other traitors. He waits until they do a wrong as he did Wilbur, then he shall strike. We Saxons well know our king, and I speak true."

When Margaret's knees buckled, Alfred held her until he could sit and place her on his lap.

"I fear. I fear for our babe, for you, for me," she whispered.

Alfred rocked her like a sickened child. He waited until her breathing slowed. He spoke softly. "The royals have begun a new policy. Half the servants, half the kitchen staff, and half the pages must be Saxon. In Winchester and wherever they stay, or they shall not visit. You know I already sent word. Everywhere you are in the castle, a Saxon will watch over you. Saxons will supervise your every bite of food, every drink. All you needs do is take food and drink only from a Saxon hand and let only a Saxon enter our room. Saxons have watched over you for me since the day after I met you. You are guarded and protected every moment, in every place." Alfred kissed her head, her forehead., her mouth. "I love you, Margaret. I protect you. Always."

Margaret's shoulders sagged, and her head drooped. Alfred carried her and stood her bedside. He removed her bliaut and her boots before he lifted her to the bed like a child. He covered her. "I go to lock the keep and return anon." Alfred tiptoed away and looked back before he opt the door. In the shadows, he saw a covered lump. When he returned, the lump had moved not. He used a burning stick to light the candles in the corners and stirred the braziers so the fires would soon die. He hung his cloak and clothes on his rack, set his sword, and climbed into bed. Margaret clutched his forearm. Alfred drew her into his arms. Margaret released a sob that tore at Alfred's heart. He pulled her close as she wept and wiped her face with the corner of a sheet. Alfred held his wife as she cried herself to sleep.

44

Preparations

The church bell rang and Alfred rolled over to face Margaret. "If you desire it, I will make excuses to Father you are ill."

"Thank you, but I want to pray in church."

"After Mass, return to bed for the day. I shall bring your food and attend you."

Again, Margaret stood and knelt at the appropriate times, but her mind was elsewhere. *Oh Lord, I thank you for Your great bounty. Despite all my wrongs and the troubles I gave You, You sent me the right people to help and guide me. Mother did the best she could and showed me a world beyond Father's gate. Caitlin has stood by me since my first breath. Jorgon risked his life to follow me. You sent the king to free me, so I could serve the queen. She taught me so much. Lord Cai"'s tale warmed my heart, and he guided me well. My knights and my Saxons helped me save this place. Alfred loves me; I am cert. Except for rank and babes, I* have everything I have ever wanted, ever prayed for. If it be Your will I am poisoned in Winchester or on my way, so be it. Know I will die happy. I thank You for my life. Before we leave, I will confess as if it is my last. Your will, Oh Lord, in all things. Margaret felt her anxious heart settle.

While eating, Margaret turned to Alfred. "My lord, when do we depart for Winchester?"

"You are resigned?"

"I follow where you lead, my lord." He smiles. Mother is right. When you must obey or when he demands, give in gracefully. It pleases him and may gain me an advantage later. Do what the king wants. Do what your husband wants. It does me ill to sigh about a woman's lot. Nothing will change it. Smile back and be resigned.

"I sent knights to Reading for two more roundseys. As we cannot leave on Sunday, I am thinking Monday, the fourteenth day. With good weather, the journey should take a week. If not, we have three days leeway."

"We will be in Winchester for Epiphany. How shall we do our gift giving?"

"If you are ready Sunday, we shall celebrate your birth date and Epiphany together."

"Six days. I needs be sewing all day, but I shall be ready, my lord." Lighten his mood. Mayhap he is as worried as I. "My lord, it is Sunday."

"I remember. No kissing or such."

"I have several questions in mind. I have chosen this week's. May I ask it now?" At Alfred's assent, Margaret murmured, "Was Elstan with you when we met?"

"Yes. I fear you are close to the answer."

"Ah-h, but I am not, my lord. My usual good memory continues to fail me."

"If you figure it not, I will tell you before Christmastide."

"I thank you, my lord, for an ending. I feared if I remembered not, you would never tell me. I can sup in the hall or with you in the keep. Whichever you choose, I will be attending Vespers."

"Syghelm, my lady wishes to return to the keep."

Syghelm went for his cloak. Margaret donned hers and greeted each man on her way to the main door. They walked in silence until halfway to the keep gate. *I am fond of him because he is devoted to me. I wonder why. Be not curious or poke at him. Be gracious and accept it. We have a bond, like brother and sister. I have always wanted an older brother, his protection, his wisdom. I have it in Syghelm. He cares for me, and I love him as well.*

"My lady, what may I do to aid you?"

"Nothing now. All is well with me, and I am glad for it. How fare you, Syghelm?"

"Well, my lady. I have both Norman and Saxon friends now." Syghelm paused. "A widow looks my way, but I am not for it. I prefer to live in the barracks."

I know her, and you are wise to avoid her. May you find a kinder woman, who will ease your life and help you smile more. "What I may do for our knights before we leave for Winchester?"

"Nothing I know of, my lady. All are well and want not."

At the steps, Syghelm offered his hand and Margaret took it. She held up her mantle front as they started. Before she climbed the ladder, she thanked Syghelm. He waited to leave until she closed the keep door.

After Vespers, Alfred kept to his side of the bed and Margaret to hers. Much later, Margaret started to thrash, but was quickly roused to such stirrings she smiled with closed eyes.

425

"I know you wake," her lover whispered.

Through her lashes, she saw his head over hers. She lowered her lids, snaked an arm around his neck and drew him to her. As his lips met hers, she flicked her tongue into his mouth and savored the taste of him. Her nails traced a path down his back. When he gasped, she retraced that path and tracked down his arms.

"Woman, you …"

"Sh-h-h. No words." Margaret hooked a leg over his and flipped him to his back. She kissed his chin, his neck, his chest. *Not ready to say the words, but I shall show you, my love.* After both were spent, Margaret lay beside Alfred and kissed his shoulder before she lay her head there. Touching Alfred neck to toe, Margaret dozed in the circle of his arms under coverings warmed by their passion. Some time later, Alfred shook her to wake her from a night terror. He whispered, "We shall risk not our babe. Next time, I shall show you how to lie on our sides away from our son."

The next morn, a cold northwest wind blew outside, but the hall was warm and filled with the noises of eating and visiting. Alfred was at his ease, and Margaret nodded to their men.

"They feel our mood and follow. Your smile, my dear, warms their hearts as much as does the fire their toes."

"My lord, I thank you for your compliment. Please remember I needs be sewing all week to be ready for Sunday. I have asked for Caitlin's help. May I ask her to dine with us?" At Alfred's nod, Margaret added, "I would think it a kindness for you to invite Cormac as well, so he eats not alone and of poor, cold fare."

"Done."

"I have an idea. "We have six days to Sunday. If we invite two knights each eve to sup with us and visit with them, they shall know we think them important; they shall know we will miss their company."

"You do like company on the dais."

"We may be gone a month or more. A fast farewell in the bailey is not enough for such good men."

"I shall think on it."

"Thank you, my lord. If you will excuse me, I must be at my needle until we dine."

Fireside in the keep, Margaret pulled a cloth from the basket. On a five-inch by eight-inch piece of cream-colored linen was stitched a Norman shield of deep blue cloth decorated like Lord Alfred's painted shield.

"My lady, this is what you have been broidering all this time!" Caitlin asked.

"We have but two completed. I stitched this pattern one for my lord. By Sunday, we must complete twelve more for the knights and one for Syghelm. Think you Cormac might like one?"

"He would be honored to wear the Dryhtenton emblem. What are the girls stitching?"

"They whip-stitch the edges of the pieces for my lord's clothes. I believe he will soon be called to his first service. I want him to carry enough clothes should he become wet or cold." She pointed. "Midryth is making the feet for his chausses. The pile in the bathing trough holds each knight's new winter mantle we just finished. After we complete the emblems, we will sew them on the left side over their hearts."

"A generous gift. Who is doing what part?"

"Cleva and Alura had whip-stitched the emblem cloths and loose-stitched the edges under to sew on a cloak. Now they do pieces for my lord. Haesel sews the straightest, so she stitches the lines for the cross and the circle at the intersection on the blue shield. Cyne cuts the threads. I broider the center of the circle." Margaret proudly displayed a bit of green ground under a one-inch brown building with a tiny gold door. "This represents the temples of the Holy Lands where my lord fought."

"Why need you me?" asked Caitlin, still speaking formal Norman.

"We are behind, Caitlin. Far behind. I have loosed-stitched back the rough edges of the shields. Will you sew the shields on the linens?

"Alura, please cut a linen for Cormac's emblem and ready it for a shield. Cyne, lend Alura the scissors and fetch a mug of broth for Caitlin."

Caitlin sat on the stool beside Margaret. She withdrew her iron needle from where she had woven it into her bliaut. Haesel first stitched a yellow circle one-third down from the shield top before she sewed the lines for the cross from top to bottom and side to side. Caitlin accepted a length of thin blue wool thread from Cyne, threaded one end and knotted the other. She held the cream cloth with her left hand as she stitched on the blue shield. She handed a completed cloth to Margaret and picked up the next piece. Because Margaret's work was small, difficult, and in three colors, Caitlin soon had three stitched shields waiting for her.

The women sewed in silence. When Cyne went to the chamber pot in the corner, Caitlin whispered, "Why is Cyne sewing not?" Margaret threw her such a baleful look of disgust, Caitlin cackled. The girls dropped their chins to hide their grins of agreement. Margaret looked up and blinked several time to ease her eyes. She gazed at her bathing trough. *Just washing now; no bathes until after the babe is born. I miss it.* She admired the stacks of gifts now filling it. *A linen tunic for Father and woolen bolts for Gytha and her children. Bolts for Caitlin, Cormac and Felamaere's family, bolts and aprons for the kitchen. Duone will love his new cap. The knights' new mantles only need the emblems.* Margaret blinked again before she took up the next emblem. When the church bell rang midday, the girls left to serve.

"Gold thread for the door is dear."

"Which is why I use my better needle from the queen and cut the thread myself. I dare not lose even the tiniest length. I am grateful he painted his shield so soon after Michaelmas. Immediately, I sent for the cloths and threads and the Epiphany bolts. I thought I had enough time to do it all, but we went to Lord Cai. Getting home took longer than I expected."

"Worry not, my girl, we will finish in time. Filling the space between the cross outlines with the yellow thread will take no time at all; three of us can do that while you finish the circles."

When they heard Scandy's call, they set down their work, dined, and returned anon. The women and girls worked until the girls left to serve supper. Margaret arched her back and groaned. Caitlin followed.

"After Vespers, ask your lord to rub your back. That should ease the tension. I am cert he also knows well how to relax your neck and everything else."

"Caitlin!"

"I shall ask Cormac for a back rub. Only he must wait do what usually follows until after I give birth and heal."

"Heal?"

"Four to six weeks. Tell not your lord of that until after your babe arrives. After five months of abstinence, four weeks more may seem not so long."

Alas, poor Alfred. Poor me. "I care not for Norman fashion. I plan to nurse our babe myself. They will think me a base Saxon. Think you I am wrong?"

"No, girl, I do not. Your milk strengthens your babe. Nursing creates a bond between you. You have done nothing usual before. Why start now and deprive your babe of its best start?"

"Thank you, Caitlin. You always give wise counsel. Sup with us if you like."

"Cormac promised me a meal."

The women parted at the hall door. Margaret waved to Cormac, who walked through the gate toward his wife.

Verel supped to Alfred's right and Pernel to Margaret's left.

Verel explained, "As leader, I ruled I go first. We placed stones in a pouch, and Pernel drew the light one. Each night, two men draw for a seat until all have won, even Syghelm."

"Sir Pernel, how came you to be a knight?"

"I was six and Louvel four when our father, a Norman knight, took us to Normandy and placed us in a monastery. He said our mother went to live in a convent, and he could not care for us. I think she died. I was a bad student and a worse future monk. I kept running away to seek a position as a page, and Louvel followed me. After the monks gave up, they found us a lord who would take us. We worked hard and ate table scraps, but we were pages, then squires."

Margaret supped and waited before she commented, "I know not how you met my lord."

"Normandy. From beside the road, we watched a party traveling to the Holy Land. We knew him to be Saxon and saluted him. They stopped on our lord's land, and we snuck out to meet him. We were knights errant in England when he returned, and we re-introduced ourselves. He sent for us the day the king signed your contract."

The foursome on the dais finished their meals and walked together to Vespers. That night Alfred was most careful to husband Margaret as they lay on their sides. Before they slept, Alfred said, "If you think we risk our babe, I will become monkish now."

"Not yet. I would we wait until it kicks me." She snuggled into her husband's arms and closed her eyes.

Each worked hard to prepare for their journey. Alfred chose men to escort them, horses, gear, food to take, and supervised the completion of Margaret's litter. The girls finished sewing their lord's clothes and packed them in a satchel separate from the couple's court clothes. Before bed Friday, Margaret commented, "When we sup on the morrow, we needs invite the final three Bertrand, Claude, and Emile."

"I sent Emile away over a week ago. I saw him not at the tourney, but he was Wilbur's man. Sent to win my confidence and spy. I had sent out an inquiry. Until I received a reply, I told Verel to give him no guard duty for fear he might op the gate in the night. When I confronted Emile, he asked to stay and promised to be faithful to me. I told him Wilbur was banished and sent him away. A spy and a traitor to his lord cannot be trusted." Alfred looked up from undressing.

Say not the wrong thing. Brag not about being right. Wound not our bond. "You were smart to withhold your trust and ask the Saxons to learn about him." Margaret commented. "I suspect Saxons know everything—or she can learn it."

"A conquered people needs learn to deal with their overlords. Will you be ready by the end of the morrow?"

"Yes, and my fingers will be grateful for the rest." *Before we leave or after our return? Before. Delay not delight.* "Alfred, I have a gift for you, but it is in the forest. On the morrow, may we go there so I may give it you?" Margaret saw his confusion. "May we go alone?"

"Two knights." At Margaret's nod, he added, "No undressing, no husbanding."

They crawled into bed from opposite sides and met in the middle to the pleasure of both.

After breaking their fasts, the party rode into the forest. At the clearing beside the river, Margaret said, "Here," and Alfred sent the men away to guard. He dismounted and helped Margaret. She gave him a fast kiss and disappeared into the trees. As he fastened the horses' reins to a low branch, she returned holding a pile of ragged fabric with mouse droppings and dead leaves clinging to it. She held it out for Alfred to take. He sniffed, grimaced, and held the mass away from his body."

"Blessed Epiphany Day early, Alfred. They look to be nothing, but they are special." Alfred furrowed his brow. "They were my running away clothes."

"Running from me?"

Margaret shook her head. "If Queen Matilda had birthed another girl, I would have come here without Caitlin and instructed my guards to stand off while I bathed." Margaret nodded at the pile in Alfred's arms. "I would have changed into those, left my garments and boots on the bank, and run into the forest. When the guards worried and returned, they would think I had fallen in, mayhap drowned. They would look down river while I raced the opposite way."

"To do what?"

"To flee. Anyone can travel anywhere in this country and never leave the forest. Likely west but not into Wales or north but not to the North Wall. I would choose a river with fish and fashion a lean-to to sleep in. Be the wild Saxon woman, dirty, unkempt, and a bit mad. No one would know me. The king would never find me."

Alfred slowly broke into a broad grin. "You truly did not want to be queen." Alfred added, "When you ran away, you would have met me. I would not have let Henry have you." Just then, something shifted in his arms; a Saxon boot fell out of the pile and a knife out of that.

As Alfred looked down, Margaret added, "After I wed, my second plan was to run off if my lord treated me ill." Alfred looked up, and Margaret gave him a neutral expression. "Now, with what I know about Saxons, you would have found me before I got five miles."

"One mile." He added, "You no longer want to run off?" Margaret shook her head. "I will burn these."

"Do with them as you will, but I suggest you permit me to cut out the coins before you do." At Alfred's "Coins?" Margaret explained, "Should I need them, I had sewed a few pennies, mostly ha-pennies and farthings into the hems of the shift and mantle."

"The accounts book reads false?"

Margaret shrugged. "Each time, I made Cormac overwrite our costs by a penny or two."

"How many?"

"Almost four shillings." Margaret grinned at his shock. "May I return the knife to the kitchen? Cook has been fretting about her loss since Lent."

"My dear wife, I am not the only one who kept secrets."

Margaret gazed into his warm, sky-colored eyes, and her heart filled. She almost spoke the words. *Not here. A better time, a better place.*

45

❦

An Early Epiphany

13 December 1103

Everyone dashed into church to escape the bitter wind and dark clouds. *Shall I pray for a storm that prevents us from leaving for a week or one that passes quickly? Neither. Your will, Oh God, in all things. Mass begins. Pay attention.*

After the service, people looked at the sky and rushed home. A large crackling fire heated the hall, which quickly filled. Alfred's guests joined him on the dais. To Alfred's right sat Father, Gytha, and Felamaere. To Margaret's left sat Caitlin, Cormac, and Erwina. So the soup cooled not in the walk from the kitchen, Nearra had moved the large pot to a tripod at the other end of the fire pit. Mouths watered at the aroma.

Father gave the blessing and led the Te Deum, and all but the servants sat. The pages filled the mugs on the dais; the girls passed pitchers down the tables and refilled them as needed.

Alfred stood and raised his mug. "To the birth of Jesus the Christ, which we celebrate in twelve days."

All repeated his words before they drank. Nerra filled bowls. With a bowl in each hand, Scandy, Hartun, Haesel, and Cyne delivered them to the head table before they served the knights. All downed the hot broth to warm their bellies. Most relaxed and chatted as they awaited the main courses. Platters of bread rounds and small wooden tubs of butter arrived and were handed out. Midryth placed the single pot of honey in front of Alfred. With the back of his left hand, he moved it to between himself and his wife. Margaret saw the knights noticed. *They note his good treatment toward me. Not for them. For me.* She smiled at her lord, picked up the tiny wooden spoon, and drizzled a bit of honey on the chunk in her hand.

From the kitchen, Hartun, and Scandy entered backward and Duone forward as they carried in the long board with half a roasted pig carcass on it. They placed the board across a side table and waited for Nearra. With a wooden board in each hand, the pages and girls lined up to receive chunks of carved meat. Duone returned with two bowls holdings boiled turnips and carrots for the head table, and left to fetch the bowls still in the kitchen. No one at the head table started until after Lord Alfred stuck a piece of meat with his dagger and pulled the meat into his mouth with his teeth. After Lady Margaret did the same, the others began eating. Conversation slowed as everyone enjoyed the feast. Ferrant sat before the dais and waited; Alfred and Margaret took turns tossing a bite to their dog. They stopped eating to watch pig bones tossed into the empty soup pot, which Duone carried away. Ferrant followed the pot. They waited for the other half of the pig to arrive. After the pork was half gone, the rest was removed to the kitchen for the staff and servants. Before the dessert of apples stewed in honey and dried lavender blooms arrived, Alfred stood as a signal for the hall to quiet. He gestured Margaret stand with him.

"Father Manntun, everyone, my lady and I greet you with our best wishes. Much has happened since your last Epiphany. By the grace of God, we met only a few hardships and all the rest was good. While we are honored to receive a royal invitation to spend Christmastide in Winchester, should we not return in time, we will miss your Epiphany celebration. With that in mind, we give our gifts now. "

Margaret, turned to accept a pair of bundles from Midryth, who stood beside the long table behind the dais. She handed them to Alfred.

"Father Manntun, please accept a bolt of fine linen for you and woolen bolts for your family."

Father rose and accepted them. "My family and I thank you, my lord, my lady." He sat.

In like manner, Alfred bestowed gifts on Cormac, Caitlin, and Felamaere. Next on the table, Margaret set before her a pile of bolts of wool cloth topped with folded aprons and a cap.

"Duone, please step forward."

He did so, but he stood before Margaret, not his lord. He did remember to pull he forelock to Lord Alfred first and then to his lady.

He has grown even taller and has gained at least a stone. I need hardly bend to give him his gift. She pointed to the pile. "Duone, these are gifts for the kitchen staff. Before you deliver them, we have a gift for you. A man needs a cap. This is yours." She handed him what she had sewn, a gray, woolen cap, peaked at his crown and shaped to cover his ears and nape. Duone's eyes widen as he accepted it and pulled it over his hair and patted his covered ears.

"Thank you, my lady." He paused a moment. "Does this mean I am now a man?"

"It does," said Alfred, "and a good one."

Duone pulled an imaginary forelock as he bent his head. "Thank you, my lady! Thank you!" Forgetting manners, Duone extended his right hand to Lord Alfred, who graciously accepted it. Duone pumped it several times as he voiced, "I am now a man. I am now a man." Standing tall and proud, Duone picked up the bundle and exited the hall to the applause of the knights. Outside, rain began to fall.

Margaret clenched her jaw to stop her tearing. *Boy no more.* She looked down the tables. *May God love you even more than I do for that kindness.* Midryth cleared her throat and handed Margaret the first three mantles, now decorated with their lord's emblem. Left of the closing leather laces was the symbol Margaret had sewn on their tunics the year before so each man would know his own. Margaret glanced up. *Raindrops make sputtering noises against the burning logs. Lord, please wet the roads, so we may stay home til my birth date is done.*

"Men, our gift to you is the same, a new wool cloak. My lady has sewn my shield emblem over your heart place. We ask you to honor our hall and wear it with as much pride as we have for each of you." Alfred called Verel forward, who nodded to his lord and to his lady, and accepted the garment. He smiled at the emblem, shook out the cloak, and donned it. Thick and heavy, it dropped to his ankles. He turned so all could see it and returned to his place. Still wearing the cloak, he sat. *They smile and admire it. They like it.* Margaret sighed in happiness. *Before yester's Vespers, Father had stacked them for me according to a system his own. I wonder what that is.* In turn, Margaret whispered each man's name for Alfred to call.

"The first I call is Arnaud. Your symbol among us is a small cooking pot because you are always hungry." Alfred grinned and waited as the men roared. "Bertrand, your symbol is a tree in thanks for your guiding my lady through the forest." The men nodded approval. Claude's mantle bore a lance; Demetre, a glove; Giraud, an arrow; Hughes, a horse. Alfred paused. "Louvel, your symbol is a log for your love of sitting close to the fire. Pernel, your symbol is the pele, for you attack it so furiously that it shakes with fear." Alfred waited for another round of laughter. Roulin's mantle bore a bow; Sauville's, a helmet, and Syghelm's, an axe. Despite the fire near their feet and the warmth in the hall, each man wore his cloak. Pages served washed soup bowls now filled with stewed apples. The feast over, singing, music, and story telling commenced. All but Alfred and Margaret left the dais for their homes. Margaret gave the pages a small head shake, and the refilling of mugs slowed.

Accompanied by Ferrant, Margaret left to visit Night. He nickered as she approached. Dressed in her best clothes, she pet him instead of grooming him as usual. "Night, you are so dear to me. Yet I can no longer ride you, and you can no longer journey as far as we must go. Shall I tell you why?" Margaret whispered into Night's ear and spoke many endearments as she kissed his cheek and petted her last tie to her mother and her old life. Memories of her beloved horse flashed. *The first time I rode you and was punished for it. Riding you when I played the ghost. Traveling to Forest Keep to meet the queen. You pranced so beautifully in the meadow after we arrived here. If I counted aright, you are twenty-three. Old friend, please be alive when I return.* She shed tears into Night's mane. *No one will touch you. I will bury you at the edge of the meadow and mark your place. Oh Night, after you are gone, I want no other Percheron. Any other kind but yours. I will tell Alfred.* Night nickered and Margaret sobbed to think of living without him. Night lifted his head and whinnied again and again; he pranced back and forth. Margaret calmed herself and wiped her face. She returned to petting, endearments, and murmuring memories of their travels and rides. Outside, Ferrant had waited for her. *The rain stopped. May it start again and wet the world too much for traveling.* She petted Ferrant. "You have changed too, my friend. I sit and am inside more, so you follow him around the bailey and beyond the gate. I may see you less, but I love you not less." Ferrant leaned hard against her and accepted her scratching his favorite places. *Too chilling to be out longer.* Ferrant escorted Margaret back to the hall. She almost burst into tears telling Syghelm what to do should Night die before she returned. Ferrant nudged her hand and followed her onto the dais. He lay across her feet.

Hours later, each in the hall received a soup of pork bits and chopped leftover and new vegetables. This eve, Cook had diced the leftover bread and dropped several chunks atop each bowl. Cyne appeared wearing her own greased skin and with Alfred's and Margaret's skins in hand. At the main door, they led the way to church for Vespers.

Locked in the keep and in their room, the couple prepared for bed.

"You prayed for this rain, so we could leave not for court," accused Alfred as he draped his cloak over two pegs to dry.

Margaret set her circlet on the bed as she doffed her seire and lifted her clothes chest lid to store them. "That I did not. I prayed to Our Lord do His will." She set her circlet atop the seire and closed the lid. "We gave gifts; they did not."

"I asked them to wait until our return should we arrive before Epiphany. If not, then after. That way, we have two celebrations. They have earned them."

Alfred pulled his greater tunic over his head and then his tunic and his waist-length shirt. Margaret hung her cloak over two pegs and yawned. She watched Alfred sit and undo his cross gartering. He hung the leather strips over one arm of the garment tree. Margaret exchanged her boots for slippers but kept her socks. Alfred removed his boots and chausses to slide his bare feet into his slippers. Margaret turned her back and Alfred stood. He stepped forward and kissed her nape as he untied her bow and loosed her laces. Margaret shook her head.

"Sorry. I forgot."

"Forgot what? I felt nothing."

"Liar!"

They chuckled, parted, and finished undressing without looking the other's way. Margaret kept her shift; Alfred removed his braies. They met in bed. Margaret yawned again.

"Roll away so I may rub your back. I shall do no more," he promised. When he heard her sigh and saw her snuggle deeper below the coverings, he whispered, "Sleep well, my love. I shall see you before the church bell."

46

Private Gifts

The walk to Mass was so bitter people's breaths made cold smoke, and the wind blew dampness into everyone's bones. After Mass, the wind was blowing away the clouds and leaving behind clear sky. Margaret frowned. *Better weather? Rain ruining the roads is what I desire.* All ate more pottage than usual, as if filling their bellies could stave off feeling the cold. Roulin reported the roads were too wet for travel. Alfred nodded and announced no travel and no practice. The men slowed their eating, and Margaret looked away to hide her smile.

"My lord, with your permission, I will re-inspect our satchels for the morrow. I emptied the rags and placed them in the rags bin. After we dine, may I help the girls cut their new garments and join them as they sew?" At Alfred's "You may," she excused herself. *Not so hard, asking permission to do what I must. He always says yes. More courtesy than permission. Telling him where I am. Anyone who hears knows I accept his authority.*

Before she supped, Margaret asked for Father, who arrived promptly and thanked her for the mug of hot broth from the fireplace pot. He followed her to the second-floor room. For propriety, she left the door op; they sat on the stools Cleva had carried from above. "Father, I know not what we will face on our journey or in Winchester. May I confess to you now, so I am prepared for Mass on the morrow?" She was a long time confessing, asking questions, and accepting both the priest's advice and the penance he gave her. Afterward, she felt more confident in her to decision to tell Alfred she cared. Father joined the couple to sup and walk with them to Vespers.

As they hung their outer garments on their pegs, Alfred announced, "We leave on Wednesday. I want you well rested before we begin." Margaret looked around the room at flickering candles in the corners. She inhaled the smell of embers in the brazier and watched Alfred add a few sticks to ease the chill from the walls. *So little time left here. I shall miss you, room.* Alfred took her hand and led her to his stool. "I have a gift for you." Alfred sat and arranged her on his lap so her backside was on his right knee and her feet dangled over his left. Alfred placed her left arm across the back of his shoulders and his right arm around her waist.

"Do you start us in a new way?"

"Mayhap later. Now a story." He lifted his heels and dropped them to give Margaret a small bounce. "Delivering Pope Paschal's letter to King Henry was my last task before returning to Lord Cai. When I arrived in Winchester, I was in such a sorry state, Sir Roger first refused me entry. He sent me to the kitchens to get clean and fed.

I washed and ate. I had refused to see the king in anything but my pilgrim's garb. They gave me clean garments while they washed mine. When I learned of Saxons guarding the keep, I sought them and found Elstan."

"Was that when we met?"

Alfred bounced her again. "We were talking when a guard arrived with a problem. I was curious, so I accompanied Elstan. Margaret, what day is this?"

"The fourteenth, the eve before my birthing date." She looked away in shame. "On the morrow I shall be seventeen years."

"Place your head on my shoulder, look behind me, and remember."

Margaret looked behind him and saw shutters closed over an arrow slit and stone wall. *Nothing unusual. What am I supposed to see?*

"And two years ago?"

"The night before...Oh no!" Margaret pulled away to stare at Alfred. She covered her face with her hands and shook her head. "No...No."

"In the torchlight, your hair glistened gold and red. You blinked against the light and squinted them shut. I so wanted to see your eyes. You were so beautiful in the moonlight you took away my breath."

"I was drunk on swill."

Alfred gently put her head back on his shoulder. "When Elstan called your name, you informed him you were dead. When he told you to op your eyes, you looked at the stars behind us and said, 'Not dead' so forlornly you hurt my heart. I wondered why such a beautiful girl wanted death. We got you stood, but we could not get you down that narrow spiral staircase. I sat down and put you on my lap. Elstan led with a torch. I saw such sadness in your eyes;

my heart ached. Remember you the light hurting your eyes and me telling him to move the torch?"

Chin on his shoulder, Margaret shook her head. An image flashed inside her closed eyes. "That was not you. His hair was in a braid; he wore a beard. By law, Saxons may have neither."

"Before leaving Antioch, I had vowed neither to cut my hair nor to shave until I was home. It marked me a pilgrim and saved my life more than once. All here thought me Norman, so I had the freedom to do as I wished. Remember you what we talked of?" Alfred bounced her again.

"I remember my stomach roiled so, I feared I would toss it."

"Which is why I took but a step or two and stopped for you to settle it."

"Of what did we speak?"

'That I was third born and you were first. When I asked why you drank, you said to forget the morrow. Of becoming fifteen with no marriage and no hope of one."

"I remember none of it."

"Remember you this?" Aldred stood her up as he had the first time and held her close. Margaret's arms hung beside her as they had then; her head lay against his chest as she faced to his left. "I promise you will be wed. Forget all but this." With one hand, Alfred lifted her chin and kissed her deeply. He withdrew and murmured, "You have the sweetest mouth. You collapsed, and I held you until Elstan returned with a blanket to cover you. I carried you across the back of the Great Hall, out the double doors and to the keep door. Elstan took you inside."

"I remember Elstan handed me to Caitlin." *Say nothing of tossing my stomach down the piss hole.* "She put me to bed." Margaret looked into Alfred's face. "I remember dreaming of blue eyes." She sounded surprised. "I thought I only dreamed being kissed." She arched away from him, but he held her fast. "You kissed me! And us not wed! How dare you!" She tried to push him away.

Alfred chuckled. "I am no dream. You are my wife. You broke no rule. I am ever the only man who may kiss your mouth." He did.

Margaret tried to push him away. When he plunged his tongue between her lips, her knees buckled. She grasped his neck and clung to him. She kissed him back and thrust her hips forward. They stripped with a speed that astonished both. Garments flew and boots skidded away. Alfred back-walked her to the bed and lay her on the coverings. Margaret lifted her arms to him. They met from mouth to knees and furiously husbanded each other. Spent, Alfred lay atop her, but she rolled him away.

"I forgot our babe. Are you all right?"

"Yes. Cold."

Alfred bounced out of bed. Margaret lifted her hips so Alfred could pull the coverings from under her. She crawled under them, and he joined her. Alfred snaked his arm under her neck and held her close.

"Better." Margaret fell asleep. In the night, Margaret woke to Alfred stroking her and kissing the hollow of her neck. "Alfred, I already have a babe in my belly."

"That is not why I do this. I wanted you the moment Elstan placed you in my arms. For a year and eight months I yearned for you every day. I want you now. I will always want you. Your smell, your touch, your smile, your voice, your wit. I love you, Margaret. I want all of you, not just this. Until the day I die." They lay on their sides, and Margaret answered him with her body. The embers in the braziers died and darkness covered them.

The next morn Margaret and Alfred shivered and blew icy smoke at each other. They giggled as they shook rushes off their clothes before donning them. Margaret had added another layer for winter, a thick woolen tabbard to her ankles and fastened close to her body by her girdle.

"I believe not how many layers men wear. It takes you so much longer for you to dress than I. Even with braiding my hair each morn, I am ready before you." Margaret put on her seire and circlet before she placed her scarf over her head and draped it around her neck and shoulders. Her mantle held down the ends. She clasped the brooch and snugged one front over the other. "You are still cross-gartering your chausses and have yet to put on your tunic and overtunic." She fetched his cloak and held it as she waited.

"Men are outside more and need the warmth of layers. I expect you to nap after we dine. This journey is harder than you think. We will stop any time you ask. I will risk not our babe. Promise me you will tell me your need."

"I promise, Alfred. I want this babe as much as do you."

Alfred fastened his second cross garter and stood. "Glad I am to hear it, my love."

"Alfred, I know who you are and of what you are capable. Say again how long have I been under your protection."

Alfred stopped and held his tunic in his hand. "Since the night we met." He pushed his arms into the sleeves and pulled it over his head. He adjusted the cuffs. He smiled at Margaret before he poked his head and arms into his overtunic.

448

Margaret asked what really worried her. "What if Wilbur had caught me?"

Alfred stepped toward Margaret. In a quiet, steady voice, he said, "His men would not have caught you. Saxons stood between him and you. They would have died before they let them pass." Alfred placed his hands on his wife's shoulders. "My darling, whether I am here or gone, you are protected. Whether you see them or see them not, they watch over you. You are a prince's wife. They will die before they see you harmed."

"Our babe, our children?" she whispered.

Alfred kissed her forehead. "The same." He enfolded her in his arms. "I know you, my love. You have not felt safe since the day you saved Jorgon from your father. You tried hard to regain his favor, to please him. You bargained your life to escape him. Defied both law and custom when you took up that sword. You have been safe for two years. When you fled Henry's court and plotted your escape, you were already safe from him. I would not have let him have you. You will be safe all your life, our children, all their lives." Alfred sighed. "I still feel you thrashing when you dream ill. It tears at my heart to hear you cry out."

"I still do that?"

"Caitlin said since you were six. When you do, I wake you. Distract you. I confess I like that part."

Margaret pushed her head into his chest. "Did I do that in the forest?"

"Yes, but I woke you not for fear to make you worse."

"What do I that I wake you?"

"Hush. No more. Now you know you are always safe. Believe it, and the night terrors shall no longer disturb your slumber." Alfred smiled down at her. "Though I plan to wake you in the night for my own pleasure." He hugged her hard as if to squeeze all fear from her. The second church bell rang.

"If I nap after we dine, will you come to me?"

Alfred stepped back and, with a smile, gave her a single nod. Margaret shook his cloak at him and held it high. Alfred turned, and she lifted it to his shoulders. Margaret leaned against his back as he laced the cloak from neck to waist and tied it.

In a light voice, Alfred chided his bride, "Come, wife, we dare not make Father wait. I liked not his penance from the last time."

During the service Margaret talked to God. *Waiting until before Midnight Mass is no longer possible. I wanted us to be home. Lord, this is harder than I thought it. I defied my father, the king, any man who told me nay. I bore any cost to have my will, including being called unnatural. You know I love him. So much. Caitlin said it aright; loving is an act of faith he will be good to me. He has been. Even this morn. He has earned my trust. Every day since our time on the steps. Oh Lord, I am going to trust in his love. As I trust in Yours. How well we do together be Your will. I choose.* Margaret smiled to herself and looked up to note Father had missed her distraction. *I choose to say the words. I needs tell him before we leave our safety, before Lord Warwick or the king calls him. Something else, Oh Lord. I know I should say Your will, Oh Lord, in all things, but in this I cannot. I beg you, Lord of Hosts, protect Alfred. Oh Lord, you know my mind. I have always protected whom I love. If anyone kills him, the king needs kill me to stop my revenge. Do not bargain with God,* she warned herself. It helped not; she did. She stopped only to take Communion and finish the service. Margaret stood and was silent as the congregation ended the service with, "Your will, Oh Lord, in all things." She never lied to God.

Margaret appeared at supper, took the dais, bowed her head when Alfred led the Te Deum and sat. Alfred looked down the fire pit and saw no one looking their way. Still looking ahead and barely moving his lips, he uttered, "I was called to the barn about the morrow. Do you forgive me?"

Following Alfred's lead, Margaret smiled and lifted her bowl to her lips. She replied, "Yes."

After Vespers."Margaret waited until they both had donned their room mantles and slippers, and she had stirred the braziers to prevent overheating and sparks.

"If you would, Alfred, please sit on your stool." Hands clenched at her sides, she paced before him. "Before we leave, I want to speak to you on a matter of import. I know not how to begin, where to start." Alfred made no response. "May I sit?" At his nod, she sat in his lap as she had the night they had met. She placed her chin on his shoulder and gazed behind him. Margaret saw flickering candles making dancing shadows and shutters closed tight against the cold and dark. She smelled fire and Alfred's man scent. Alfred's arms around her were light. She inhaled deeply and started. "I have been thinking something for a time, but I have spoke it not." Into his ear, Margaret whispered, "I love you." She froze; Alfred moved not. She kissed his cheek. "I love you." Margaret's husband turned his head. Their kiss was unhurried, sweet. They gave their hearts fully into it. No need to clutch each other, no need to rush the thrill coursing through them. They parted slowly and gazed at each other with half-opt eyes and gentle smiles. In a soft voice, Margaret murmured, "I love you, Alfred." Margaret lay her head on his shoulder and inhaled the scent of his skin. In the silence, she felt something so new she struggled with it. *My heart eases. No.* Margaret closed her eyes and relaxed against her husband. *My whole body is… calm. The lock around my heart. Gone. Fears fade to nothing.* Her sigh was slow and long. *I feel something new. What is it?* "I expected not that," she murmured.

"What?"

"Peace." Margaret leaned more deeply into Alfred's arms.

Against his chest, Alfred felt and heard another long, slow sigh. He gave her a small squeeze and time for her to savor her emotions. Margaret's husband promised himself never would he spoil the memory of this moment by revealing he already knew. For weeks, her soft, warm gazes, her tone of voice, and the way she husbanded him revealed her heart. "When did you decide you love me?"

Always the truth with him. "The night I almost drowned."

"Because I saved you?"

"No." She paused. "When the lake was trying to pull me under, all I could think was your name, reaching you. That startled me. I realized how much I cared for you, wanted to be with you." She kept speaking halting sentences. "Later. In the hut. You warmed me with your body. Against my skin, I felt your desire, but you did nothing. You did what I needed, not what you wanted. A sign." She explained. "I knew you love me."

Alfred frowned. "All this time, I was doing things to prove I loved you. Your proof was what I did not?" Margaret nodded against his shoulder. "Is that why you woke me in the night?"

Margaret nodded again. "For the first time, I thought the words, but feared saying them. To show you how I felt."

Alfred hugged his wife. "I love you, Margaret. You are mine heart."

Margaret's eyes filled. She lifted her head to meet his loving gaze with hers.. "And I love you. Alfred, you are mine heart."

Their smiling lips met. Margaret held his head to hers. Alfred's held her as if she were delicate, precious, breakable.

"I pray you forgive me my harshness."

"For what, my love?"

"On the steps that day. I said 'I love you' meant nothing. Deeds counted, not words."

"You spoke aright. Well, mostly aright. Deeds may needs come first, but the words are good to give and to hear."

"Yes, they are. After that day I started toting your kind deeds from the time I agreed to wed you. Your gifts. Your greeting. The warmth in your hands. After that night, I added to it, and my list swiftly grew. At each deed, I trusted you more, believed you. When Lord Cai's daughter demanded the brooch, you stood with me. Only someone who loves me would have challenged another for me." She kissed him. When they parted, Margaret murmured, "May we sit like this again?"

"As often as you like."

The bishop said we were joined as one. Love makes it so.

In silent agreement, they stood. Alfred walked round the bed to set his sword in its brackets. Margaret followed. They unclothed each other without hurry and let them fall. Naked, but warm all over, she watched him crawl abed. He lifted the coverings in invitation, and she joined him. As brazier fires faded to coals and one candle died, they made love at a luxuriously slow pace.

47

To Winchester

After Mass, Father blessed Alfred and Margaret and asked God to pour His grace and protection upon them. The couple and their escorts hurried to the hall. Without removing outer garments, they ate standing at the end of the fire pit. Their men left first and headed to the barn. As the couple finished eating, they heard noises from the bailey. Giraud rode out to scout the road.

"My lord, did someone tie Ferrant so he follows us not?"

"Done," replied Alfred between spoonfuls. He waited until Margaret had finished eating to set down his bowl and empty his mug.

"My lady."

"My lord," Margaret replied as she took his hand. Once out the door, she placed her hand on his forearm.

Knights, staff, servants, and villeins ringed the bailey. Margaret nodded right and left as she approached the litter. *Four roundseys.*

Sailcloth cover. Who stitched the border band above the hem? She smiled at the larger version of the band on her marriage bliaut. *Caitlin.* She caught sight of her rosy-faced friend, smiled, and nodded her thanks. Caitlin smiled and nodded back. *The cover goes from the bottom front, to make a canopy, and drops to the bottom of the back. It is tied to the side and top poles. The sides are sewed to the top. The ends extend below my seat. I can get air at the poles, yet the covering will stop the wind.*

"Well done, my lord. It looks fine."

"Father blessed it last morn. The inside is appointed as well."

"Need I say anything before I climb in?"

"I shall do it."

Shovel in hand, Duone approached and gave obeisance. Margaret's eyes glinted at seeing he was wearing his cap. From the shovel, he picked up a piece of leather in each hand, he reached inside the litter, removed a rock and a piece of wood with a burn mark on it, and placed them on the shovel. "My lady, it is warm inside."

"Thank you, Duone. I will return as soon as possible."

"Yes, my lady." He picked up the shovel and returned to stand next to his aunt.

Alfred held up the side curtain. *Two satchels left, one right. Folded blankets. and a wolf pelt for my backside.* "Very well appointed, my lord. I look forward to traveling in it." She sat over a small lip, and the horses shifted. The litter swayed. Margaret swung her legs into her conveyance and faced forward. She smiled at Alfred. "One face, my lord."

Alfred smiled back and replied, "One face, my lady," before he dropped the curtain.

Margaret tied the fabric strips top, middle, and bottom. *Light only in the open slits at the poles. Too dark to sew. Oh well. My backside* touches the back satchel and my feet touch the front ones. Long enough. Margaret reclined with her arm atop the satchel behind her. *Warm too.* She looked at the blankets. *Mayhap later.*

"Father Manntun, knights, those of the bailey, villagers, my lady and I depart to Court. We had planned to enjoy Christmastide with you, but our obligation to King Henry and Queen Matilda is first. We hope you have a blessed holy season. We look forward to returning home as soon as possible. God be with you."

Father Manntun gestured, and everyone replied, "God be with you."

Alfred mounted Garhard. Verel, Sauville, Bertrand, and Pernel, mounted and Pernell took the leads for the front roundseys from Jorgon. The caravan proceeded out the gate and down the lane. They were followed by Roulin and Arnaud, who were changing sentry duty with Hughes and Claude. Demetre ordered the gate secured. Alfred looked back to see Syghelm standing guard beside the closed gate.

Under the trees in the lane, Margaret's space darkened. She felt them turn left, and her space lightened. The roundseys increased their stride to an amble, faster than a walk but slower than a trot. *I heard they can keep this pace for hours. I am more comfortable than I thought I would be.* The ponies' clopping and the gentle sway of the litter soon lulled Margaret into half-closing her eyes. She reached for the blankets, covered herself, and lay her head on the satchel. She yawned and drew her legs up so her feet touched the other satchels. *I am eager for Newbury Inn and Fayme's good cooking.* Although Margaret tried to stay awake, the warmth and the swaying put her to sleep.

A horse's neighs woke Margaret. Afraid, she sat upright and reached for her dagger. The roundseys continued their same pace. *I cannot see where is the sun to know if it is midday, but my stomach tells me it is so.* She caressed the wolf pelt on her hip. *Warms me well. Only slits of light at the corners. Just satchels and shadow.* A dash of light lit something new. Between the satchels, she spotted the cork top of a flask. When she reached for it, she also saw something wrapped in sailcloth. She picked it up and felt bread inside. *Thank you, Alfred.* She grasped the leather flask and set both items beside her. Sitting upright, she sipped from the flask and re-corked it. The round had a slit in the top. When Margaret broke the bread in half, a thick slice of cheese fell into her lap.

"My lady, have you found your food and drink?"

"I have, my lord. Thank you for thinking of it. Is it yet midday?"

"It is. We are eating while riding. We want to arrive before dark."

"I am warm, comfortable, and soon fed. Thank you."

"I am glad for it."

Margaret heard his voice fading as he addressed Pernel and moved forward. *Leading as he should.* Margaret pulled free a chunk of bread and started. *These days I am hungry all the time. This babe must be growing fast.* She picked up the cheese. The meal was soon gone, but she saved half the ale.

Hours later, Margaret watched the slits fade and darken to night. She sat up. *Noises. Geofroi's voice. We arrive.* Margaret draped her scarf over her hair and around her shoulders. The ponies stopped. She heard gates creak and bars fall into their brackets. She untied a satchel and pulled out a parcel.

Alfred announced, "My lady, we have arrived."

Margaret untied both sets of ties. Alfred lifted the curtain and threw it over the top. She gasped at the cold air. He extended his hand and helped her out. Margaret grasped the platform.

"Steady." Alfred put his arm about her waist.

"I have been sitting or lying a long time, my lord." She straightened and turned back to pick up her parcel. Margaret looked around, but the dark hid everything familiar. She spotted the inn door opening and light streaming toward her feet. Someone took the ponies toward the barn. She accepted Alfred's hand as they walked to the covered porch.

Inside, the great room was filled with travelers. Two tall, well-dressed men stood to the right of the fireplace. They glanced at the newcomers and returned to their conversation. A man and three women sat at one table and gawked at Alfred and Margaret. They put their heads together and whispered. The couples' children and their nurses filled another table. The dark-haired ones looked to be the offspring of the dark-haired woman, and the light-haired ones to the other. Four unknown men had already taken to their blankets and had rolled against the left wall of the great room. They stirred not. A lord and a small boy sitting alone a table watched Alfred's group.

Only one table was set for eating. The knights stood two on a side. Alfred escorted her to one end and took the other. They all crossed themselves, and Alfred led Te Deum. Verel seated Margaret and sat to her right. Each place had a small round on a wooden dinner platter. The party broke bread. A vegetable broth and ale arrived. They were followed by two platters of fried fish and two bowls of boiled vegetables. Alfred started at his end of the table and passed to his right. Margaret did the same. *Fish. Three days more until meat.*

"Sir Verel, how long since you left the estate? Are you glad to be traveling?"

"As leader, I thought I should stay. I have not seen Winchester since you and I left it over two years ago. Yes."

Margaret passed the bowl. "I am glad you came."

"Demetre is leading in my absence," he commented.

Margaret nodded and returned to eating.

Geofroi's wife approached. She still wore her dark brown hair in a bun and wore a clean apron, now over a green gunna instead of her workday brown one. "My lady, we are full. The bed we reserved for you in the women's room is ready."

"God give you a good eve, Fayme. How fare you and your family?"

"We are well, my lady, and glad to see you again. Since your visit, both Norman and Saxon now stay here. We are grateful for your lord's good comments about us."

He values good service over the prestige of staying at the King's Inn. He need not prove his worth.

"Is a pitcher of water there? I want to wash my face and hands."

"I will send it anon."

"Thank you, Fayme." From her lap, she picked up the parcel, a length of fine linen rolled and bound with a rib of hemmed linen tied in a bow. "My Saxon Elstan and I thank you. He is healing well. My lord and I are grateful for your service."

Fayme accepted the roll. "Thank you, my lady. You are most generous and kind to us."

"May God give you good rest, Fayme."

"A good rest to you, my lady." Fayme left for the kitchen.

"My lord, I would like to retire."

Alfred stood. They met at her end of the table. He escorted her to the bottom of the stairs. Margaret took one step to be as tall as he. *I like standing eye to eye.*

Margaret whispered, "We left in such a rush. I lack privacy." She leaned a little toward him. "I love you."

"You may say it every day if you like," he whispered back. For a moment he placed his hand atop hers on the bannister. She turned and took the stairs. *I need not look back; I know he watches.* She took the walkway to the first door.

Margaret stepped into the women's room. She held the handle as her eyes adjusted to the dark.

"Shut that door," demanded a harsh voice. "You are losing our warmth."

A girl followed Margaret inside and shut the door with her hip. She handed Margaret a clean cloth and moved to the only table. She sat the empty pitcher on the floor, and replaced it with a full one. She poured the used water from the bowl into the spent pitcher and took it away as she slipped through the doorway and closed the door behind herself. Margaret saw Fayme's youngest dangling her feet over a double bed topped with a cream blanket with green stripes at the top and bottom. She washed her face and hands with warm water and draped her towel over the pitcher. As she turned toward her bed, the harsh voice assailed her.

"Who are you that you get a clean towel, fresh water, and the other bed?"

"The Lady Margaret of Dryhtenton." She stepped beside her bed.

The woman harrumphed her disgust. "The one who married a Saxon and made him a lord!"

Margaret ignored the woman's next comment, an insult. She watched the woman turn her back to the room. *Become accustomed to it.* Margaret looked through the shadows for an older woman on a floor pad. She spotted a young woman great with child.

"My lady, might you like a soft bed.?I am willing to share mine."

"Thank you, my lady." She rose to her knees. Margaret stepped forward and offered her hand. The woman stood and Margaret released her.

"I am the lady of Lord William du Lac."

Margaret gave obeisance. "I am honored to meet you, my lady. Would you like the wall or the room side?" She turned. "Thank you, Blithe. You are excused." The girl jumped off the bed, curtsied to each lady, and left.

Margaret pulled off her boots and set them in the corner atop the coverings. *No one can spit in my boots in the night.* She removed her mantle and scarf and draped them on her half of the bed. *Another layer.* She crawled under the coverings and settled against the wall. Lady du Lac climbed into bed. On her pillow, her sun-colored hair splayed behind her as she lay on her side and faced Margaret. A three-wicked candle flickered on its stand, and the room quieted. The women whispered.

"I asked, and she refused to share. Is your lord a good man?"

"He is. And kind."

"As is mine. He has a three-year-old son from his first wife. They are below." She hugged her belly. "This is our first. Have you children?"

"We are married four months. Not yet."

"I will pray you have a healthy son. God give you a good sleep, Lady Margaret." Lady du Lac rolled toward the room.

"God give you a good sleep, my lady." Margaret added the Lady du Lac to her prayers.

Before dawn, Margaret woke to a soft cough from the hall. She crawled around her bedmate's feet and reached for her things. When Lady du Lac opt her eyes, Margaret gave her a nod and carried her

462

things out the door. She held Alfred's hand as she slipped into her boots. Alfred kept her scarf and mantle over his arm as he walked her backward to the wall and pressed against her. Margaret snaked her arms around his waist and kissed him back.

"In Winchester, we shall have a whole house to ourselves." He kissed her again. "Follow me." Alfred led her on the walkway opposite the way she had come and down the back stairs. At the bottom, Alfred turned right. "We have eaten. The litter will be ready anon." He left by the garden door.

Standing away from Fayme and the cook, Margaret ate her pottage and drank hot broth. She arranged her scarf and fastened her mantle. "Thank you, Fayme." She slipped out the door and saw dirt, frozen stalks, and bits of plants on either side of the path as she walked around the building.

Giraud stood beside the litter. Alfred and three others waited on their horses. *He sits so tall. His cloak may be the same as the others, but his air of command marks him. I do have a handsome husband. This morn Sauville must be ahead.* She accepted Giraud's hand, sat on the edge, and swung her legs inside. Giraud lowered the side curtain, and Margaret tied it.

On the road before the inn, the group turned south. Margaret shifted and felt something bite her hip. *What is so hard?* She lifted the pelt and blankets, touched a hilt, and smiled. *Only a common, black iron short sword. Not fine like his. Still, pointed to pierce and sharp enough to cut. A good husband indeed.* Margaret covered the weapon and lay on her side. She pounded the satchel to shift the clothing inside and lay her head in the dimple. She covered herself and slept.

That evening, the Rooster's Nest great room was crowded. They supped on a stew rich in cod, white fish, mussels, and clams. The bread was hot, delicious, but butter free. The ale had a light bitter bite that complemented the creamy stew broth. Margaret felt surfeited. Again, Alfred walked her to the walkway steps. They whispered.

"I thought you wanted me swordless."

"I said not that. I just wanted you to have not that one. We are on the main road and beyond friends."

"Do our men know?"

Alfred shook his head. "Neither do our enemies."

"I shall keep it hidden until a need. Thank you, Alfred."

"God give you a good night, my lady," replied Alfred loudly enough for others to hear.

"God give you a good night, my lord."

Margaret took the stairs and looked down over the crowded great room. A man glanced up, and Margaret shrank back. In the women's room, only two floor pads remained. She took a spot against the wall and immediately knew why it was bare. *So cold, but no one at my back.* She kept her boots and used her mantle and scarf as her blanket. She made a pillow of one arm and held her dagger in the other hand, which she kept hidden under her mantle. Everyone seemed to ignore her, so she lowered her lids and watched for a time through her lashes. *No one approaches.* One of the candles sputtered, leaving her half of the room dark. She closed her eyes.

Again, Alfred woke his wife before dawn to repeat leaving early. As he walked her to the litter, he explained, "Three litters at Newbury, six here. More nobles each day to Winchester. I ordered a sleeping pad for you, but they may sell it from under you to someone of higher rank."

"I will be the envy of the room if I sleep on my soft wolf pelt. If I must, I will draw my dagger and demand space on the floor. Fear not, my lord, my reputation for a temper will aid me."

Alfred chuckled as he lifted the curtain for her. "That it will," he averred, "and I am glad for it."

The innkeeper's wife had saved a pad for Margaret by hiding it in the kitchen. Her eldest daughter held it as she stood beside her mother.

"Thank you for saving a pad and a place."

"My lady, on your journey from Winchester over two years ago, you showed me a kindness. I am returning it."

The girl followed Margaret, who asked women to shift their pads. After she had placed the pad against the exterior wall, Margaret thanked the girl, who curtsied and left. She nestled under her mantle in the last bare spot in the large women's room. She watched the others through her lashes as she recalled her journey home from Winchester. *I remember our stay. I had asked her about the ditch women I had seen. She sought information about a babe. I thought she knew one of them but told me nothing. Those poor women. To You, Oh Lord, I vow I shall see a daughter never becomes one.* Margaret closed her eyes.

The road was crowded. The nobles had demanded they queue by rank. Alfred's party was last. Workmen's wagons followed him. Margaret tasted dust and drank ale to cleanse her mouth. She draped her scarf over her head and huddled beneath a blanket to keep her hair and mantle clean. She woke to men loudly commanding, horses neighing, and her litter stopped.

Margaret sat and peeked. When she saw nothing, she undid the top and middle curtain ties and widened the hole. She saw a tall palisade of new wood and roofs beyond it. *Not the Half Moon I remember. Did they rebuild it?* The litter moved forward, and Margaret saw a crowd of horses and litters in a yard and a double gate being closed. Above it, she spotted a white flag with a cluster of large flowers in the center. The blooms had been painted red, pink, yellow, and blue. Before she could close the hole, Bertrand's horse blocked her vision.

"My lady, most stopped at the Four Flowers Inn. We are now second. The Half Moon is three miles ahead. We will arrive in darkness."

He rode ahead, and Margaret retied the curtain strips. She lay back and smiled. *We are now traveling our regular speed. Mayhap the Half Moon will not be so crowded.*

The older inn hosted two other noble couples and their children in addition to families of lower rank, and men hauling goods. The tasty fish soup included onions, turnips and carrots and was served with bread and two cheeses. The innkeeper stopped at each table and promised his guests a sumptuous Sunday dinner of roast pig, duck, and chicken if they stayed.

The next morn, several drivers took their wagons to Winchester despite it being Sunday. Everyone else walked a half mile to attend Mass. The innkeeper's family stood in back so they could rush back. Inside the inn, the ranked sat close to the fire; the others arranged themselves at other tables. The two Norman couples and their eldest sons visited at one table. Their other children filled another table supervised by three nurses. Several times the ranked glanced at Alfred and Margaret, who sat at their own table.

"They gossip because we sit with our knights while theirs sit separate," Alfred commented.

They gossip because last night in the women's room, the women asked our names. Margaret nodded agreement. Bertrand reported Sauville was in the barn guarding their horses and the litter. He sat beside Verel, who volunteered to relieve Sauville.

"I saw nothing on the road," admitted Margaret. "Have you news?"

The men talked of the new inn three miles north. How large it was and how fine it looked. Pernel reported he had guarded the materials while it was built. He told them the upper level had a women's room in the front with four smaller rooms for couples or families behind it.

"With a matching set above both sides of the great room, it can host eight couples or families in private rooms. I suspect that is why so many noble families stopped there." He added, "It is new and expensive, so it is counted fashionable."

They speculated what might become of the Half Moon with such formidable competition. A boy refilled the mugs at the other table and left the pitcher. He returned from the kitchen and did the same for Alfred's table. The meal was as sumptuous as the innkeeper had promised. Each table received a platter of bread rounds warm from the oven and a generous tub of butter. Servers placed a bowl of meat broth before each guest. The innkeeper set platters of roasted pork, duck, and chicken at each table, steam rose from the sliced meat. A pretty fair-haired girl carried pairs of bowls of vegetables to each table, pale orange carrots and white parsnips. Ale flowed. Conversation became desultory as guests enjoyed every bite. Margaret buttered a bread chunk. *This meal is good. Only four more days of fish. Then a Christmas Day feast at Court. How I look forward to that meal!* Verel left and Sauville arrived to dine.

"My lord, with your permission, I would rather sit here than in the women's room. Last night, there was hardly room to step for so many bodies. Children unable to play get restless, make noise, and cause trouble. This corner will be quieter."

"I am happy to be your company."

The knights took the hint and made excuses to leave. Alfred gestured, and servers cleared the table and brought a fresh pitcher of ale.

"May I know what happens on the morrow?"

"As His Majesty may not hunt or do anything today, we must tarry here, so as not to be required to appear at Court. The two-mile ride shall not be long, but we must travel west along the city wall. The house I rented is modest and on a quiet lane near the northwest gate. Before dark and the gates are locked, we enter town through that gate so few shall spot us. On Monday morn, we must rise, be dressed, fed, and at the castle barbican before the city gates op."

Either he *has a plan or he is plotting.* Margaret smiled not. "Am I to know more?"

"Margaret, you shall be severely tested by the Court. With my rank, you needs give obeisance to every Norman woman there. They know your temper and shall act badly so you give it rise. You must fail their traps."

"My lord, I mean not to cause trouble, but I have done so each time I was at Court. Her Majesty has chastised me for it." At Alfred's frown, she continued, "My lord, I shall obey your instructions and be the modest, obedient wife, whose actions bring you credit."

"Margaret, what is in the third satchel?"

"Alfred, I shall not tell you until this night." Margaret changed the subject. "Now that Elstan is free, what think you shall become of him?"

"We agreed. He shall stay with Mother and work our land. When I clear the first virgate of our new land, I shall give it to him. Elstan shall work my land; I shall work his. We have agreed at the end of each harvest, we shall send half of whatever we have to the other.

As a landowner, he can marry, attract a good family who can provide a bountiful dowry for their daughter. He shall prosper." Alfred smiled. "Mother is already inviting families with daughters to visit."

"He shall attract many a girl, for he is both charming and landed."

"And he is an 'el.' That still means something in our world."

"What shall become of the house after Mother…" Margaret looked away.

"Elstan and his family shall stay until you decide what to do with it. Mayhap make it part of a daughter's dowry, give it to our second or third son. Whatever pleases you."

"I am glad it shall be lived in. I would not like to see it unused and falling apart. I shall think on it, plan what I shall do."

"Plan," he murmured. "I planned not. Not to meet you. Not to love. Not to build and wait for you. Not any of this. Be careful, my love. You know the saying. 'If you want to hear God laugh, make plans.' Were I you, I would wait to plan. You never know what God plans for you."

"You plan. Knights becoming landed. Dryhtenton becoming a town."

"I think of it as hoping. I want not to make God laugh." He reached under the table to squeeze her knee. "After all, He sent me to you. So far, I am very grateful for the plans He has made for us."

48

❧

To Court

In Winchester, the homeowners had prepared a meal and readied the table. After welcoming Lord Alfred and Lady Margaret, they departed to the their son's home. Alfred and Margaret supped with their knights. Pernel left to guard their animals and gear at the nearby stable, and Bertrand arrived to sup. As they entered the nearest chapel for Vespers, Margaret noted the city was warmer because close buildings blocked the wind and rising smoke warmed the night air. The knights slept on the main floor. Alfred led Margaret to their room above. He gestured she enter first.

"Oh, Alfred, a half barrel! Hot water, soaps, linens. You are so kind!" She turned and hugged him. Alfred locked the door. "You first, my love. I bathe in cold streams, so warm water will suffice."

"I need help to wash my hair."

Alfred sat on the bed and watched Margaret stand in a corner of the tiny room and strip to her chemise. He wondered why she kept it when the thin linen displayed everything beneath it.

"You are grinning at me," she commented as she removed her ties and loosed her hair.

"I am admiring how quickly you undress."

Margaret turned from him and crouched beside her satchel. She rummaged until she found her boar's hair brush and bone comb.

"I shall do that."

When Margaret reached him, he put his hands on her hips and pulled the shift taut. He lowered his head and kissed her slightly bulging belly.

"You do this every night."

"I ask God's blessing on our babe."

"Will you love it if it is a girl?"

Alfred gazed into his wife's eyes. "If she has her mother's spirit and cleverness, I shall love her almost as much as I do her mother." Alfred kissed Margaret's breast.

"The water is cooling."

Alfred chuckled. "You want me to cool as well." He turned her; Margaret sat on the edge of the bed between his legs. *I do enjoy this ritual. By next Christmastide, my braids will do more than peek out of my seire.*

Alfred pushed the barrel toward the wall and stopped Margaret from lifting the pails. Into the barrel, he poured one pail of hot water and some of the cold. Margaret knelt with her head over the barrel edge. Alfred wet her hair with a full mug of water. soaped her head, and rinsed it. He repeated the steps and was left with but a sliver of soap in hand. Margaret asked for the small bowl beside the candle on the table. She scooped a handful of cold water into the bowl to dilute the vinegar before she rinsed her hair a final time.

"Why do you that?"

"For shiny hair." As Margaret squeezed her hair over the barrel, Alfred reached for a linen. Margaret dabbed her hair and bound it in the cloth. After stripping, she grabbed a second cube of the green-flecked turino soap and the rag it sat upon. She climbed into the barrel and discovered it was just large enough for her to kneel if she curled her toes. She dropped the rag into the ankle-deep water and used it to wet her face. She accepted the second soap cube from Alfred and soaped her face, neck and shoulders before rinsing. She sloshed water from her neck down. She shivered and soaped her body and legs. Margaret accepted Alfred's offer and covered her breasts with her arms as he washed her back. After he rinsed her, Margaret stood and lifted each foot. *They are clean enough.* Alfred wrapped her in a sheet and lifted her out of the barrel. He rubbed her arms and back. Margaret stepped away and dried herself before re-donning the chemise and tending to her hair

Alfred knelt and drooped his head over the barrel. Margaret soaped and rinsed his hair twice. *I like doing this.. Being wifely.* She messaged his scalp to his soft groans of pleasure. Margaret grabbed a sheeting and dried his half-head of hair. *It curls at the ends when it is wet. Darker at the roots now the sun is weaker. His hair looks the color of wet sand.* Alfred stood and added the second pail of hot water to the barrel. He undressed and took his turn. Too long-legged for kneeling, Alfred bathed standing. Margaret soaped his back and watched rivulets trail over his backside and down his legs. With the soapy rag, she followed the path to his ankles, making circles and swirls as she soaped his muscles. *Caressing his body.* She smiled to herself. She handed the rag around to Alfred, who started with his face. Margaret turned to pick up her rinse rag. As Alfred reached his belly, she soaked the rag and rinsed his back and backside.

As he washed, he commented, "You know Queen Matilda shall to ask you if you are happy."

Margaret rinsed the back of his legs. "Does your well-being depend upon my answer?"

"You know it does."

Alfred finished his bathe. Shaking out the last sheet, Margaret held it for him as he stepped out of the barrel. She watched him swath himself in it and saw patches of wet cloth stick to his skin.

"Then I had best answer aright."

"Which is?"

"Alfred, you know the answer."

"I want to hear it."

She kissed his moist arm and said, "I am happy."

"How happy?"

"You do dig."

"Yes." He faced her.

"She shall ask. I shall blush. She shall know." Margaret paused. "I am happier than I expected to be, and I am rather pleased about it."

Alfred swooped and kissed her. She pushed him back a step.

As Alfred wiped himself dry, he asked, "Did I wet you?" At Margaret's "No," he requested, "Please shave the back of my head. I have no time to see a barber before Court." Alfred donned his braies and took the only stool.

Margaret picked up the last sliver of soap and squeezed water from the washing rag. She moistened the back of Alfred's head and soaped the stubble from his crown to his nape, from ear to ear. She accepted his dagger. "Why do knights shave the backs of their heads? Is it to appear normal from the front and frightening from behind?"

As Margaret worked, Alfred answered. "Practical. Normans shave their heads to make room in their helmets. They are padded top, sides, and back to protect us from head blows. The back is padded double should I fall that way. I dress like a Norman lord; I needs my head shaved like one."

Margaret rinsed the rag in the barrel several times as she wiped soap and stubble from Alfred's head. She nicked off stray hairs until his scalp was bare, and dried his head with a corner of her sheet. Margaret kissed his baldness and declared, "Done." *You look and dress Norman, but I like that you think Saxon and we live their ways as well.* By feel, Alfred shaved himself. In the cold room, Margaret wrapped her mantle about her. She handed Alfred his.

"You gifted me early with my litter. I am gifting you early as well." Margaret dragged the third satchel to Alfred's feet.

She sat on the bed and watched him undo the ties. "I stitched more garments for you and made a plain cloak." As Alfred pulled items out of the bag, Margaret listed them. "A spare pair of long boots, a pair of short boots. Jorgon made them. Two hemmed loin cloths. Two braies, three chausses, leather for cutting new garter strips. Three shirts, and a spare tunic. I had not enough for a spare outer tunic.' She beamed with pride as she added, "You gifted me so much clothing. I want you to have enough clothing should you get wet or need them for warmth."

Her face fell, but she lifted her voice to sound casual. "I expect Lord Warwick or His Grace will send you to your annual required service immediately after your loyalty pledge on First Day. I want you ready."

The satchel empty, Alfred sat with clothing draped over his legs, boots at his feet, and a smile on his face. "My love, you are a wife of surpassing excellence. You stand at my back, protect me from the king, and give me respect at home. Ask and order not. Care for my heart. Promise when I ask you. Now prepare for my welfare away from you." He shook his head. "The men who ignored you were fools. They saw you not. I am more clever than they, for I did see you and now you are mine."

Margaret had blushed bright pink. "May I repack that for you?"

"Please."

Margaret knelt and placed the boots at the bottom. She took each item from Alfred and rolled it before filling the corners first.

Alfred savored every moment of his wife's movements and committed them to memory. He was cert he soon would be parted from her. As she worked, Alfred told her, "My darling, we owe a debt to the king. Knight's service, the forty days each year a lord must pay in men to the king's army, one for each hide of land. Come First Day, we owe twenty knight's service."

Margaret halted and looked at her husband. "We own ten hides. Ten hides, only ten services."

"You have forgot. When King Henry awarded you the estate, he delayed the services owed until you had a lord. Five hides in 1102, five this year, and ten for next year. Twenty."

"With eleven knights, we cannot pay the debt and keep the estate protected."

"Cormac and I figured it. Three knights six times until early 1105. Then two or three knights the rest of that year. We shall be debt free before 1106, owe ten-knights' service for that year, and every year beyond."

"At Court, you shall remind King Henry of our debt and offer your solution for repayment." *Eight knights home at a time for two years. Are they enough? They needs be.* At Alfred's nod, Margaret asked, "How many times will you be gone?" Margaret stuffed the plain cloak atop the rest and tied the satchel. She sat back on her heels and gazed at Alfred. He extended his hands and accepted hers. *Hold not too tight, or he will think me fearful.* Alfred drew her upward and onto his lap. Margaret lay her head on his shoulder to hide her distress.

"Twice each year. Go now, be home for our babe's birth, go again before Michaelmas and be home for Christmastide. With Cormac's help, you ruled the estate for a year and six months more. We can do this, Margaret. Mayhap ten days travel to the appointed place, forty days service, ten days home."

Margaret shrugged. "If we must, then we shall do it." Alfred gave her a squeeze. Outside, the covrefeu bells rang from every church steeple. "We must douse the candle. Do the knights know to spread the fire's coals and watch until they die?" Alfred nodded and blew out the candle.

In the blackness, Margaret said, "I ask you grant me three desires."

"Done."

"Whether you are home or gone, I may send for your mother for my lying-in time and our babe's first weeks."

"Of course."

"If you leave after First Day or Epiphany, I may return home, ordered by you should a royal object. I want not to stay at Court while I wait for you. Two knights' escort?"

"Three knights. I need only one with me. What else?"

"I want not to be husbanded in the castle unless we are behind a bolted door. Not safe. Our babe should come alive by the end of January. If you leave soon…" Margaret stopped.

Alfred lifted her chin and kissed her cheek. "My thought exactly."

His lips tracked their way to hers. They stood and begin their lovemaking. Soon mantles, chemise, and braies dropped. They dashed into the bed, and warmed the sheets. Margaret slowed his hands on her to increase their desires. She used what he had taught her to drive him into a frenzy. Their joining was ecstasy. Afterward, they lay in each other's arms and whispered love words and promises. Before they slept, they made love again.

Well before dawn, Alfred used his flints to create a spark and lit the candle. The room was more shadows than light. He washed before he nudged Margaret. "Cold water, but I washed. If you would wash, you needs rise now." Alfred turned his back as he dressed. Margaret washed and donned a clean chemise. She unrolled her dark green bliaut, her second best winter garment and its matching mantle. *I shall save the blue with its matching shoes and mantle for Midnight Mass and Christmas Day.* As she dressed, she worried about coins. *I have my ha-pennies and farthings in my satchel. Two bliauts are sufficient for my rank. How is he paying for the inns, this house, and the rest? Lord Cai's gift? Ask not.*

The men were already eating when the couple joined them. A cold wind blew into the room with Sauville, and again when Giraud left. Margaret heard horses outside, so she finished her ale and stood without finishing her pottage. She arranged her scarf over her seire and circlet, swung her mantle about her, and fastened her brooch. Margaret pulled leather gloves from an inside pocket and donned them. She followed Alfred and the wind swirled her mantle about her legs. She climbed into the litter and tied the curtain. *As cold inside as out. Wish Duone were here with his hot rock.* She pulled the blankets and pelt over her legs and lap. The litter moved, and Margaret grasped the lip to steady herself and stay upright. *I must look unruffled and at my ease when we arrive.* She felt for her sword. *Still here.*

Alfred led the party with Verel behind him, Giraud leading the roundseys, and Pernel, Bertrand, and Sauville following. At hearing the sound of hooves on stone, Margaret knew they were on the street leading to King Henry's palace. They wended their way south and swung left for a bit before turning right. *At dawn, they are at Mass. Do they op the barbican after Mass or after they break their fasts? Why are we so early?*

The litter stopped and the roundseys made a quarter turn. Margaret peeked and saw the portcullis. She leaned against her satchel, tucked her hands inside her mantle, and crossed her arms to hug herself warmer.

The slits lightened and then brightened with the day. The distant sound of horses increased. Margaret used her fingers to widen the space between ties but saw nothing. She heard an angry voice.

"Move away, Saxon. I outrank you and will enter first."

"God give you a good morrow, my lord. As I am here first, I will stay."

"This day's honor should be mine, not yours. You have no honor!"

What honor?

"I will cut you down! Your lady will die."

"Battle before His Majesty's gate? Where is honor in that, my lord?"

Margaret heard the familiar voice above her. She looked up to see only sail cloth.

"God give you good morrow, Lord Alfred. I declare you first this day. All others will follow you into the bailey."

"I thank you, Sir Roger. We await your pleasure."

The king's constable. He saved Alfred from being beaten to death before we were churched. Margaret sat up and arranged herself. As the noisy portcullis rose, the roundseys backed and turned to face the gate. *Alfred enters first to receive what honor?* The roundseys walked through the barbican and acrossed the bailey. Margaret heard saddles creaking. Two pairs of hands undid the ties and lifted the curtain. Margaret blinked and squinted against the light. Alfred extended his hand and helped her leave the litter. *Look not for the troublesome man.* She smiled at her husband. *Remember. One face. Follow. Be a proper wife, Norman style.*

She placed her hand on Alfred's forearm and give it a quick squeeze. They approached the steps to the Great Hall with Sauville, Giraud, and Verel following. The great hall doors stood twice a man's height and was framed with thick boards edged with big, black iron studs. The oak center was richly carved with a tree trunk half on each side of the split and branches and leaves that reached the top. The door was finished with tall iron handles.

Older pages in the king's livery of black with gold-colored trim opt the outer doors for them. Behind them, other pages removed their satchels from the litter and took them away. Bertrand and Pernel escorted the hostlers, taking their horses and the litter around the right side of the hall to the stables. Margaret heard the voices beyond the inner doors. *Have they finished breaking their fasts? Where is she?*

Other pages opt the inner doors, and the king's seneschal asked their names. In a loud voice, the seneschal announced, "Your Grace, members of the Court, honored guests. The first to enter this day is Lord Alfred of Dryhtenton, his lady, the Lady Margaret, and Sirs Verel, Sauville, Giraud."

The party stepped into the room as courtiers stared. A few persons applauded lightly and stopped. At the far end of the room, King Henry, surrounded by men and advisors, gave a desultory wave from the dais and continued conversing with a man to his right. Alfred escorted Margaret between the two lines of tables in the hall. *He takes charge of the room. Smile not.* People cleared the way. At the dais, Alfred waited to be recognized.

King Henry said, "God give you a good day, Lord Alfred." Alfred bowed; Margaret lowered her chin, curtsied, and stayed down. *Look not at the king unless he speaks my name.*

"Your Grace, it is a good day indeed when I am in your presence."

"Join us. We are in council on several matters of interest to you."

Alfred tapped Margaret's shoulder. She stood and stepped to the wall. When she turned, Alfred lifted her hand to his lips. He took the dais stairs and joining the half dozen men around the king.

"My lady, God give you a good day."

Margaret gave obeisance to Lady Perrine. "Thank you, my lady. Glad I am to see you."

"This page will follow you all day. Order him as you will." Lady Perrine walked away.

Margaret looked into a smiling Saxon face under a towhead mop. She removed her gloves and put them in her inside mantle pocket. She undid her brooch and pinned it to her mantle before removing it and draping it over the boy's arms. She unwound her scarf and lay it atop her mantle. "To our room and return." The boy nodded and walked toward the entrance to the queen's wing. Margaret looked around. *Glad they ignore me. Safer.*

She peered behind the dais and saw four women standing around a large braided rug laid within the warmth of the fireplace. A richly dressed girl sat with a painted wooden soldier in hand. A nurse stood between the girl and the fireplace. *Princess Matilda! Almost two now. Coloring like her father.* A pregnant woman stood behind a small boy playing with a wooden horse. *They play nearby but not together. Each child has a woman supervising it.*

Margaret looked up and smiled. "God give you a good day, Elric. Glad I am to see you."

With his left hand, Elric pulled his forelock and nodded. He handed her a goblet of ale. "I poured it myself. God give you a good day, my lady. How fare you?'

"Well, and you?"

"Well. His Grace invited us to Christmastide." He whispered, "We are on display to show the Court a Norman and a Saxon can produce a normal child."

"We?"

He pointed to the pregnant woman. "My wife, Aurore, and our son, Eldun."

"She is beautiful, and he is a handsome little fellow."

"Thank you, my lady. Your drink is safe. I got the pitcher from a Saxon page."

He knows. She sipped the brew and declared it excellent.

49

Small Victories

"My lady, may I offer a suggestion or two?

"Yes, Elric. You gave me good counsel at Forest Keep, and I trust you."

"Finish your goblet. Set it down and lift it not again. Also, I learned Court etiquette. We needs give formal obeisance the day we arrive. For the rest of the day, you stop, let them pass, and speak not to them except to answer should they speak to you. I recommend you hug not the wall. Stroll about the room. These biddies are eager to make you show them obeisance, belittle you for your low rank. Complete the task before we dine, and you can rest afterward. Every day after this, you curtsey as they pass and snub you." He added, "Aurore does it. I needs do it to the Norman men. An easy task, quickly done, and soon forgot."

"Good advise, Elric. As I have no friends among them, no one will speak to me."

"Aurore and I will, after we give you formal obeisance. You rank higher than we."

Margaret nodded. "You two are the only ones." Margaret finished her ale. "Please tell your lovely wife I look forward to meeting her. At her leisure, of course." Margaret leaned in and whispered, "She may know it not, but you know we are family." She raised her brows at Elric and stepped to the nearest table to set down her goblet.

Margaret walked down the row and passed through an opening in the tables toward the middle of the hall. Two steps later a woman stepped in her way. Margaret curtseyed, murmured, "My lady," and waited. The woman snorted her derision and passed. Margaret stood. Two steps later, she did it again. Every two or three steps she repeated giving obeisance. *I think they made a line for me.* She need not look into their faces; every Norman lady in the land outranked her. Each time she saw a different chest, neck or chin she gave obeisance. *Count each curtsey a small victory. I do what I must. It means nothing to me.* Margaret finally reached the double doors. She turned right and proceeded up the space between the second row of tables and the wall, giving obeisance every few steps. A chin stopped her. Margaret gave yet another respectful obeisance to the body before her.

"Lady Margaret."

She looked into a Saxon face and hard eyes. *His lady.*

"I would speak with you."

"I am honored you deign to do so, my lady." She bobbed a tiny second curtsey and placed one hand in the other at her belly.

"I am the Lady William of Avondale."

"Congratulations on your marriage, my lady. I wish you every happiness."

"My daughters," continued the lady in Saxon as she pointed to a pair of well-dressed girls sitting alone at a table. "Girls walk past them, snigger or sneer. They speak not to them and walk away laughing."

Margaret looked at their unhappy faces and pitied them. "To insult you and make them miserable."

The lady nodded. "I have questions."

"I am eager to be of help, my lady."

"When I give these women obeisance, they insult my clothes, my accent, move away, and laugh. I am well dressed; I speak Norman. Why?"

Margaret's eyes popped. Astonished, she asked, "You give obeisance?" Lady Avondale nodded. "That should not be! After the royals, your lord is sixth or seventh in rank in all the realm. His blood, his wealth, and the king's favor make him so. His rank is yours. Yours and your daughters'. Almost every woman in this hall owes you obeisance."

Lady Avondale whined. "He never told me. How was I to know?"

"Your lord knows etiquette among men. His first wife needed only to be pretty and produce sons. You needs navigate the dangerous waters of court women. They will sink you if they can. May I help you?" At the lady's nod, Margaret began. In detail, she reported how to behave, including the fact only Norman or Latin was spoken within the castle. "That we are speaking Saxon enrages them because most know it not and assume we are insulting them. After we part, you must only speak Norman, even to the Saxon pages." Margaret continued and was pleased at how quickly the Lady Avondale caught the nuances of behavior.

"Let me show you, my lady. Place your arm across your waist." Margaret raised her right hand and did so. Lady Avondale followed.

"See how the bell of your sleeve is much long than mine? Her Majesty's system of marking ladies' ranks when they are not with their lords. If a lady's sleeve is longer than yours, you owe her obeisance. If it is shorter, she owes you. If the lengths are the same, you nod at each other and either of you may speak first. When your girls are with you, you receive obeisance first. Then you say, 'This is my daughter her name.' The woman must give your girl obeisance because she too carries Lord Avondale's rank. You do the same for your second-born daughter. At your request, the woman is then forced to introduce her girls. Yours will outrank hers." The women grinned at each other. "Your girls can force conversations with any girl they outrank. After all, their sleeves are as long as yours."

"I wondered about the fashion and various lengths. How do I repair the damage done to me and my girls?"

"When your girls do something poorly or not at all, how do you punish them?"

"I dare not smack ladies of rank!"

Margaret smirked. "Yes, you can! Not with your hand but with words and deeds. What they fear most is being embarrassed, insulted, or ignored. Use it against them. Take your girls with you and re-walk the room. Walk toward a woman with a shorter bell, show your sleeve, stop, and glare. Her obeisance will likely be sloppy or done with disdain, but no matter. Say 'Again!' loudly and in the voice of a queen being insulted. You have embarrassed her, and she must redo it properly. Everyone within hearing will look and know."

"Know I understand my rank and will use it against them if they treat me ill."

"Exactly. When you introduce your daughters in turn, she must give your family obeisance twice more. If you ask, 'Your daughters?'

She must call them over and they give three obeisances as well."
Margaret leaned in and whiispered, "Do this once or twice before
we dine, and they will flee you!" The women laughed together.
"Remember, my lady, you stop not walking for those beneath you.
They must clear the way and curtsey as you pass. The only ones who
can hurt you or your girls are the few above you. To them you must
be as subservient as those below you must be to you. Do that, and
they will respect you even if they befriend you not."

Lady Avondale switched to Norman. "He gave us Norman
names. You may call me Lady Pensee. My daughters are Cherise
and Claudine."

"Thank you, Lady Pensee. Would you like to summon your
daughters and practice on me?"

Lady Pensee did so. After she explained what the girls were
to do, Margaret gave proper obeisance to the girls, much to their
delight.

Lady Pensee straightened her back. "Girls, stand tall. Follow us."

Lady Pensee drew Margaret's arm through hers and walked
toward the end of the hall. "Walking arm in arm shows my favor
toward you?"

She walks now with authority. Even her voice has changed.

"Yes. I thank you for the honor you bestow upon me. This can
also be a way to confer favor on one of lesser rank or a way to start a
friendship. Those of lesser rank must be polite in public."

"I was prepared to hate you, but you are as good a person as he
said." Lady Pensee placed her head close to Margaret's and whispered. "We do not well together."

"Here you have him trapped, and he must do better." Lady Pensee
stopped and looked confused. "My lady, we are both on display as

is the farmer Elric and his Norman lady, Aurore. The royals want to advance more marriages between our peoples to create Englishmen. Elric has almost no rank; we are only a bit higher. You and your lord are the most important because of your high rank. Their Graces are using us to demonstrate marriage between Norman and Saxon can be happy. Elric is happy; I am happy."

"What do you suggest?"

"When alone, explain to him. When Lord William is in your sight, near you, with you, he must display his respect and regard for you. He needs be courteous, deferential, doting. On your part, you must gaze at him lovingly, speak to him warmly, touch his arm as you talk, and do other sweet gestures and words in public. If you glance a royal's way and see a smile, you know you are gaining even more favor because you two are doing as they wish. Did you see my lord kiss the back of my hand before he left me and my blush and doting look after him? We do like each other. It was not an act, but it was also done to gain the king's approval. He saw it and smiled even as he was listening to a man."

"You have the Court noted well even if you lack their rank. Lady Margaret, you have given me great service. I will remember."

A young woman walked toward the group. *Lady Claire's daughter by the look of her.* Margaret whispered, "Her sleeve. You outrank her. She addresses you first. She outranks me. Afterward, I address her."

After being given obeisance, Lady Pensee introduced her daughters, who were also honored. "Your name?"

"Lady Clarice, my lady. Daughter of Lord Roland of York Downs and the lady Claire." She looked down her nose at Margaret.

Margaret curtsied low and intoned, "My lady." She kept her eyes on the girl as she rose.

"Her Majesty is ready to see you." She omitted the honorific. To Lady Pensee and her daughters, she bobbed a curtsey as she said, "My ladies." She backed away after looking at Margaret as if she were a leper.

Am I in trouble again? I have done nothing wrong. Oh yes. Am I happy?

"Lady Pensee, if you will, where is the nearest chamber pot?"

"Between the double doors. Women to the left, behind the tall screen painted a garden scene. We will talk again, Lady Margaret."

"Thank you, my lady," said Margaret as she curtsied. At the inner doors, Margaret stopped her page. She passed through, and the doors closed behind her. She stepped behind the garden scene. While meeting her needs, she heard a group enter the hall. When Margaret returned, the page followed her. She stopped at seeing Lady Pensee stride up the aisle between the rows of tables with her daughter's trailing.

Lord William's wife stopped, faced the woman standing to her left, showed her sleeve and glared. Margaret saw a sloppy curtsey and heard a loud, imperious, "Again!" She spotted a dozen women turn to watch. The woman curtsied and spoke to Lady Pensee's satisfaction. After properly performed obeisance to the girls, the woman called a girl to her, who was also forced to give three proper curtsies. Lady Pensee spoke, "Better. Remember me." She turned away to trap the next woman.

Margaret took two steps toward the door to the queen's wing. A lady approached. "Lady Margaret of Dryhtenton?" Margaret gave obeisance to the roundness before her. As she rose, she received a blow to left side of her face. Spinning right, without thought, Margaret drew her dagger.

"MARGARET, NO!" roared Lord Alfred from the dais. He jumped off the dais front and dashed to her.

Everyone in the hall stopped. A few looked at King Henry; most eyes followed Alfred.

As Margaret spun, she flicked her dagger upward and brushed the woman's breasts with the backs of her fingers. Seeing the dagger almost remove the tip of her nose, the woman jumped back, lost her balance, and landed on her backside so hard her head slammed against the rush-covered stone floor. Her husband raced to her aid. He helped the shaken, ponderous woman stand. No one in the hall spoke or moved.

"Your lady is a monster! She attacked my lady. She almost killed her!"

Alfred's arm touched Margaret's shoulder as they stood together. "My lord, if you saw it, you know your lady struck mine. A blow so hard my lady spun about. That my lady defends herself is well known. Your lady risked her life to harm her."

The lord sputtered as his lady's knees buckled. With effort, he held her upright.

Alfred's voice was loud in the silence. He announced, "I expect anyone who touches my lady to die. Your lady is fortunate she lives. Should your lady touch my Margaret again, I will not save her. Or you. Or anyone." He paused and vowed, "Anyone who touches or harms my lady meets my sword."

In the back of the hall, Verel stood, as did Sauville and Giraud. Because they were only knights, they could not speak at Court unless they were first addressed. To show their support of their lord and lady, the men placed their right hands on their hilts and stood tall and menacing. Their glares warned all they would defend their lady

490

as well. To break the tension, King Henry loudly coughed, picked up his goblet, and drank.

The lord sat his lady on a bench and stood over her. The courtiers turned away and visited in hushed tones.

Barely moving her lips, Margaret whispered, "The queen sent for me."

Alfred offered his arm and escorted her to the door. The guards opt it. Leaving her page behind, Margaret passed through. After the guards closed the door, Alfred faced the hall and noted none looked his way. He climbed the dais stairs and approached the king. The other men on the platform stepped away and listened. Alfred apologized for the disturbance. He ended with, "Sire, I pray we upset you not."

Henry looked into Alfred's eyes and shook his head. "She is still as dangerous as ever, my lord."

"For which I thank God."

The men smiled at each other. Alfred moved away so others could approach the king to finish their business.

50

Queen Matilda

Trying to calm herself, Margaret walked the hall slowly. *Mother, you told me we ranked high, but the ranked wanted you to midwife them only because you were Norman. Hired, not a friend. Mother, because of you I assumed a height Father lacked. How proud and haughty those above me must have thought me. Now I rank lower than you did, even as I rank high in the Saxon world. Two different ranks, and I must live within both worlds of them.* Margaret sighed and shook her head. *A luxury I should not have had. Here, I must abandon pride.*

At the door to Queen Matilda's chambers, she straightened her garments and adjusted her serie and circlet. Her knock was soft, tentative. A young woman unknown to her opt the door, and she slipped through. She stood behind the cluster of the queen's ladies and saw Lady Clarise addressing the queen. In her high-backed armchair, Queen Matilda was regally attired in a deep blue bliaut with gold sleeve linings that gleamed as bright as her coronet. Her slippered feet rested on a brightly broidered cushion, which also shone in the sunlight streaming from the clerestory windows. Clarise glanced Margaret's way, said something to Her Grace, and backed away three steps before she turned toward the group. As she joined them, she threw Margaret a look of smug satisfaction.

"Lady Margaret, approach."

The girls parted. *She sits so straight because I caused trouble. No footstool between us this time. Be not so close she strikes me. That I could not bear.* Margaret curtsied, stayed with her head down, and uttered, "Your Grace."

"Stand." Queen Matilda inhaled deeply. She roared, "What did you this time!"

Margaret clutched her hands together. She bobbed a curtsey and answered, "A lady I know not struck me. I tried to defend myself."

"Leave us!"

The ladies walked out slowly so as to hear Lady Margaret before the last girl closed the door.

Margaret rushed out, "Your Grace, I gave respectful, humble obeisance to every woman in the hall. I did the same for her. I was modest and subservient. I swear I know not how I gave offense. I know not why she struck me. I beg your forgiveness for my offense to your Court."

Matilda waited to speak until the door closed. She calmly murmured, "She struck you because she is the sister of Lord Wilbur's lady, who went into banishment with him. Her sister resides somewhere on the continent. Likely, she fears she will see her sister never again."

"I did nothing to Lord Wilbur or to his lady. He chased me to kill me."

"His Grace informed me. Lady Trematon is angry. She cannot strike our king, who banished them, so she aimed lower and attacked you." The queen called, "Lady Clarise," and the door opt immediately. Margaret stepped back so Clarise could attend the queen.

She curtsied and intoned, "Your Grace."

"Go to the Lady Trematon and express my deep regret she injured herself. Inform the lady I expect her to take to her bed to rest and recover for the remainder of this day and all the next. Explain her meals will be brought to her. Then see to it. Keep her company until Vespers. Report to me anything she says about Lady Margaret today and for as long as she is at Court. Tell Lady Trematon when she is recovered, I will see her attending Mass. On the morrow, assign another lady to attend her all day. Go to her and stay."

A polite banishment for a time accompanied by a subtle threat against gossip. She is so much a queen.

When the door again closed, Matilda gestured Margaret forward and demanded, "Why do you attack?"

Margaret clenched her hands tighter and rocked forwards then back before she stopped and straightened. She spoke softly, "Your Grace, I doubt you have been hit. Struck with a fist, beaten, ribs broken, kicked in the head. Beatings make you strange, Your Grace. Some cower at the slightest sound, ever fearful of another blow. They become mice, running away and hiding from everything. When I am struck, I attack. To prevent another blow. To stop a beating. To... to" Margaret stopped and dropped her chin to her chest.

The queen spoke softly as well. "To protect yourself. You kept the sword not because you wanted to be like a man, but to protect yourself from men." Without lifting her head, Margaret nodded. "Knows Lord Alfred you attack because of beatings?"

"I think he knows."

"Tell him. He will understand you better."

"Yes, Your Grace, I will tell him." *Not now or here. When we are home, and in an empty keep.*

"Please fetch a stool and sit."

Margaret placed the stool where the queen pointed and sat with her knees almost touching the queen's.

"Palms down, extend your hands." With a stern face, the queen lightly tapped them once. She grinned and grabbed Margaret's hands. "There. I have severely punished you. Should anyone ask, inform them I did so." Matilda held hands, not queen to subject, but woman to woman.

Margaret nodded. *Cry not at her kindness. Smile.*

"Worry not over Lady Trematon. She is a crabby, disagreeable women, seldom complimented and much disliked. All I hear from her are ailments and complaints. You enabled me to remove her from my presence, even if only for two days. Thaes hal, Margaret," said the queen in Saxon.

For a moment, Margaret's mind switched to Saxon. *Dare I answer in Saxon?* "Thaes hal, min cwen." Margaret returned to Norman. "If you never invite me to Court, I would not be here to cause trouble," she offered.

Matilda squeezed Margaret's hands and refused to release them. She too returned to Norman. "Ah-h-h, Margaret. If I called you not, how dull Court would be." She squeezed Margaret's hands again. "Glad I am to see you. How fare you?"

"Well, Your Grace. Glad I am to see you."

"Your news?"

Margaret smiled and stalled. "God, in His goodness, bestowed upon us a huge harvest. We built two more grain bins. Our animals multiplied, and our smoke house is brimming. Our people are well, the children fat and healthy. We were fortunate to reach Lord Cai before he died. He talked with me and awarded me a beautiful brooch he once gave his lady. I will wear it to Midnight Mass and on every special occasion after."

"What of Lord Alfred?"

"He is well. He added four knights to our estate, good men. His knights respect him. My lord controls the estate and runs it well."

"Margaret," chided the queen. "How are the pair of you together?"

Margaret started pinking. "Your Grace, you were right about my lord. He is from a good family." She gave her queen a look. "A very good family." *She knows I know.* The women grinned at each other. "My lord is a good man, and kind. You were right to match us. We are well suited to each other."

"Are you happy?

Margaret nodded vigorously and blushed.

"You know I expect to hear the words."

"I am happy, Your Grace. More happy than I expected," admitted Margaret.

"Then Lord Alfred pleases me." She surprised Margaret with, "Have you learned your lesson?"

"Lesson, Your Grace?"

"That being loved every day is far better than rank while at Court once a year."

"Yes, Your Grace, I have. You are right about that as well."

"Good." Matilda released Margaret's hands and sat back in her chair. "I was informed Lord Alfred and you entered the grounds first. His Grace decreed each day from Fourth Advent Sunday to

Christmas Day the first to arrive dines and sups with us on the dais. Your lord sits beside His Grace, and you sit beside me."

"You bestow great honor upon us, and we are grateful for your favor."

Matilda cocked her head and considered before she spoke. "A queen should not have favorites, but I think you know."

Margaret pulled her lips between her teeth to stop her grin. That her eyes sparkled announced her pleasure at the queen's admission. The women gazed at each other with bright eyes and warm hearts.

At a knock, Margaret jumped up, replaced the stool, and stepped back from the queen. *I should have bumped against the prince's cradle. Where is he? At four months, is he already in the nursery? I could surrender not my babe to a nurse so soon. Poor Matilda, to be without her children.*

Lady Perrine entered. "Your Grace, His Grace asked me to inform you he hungers. He waits at your door for the promenade and asks you to hurry."

After Lady Perrine closed the door, Matilda pointed, "Margaret, I need my matching blue shoes. My seire is in that chest."

As Margaret attended Matilda, she commented, "I recognize Lady Perrine, but your other ladies are new to me." She removed Matilda's slippers to put on short boots and fasten them.

"I replaced them all. One of my wishes, remember. Perrine will be gone after Epiphany to marry well. With His Grace's permission, I arranged it."

Margaret held the coronet as Matilda positioned her seire. "May I?" Margaret adjusted the cloth with one hand before she handed over the coronet.

"I like their young, hopeful faces. They are eager to please me because I hold their futures in my hands. I plan to find matches for each one. Clarise is Lady Claire's."

Margaret held the queen's metal viewer for her. "I noticed the resemblance." *If her disposition is the same, she will be sent home as well.*

"She understands her position is precarious because of her mother. I have warned her. We will see about her."

Margaret turned out the bottoms of Matilda's bell sleeves to a wide cuff so the gold lining showed. She nodded and stepped back. From the side table, Matilda picked up her viewer for Margaret to see her appearance. *Such a personal service. I must use it so as not to hurt her feelings.* Margaret shifted her circlet and seire and returned them to be straight again. She accepted the viewer and placed it on the side table.

"Thank you, Your Grace." Margaret stepped aside, followed, and moved to hold the door for her queen. As the door opt, the ladies stood with their backs to the walls, waited, and followed.

At the entry door, a Saxon woman coughed loudly. The door opt and the queen took the steps.

"My queen, you are as beautiful as ever." Henry offered his forearm, and Matilda placed her hand upon it. Everyone in the hall stood before the couple turned toward them. The royals started down the aisle between the wall and a row of tables, nodding right at courtiers and welcoming guests as they walked the customary promenade.

Alfred offered Margaret his arm, and they followed the royals. The courtiers' faces switched from friendly to neutral. The couple noticed not.

From his half smile, Alfred whispered, "Am I safe?"

Margaret broke her half smile and recovered. "She is pleased with you."

"Thank you for my life, wif," he whispered in Saxon.

She returned in Saxon, "Please keep it for decades, husband."

The royals turned and walked the center aisle while speaking to those on their right. At the dais, they turned left and walked down the other outside aisle. Alfred and Margaret smiled at Elric and Aurore, who sat last at the end table. At the double doors, the foursome again took the center aisle, this time the royals greeted couriers and guests to their left. Thus, everyone had seen the royals and been welcomed. At the dais steps, the Bishop of Winchester followed the royals. Alfred and Margaret followed him and took their positions. The hall saw a line, Lord Alfred, King Henry, Bishop Giffard, Queen Matilda, and Lady Margaret.

To the hall, Bishop Giffard remarked this day was the shortest of the year. The birth date of the Christ was in three days, marking the event Our Lord had arranged for the forgiveness of sin, and for bringing light to the world on Easter. Henry cleared his throat. The bishop stopped his sermon, gave the blessing, and led the Te Deum. *The song fills the hall. I hear an echo from the ceiling. Beautiful.* They sat in order, Bishop Giffard, the king, the queen, Alfred, and Margaret.

They look to the king to lead. Some look at the queen. As we are nothing to them, they regard us not. Lady Pensee and her daughters smile at me. How kind. So many pages line the walls. From which door comes the food? Who serves the dais?

"Honored guests, barons, earls, lords and all your ladies. Welcome. Lord Alfred will give our toast."

Alfred stood and nodded to King Henry. "Thank you, Your Grace." He leaned forward and said, "Your Grace" to Queen Matilda.

Alfred faced the hall and paused. "I know warriors so fearless they laugh at death. So brave they fight without sword or shield, helmet or mail, lance or horse."

They frown and shift in their places. They think he will name Saxons and dislike him for it. Some angry, most confused. Not a friendly face among them.

"These warriors are strong and carry burdens most of us would not. They do battle time and time again. We are alive because of them." Alfred lifted his goblet to his sovereign. "Bishop Giffard, Your Grace, honored guests, nobles, knights, men, let us toast the bravest people I know. To our mothers, who birthed us through pain and blood. To our wives, who birth our heirs that we men might live on. To the bravest of them all, Queen Matilda, who thrice risked her life to help England have a future."

They are stunned.

Henry stood and lifted his goblet.

Now *every man stands. Well done, Alfred.* She smiled at Queen Matilda, who was looking at Alfred.

"To our mothers!" roared Henry. He turned, and touched his goblet to Alfred's. They sipped in unison. The men in the hall repeated Henry's words and drank.

"To our wives!" Henry and Alfred repeated their actions. The hall rang with the toast.

To Queen Matilda!"

Such an outcry! She is much loved.

After emptying his goblet, Henry gestured all to sit. When the room quieted he slapped Alfred on the back. He announced. "Lord Alfred, well done. Best toast I have heard in many a month." Henry sat and Alfred followed. As the pair talked, the volume in the hall rose and fell.

Margaret beamed. *Look toward him not. Be like her.*

Matilda commented, "An excellent toast. Unexpected. Others praise His Grace or me. Your lord has gained favor in the hall. A few men and women even smiled at him."

"Thank you, Your Grace." *He knows how to gain favor and persuade. He convinced you to marry us.*

Two pages and a man dressed with the king's emblem on their tunics took the steps and walked before the dais table. The man picked up a pewter bowl with a spoon handle showing. With both hands, he placed it before the bishop.

A Norman chooses my bowl. I am not safe as Alfred promised. The Saxon page before us women can do nothing. Oh Lord, please protect me.

Margaret watched the bowls. When the Norman reached for a bowl, the Saxon page shifted his tray, so he took the bowl closest to him and placed it before the queen. The boy gave Margaret a knowing look and glanced down. The last bowl was hers.

Saved! She gave the boy the tiniest nod of thanks. She looked up to see those at the tables were being served as well. After King Henry lifted his spoon to his mouth, everyone started.

Delicious! What are these pink and white bits? I have tasted not this fish before. The vegetables cut into flowers, stars and crescent moons. The broth has both a sweetness and tartness to it. Honey and a dash of wine or is it vinegar? How special. I am going to enjoy eating here. Margret looked to the queen and noted she must scoop the broth with the spoon, not drink it from the bowl. She saw those in the hall using spoons as well.

Queen Matilda pushed her empty bowl forward. "Lady Margaret, I have been thinking your lord's toast is part announcement."

"Your Grace, I know not what you mean." *Please go no further. I must protect our babe.*

"I see now your face has changed; you are not as slim. When?"

She knows I dissemble not. Evade. "Your Grace, your enemies are mine enemies. Away from home, I fear poisoners. Some hate my lord, and I have been chased. I dare speak not to give them power to harm us." Margaret smiled to hide her fear.

Matilda smiled back so those in the hall would suspect not. "You refused to come. He made you promises of safety, and he asked me to help him keep them. Now I know why. When?"

Margaret hung her head. She whispered, "The first fortnight in June."

"Those who poisoned me are dead. Any remaining allies quake at being charged with treason. I can keep you safe. You are now under royal protection. Watch."

"Please say nothing," she begged. *You are royal, and they entered your inner circle and poisoned you. How much easier I am to reach.*

Matilda raised her voice and announced, "Sire, I have happy news."

My babe! Now I must neither drink nor eat neither here nor on the way home.

The hall stopped eating and looked to the dais.

"What is your happy news, my queen."

"Your will, Oh Lord, in all things. Your will, Oh Lord, in all things. Your will, Oh…"

"I am going to be a godmother."

"Who is the child so fortunate to have your love and protection?"

All in the hall saw Matilda grasp Margaret's hand.

"The firstborn of my dear friend, the Lady Margaret."

Alfred saw the stunned expressions in the hall. Even he knew the queen had never before called anyone a friend, not before she became royal and cert not in the three years since her coronation. The Court applauded as they must, but their faces showed confusion.

Henry slapped Alfred's back. "Well done!" he bellowed. "Another Englishman soon born."

Matilda astonished Margaret when she leaned and kissed her cheek. "Now no one dare touch you."

Fearing the queen's innocence, Margaret barely managed, "We are more honored than I can say, Your Grace."

The bowls were replaced with trays of baked and fried fish. To the side, four pages held bowls of boiled vegetables ready to serve. Queen Matilda placed a fillet on her plate. She murmured to Margaret, "Fear not, you are now safe. You and your babe." Standing before them, a Saxon page hid them from the Court. Queen Matilda lifted a fillet from the serving tray and set it on Margaret's plate. Barely moving her lips, Matilda smiled and whispered in Saxon, "You are an el's wife and my family. Cousin, well you know we Saxons protect and defend each other. "

Epilogue

Dryhtenton
1 August 1012 A.D.

"Mother, think you Father has found me a fostering place so I may be a page? I am of age."

Just like me at eight. Eager to leave home and begin his path to adulthood. Cai soon shall follow. As much as I shall miss them, they need associations with Norman families and proper training. Hopefully, Norman families shall accept them.

Margaret kept searching the distant trees for color, so she looked not at her firstborn to her right. "Your father will tell you in good time, Fred."

A battle near the North Wall to drive back Scots is always dangerous. I pray the message is wrong. Two dead, but why said they not who? My love injured. Others too. Why no details?

Margaret nuzzled her youngest, fifteen-month Elsworth, who was sucking his thumb and looking about. Margaret shifted him from one hip to the other as she waited. Her braids brushed her backside as she moved. She looked left to admire the village now treble in size. Their land, long cleared, was now fields ready for harvest. Ripe grains swayed all the way to the inn beside the road and north past the river, where a second, larger mill stood. The villagers, who lined the road to the bailey, chatted in as they waited. A few waved to the family. Margaret nodded back. *Be not too cheerful. I know what is coming.* Across her right cheek, Margaret felt the kiss of the summer breeze as it cooled her sun-lit face and ruffled her seire. Margaret admired her sons, colored like their father and trim like her. Though she dressed them in chauses and tunics of the same color, she knew how different they were. Alfred was more serious, and Cai more adventurous. She tilted her head at spotting a tiny blue flash through the green. Margaret saw more color as the boys raised themselves on tiptoe and began waving.

"Stand still!" she commanded. "Wave not."

"We want to show Father a happy welcome," explained six-year old Cai, as he and his brother did as they had been told.

"Be not cheering your father's return when one or more of your friends in the village soon may mourn." She glared at Alfred and Cai.

"No, Mother," said the boys in unison. They pushed back their shoulders and froze.

Margaret smiled at the straight stances and serious demeanors of her daughters. Beorhti, five, had her mother's coloring, but her hair was curlier and light, as her grandmother's had been. Three-year-old Rosamonde, who copied her sister at every turn, was sandy-haired like her father and still carried baby fat. "Well done," she whispered to them. The girls beamed at their mother for her infrequent praise.

Beorhti spoke for the pair. "Why is Father's banner backward?"

"A warning, Beorhti. Someone is not coming home.

Lord Alfred came into view. His left arm was in a sling and his left leg heavily bandaged. Alfred struggled to wobble not in his saddle.

Elbeorht slipped her hand into her mother's as she whispered, "Father is hurt."

"Yes, child. Mayhap others."

From the bailey gate opening, Margaret watched the party leave the trees. Behind the banner and her beloved rode a single line of knights on their roundseys and leading their battle horses. Because they were empty, the supply wagons behind them made a racket as they bounced on the cobbled-stone roadway. She spotted Caitlin, her simples box in hand, slip away from Cormac and their three children to wait beside the lane for the line to pass. *She may be plumper these days, but she still works hard and will serve the others before she comes to help me. Good Caitlin, so skilled and always ready.*

Margaret returned to pouring her love and strength toward her beloved. *Love, I will you to stay in the saddle until you reach me.* Alfred spotted her in the distance and gave a brief nod. Margaret forced herself to smile and give her head a soft tilt so he would believe she was at her ease. Without looking away from Alfred, Margaret issued orders to the pages behind her. "Fetch Jorgon and his crew. Tell the kitchen to send hot water to the hall and place it near my simples box, which you shall fetch from the keep. Return for more instructions." They scurried away.

The meal must wait. "Alfred, when your father dismounts, stand on his good side. Only smile at him. Ask no questions and look worried not. If he pats your head and walks beside you, continue with him. If he pats your shoulder and leaves his hand, be his crutch. If you are able, seat him on the dais so I may tend him." From the corner of her eye, Margaret saw Cai's hopeful look. "Cai, stand on his injured side. Protect him so your father strikes not his injuries on the doorway, so he does not fall toward the fire pit. Boys, if Father stumbles, grab him at his waist and hold him upright until men can help you."

"Yes, Mother," replied the boys in unison.

Margaret's heart warmed at seeing Cai's prideful smile. She looked left. "Elbeorht, you are old enough to greet the knights errant as they arrive. Would you like to say, 'Welcome home' after me?"

Elbeorht nodded; she too stood tall. Rosamonde whined about being left out.

"Rosamonde, stop! Your task is to keep your brother happy. Nurse, attend them. To the keep for the day. Feed them, and stay close after you put them to bed." At Rosamonde's, 'But Mother, I want …" Margaret set down her son, lifted her arm, and pointed to the keep without taking her eyes from her husband. The nurse picked up Elsworth as he toddled off. With chin to chest, Rosamonde dragged her heels as she followed the pair across the bailey.

Margaret poured her love toward Alfred to give him the strength to reach the bailey. *Know you how much I love you? Need you? I shall heal you. I promise. Stay in your saddle; stay strong. Reach me, my love. I shall do the rest.*

Margaret watched Alfred slow his horse; she held her breath. Alfred stopped and bent right to speak to the Lady Arabelle. She collapsed into the arms of her friends; her children clutched her skirt.

Please, God, no! Not Verel! Margaret's clenching her jaw tight did nothing to stop tears coursing down her cheeks. *Oh Verel. Ever good, honest, kind. And her with child again. Oh Lord, why Verel!*

Alfred stopped again. Through her tears, Margaret watched

Pernel's son clutch Lady Calandre's hand as she nodded and turned away. Villagers surrounded her. The landed knights peeled away from the column as their wives and children rushed to them.

Worse than I feared. I must be grateful for the living. Say it and mean it. Your will, Oh Lord, in all things. Thank You, God, for letting him live. Margaret wiped her cheeks with her sleeve. She stood on tiptoe and then settled herself. *Feel my love washing over you, my darling. Soak in the strength I send you. Reach for me, Alfred, as I am reaching for you. You shall rest in my arms.*

Alfred kicked his roundsey forward and looked up the hill at the gate framing Alfred, Cai, Margaret and Elbeorht. He smiled to see her right hand on her bulging belly. He thought her tears were joy at his homecoming. Alfred's horse began the switchback toward his family. Even as Alfred's heart leaped up, he winced in pain. As he reached the bridge over the water moat, Alfred's eyes were only for his wife, her face framed by her circlet and seire. Her loving look warmed his whole being and gave him strength. Alfred urged his horse across the bridge as he thought, *Still my bride. You are my heart, my life, my beacon.*

Author's Note

In 1105 C.E., King Henry turned over the regency of his two-year-old heir, Prince William Adelin, to his wife, Queen Matilda, and invaded Normandy. While she ruled England, he took control of the cities Bayeau and Caen before returning home to settle a dispute. Henry again invaded Normandy in 1106 because his brother, Robert Curthose, Duke of Normandy, was massing an army to invade England as he had in 1101. Robert still wanted Henry's crown. This time Henry took the fight to Robert's lands. In the one-hour Battle of Tinchebray on 28 September, Henry defeated and captured Robert. Henry imprisoned him for life. First, Henry held Robert in Devizes Castle in Wilshire, England, and then in Cardiff Castle in Wales. Robert Curthose died at 83 in 1134, one year before his brother.

Robert de Belleme, former Earl of Shropshire and Shrewsbury, whom Henry had charged in 1102 with 45 counts of treason and other crimes, had fled England to his estate of Ponthieu in Normandy. In 1106, De Belleme fought with Robert Curthose's army against King Henry. He chose to command the rear guard, and led them to retreat to save himself from capture and death. One historian commented de Belleme and his men had waited on a hill to see how the duke fared. When it was apparent the duke would lose, de Belleme departed with his men and "faded into the mists of history." I consider his comments about de Belleme to be legend until I can verify that historian's story with another historian's documented account.

In 1106, Queen Matilda again had been regent for her son, Prince William Adelin, and had ruled England while her husband fought the Battle of Tinchebray. After Henry returned, he praised Matilda for her good administration of the country during his absences. In her court, Matilda supported music and literature and was interested in architecture. She was much loved by her subjects for her piety and charitable works. A strong supporter of the Church, Matilda ordered cloisters and hospitals built. Queen Matilda was the daughter of King Malcom III of Scotland and the Saxon princess Margaret. No written records exist that prove Queen Matilda supported Saxon ideas, but as she was half Saxon herself, I cannot help but think her good works on their behalf are evidence of her support. One historian claimed she had three children after Prince William Adelin, but none survived. As I could not substantiate that information, I only share it for your interest. Queen Matilda died in 1118.

By the end of 1106, King Henry had dispensed with the greatest threats to his kingship. After Robert de Belleme had been banished, the other barons, earls, and lords fell into line. Henry's brother Robert was in prison. Queen Matilda had brought Henry and Archbishop Anselm together to negotiate peace. Henry conceded the archbishop's right to choose the nation's bishops and to lead the Church in England. However, Henry removed the Church's power over all matters civil including trying cases. Henry moved those rights to his Royal Courts, the Saxon courts, and to himself and his Privy Counsel. Henry restricted the Church to priestly and religious matters only. The Church lost much power. Because I wanted to show how determined and forceful Henry was, I moved those events to within *Lady Margaret's Challenge Book Two* and 1102/1103 instead of their actual dates, which had occurred during the years 1102-1106.

King Henry and Queen Matilda named their heir after his grandfather, King William I (the Conqueror), and added "Adelin," which is not a middle name but a title. "Adelin" is the Latinized version of "Aetheling," a reference to his lineage to ancient Anglo-Saxon royalty through his mother.

When Henry's grandson became King of England on 9 December 1154 C.E., he was crowned King Henry II. Historians returned to their accounts and renamed Henry, King Henry I. In the early thirteenth century, historians re-examined King Henry I's reign, his accomplishments, and his legacy. Several historians started adding the surname, Beauclerc (good scholar) to Henry I in tribute to his many accomplishments. King Henry I had created a centralized power, formed a legal system that incorporated many Saxon laws and customs, added a judge (called a justiciar) to the 12-man jury Saxons used, introduced traveling justiciars (royal judges) to settle disputes unresolved in lower courts, and began the separation between Church and State. Those are just a few of Henry I's contributions to England. We now call him King Henry Beauclerc or King Henry I (Beauclerc).

King Henry II is considered one of England's greatest kings, but his grandfather, after whom he was named, is seldom counted one as well. I opine Henry I turned England from a country of invaders into a nation of citizens of law. Henry's father, William I (the Conqueror), invaded and parceled the land to his supporters. He brutally subjugated the rebelling Saxons. His favorite son and heir, King William II (Rufus), treated England as his personal playground and his subjects as toys. Henry I reinstated the laws he liked from his father's reign, made peace with the Saxons, who then supported him, and calmed the Church's rage over his brother's depredations of their properties and rights.

King Henry I died 1 December 1135 after 35 years on the throne and was buried at Reading Abbey, which he had ordered built in 1021. Henry left behind a powerful nation of laws, peace among his peoples, and a burgeoning economy that used a monetary system respected at home and abroad. I often wish those who followed King Henry I's reign had continued his wise policies, excellent decisions, and robust sense of justice. Unfortunately, a civil war ensued.

If you are curious what became of Prince William Adelin and Princess Matilda, I recommend you read *When Christ and His Saints Slept* by Sharon Kay Penman, one of my favorite authors. I so love her book I have reread her account at least five times. I am in awe of her story-telling abilities.

In an effort to create the peoples Henry called "Englishmen," he began intermarriage between Normans and Saxons. Henry's efforts were met with vociferous objections and sometimes outright defiance. I used the fictional characters of Lord William of Avondale and Lady Pensee, Lord Alfred and Lady Margaret, and Elric and Aurore to represent Henry's early attempts. One hundred fifty years after Henry died, a historian commented that Normans and Saxons intermarried "at every level of society." In the fourteenth century, a man admitted he was an Englishman when he wrote, "A true Englishman drinks only ale, not that vile brew from the continent" (beer). When I read those words, I smiled and thought, "Henry, you succeeded twice more."

The blessing Bishop Giffard gave Margaret and Alfred at their church ceremony is over one thousand years old. In 1993, a Catholic priest gave me the English translations for three Latin versions of this ancient Catholic wedding prayer, a short, a medium, and a long one.

As I liked parts from each version, I combined them into a single prayer. I think it reflects the Catholic Church's beliefs about marriage in the tenth, eleventh and twelfth centuries as explained to me by the priest I had consulted. What I wonder is if the old "kiss of peace" at the end of the ceremony became the modern "You may now kiss your bride." Unfortunately, I forgot to ask him.

Though fictional, Margaret and Alfred represent two groups in this era. Norman women were property, first their fathers', then their husbands', and, in some circumstances, the king's. Women's lives were restricted, confined, and never their own. No one was going to permit Margaret to choose her own husband. Hers would have been a cautionary tale to other Norman girls: "Defy our social order and suffer the consequences."

At this time, free Saxons were rare. When Alfred became a lord, he gained self determination and freedom from all legal restrictions Normans had forced upon all Saxons after they had conquered them. Alfred's cost was social rejection from Norman society.

What became of Lady Margaret, Lord Alfred, and their children I leave to your imagination.

Coming Soon

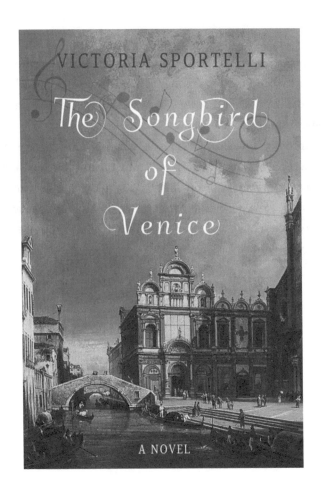

An orphan seeks a better life.

"Grazia, why won't you sing for Padre Vivaldi? He came especially to hear your voice."

I stared at Mother Superior and decided. *Silence is not a lie.*

Grazia, known as the songbird of Venice for her perfect pitch and pure voice, has been trained to be a nursemaid or housekeeper. Instead, Grazia dreams of leaving the orphanage to marry a shopkeeper or a merchant and have a family.

Antonio, a wealthy businessman, proposes marriage. Then Grazia receives a second proposal from a man whose social position is even higher. Unbeknownst to Grazia, the men are enemies.

After Grazia marries, she attempts to fit into Venice's exclusive society, but secrets and the disappointed suitor's revenge could unravel the life she has begun.

Acknowledgements

My writing partner, T. M. Evenson, has been with me during every step of my writing the prequel, Lady Margaret's Disgrace, and the Henry's Spare Queen Trilogy. She gave me encouragement, ideas, editing tips; she even taught me how to be published. Dear Sister, I am forever grateful for all you have taught me and your help, all the while you launched *Emergence: The Journey Begins,* Book 1 of *The Destiny Saga.* You keep writing about the future while I keep writing about the past.

Kathy Carlson took every call for ideas and help. She cut to the heart of every matter, asked the right questions, edited my writing and book descriptions, and gave sound suggestions. I could not have competed this trilogy without her input and advice. Kathy, you are a true friend and my sister-of-the-heart. I am more grateful for having you in my life than I have words to express.

Thank you to Dawn R. for all your help. Thank you Lindsey Grassmid for your fine maps, and T. Wiering, for helping me locate Creazzo Publishing.

Any "horse sense" in this story comes from my friend Joyce sharing her equine knowledge and from my meeting her American saddle-bred horse Gizmo.

Producing a good-looking book is best be done by finding the right people. Thankfully I have. Thank you, Jenny Q. of Historical Editorial, for book cover designs I am proud to call mine as well as for your patience with me when I wanted new versions. Margaret Diehl, my book editor, "gets" me. She not only edits copy, she also writes me pages of single-spaced notes, explaining what I need to do to add depth to my ideas. If my writing has improved, it is because of Margaret's able assistance. Wordzworth is an interior book design company that understood what I meant when I said, "I want my interiors to meet the industry standards for historical fiction novels." Wordzworth is so good at it that I plan to continue to use their services. Jenny, Margaret and Wordzworth are exactly whom I want for my upcoming novels.

Glossary

Advent. A time of prayer and fasting from the fourth Sunday before Christmas to midnight Mass on Christmas Eve.

All Saints Day. November 1. During this period, the Church counted this to be the first day of the new year.

All Souls Day. October 31. Also called All Saints Eve by the **Church**.

A.D./Anno Domini. Latin for "In the year of Our Lord." We now use C.E. (Common Era).

Aetheling. Old Saxon. Prince or princess. Royal.

anon. Immediately.

bailey. A large area, usually protected by a dry or wet moat, surrounded by a tall wooden or stone wall called a palisade, which encircles the hall, keep, kitchen, garrison, chapel, and other buildings where a lord, his family, and his retainers reside. Part of an early Norman castle.

barbican. A fortified entrance to a castle or a town of towers on either side of a passageway to enable guards to shoot arrows, or drop rocks or boiling water over invaders. They may also drop a **portcullis** to stop an invasion.

bed and board. Payment in the forms of a place to sleep and a wooden plate, which means you will be fed.

betrothed. A formal arrangement of a marriage with the first step of a contract between families. The second step is a blessing of the couple by a priest; the third step is the couple bedding together, and the woman proving she was a virgin.

bliaut. *(pronounced blout)* A Norman-French word for a woman's outer garment to the wrists and ankles, fitted to the elbows for fashion, then flared to the wrist and fitted to her hips, then flared below for easy walking, usually wool in winter and linen in summer.

boon. A gift or favor granted by one person to another.

braies. (bray-is) Old French. A loose male undergarment, usually to the knees, fastened with a belt, and worn under chausses. Imagine modern men's boxer shorts.

broider/broiderie. (to broider, verb/broiderie, noun) An Old French term from which becomes our modern "to embroider" and "embroidery," an ancient practice of embellishing fabric with additional stitchery.

C.E. Common Era is the modern term used to describe years. It replaced "A.D." (Anno Domini): Latin for "In the year of Our Lord." Some still use A.D. I use C.E. when speaking you and A.D. within the novel.

Casteela. A region on the Iberian peninsula where scented, gentle soaps were first created in the eighth century. The modern spelling of this region of Spain is Castile.

Catholic. A person who follows the teachings of Jesus the Christ but does so through the **Church**, whom he/she considers as the path to Jesus. A Catholic believes in the special authority of the pope.

cert. The medieval word for certain. The opposite is uncert.

chatelaine. Usually the landholder's wife; she is responsible for everything on the estate except its safety and men's hunting practices.

chausses. (Old French) Loose-fitting covering for the legs and feet and part of a Norman male's clothing. It is often held close to a man's legs with strips of cloth or leather called garters or cross garters. Think modern men's pants without bindings.

chemise. A soft undergarment of linen or wool slightly smaller than a **bliaut** worn by a Norman woman to protect her skin from chaffing. Called a shift by Saxons.

Christmastide. The days from Midnight Mass on December 24 through the Epiphany on January 6.

Church. The one, catholic, true religion taught by Jesus the Christ and practiced throughout Western Europe with the pope in Rome as its head; it is also called the Christian Church. After the Protestant Reformation it was renamed the Catholic Church.

cloak. A hoodless, sleeveless warm outer covering worn by men, which we now call a cape.

close. A piece of land held as private property, usually walled and gated. European cathedrals and churches are often surrounded by a close that may also encircle other buildings, such as a convent, abbey or other religious place. Because a close may be locked, it protects the religious from attack.

Communion. Shortened form. See **Holy Communion.**

Confession. A requirement to state one's sins to a priest, to receive absolution, and to do penance before being permitted to receive **Holy Communion** during Mass.

constable. A man in charge of a castle.

convent. Enclosed buildings and its surrounding property which houses women who have chosen to become servants of God and are called nuns.

coronet. A relatively small metal crown consisting of a band with only one peak, which may be plain or decorated, especially with a gem or jewel.

corps d'elite. An inner circle of knights King Henry kept close to him to guard his person and family; he also charged them with special projects. In turn, Henry promised them special privileges and to award them land after five years of good service. With permission from his overlord, any lord could create such a group as well.

cotte. (cot) The **cotte** (or cote) was a medieval outer garment, a long sleeved tunic (male or shift (female), usually girded. Synonyms included tunic or gown and was an outer garment In medieval texts, it was called a "tunica "or "chiton."

courses. A euphemism for a woman's menstrual cycle during which her uterus sheds its bloody lining.

covrefeu. (*Cuv rey few*) Old Norman-French for "cover fire." With most buildings of wood, a single spark could burn a town. During this time in England, all fires in homes in a town had to be doused every night at dusk. From this word and custom we get the word "curfew."

cross garters. Strips of cloth or leather which keep the loose legs of chausses close to a man's legs. The two most common patterns are two strips that cross in Xs in the front and back of the man's legs or spiraled like the red of a barber pole.

curtsey. A woman's or girl's formal greeting and/or sign of respect made by bending the knees with one foot in front of the other to one who is of superior rank. What one does as part of giving obeisance to one of higher rank.

cwen. Old Saxon. The original spelling of "queen." The pronunciation has not changed in over 1,500 years.

dais. (die s) In a hall, a platform two to four steps high upon which sit a table and benches, stools or chairs and from which the lord of the estate and his family dine and rule. Used both indoors and out.

daub. Any mixture of mud, straw, and other substance used to cement items together or to fill in holes. The term is part of **wattle and daub.**

ditch woman. A girl/woman whose father/husband has thrown her out of her family for unacceptable behavior, such as disobedience, having had sexual relations outside marriage, running away, etc. She lives in fear of her life because anyone can do anything to her. See also **pariah.**

donjon. The below-ground level of a **keep** or medieval castle which originally was a storage room for food, weapons, and other supplies. Later it became a prison. The modern spelling is "dungeon."

doth. (dawth) From Old Saxon. Does.

dowry. The money, goods, and other items a woman's family agrees to give so she can bring it to her husband and her husband's family at her marriage. The amount of wealth she brings often determines her value as a wife. The verb form is "to dower."

Epiphany. January 6. The twelfth day after Christmas, believed to be the day the Magi visited the Christ Child and gave him gifts; a time of gift giving and feasting.

ere. Before.

farthing. A coin equal to one/fourth of a penny. The obverse side was scored with a cross so a penny could be broken in half, a ha-penny, and then again into a farthing (a fourth thing.)

fasting. The restriction of the intake of food and/or drink for a stated period of time.

feudalism. All of England was owned by the king. He portioned out some of it to be held by those beneath him, who worked and protected it on his behalf. A baron held vast tracts of land and answered directly to the king. With royal permission, a baron could separate his lands into earldoms and raise a lord or knight to that station. In turn, either the earl or lord could then assign land within the property he held to a knight who could then marry because he was a landholder. Each rank owed military service and taxes to the station directly above his.

flagon. A portable leather pouch with a wooden or cork stopper used to hold drinking liquids.

forelock. The front portion of hair, which a Saxon male grabs and pulls down over his forehead when he lowers his head as a sign of respect toward a Norman or to one who is of superior rank.

foster. The Norman practice of exchanging sons or of taking in someone else's son in order for him to learn skills and about the customs and practices of another household. Often it was also used to introduce a young man into a household from which he might take a wife.

freeman/freewoman. A Saxon who had been a villein and has become a free individual. He/She may now buy land, make contracts, sue in court, move freely about the land, and, of course, pay tithes and taxes directly to the Church and Crown.

froward. The medieval form of forward. The act of behaving in an outrageous, unbecoming, unacceptable manner.

geld. Old Saxon for "gold" or "coin."

gelding. A castrated male horse. Generally ridden by men. A woman rode a palfrey, a docile or female horse.

girdle. A belt of leather or stiff fabric, decorated or not, that women wear around their waists. They hang their personal dagger, a scissors, household keys etc. from it. We now call it a belt.

girl. Any unmarried female no matter her age.

Grand Crusade. In 1097 Pope Urban II called all of Christendom to a crusade to free Eastern Christians from Turkish rule and to take possession of the Holy City of Jerusalem. When Jerusalem fell to the Turks in 1147, a second Crusade was called and the custom of numbering the Crusades began; this one was then renamed the First Crusade.

Grace. Always used with Your as "Your Grace"and only for the king and queen of England. It is the title of address until 1534 C.E. when King Henry VIII was the first English royal to require the use of Your Majesty.

grub. To turn over the earth before planting a crop or to dig a hole.

gunna. (*pronounced goona*) An Old Saxon word for a long-sleeved woolen dress worn to the ankles and fastened to the body with a girdle (belt). Most Saxon women owned only one, which they wore until they were annually given cloth by their lord to make another one in preparation for Easter. Similar to a bliaut, but straight from shoulder to hem and shoulder to cuff.

ha-penny/half penny/half pence. A silver penny with a cross on the obverse side that can be used to cut it in half or quarters. See also **penny/pence**. The Old Saxon word was "pfenning."

hall. The building where the Norman owners of an estate dine and conduct business.

hand. One hand equals 4 inches. A measurement of a horse from the ground to the top of its shoulder.

High Mass. A regular religious service led by a priest or higher member of the Christian Church for a special occasion to which has been added additional elements such as a procession, special prayers and the use of incense.

hide. A unit of land comprising about 120 acres.

hill fort. Thousands of human-made mounds can be sighted in England today. They are believed to pre-date the Saxons and Romans, who found and built upon them as high places from which to spot enemies.

Holy Communion. A piece of bread and a sip of wine transformed into the body and blood of Jesus the Christ by a priest during Mass. The ceremony unites all of Christendom, and only those in good standing with the **Church** may partake of it.

hostler. A person who trains, works, and takes care of horses.

Hure e Crie. Old Norman-French for "See and Cry." To order a Hure e Crie was to command that any person seeing a danger must inform all the others in the area. This phrase is our modern "Hue and Cry." See **Seon und Heour** for the Old Saxon form.

husband. (hoos-bond) Old Saxon word for the male in a marriage. As a verb, it means to manage and/or conserve wisely, as in "He husbanded his resources." This is one of the approximately 25 percent of English words that come from Old Saxon.

jerkin. A sleeveless jacket that evolved into what we call a vest, usually leather with metal rings tightly sewn together as a form of armor. Used by one who could not afford mail/chain mail

keep. A square building usually of stone, sometimes of wood, where the Norman lord and his family may flee for safety if his estate is attacked and his bailey is breached; generally the family lives and sleeps there. It is built on a motte, a hill, either natural or man-made.

kneeler. A bench for kneeling on with an upper part upon which one may rest her/his hands.

kneeling cushion. Attendees of Mass at their local chapel or church stored a cushion upon which to kneel on the cold dirt or stone floor. Poor persons usually did not have them and knelt on a corner of their **mantle** if they had one.

knight errant. Designates a fighter in arms who serves or is hired by one of rank without his being given land; he is called "Sir" out of politeness but bears no rank.

knight landed or just **knight.** A knight errant who has been given land and who may now marry; he serves a man of a noble rank above him he is the lowest noble with the title of "Sir" during these times. See also **titles.**

linsey-woolsy. A textile made with a flax warp and a wool (worsted) weft.

litter. A canopied, curtained conveyance for a lady of rank. She sits or lies among cushions, blankets and furs on a wooden platform while the device is attached to horses front and back. No real lady rides unless she must.

mail. a hood and/or body covering comprised of small metal rings linked together to protect a fighter from swords and other piercing devices. On his way to knighthood, a boy started wearing mail day and night to strengthen his body and to prepare him to think of it as his second skin. Protection in battle.

mantle. A hoodless, sleeveless warm outer covering worn by women, which we now call a cape.

mark. A measure of money equivalent to 160 pennies. In 1096, 10,000 marks was 1.6 million pennies when two pennies bought an adult boar pig, one penny bought a sow, and piglets were two for a penny.

marriage chest. A wooden chest, carved, painted, or plain, into which a girl placed the linens she has hemmed and all manner of clothing, fabrics, household goods and items she has made or acquired and will take with her to her new home as part of her **dowry.** During the 20th century, it was called a "hope chest."

Mass. A religious service led by a priest or higher member of the **Church** to which Christians attend and those in good standing with the Church receive **Holy Communion** as a way of uniting all Christendom and of keeping its members faithful.

May Day. May 1.

mayhap. The medieval word meaning "maybe."

merlin. The solid part of the top of a wall that is separated by spaces called crenels, part of the top of the battlement of a castle or the top of a keep.

Michaelmas. September 29.

Midsummer. The summer solstice, usually June 21 or 22, depending on the moon cycles in that year.

min. (mine) Old Saxon. The original spelling of "mine." The pronunciation has not changed in over 1,500 years.

minstrel. A servant who was the entertainer of an estate or was the court musician for a king. Men who traveled as minstrels were for hire. The word 'minstrel' means "little servant."

morrow. The medieval word for tomorrow.

motte. A mound topped with a tower called a **keep,** which is within a **bailey,** the whole of which comprised an early Norman castle. Motte and bailey are the modern terms for this kind of castle arrangement.

mortal sin. A misdeed that will cause your soul to be sent to Hell if it is not forgiven by the **Church** and which is more serious than a venial sin, which is a misdeed and a minor offense against God and/or the **Church.**

Norman. Both the name of the group and the language the Normans of England and Normandy spoke during the twelfth century. We now call the language Old Norman-French.

nonce. "For now" or "for the time being."

offal. Excrement from a human or an animal.

oft. Often.

op/opt. (sounds like oap/oapt) The medieval words for open and opened.

over tunic/ super tunic. An ankle-length second tunic over a tunic of knee length. Sometimes sewn on it was the lord's emblem. Whether armor was layered between the tunics or only over the over tunic varied by personal preference and the weather. In later times, this garment was also called a surcoat.

page. The first step toward knighthood begun when a Norman boy was 6 to 8 years old. He was trained by the chatelaine to serve at table, learn manners and customs, run errands, as well as to begin wearing chain mail to strengthen his body and to begin sword practice. At 14 he was eligible to become a squire and begin preparing for knighthood. Saxon boys could only rise to becoming a squire without chain mail or sword training.

palfrey. A female horse only women and priests ride. Sometimes called an ambler if it is a **roundsey**.

palisade. The wall of wooden timbers or of stone which surrounds the bailey and all within; usually has either a dry or wet moat around it for further protection and only one gate for entrance. Also called **ramparts**.

pallet. A low contraption of sailcloth and wood so one can sleep off the ground. Modern military calls it a cot.

parcener. Old Saxon. Partner.

pariah. A person who is despised, avoided and treated badly. During this time in England, anyone declared a pariah could be hurt, maimed or killed without any penalty. It was not a crime to kill a pariah.

parchment. Sheep skin that has been pounded thin and stretched and upon which records are written. Sometimes also called **vellum**.

pele. Old French. A tall thick pole buried into the ground knights use in practice to attack and practice sword blows.

penance. Prayers and good deeds which must be completed before one's sins are expunged and before one can receive **Holy Communion** during **Mass**.

penny/pence. A coin/coins of the realm. Pence was also another word for a penny; the word is sometimes used for a single coin or a number of coins, as in "six pence." In Old Saxon the word was "pfenning."

people/s. A group of persons related by common elements such as descent, heredity, history, language, cultural traits, social norms or geography. In the early medieval period, the chief determiners of a people were language and geography, so the people were: Saxon, Norman, Scot, Irish, etc. One of the most shocking of King Henry I's policies was his mixing of Saxons and Normans through marriage to create a new people he called English. In later centuries this word was changed to race.

Percheron. A horse, usually black but sometimes gray, from Perche, a region in northwestern France.

portcullis. A strong, heavy metal grating that can be lowered down grooves on each side of a gateway or a **barbican** to block entry.

pottage. Soaked grains such as cracked wheat, cracked rye, smashed oats, or a combination of grains into which can be thrown leftover vegetables and meats; it is cooked and turned into a soup/stew and served in the morning. This word was later changed to porridge.

pound. A unit of money in silver pennies/pence. In this era 240 pence equaled 1 pound.

pull your chin. Before William the Conquerer's invasion in 1066 A.D., all married Saxon men wore beards. They pulled on their beards as they swore oaths to seal them. When King William ruled, he ordered that all Saxon males must be clean shaven "because with beards they all look alike." After the King's new law, Saxons started pulling their chins as if they still wore beards when they swore oaths.

Purgatory. A middling place between Hell and Heaven to which souls went for a time. For a soul to reach Heaven, those on earth had to pray or do the good works the dead person needed to complete before her/his death. During the early 21st century, the Catholic Church removed Purgatory from its religious practices.

ramparts. Another word for **palisade**. The wall of wooden timbers or of stone which surrounds the bailey and all within; usually has either a dry or wet moat around it for further protection and only one gate for entrance.

rank. See **titles**. Within each title, men are ranked according to how much land they held, their level of wealth, and how the royals favored them. Wives, sons, and daughters held the same rank as the head of their household.

reeve. On an estate, a man who has been elected each January by his fellow Saxons to oversee all the assigning of land, planting, growing, and harvesting of crops. Rather than speak his name, people often just said his title. Traditionally, he may elected only three times before another man must be chosen.

rib. Any narrow strip of cloth. See **wedding rib**.

riding platform. A platform that was n early medieval woman's saddle, upon which she sat sideways with her legs to the left side of a horse with a sandbag counterweight behind her on the other side of the horse. No self-respecting or honorable woman spread her legs around a horse's back.

roundsey. A very strong horse who was the size of a large modern pony. Not only could it carry heavy weights, its five-gaited walk was much desired. In addition to walk, trot, canter and gallop a roundsey ambled, a gait the pony could maintain for hours. This created easy riding for humans because it was so smooth. Roundseys still exist and are now called Icelandic ponies.

rushes. The general term for any hollow stalks, which, after the harvest, were strewn on the floors of halls, keeps, and other buildings to keep down dirt/dust and to catch food and other fallen debris. In addition, they were also strewn on barn floors for animals to stand upon. After rushes dried, they became a fire hazard.

Saxon. Both the people of England who were invaded in 1066 by King William I (the Conqueror) and the language they spoke. We now call their language Old Saxon.

scabbard. A sheath for a sword, usually of leather or cloth-covered wood.

scythe. A metal curved blade attached to a long wooden pole, which is used to cut grain stalks during harvesting.

seire. (Old French) Silk cloth from Seire (China). The word came from **Sericum**. In Late Middle French the word was changed to "glossa."

seneschal. The man who leads the estate and sees that the Lord's and Lady's commands and wishes are followed. Think of a foreman on a ranch.

Seon und Heour. Old Saxon for "See and Tell/Announce." To order a Seon und Heour was to command that any person seeing a danger must inform all the others in the area. See **Hure e Crie** for the Old Norman French form.

serf. Term for a person tied to the land owned by the king, earls, barons, and lords, as part of the feudalism system common on the European continent. Usually serfs are not free, but they neither are serfs bought or sold as if they were slaves. This term was used on the European continent, not England, where they were called a **villein**.

Sericum. The 12th century Latin for China. Most likely, silk cloth traveled from Sericum over what we now call the Silk Road and into Persian and Arabic lands.

shift. A soft undergarment of linen or wool slightly smaller than a gunna worn by Saxon women to protect their skin from chafing. A Norman woman called it a "chemise."

shilling. During this time period, a unit of money comprised of 12 pennies.

shriven. Being assigned a penance after confessing one's sins and misdeeds to a priest.

shroud. A soft coffin. Any cloth wound around a dead body or cloth covering a dead body and sewn together.

simples. Ointments, creams, powders, and other remedies for a variety of illnesses and ailments; most used pig fat as a base.

Sire. Title of address of a person of rank to the king until about 1534 C.E. Considered slightly less formal than Your Grace and used only in personal or private conversation with royal approval. Can be used as an alternate to Your Grace, which was used for the kings and queens of England until the mid-16th century. King Henry VIII was the first royal to require the use of Your Majesty.

sokeman. A Saxon who ranks above a villein. He owns his own land, can go to court on his own behalf, and pays tithes and taxes directly to the Church and to the Crown. He is still supervised by the ranking nobleman, who controls the estate.

solar. The English form of the Latin word "solarium," a room in which the sun shines during a major part of the day.

squire. The second step toward a Norman boy becoming a knight after having served as a page. Usually a squire began this position at the age of 14. A Saxon might become a page or a squire, but he was never permitted to wear chain mail, learn swordsmanship or to rise to knighthood.

stone. A unit of weight equal to 14 pounds.

surcoat. A man's loose robe worn over armor, a sleeveless garment worn as part of the insignia of an order of knighthood, or an outer coat of rich material worn by a man of rank.

swill. Usually contains the wine and lees from the bottom of a barrel of wine. It tastes terrible.

tabbard. A strip of cloth with a hole in the middle for the wearer's head to be worn over armor or one's clothing for protection and warmth. Often it was also belted. By the late 12th century, a man's tabbard was often emblazoned with a coat of arms. In winter, Norman women wore plain woolen ones to keep warm. Now it is spelled "tabard."

Te Deum. Literally "To God." A prayer or song of praise to God, often used as a blessing before a meal.

Thaes hal. (thay-us hail) Old Saxon greeting, loosely translated "thus hail." Today we say, "hello."

thrupence. Three pennies.

ticking. Cloth case for a mattress or pillow into which is stuffed hair, feathers, straw or the like.

tithe. The Church's demand that ten percent of one's wealth must be paid to the Church annually on September 29.

titles,   **Royal:**   King/Queen
                           Prince/Princess
         Noble: Baron/Baroness (called Lady)
                           Earl/Countess (called Lady)
                           Lord (sometimes addressed as Sir/Sirrah)/Lady
                           Sir (Sirrah)/Lady (a knight who owns land)
                           During these years, titles of address were fluid.
                           All the nobles except for knights landed could

be—and often were—addressed as "Lord"—even the barons and earls. Many times the barons/earls and lords were informally addressed as "Sir" by their equals. "Sirrah" was its most informal form.

treble. Another form of triple.

trestle tables. A wooden table composed of a top of boards set upon a triangular A-frame (think sawhorse).

troubadour. A Norman-French word for a composer and performer of lyric poetry who usually accompanied his works with a musical instrument such as a lyre or psaltery. The Old Saxon word is scop.

turino. During the medieval period, a region in what is now north-western Italy. During the ninth century, a man stole the process for making soft, body soap from what is now Castile, Spain, and took the knowledge to this area. Because the climate did not support roses well, he used pine needles and sap to scent his soaps. The principal city in the area is now known as Turin in English.

uncert. The medieval form of uncertain. The opposite is "cert."

vassal. Under the feudal system, any person who holds land and owes taxes, homage, fealty and/or military service to an individual of higher rank. In England all are vassals except the king.

vellum. Sheep skin pounded thin and written upon. Sometimes also called **parchment**.

vespers. At dusk everyone on a farm or estate or in a congregation meets for evening prayers before going to bed.

villein. Term used in England for those tied to the land, who are not free, but they neither are they bought or sold as if they were slaves. See also **serf**.

virgate. A medieval unit of land, almost 30 acres. They counted four virgates per **hide**.

walkway. Structure attached to and behind the palisade upon which guards may stand and defend the bailey.

wattle and daub. A form of construction using softened willow sticks woven together (wattle) and a mud of dirt, straw and other debris (daub) to form walls of a hut that is then roofed with thatch and whitewashed with a lime water solution to protect it from rain. A common type of home for Saxons during this era. Wattles were also used as fencing and screens.

wedding rib. A strip of woven, lightweight cloth 3 to 6 inches wide that is used as decorative trim on clothing or is wrapped around a married woman's long hair when she wears it in two braids. Thinner ribs are often woven into braids for decoration. We now call them ribbons.

wench. A female servant, whether girl or woman.

wergeld. Means "man payment" in Old Saxon. It is the amount of compensation paid by a person committing an offense to the injured party, paying for a person's freedom, or, in case of death, to his family.

white wash. A liquid comprised of ground lime and other substances used to cover and seal walls and buildings from moisture and rain, also painted on wattle and daub huts to protect the structure. In modern times it is used metaphorically and means to cover one's deed, lie, or deception with untruths that make the person or event appear good.

wif. (wife) Old Saxon word for the female in a marriage. Later the "e" was added to indicate the long "i"sound. It is one of the approximately 25 percent of English words that came from Old Saxon.

wimple. A woman's head-cloth drawn in folds about the head and around the neck; it usually covered the forehead as well. Originally worn out of doors, it later became popular for covering one's hair indoors. Nuns started wearing it to cover their hair from being seen by men.

withies. Thin willow branches, soaked and woven together to build exterior walls called wattles. They are then covered with mud and straw mixed together to form house walls and white washed to inhibit rain damage. See also also **wattle and daub**.

wroth. The Old Saxon form of the word "wrath."

About the Author

Ms. Sportelli is a life-long Anglophile, who loves British history, culture, manners, folklore, customs, and humor. How women worked and struggled, what they wore and ate, and how their families survived are the focus of her novels.

She has been to the places she writes about. One of her exciting finds is in the hall to the Queen's Wing of the Great Hall, which is all that remains of the large castle in Winchester. Hanging there is a photograph of a royal treasury chest King Henry I used.

During 25 years of reading and research, she concluded that Henry I of England was an under-rated king. She found compelling King Henry's struggles, and the dangers he faced amid the conflicts between the Normans and the Saxons.

In college she majored in English with a special interest in the Anglo-Saxon and the early Medieval periods. She learned to read, write and speak basic Anglo-Saxon.

Now Ms. Sportelli off to Italy to research her next historical fiction novel, which is set in Venice.

Find Victoria online and on social media:
Author Website: *www.victoriasportelli.com*
Facebook: Victoria Sportelli
Pinterest: VictoriaSportelli
Twitter: Victoria Sportelli

Dear Reader,
The author will be grateful
if you leave an honest review online.
Thank you!

Made in United States
Troutdale, OR
10/13/2023

13676345R00336